THE HAUNTING OF TULLABEG

TONY WALKER

CONTENTS

ARRIVING AT THE CASTLE

Through the heart of Ireland across the Bog of Allen at October's end with flood-water covering the one-tracked road and the fog thickening like a veil, dim headlights peering purblind forward, the car with its four passengers approached its goal.

Still invisible in the vaporous air, the anticipation of the castle and the sheer mythic presence of its blood-soaked history brought a delicious anticipation. From its reputation, **it** was a place full of ghosts and legends and therefore ideal for their purpose.

As the car crawled on, the marshland stretched on both sides for miles beyond imagining.

Claire leaned forward from the back, her skeletal hands clamping a Sunday School Bible as old as she was, as she strained for a better view. Her tongue moistened her lips and she muttered, "Sin slips in while the conscience sleeps, and, make no mistake, this is a place of sin."

"Is that a premonition, or are you being your usual sunny self, Claire?" Tristan sat in the front passenger seat, freckled, dark-haired, and young. He winked at Gwyn in the driving seat beside him, the other man older, once black-haired and now grey.

Claire fixed Tristan with glass-blue eyes. "Don't mock what you don't understand, boy. The Lord punishes pride most of all."

Next to Claire in the back seat was Iseult. She took out her ear-buds and threaded her long blonde hair into a ponytail through a gauzy blue scruncher. Yanking it straight, she leaned forward over Tristan's shoulder and squinted through the windscreen. "Is that where we're going?" Her finger pointed through the gathering fog.

Gwyn nodded. "Tullabeg Castle. We can't see much of it yet, but you've got to admit **it's** impressive, isn't **it**? I hope the guests think so too." He turned. "You'll agree I've picked somewhere special this time."

Tristan said, "You picked well, boss. I can't imagine anywhere better to be for a ghost hunt."

"And for Halloween too," Iseult said.

Gwyn grunted. "The owners sort of picked us."

"How so?" Tristan said.

"They did their research, I guess. There must be outfits like us a bit closer, but they must have wanted the best."

Iseult said, "We've done private parties before."

Gwyn said, "**It's** not private. They're selling tickets to the public."

"Did they give you a deposit?" Tristan asked.

"No, she said something about my bank details not working."

"Pity." Tristan said.

Gwyn shot him a glance. "I know."

Tristan held up his hands and Gwyn softened. "But don't you worry about that, pretty boy. You sort out the technical side and leave the cash to me."

Tristan said, "I want an easy life. Do the job. **Get** paid. Go home."

Gwyn punched him on the shoulder. "Don't worry. This is going to be a cake-walk."

They were doing less than thirty miles an hour, and the castle was still only a silhouette about half a mile off across the flat landscape.

Through the window, Tristan considered the line of battlements against the darkening sky. The castle's broken central tower spiked up from its crenellations, with smaller towers flanking **it** on both sides.

The left tower looked solid, but the one on the right had a hole at the top like **it** had been blasted by lightning.

The beat-up Ford Focus crawled along the narrow road while daylight failed, and gloom gathered.

Tristan had hoped they would be at the castle before dark, but stormy weather over the Irish Sea delayed their ferry. **It** had been a long day.

The fog thickened by the minute as the wiper tick-tocked across the windscreen, pushing away beads of moisture. Gwyn clicked the headlights on, but the beams mostly bounced back from wreaths of fog. Gwyn cursed and hunched over the the wheel.

☙❧

TO THEIR LEFT A RUIN EMERGED FROM THE FOG LIKE A GHOST.

Tristan tapped on the car window. "Hey, take a peek at that!"

Gwyn peered. "What is **it**?"

"**It's** an old tower—very Gothic. That would make a fantastic Instagram shot. Can we stop?"

Gwyn glanced over at the dark shape. "**It's** a heap of stones. I don't want to delay getting to the castle."

Tristan said, "The tower looks great in this mist. **It** would do as a new cover for the Facebook page. **There's** maybe enough light."

Gwyn groaned. "More Social Marketing shit. I don't know about **it**, and I don't care much about **it** either."

"But it boosts the business. C'mon, boss! Let me stop."

Gwyn sighed. "Five minutes only. "

Gwyn stopped the car. "Like I said: five minutes." He pressed a button, and the window wound down. He tried to light a cigarette with a red plastic lighter, but the damp breeze blew the flame, and **it** wouldn't catch.

Tristan pushed open the car door with his boot and dragged his camera by the strap from the well of the seat as he stepped out. He went to the road edge by the ruin and called, "I bet **it's** medieval."

"I don't care," Gwyn said, his cigarette finally lighting.

Iseult opened the back door of the car to go after Tristan. "I'm coming too." As soon as she got out, she hugged herself through her white silk blouse and shivered. "**It's** cold." The gold cross around her neck glinted in the car lights.

Gwyn blew out a cloud of smoke through the open window. "**It's** the end of October in Ireland. Of course, **it's** cold."

Rain pitter-pattered on the ground, dotting puddles and streaking the car windows. The fog was so thick **it** was hard to **see** far in front. Tristan descended from the road onto the remains of an ancient staircase. Iseult followed him.

The stones here were wet and slippery, and moss grew in crevices between cracked rocks. Iseult nearly slipped and put out her hand. Tristan grabbed it.

"Thanks, I thought I was a goner then."

"No problem." He dropped her fingers.

Going down a few steps, he crouched and pointed. "Brilliant! **There's** a tunnel here."

"Only five minutes, remember," yelled Gwyn from behind from the car.

Claire sat in the back seat, muttering something to herself.

In the ruin, Tristan squinted down and sighted his camera through the arched entry of the stone passage. It was too dark for a clear shot, but **it** was worth reconnoitring the place.

Rain dripped from grey lichen onto the stone floor, and rushes grew from the mire into which the slabs had sunk. He couldn't **see** far into the tunnel but had the impression **it** extended a long way.

"Wonder where that leads?" Iseult said, appearing beside him. She placed her hand on Tristan's back as if to steady herself on the slippery stones. Without meaning to, Tristan stiffened, and she took her hand away. But she still stood close.

Tristan said, "**It** could go all the way to the castle. Wouldn't that be cool?"

Iseult stared. "Cool and damp and dark and dangerous."

He put down his camera. "Come on, let's **get** back."

He glanced round and saw her standing there. Her blue eyes met his and he turned away.

Iseult trembled from the cold. Her chin shuddered. "What if we come back and **get** some shots tomorrow when the light's better? You and me if Gwyn and Claire won't come."

Tristan grimaced. "I'm not sure. Me and Gwyn will be busy setting up for the show."

"Yeah. Of course."

"Probably won't have time."

She hesitated. "Tristan..."

He pushed his hand through his hair and walked back, making his way up the steps.

She said, "Wait. Help me."

He stopped, turned, and Iseult stretched for him to take her hand and steady her. He seized her slender fingers and pulled her up the step.

Gwyn had got out of the car and stood waiting beside **it**. Seeing them come back, he finished his cigarette and threw the butt down, grinding **it** with the heel of his boot.

Iseult stood, still shivering, and Tristan said, "Thanks for stopping, boss. **It** was good."

Gwyn said, "Got what you needed?"

"Too dark. But I can come back."

"Doubt we'll have time. Still, are you happy?"

"Sure. Of course. Happy as a sand boy."

Gwyn said, "Whatever that is."

Tristan gazed around him. "Man, **it** got dark quick."

Gwyn said, "Happens every night."

Tristan nodded. "Ideal for us. Night."

Claire said, "Yes, the darkness is for hiding things that shouldn't **see** daylight."

☙❧

TRISTAN GOT IN THE FRONT. ISEULT CLIMBED INTO THE BACK BESIDE Claire, who was now gazing out of the window at the gathering gloom, her eyes flicking every way as if she saw shapes in the fog.

When they'd closed the car doors, Gwyn turned the key. The engine coughed, sounded like **it** wouldn't fire, then spluttered into life.

Tristan smiled. "All's well that end's well."

Tristan gazed at the bog that stretched for miles around them. Shifting curtains of mist, grey in the car lights, made **it** difficult to **see** further than a few yards, but the headlamps lit up the sheets of water that were seeping onto the road.

"All that rain didn't help," Gwyn said. "**It's** flooding."

The rising water shone petrol blue with oil from the peat. Gwyn hunched forward over the wheel. **It** was a poor road with an uneven surface, and the passage of previous vehicles had churned the road verges to slippery mud. The potholes were filled with mud and water. The car's wheels whirled until they got a grip on the asphalt and moved on again.

A shadow shifted across the road ten yards ahead. Tristan blinked. Someone stood in the road. The mist blurred the outline, but **it** looked like a woman.

Gwyn slammed on the brakes. Stomping the pedal made the car skid, and he jerked at the steering wheel to regain control, but they were sliding forward. Tristan grabbed the handle on the car's ceiling to brace himself as they veered. They left the road, and marsh loomed out of the darkness as the car bonnet lifted and plunged into a pool. There was a splash. Steam hissed. Wheels whooshed and water churned. The bonnet dropped, and Gwyn mashed the car into reverse. The engine revved up to a scream as he pumped the pedal, but they got nowhere.

Gwyn took his foot off the accelerator. More steam boiled up as the engine shipped three feet of bog water. The vehicle stopped dead: silence. Gwyn hammered the steering wheel. "Fuck, fuck, fuck, fuck!"

"No need for profanity!" Claire snapped from the back.

Tristan turned to Iseult. "Everyone okay?"

Claire pursed her lips and gripped her Bible.

Iseult smiled. "Yeah, I think so."

Gwyn's eyes blazed with futile anger. "How are we going to **get** the car out of this mire?"

Tristan squeezed his shoulder. "Never mind, boss. Worse things happen at sea."

Gwyn snarled. "Like what?"

Tristan met his boss's watery blue eyes with his calm brown ones. His gaze didn't waver as he smiled and shrugged. "**It's** only a saying."

"I know **it's** a fucking saying. For fuck's sake."

Iseult reached forward and stroked Gwyn's face. "Calm down, darling."

Gwyn's fingers wrapped around the steering wheel as if he wanted to yank **it** off.

"We'll have to walk. **It's** not far," Tristan said.

Gwyn exhaled.

"Come on." Tristan opened the door. The chill fog flowed in, full of smells of damp and decay and the bubbling sound of water.

They sat for a second, quietened by the accident. Tristan was about to say something when Gwyn blurted, "Put a coat on, Iseult."

Iseult reached into her overnight bag to drag out a brown leather jacket. She pulled **it** on over her white blouse. **It** was awkward to do in the back seat of the car, and as she tugged **it** straight, Claire shuffled and twisted beside her. Iseult untwined a red silk scarf and wound **it** around her neck. "Okay."

She tucked her gold cross under the scarf.

Tristan stepped out of the open door and sank to his calves in the peaty mush. "Oh!" he exclaimed. "Wait a second." He sloshed his way towards the back door where the ground was more solid. He dragged the door open and stretched to help Iseult out. She stepped in the water, half-way up her knee-length boots and laughed.

"Glad you find **it** funny." Gwyn gripped his front door handle but didn't yet open **it**.

Tristan said, "Easy boss, **it's** deep at the front,"

Gwyn hesitated.

Iseult whispered. "He hates water."

Tristan turned back to the car. "Maybe climb over the seats to the back, boss, and **get** out that way? **It's** easier."

But Gwyn was standing on the lip of the open door.

Iseult said, "Please, Gwyn, climb over and **get** out the back door."

Gwyn launched himself from the front seat. Tristan heard the splash as Gwyn landed in a bog pool. He waded his way round, so he could **see** what had happened. Gwyn had gone right in. Stinking bog water dripped from him. He waded out of the pool, streaked with peat.

Iseult reached for Gwyn, but he held up his hands. "No, I'm soaked." Gwyn shook his head like an old dog, drops flying off his hair, rivulets running down his face and chin. "I don't want to ruin your outfit." He cursed, "That's fucked my cigarettes and my phone." He spat. "I think I mind the cigarettes more."

Claire shivered. "Where's the castle? I'm cold."

"Get the bags from the boot of the car, Iseult," Gwyn said. "Just take what we need for tonight."

Claire repeated, "Where is the castle? How far?"

Tristan said, "Not far." He pointed to the dark bulk in the shadows ahead of them. "It's that big dark thing over there."

2

THE LADY OF THE CASTLE

The castle loomed out of the mist in front. Tristan tipped back his head to study the three towers barely visible in the ever-shifting fog. He yelled back to the others, "It's just here."

A curlew's call came from way out over the marsh as if announcing their arrival.

Gwyn was drenched, and Iseult squeezed her arm round his shoulder as they walked. Claire trudged along the road behind them.

The central part of the building was in good repair, but the rest looked ruinous. Lights gleamed weakly through diamond-shaped panes of antique glass, but only a few windows were lit up.

They stood at the door. Gwyn stopped, water running from his pants to pool around his feet. Teeth chattering, he muttered, "Doesn't make a good first impression."

"Let's get inside. It's freezing." Tristan trotted up the five stone steps and lifted the iron knocker shaped like a wolf's head then brought it down heavily. The knocker thudded against dense wood, and its echoes sounded in the room behind. After a few minutes, rapid footsteps came, then the grinding noise of a bolt being withdrawn, and the door swung slowly inwards.

A woman of medium height was silhouetted by a dim electric chandelier hanging in the hall behind her. Her jet-black hair was piled up, and her skin looked pale in the electric light. Her elaborate black dress was decorated with a high lace collar. Unexpectedly, she had an American accent. She said, "Hello, I'm Sorcha O'Connor." She extended her hand to Tristan. "You're Gwyn James, right?"

Tristan jerked his thumb at Gwyn shivering behind him. "No, he's Gwyn."

Sorcha switched her attention to Gwyn. She stopped a smile halfway before it broke out into a laugh. "Have you been in the bog?"

Gwyn said wearily. "An accident. We skidded."

Iseult said, "There was a woman on the road, so he hit the brakes."

Sorcha raised an eyebrow. "A woman? On the bog road tonight?"

Iseult shrugged. "I didn't see a woman. But it was something."

"Something evil." Claire spat the words.

Sorcha smiled at Claire. "You must be the psychic." Sorcha stepped forward to greet Claire, but the thin woman's her arms came up, brandishing the Bible like a shield.

Sorcha raised an eyebrow. "And a Christian psychic at that."

Claire fixed her with beady eyes. "I'm a Christian spiritualist. My mission is to lead tortured souls to the light."

Gwyn raised a hand. "Yeah, but not too soon. We need to make some money first." Walking up to the steps to the door, he said, "Mind if we go inside? I'm freezing to death here."

Sorcha smiled. "Of course. You're very wet. I'll get you some of my husband's clothes. You're a similar build, though he may be taller."

Iseult said, "I've got a change of clothes for him."

Sorcha appraised Iseult as if she were a pretty brooch. "I take it you're this handsome young man's girlfriend."

Tristan blushed. "She's married to Gwyn."

Iseult's mouth tightened. "I'm Gwyn's wife."

Sorcha grinned. Tristan saw a hint of mischief in her eyes.

Iseult's brow furrowed. "Is it so astonishing?"

"I guess I got lucky," Gwyn winked at Sorcha as he entered the castle. Iseult followed him, her hand reaching for his arm.

"Sorry about the drips," he said.

Sorcha pointed. "The floor's made of stone. It doesn't mind a little water."

⚜

THE PARTY ENTERED THROUGH THE HEAVY WOODEN DOOR, GAZING around, gaping mouthed. Grey limestone flags formed the entrance hallway floor and dark oak panelled the walls. Heraldic shields with various painted designs hung all around its borders, and a sweeping stone staircase ascended directly ahead. On the landing at the staircase's top stood an authentic-looking suit of armour. But here, at ground level, corridors led back into the castle's heart, and to the right and left dark doors flanked both walls.

Sorcha beckoned them to follow. Gwyn and Iseult started after her, then Claire. Tristan turned around as he walked, trying to take in the castle layout. He liked to suss out the exits and entrances--an old army habit. You couldn't be too careful in a new place. You never knew what was coming for you.

Sorcha opened door after door, and they followed her through endless rooms of forgotten heirlooms and tatty chairs, and it seemed the castle was an endless labyrinth, but at length, they came to a library.

The library walls were lined with shelves of ancient books whose covers bore faded gold titles. The room smelled of old words and damp wood. These books were so ancient that Tristan wondered whether they would crumble to dust when he pulled one from where it had nestled for years, perhaps centuries. Another chandelier swung from the ceiling, though half the bulbs didn't work.

Two long tables dominated the middle of the space with a three tarnished candelabras standing down each of their middles. The candles were of black wax but were pristine, and obviously never yet lit. On the nearest table was a skull. The bone was brown, and half of the teeth were missing. It didn't look fake. Towards the end of the farthest table was a Ouija board.

A massive fire was just starting to burn and spit in the hearth between the bookshelves. Flames licked the logs, and a column of smoke from the dank wood rose up the chimney, fluttering in an unseen draught.

Tristan observed Sorcha watching each of their reactions as they took in the room. She noticed him looking at her and held his gaze. A mysterious smile haunted her lips like an Irish-American Mona Lisa.

Now they stood still, Iseult put up her hand tentatively on Gwyn's shoulder. Whether he felt it or not, he stepped closer to the fire, and her hand fell away. Accident or not, she looked bereft. Gwyn just looked like he wanted to get dry.

Tristan said, "Is? You okay?"

She smiled wanly. "Pre-performance nerves." She nodded. "I like your watch. I meant to say that."

Tristan showed his wrist. "This? It was my dad's. **It's** the only thing of his I've got."

"He was a soldier too, wasn't he?"

"Yeah, though I didn't join up until he died. Before that I thought of myself as a perpetual student." Tristan paused, remembering. "He was a good man: honest, loyal and brave."

"Just like you," Iseult said.

Tristan laughed. "I wish." He glanced toward Gwyn was steaming nicely by the fire.

Iseult saw him looking. "You don't need another dad, Tristan. **It's** time to show courage and take what life wants to give you. Stop waiting in line like an obedient boy."

Tristan avoided her gaze. "I don't think **it's** as simple as that," he said.

Claire had her chin tilted up, looking around as if expecting to see something in the shadows by the ceiling.

Tristan indicated the black candles, the skull and the Ouija board. "This is for our benefit?" He said.

Sorcha gave a small shake of her head. "For the event. For the guests."

Gwyn stood by the fire, his pants and shirt steaming. He said,

"Normally we handle the ticket sales, so forgive me fretting, but they are all coming tomorrow? Or on Halloween itself?"

Sorcha nodded. "Some will arrive tomorrow, I'm sure. Most on Halloween itself."

Tristan said, "**It's** better that we've got a lot of preparation time. We don't often have that luxury."

Sorcha said, "I paid for the extra time, because I want you storytellers to settle in here. Tullabeg is an old place and full of wonders. It wants to get to know you before it lets you wander around its corridors untouched."

"Sounds ominous," Iseult said. "But we're not storytellers as such."

"More a travelling show," Gwyn said. "Specialising in putting on ghost hunts for paying customers."

"But you tell ghost stories as part of the show?"

Gwyn said, "Sure."

"Well, Ireland is full of tales and legends. I'm sure you'll find some suitable ones to enthrall our guests, and maybe yourselves."

Gwyn asked, "Still twenty punters?"

"I think so." Sorcha busied herself moving along the tables, lighting the black candles with an expensive silver lighter.

"Okay, yep," Gwyn said. He stepped over to her. "By the way, I couldn't bum a cigarette off you?"

Sorcha pulled out a packet of cigarettes from somewhere in her dress and offered Gwyn one.

"My lighter got wet."

She lit it for him and offered the pack to Iseult, who shook her head.

"You're sure nobody has dropped out?" Gwyn said.

"Of what?" Sorcha said.

"The guests for the gig."

She shook her head again. "Don't worry. Coffee? Or something stronger?"

Gwyn smiled. "I'll always take a whiskey if you have it, or vodka, or gin, or brandy..."

"Peach schnapps?"

He wrinkled his nose but shrugged. "Sure."

Sorcha said, "Was joking. We don't have any schnapps. We have whiskey, though. Irish, of course."

"It all works."

"Red wine for me," Iseult said.

Tristan absent-mindedly stroked dust off the table. "I'll have a whiskey too."

Sorcha turned to Claire. "Sorry I don't know your name. Would you like a drink?"

"Claire Foster. Just a tea please."

Sorcha smiled. "You're in Ireland now. I can't tempt you to anything stronger?"

Claire was po-faced. "Tea please."

Sorcha smiled again and left the room by the far door.

⁂

GWYN RUBBED HIS HANDS IN FRONT OF THE FIRE TO WARM THEM, and Iseult stood by him, making another attempt to put her hand on his arm. He let it be and even stroked it, like he might his pet dog. The orange light of the fire made the difference in their ages more apparent.

While husband and wife stood before the fire, Tristan and Claire walked to different bookshelves and pored over the volumes. Tristan pulled out a Victorian book entitled "A Historical Survey of the Townlands of Clonaghmore and Tullabeg Castle." He flicked through the yellowing pages until he got to the entry about the castle. He skimmed the history section, not taking it in. Then he found a map. "Hey," he said. "There's a tunnel on this map leading out from the castle. I bet it goes to that chapel thing we stopped at."

Gwyn crossed over to Tristan and peered over his shoulder. "How would they keep the tunnel dry?"

Tristan laughed. "Line it with clay? I don't know. But they must have somehow."

"And they'd need to pit prop it to stop it falling in," Gwyn said. "This castle is made of limestone, so that's the underlying geology, but there must be a layer of glacial boulder clay on top that stops the bog draining away. Looks like magic, but it isn't."

Tristan whistled. "Once again, colour me impressed the way you know so much random shit."

Gwyn winked. "24 Commando Royal Engineers before I joined your mob, boy. Anyway, most of these tunnels are just figments of the Victorian imagination. Believe me, I've been to more castles than I can shake a stick at since starting this ghost hunt lark, and they always say they have secret tunnels."

Iseult laughed. Her husband amused her, and Tristan glanced over. He turned back and snapped the book shut, shoving it back in its place, and then touching the spine as if ashamed he'd treated it so roughly. He looked back at Gwyn and Iseult standing by the fire and nodded. Gwyn smiled and steamed.

❧

Iseult left Gwyn and wandered over to the Ouija board. She moved the planchette idly, but Claire rushed over and knocked the young woman's hand away. Claire' stuck her face in Iseult's, her eyes gleaming and Iseult stepped back.

"Don't touch that thing!" Claire hissed.

Tristan noticed that she'd put the Bible down and was holding a small battered volume.

"What's the book, Claire?"

The psychic's eyes narrowed. "The Christian's Guide to the Seven Deadly Sins."

"Sounds fun," Tristan grinned. "You found that on the shelf?"

Claire nodded.

Gwyn laughed. Iseult was still shocked by the assault, staring at Claire as if the older woman was unhinged.

"So what's the worst sin in your opinion, Claire?" Tristan teased her.

Without hesitation, Claire blurted, "Idolatry."

"What do you think, Tristan?" Iseult said, not looking at him.

He shrugged. "Disloyalty."

"That's not one of the Seven Deadly Sins," Claire said.

"Neither's idolatry, but I didn't mention it because I'm not a pedant." He frowned. "Sins aren't my interest. If we're talking virtues - loyalty is the greatest."

Gwyn said, "Loyalty, yes. You stick by your mates, don't you Tristan?"

Iseult muttered, "You still talk like you're soldiers."

Tristan smiled. "You can take the boy out of the Army, but you can't take the Army out of the boy. Isn't that true, sarge?" He looked at the older man.

"I'm not your sergeant now, Tristan."

"You're my boss in this outfit."

Iseult broke the silence. "What about you, Gwyn? What's the worst sin? Wrath, envy, gluttony, lust?"

The door opened, and Sorcha re-entered carrying their drinks on a silver tray. She handed Gwyn his whiskey in a crystal tumbler. "We're talking sins?"

Iseult nodded. "Gwyn hasn't told us yet what he thinks is the worst sin."

Gwyn took a slug of the whiskey. Then another. The glass was empty when he placed it back on the tray. "I don't know—coveting thy neighbour's oxen?"

Sorcha gave a half-smile. "What about coveting thy neighbour's wife, that must be worse?"

Gwyn winked. "No offence, but your husband's not my neighbour." He paused for dramatic effect before adding, "And you're not my type."

Sorcha frowned but nodded towards Iseult. "You're already punching above your weight."

"Murder's a sin," Tristan said, his mind still on the conversation about sins.

Sorcha chuckled. "If we have any murderers in the house, let me know, Mr Gifford. But I'd say the worst sin is cowardice."

Tristan stared at her. Once again, he had the feeling that Sorcha knew things she shouldn't.

Tristan stepped over and took two cut-crystal wine glasses from the tray. He handed one to Iseult and sipped his own. "You seem an intelligent woman, Sorcha. Don't tell me you believe this castle is haunted?"

"You tell me," she said.

In that instant, all the candles blew out, and the electric chandeliers winked off. The room was plunged into darkness.

3

MAGIC TRICKS

Standing in the dark, Tristan began a slow handclap. "Bravo," he said. "Neat trick. You have an accomplice somewhere, I take it?"

"No trick," smiled Sorcha: "Magic."

"Magic? Don't believe in it," Tristan said.

"Well, you might be the sort of man who lays his faith in gadgets and machines, but true power arises from the deep—true power comes from manipulating ancient forces."

"What ancient forces?"

"Only the ignorant call them supernatural."

Tristan said, "Well, if it's all the same to you, I'll put my faith in technology."

Sorcha laughed softly. "One day soon you will believe in magic, Mr Gifford. One day soon, you'll even come to rely on it."

"I doubt that."

"Will someone put these lights back on?" Iseult said.

A click echoed, and the lights went back on. Standing behind Sorcha, with his finger on the light switch was a tall, rangy man with long grey hair. He had hollow cheeks and watchful eyes, and, as he breathed, he opened his mouth, showing yellow teeth. The man wore a three-piece tweed suit, which had seen better days, and scuffed brown brogues.

"Magic is tricks," Tristan said to Sorcha, but she was not listening to him. She beckoned the grey-haired man to come to her. He stepped forward, and they linked arms. "This is my husband," she said, "Mr Dudley."

Dudley spoke in a heavy Irish accent. "Pleased to meet ye."

Sorcha laughed. "He came with the castle when I bought it."

Dudley turned to Sorcha and spoke in a language that Tristan guessed must be Irish. She nodded and said, "Mr James, is your car locked? Dudley will recover it from the bog if you give him the key."

"What is he, magic?" Gwyn said.

"Oh, yes." Dudley grinned, showing his teeth.

Sorcha said, "We have a landrover with a winch. Vehicles often drive into the bog. He can fetch your equipment. And here are some dry clothes."

Under Dudley's arm was a change of clothes for Gwyn. Tristan inspected the Irishman. Despite what Sorcha said about his build, Dudley was about five inches taller and a lot skinnier than Gwyn was.

Gwyn shook his head. "I've got clothes in my holdall in the car. I'll come with you. I'll help you haul the car out of the bog."

Dudley said, "I don't need your help."

Gwyn winked. "It's my car, mate, one of my few assets. Not that I don't trust you."

Dudley smiled. "You put it in the bog, not me. Mate."

Tristan said, "Want me to come too?"

Gwyn waved him away. "Nah, you enjoy yourself with the ladies. And fill up my glass for my return."

Claire had sat down uninvited at one of the tables, poring over her book of sins and Iseult stood by the fire. Tristan glanced over and she smiled.

He asked Sorcha, "Have you many servants?"

She took a sip of wine. "None. Only Dudley and I live here. And the ghosts of course, though they can't be said to live exactly." She had a deep laugh, and her smoky American voice sounded husky from too many cigarettes and too much alcohol.

"They're not happy," Claire said, staring at Sorcha with intense concentration.

Sorcha tilted her head. "The ghosts?"

Claire nodded rapidly. "Their spirits are troubled."

Tristan rolled his eyes.

Iseult came up beside him. Sorcha pivoted to register the two of them standing close. A smile appeared on her face, and she turned to Claire. "There's only one ghost that causes us trouble."

Interrupting them, Tristan gestured to the portraits on the walls. One of them in particular, a haughty looking woman with a thin face and evil eyes looked like she was staring directly at him. "Are these your ancestors?"

Sorcha said, "Goodness, no. These are the Mortons who originally built the castle. They left for England after the setting up of the Free State in 1922." She said, "I'm a native by blood if not by accent, and I don't think the Mortons like the castle being in the hands of the Bog Irish, but it is, and if us being here troubles their ghosts, their ghosts can leave."

Claire frowned at Sorcha, as if she recognised her from somewhere.

Gwyn came back into the library, hefting two heavy bags of equipment. Behind Gwyn, Dudley had more bags slung over his shoulders.

Tristan asked. "Get the car out all right?"

Gwyn said, "Hooked it up to Dudley's landrover. He pulled it out easy enough."

"Does it go though?" Tristan asked.

"Not as such."

Sorcha said, "We'll ring a mechanic tomorrow."

Gwyn gestured at his empty glass. Sorcha smiled and said something in Irish, and Dudley nodded and left the room. He returned within minutes, carrying a decanter of whiskey. Dudley refilled Gwyn's glass, and Sorcha said, "Dinner in an hour or so?"

"We can talk about business while we eat."

Gwyn took Iseult's hand for the first time, slipping his hairy fingers through her slim white ones.

"Of course. Dudley will show you your rooms. I'll get on with the cooking."

Dudley gestured. "This way."

Gwyn took his whisky with him.

⬥

DUDLEY LED THEM OUT OF THE LIBRARY AND ALONG A PANELLED corridor floored with red and black tiles. The blank faces of closed doors flanked the passage. Even carrying their heavy bags, Dudley walked fast, and they hurried to catch up. Gwyn was breathing heavily, so Tristan reached to take a bag off him, and Gwyn grinned his thanks.

"You need to give up the cigarettes, mate," Tristan said. "They'll kill you."

"You've got to die of something, Tristan. Not sure you get that yet."

Tristan twisted round to check Claire was following. She walked last of all, staring around her, her eyes wide as if she saw invisible birds fluttering around the ceiling.

"Wow, that woman's weird," Tristan said under his breath

Gwyn nodded. Still not able to breathe enough to speak in full sentences.

"Leave her alone," Iseult said.

"What?"

"You were muttering about Claire. She means well. Leave her alone."

Tristan laughed. "Does she?"

Iseult reached back and swatted his arm. She grinned. "Yes!" She called back. "You okay, Claire?"

"There's so much here," the older woman muttered. "So much evil."

Tristan smirked and shook his head.

They arrived at the first floor hallway. There was a bronze bust of an unknown man on a pedestal. He looked haughty. Dark corridors with wooden floors led off to the left and right, and stairs mounted up in front of them to further levels of the castle.

Claire pulled her thin anorak around her. "Is there heating in this place?"

"Some," Dudley said. "Some plumbing too."

Tristan jerked his thumb at the Irishman. "Funny. He's a funny guy."

Iseult smiled. Gwyn was still catching his breath from the stairs.

"Some are left, and some are right," Dudley said.

Claire's head jerked around. "What's that?"

Everyone jumped except Dudley.

"What's what?" Tristan said.

Claire pointed into the gloom.

"There's something down that corridor."

Tristan's heart hammered despite himself. The stupid woman and startled him. "I see nothing."

She said, "It was there."

Dudley said, "There are four rooms. Take your pick."

"We only need three." Gwyn reached out and took Iseult's hand.

Dudley looked at Gwyn's fingers wrapped around Iseult's slender hand. "Ah, you've both got wedding rings."

"Yes," Iseult said.

"And you're married to each other, eh?" He gave a toothy smile. "Then you two go left," he said. "Take the first one."

Dudley glanced at Claire and Tristan. "Are you two married as well?" Dudley smirked. No one could fail to notice the difference in years—a good two decades—and in attractiveness. Tristan still had his soldier's build. He was tall, and dark-haired while Claire was stooped, her face lined and pale, her chestnut hair obviously dyed.

Tristan didn't dignify the comment with a response.

A smile played around the Irishman's mouth "Well?"

Claire growled, "Of course not. Please show me to my room. I need to meditate."

Tristan took the bag of equipment from Dudley. In his other hand, he had the holdall with his personal things. He watched while Dudley showed Claire the door to her room. It was next to his. He turned to see Iseult and Gwyn about to disappear into their room down the corridor and called, "Gwyn, maybe we should have a recce? Just to get a notion of where to put the equipment."

Gwyn nodded. "Okay, I'll see you out here in fifteen."

TRISTAN TWISTED THE COLD CERAMIC KNOB OF HIS BEDROOM DOOR. The room revealed behind the door was small. A four-poster bed stood against one wall, and white chiffon drapes hung down, pulled back to reveal crisp linen sheets under a bedspread with two linen-covered pillows. Beside the bed was an antique table with a two-headed candelabrum. Melted wax from the candles had streamed down and flowed into the bobèche creating lava runs of hard white. There was a notepad, and a fountain pen on the bedside table.

Tristan muttered. "That must be for visitors to write down their nightmares."

He threw his holdall onto the bed. The room smelled of damp and long burned out fires.

A connecting-door led to Claire's room. He grimaced. He wouldn't be sneaking through there in the night, or any other time either. The old iron key was in the connecting-door lock, and Tristan turned it to make sure it was locked. He unzipped his holdall and rummaged through the neatly ironed t-shirts, a clean pair of blue jeans and some earphones for his iPhone.

He pulled out two books: Mícheál Ó Siadhail's *Learning Irish*, and a children's edition of *La Morte D'Arthur*. He put them on top of the writing pad, got the equipment bag, and looked over the infrared cameras and the speakers. Tristan had a dongle he could plug into his laptop so they could broadcast the ghostly groans and rattling chain sound effects to the wireless speakers he would place out of sight. That was after all what the guests paid good money for: to be scared shitless.

He then moved the bags and lay on the bed, making it sag in the middle and wondered what Iseult and Gwyn were doing. He shook his head for thinking of it, sat up, opened his book, turned to the story of Lancelot and Guinevere, but he couldn't concentrate on it so began to leaf through Ó Siadhail's chapter on Irish phonetics.

Distraction was the key, that and self-discipline.

Ten minutes went by reading about broad and slender consonants, and then, he didn't know why, but he looked up from the book. A strange feeling permeated the room. He shivered. The temperature had dropped at least ten degrees. He glanced around and saw his breath hanging in the suddenly frigid air.

A movement caught his eye up on the ceiling. A phosphorescent ball burned bright against the wooden panelling. Tristan blinked, but it didn't go away. He stared at it in wonder and fear. In all the places they'd been, he'd never seen a genuine supernatural sight. He frowned: another of Sorcha's magic tricks. She was going to a lot of trouble to convince them the place was haunted.

Then a loud crack rang out. "What the hell is that?" he said out loud.

$$ \maltese \quad 4 \quad \maltese $$

DINNER THE FIRST NIGHT

e jumped up, but the noise wasn't repeated. It had sounded like wood cracking, but there was no visible damage. It must be just the old place settingl. Still, there was that damned orb. How the hell did she do that?

There was a knock on Tristan's door but all the while the light orb hovered on the ceiling. Tristan leapt out of bed and yanked the door open where Iseult stood beaming at him. He grabbed her wrist and tugged her into the room. Her eyes widened, and Tristan jabbed his finger upwards. "What the hell is that?"

She glanced up and gave a faint smile as if he was losing his mind. "What?"

He let go of her wrist. He couldn't believe it. The orb was gone.

"There was a ball of light there. Up hovering by the ceiling. Honestly."

She grinned. "I thought you didn't believe in ghosts?"

"I don't believe in them. It wasn't a ghost."

"I thought you said 'the only ghosts in that castle will come out of my speakers'."

"Don't make fun of me, Iseult."

She put her hand to his cheek. "I like you when you're sulky."

He took her hand away. "Don't do that."

"Don't you like it?"

He sighed. "I can't like it. Where's Gwyn?"

"He sent me for you." She smiled shyly. "Well, I volunteered."

He stepped away from her. "We can't, Is. You know that. It's not good. I can't deceive him. I owe him too much."

"We haven't done anything."

"Not done anything, no."

She gave a sad smile. "I can't help it. It seems I want to have my cake and eat it too."

He said, "Let's go."

Tristan stepped out of the door to find Gwyn, and after lingering, watching him go, Iseult followed.

⚜

GWYN WAS STANDING IN THE PASSAGE OUTSIDE HIS ROOM. HE scratched his chin. "We need to work out a route to lead the guests. Then rig it with our little tricks."

As they approached, Iseult grinned. "Tristan just saw a ghost."

Tristan blushed. "No, I didn't."

Gwyn raised an eyebrow.

Tristan changed the subject. "We've been through our routine so many times. You must know it by heart."

"Pretty much," Iseult said.

Gwyn said, "Piss poor planning leads to piss poor performance."

Tristan said, "So we're doing a walk-through?"

"As usual," Gwyn said. "Standard operating procedure. Tonight."

Iseult said, "Tonight, really? We've got loads of time. We don't have to do it tonight."

Gwyn said, I just want to get the lie of the land."

Tristan asked. "Are we taking Claire on the walk?"

Gwyn said, "She's still meditating. I just knocked."

Tristan said, "Do you believe her?"

"Believe her what?"

"The ghosts: she makes it all up, surely."

Iseult shrugged. "She believes it."

Tristan said, "Yeah, she believes it. But she's crazy."

Gwyn was already moving. "Leave her for now. Let's walk the ground, starting in the entrance hall."

"Can you find your way back there without Dudley?" Tristan asked.

"Yes, corporal, I think I can. Do you remember my sense of direction?"

Tristan laughed. "I do. Very well."

"More war stories?" Iseult said.

"Did I ever tell you about the time..." Gwyn joked.

Iseult rolled her eyes. "Yes. On multiple occasions."

❧

THEY TROTTED DOWN THE STAIRS, THEN ALONG THE RED AND BLACK tiled corridor until they were in the library. There was no one else there. One of the black candles still smoked, a thin plume of grey twisting up towards the ceiling.

"The whole place stinks of candles," Tristan said.

"And damp. And bog," Iseult added.

"And old." Gwyn gazed round. "It's a great spot. I can almost feel the threat coming out of the walls."

Gwyn led them back into the Entrance Hall. He switched on the light. The electric bulbs in the chandelier were faint. The heavy oak door to outside was bolted shut. Gwyn was about to open it, but Tristan said, "Don't. You'll let the night in."

Iseult shivered. "This place gives me the creeps."

"Good," Gwyn said. "That'll make your performance authentic."

Tristan turned and ran up the main staircase. At the top, he tapped the suit of armour. "I saw this before. I want to put a speaker in this." Then he reached down and drew the sword a couple of inches from the scabbard. "This even looks sharp."

The sword hung on the suit's left side, on the right was a knife in a smaller sheath. Tristan pinged the steel helmet with his index finger. "Yes, this armour is a perfect prop. You're right, boss. Tullabeg is a great setting."

Gwyn said, "The venue is seventy per cent of the experience. This place is so Gothic; plus Sorcha in her getup; it's a winner from the get-go."

Tristan laughed. "The sound and projectors will make them see ghosts snapping at their heels."

Iseult called up to him. "For a man who prizes honesty above all things, you sure get off on tricking people."

Gwyn snorted. "It's not tricking them; it's entertainment. They want to be tricked. They collude in our deceiving them. It's fun. Remember fun, Iseult?"

"Not for some time."

Gwyn peered out of the mullioned windows. "It's so black out there. There can't be another house for miles."

Tristan descended the stairs again. He said theatrically, "We're all alone in the heart of the Bog of Allen. No help will come for us."

"And no mobile phone signal," Iseult said.

"My phone got ruined when I went for a dunk if you remember," Gwyn muttered. "Thank God it's insured. I nearly cancelled the insurance last week too."

Iseult stroked his arm. "This could be us turning a corner. We could generate a lot of word-of-mouth business from this if the gig goes well."

While the men poked around looking for possible locations to hide speakers, Iseult sat on a threadbare armchair by a table to the left of the door. On the table lay old editions of *Irish Country Life*. She leafed through them, looking up to say, "Do you think people really sit in this gloomy hall and read for pleasure?"

Tristan said, "I can't imagine anyone comes here for pleasure."

Gwyn gave him a high five. "They will tomorrow. They better anyway."

"Has she paid you yet?" Tristan asked.

Gwyn lit a cigarette. He shook his head.

Iseult said, "Hey, here's an article about Sorcha. Says she's from Boston. Apparently, she wanted to reintroduce wolves onto her estate, but the Irish government prevented it."

Gwyn wasn't paying attention. With his cigarette nipped between his nicotine-stained finger and thumb, he pointed. "So, Iseult. I want you to be here in your black dress, the low cut one—all made up—full Queen of the Night, you know? We have to make the most of the setting. Then when the first guests arrive. I'll open the doors, and you'll greet them in your role as Chatelaine of Tullabeg."

Iseult stood and went to the door, running her fingers over the heavy iron bolts. "Yes. When these go back." She ratcheted the bolts back for effect, and the grating sound of metal echoed in the hall. "I'll be here. All dressed up. Queen of Halloween—just like Sorcha!"

"Yeah, except you're better looking," Gwyn said.

Tristan watched her play-acting, her blonde hair back over her shoulders, and the look of mischief in her eyes. If the world were different, then things would be easy, but it wasn't, and they weren't.

৩৯৩

THE DINNER GONG RAN OUT, ECHOING DOWN EMPTY CORRIDORS.

"Hark!" Tristan said. "Grub is up."

Gwyn said, "Man, I thought we'd have more time for a run-through."

Tristan said, "Do it tomorrow. We won't be so tired. I'm starving."

Iseult said. "Guess we're not dressing for dinner then?"

"Well, I'm just lucky that I salvaged my own clothes or I'd be wearing Dudley's duds," Gwyn said.

"And they wouldn't fit," Iseult said.

They made their way towards the library where Claire was waiting. She had changed into a brown woollen skirt and jacket with a cream blouse and a pearl necklace. She'd left her Bible behind.

Dudley stood by the brass gong, the padded hammer in his hand. "My lady is waiting for you in the Room of Blood."

Tristan whispered, "Are they for real?"

Iseult chuckled.

"I mean they're even more theatrical than us—'my lady' is in the Room of Blood for goodness' sake..."

Gwyn shook his head. "No, it's good. The guests will lap this up.

It's showbiz, Tristan. You need to relax your pent up bones. Not every-thing has to be classy; they feed the masses with corn."

"Yeah, and this is pretty corny."

Iseult turned to Claire as they walked down another wood-panelled corridor. "Did you have a sleep?"

"I was meditating, Iseult. It clears the mind so you become more perceptive. You should try it. "

"Thanks for the tip. I might just do that."

Tristan glanced at Iseult, who didn't appear to be being sarcastic.

They mounted a short flight of wooden stairs, and Dudley opened the door for them. The room inside was lit by a blaze of candles hoisted inside the tiara of a crystal chandelier. The chandelier was held up by a mental chain, fastened to the wall with a strong iron clasp. The walls themselves were ruby red, and the ceiling was white.

Tristan stopped in his tracks. "Wow!"

"You have to admit that's pretty impressive," Gwyn said. "They'll love it. They're gonna think this place is worth every penny."

Tristan lowered his eyes from the fiery candles and saw the table, obviously antique, was laid with black linen. On the linen were sets of knives, forks and spoons in sterling silver and wine glasses of cut crystal. Tall backed chairs flanked the table, and at its head, Sorcha stood, dressed in white like she was a bride. She curtsied. "Greetings!"

Sorcha had a good figure, and the dress showed it off. Iseult glanced over and saw Tristan's gaze on Sorcha. Her mouth tightened, and she went to sit down next to Gwyn.

In the wall to the left was a log fire. The heat and light were a welcome antidote to the dank and dark that haunted the castle.

Sorcha sat. There was no place for Dudley, and it looked like he would be the waiter. Tristan sat beside Claire. He took the crisp black linen napkin and unfolded it to put it on his lap. Claire had brought her napkin to her nose. "I love the scent of clean linen."

Tristan stifled a laugh. "Fresh linen's nice," he said, grinning.

After a brief round of conversation, Dudley brought the starter of smoked salmon with Irish potato farls and horseradish. He served a chilled white wine. Tristan saw from the label it was a Vouvray.

Sorcha held out her hands expansively. "We grow the horseradish ourselves, and the salmon's from the West Coast. Please, eat."

Tristan studied her. "You said earlier you were a native by blood if not by accent. You sound American."

Sorcha smiled and brought the dainty silver fish fork to her mouth. "It's not illegal."

"Where are you from?"

"My people are from here. We took a couple generations vacation in the States. I'm one of the O'Connors of Clonagh. Do you know it?"

He shook his head. "Clonagh? Should I?"

She sipped her wine. "It's near the Hill of Allen, the seat of Fionn Mac Cumhail and his warriors in ancient times. Do you like legends, Mr Gifford?"

"Tristan."

"An appropriate name," she said.

"For what?"

"For the legend we are about to re-enact." She lookd down. "But then there are no coincidences, not really."

"I don't know what you mean."

"No."

"But yes, I like legends."

"Good. There's a book in the library, written by Lady Gregory, a friend of WB Yeats, of Irish Legends. May I recommend the Story of Diarmuid and Gráinne?"

"I'll take a look."

"I think you'll find it very interesting. Some people may get to choose their stories, but for most their stories choose them."

"Very wise," Gwyn said. "I choose more drink though please."

The party finished the fish, apart from Iseult who picked at the salmon and left most. When Dudley came round, she smiled and told him he could take the plate.

Sorcha put down her glass. "I would be very interested to know a little about each of you now you are my guests, even for a short while."

"You know me," Gwyn said.

"I know your business persona, but I don't know who you are inside."

Gwyn knocked back his wine. "Who I am inside, stays inside. No offence." He waggled his glass. "You got any more of this? It's lovely."

Dudley had left the bottle in a silver ice bucket on the table. Tristan took it out and handed it, dripping and cold, to Gwyn. Gwyn filled his glass and placed the bottle on the tablecloth beside his knife as if daring anyone to take any for themselves. A wet circle soaked the linen out from its base.

Tristan coughed. "I'm the tech-guy. I place the speakers and other trickery. Just to create the experiences for the paying guests."

Sorcha fixed him with her brilliant blue eyes. "You needn't hide behind your tricks here, Tristan. This is the real deal—a genuine haunted Irish castle. Are you genuine, Tristan? Is this the real you?"

Tristan twirled the silver knife in his hand. "A genuine haunted castle, eh? If you say so."

She tilted her head. "And you don't look like a technician. You're too tall and broad-shouldered."

"I was in the Army with Gwyn. He was my sergeant."

"A warrior! Where did you serve?"

Tristan said, "We're not allowed to talk about it." He looked to Gwyn for support. The older man had his head tilted back and was examining the chandelier and sipping more wine.

Tristan looked back at Sorcha. "I couldn't get a job after I left the Army. I didn't have many transferable skills. Being honest, I think Gwyn created this job for me."

"Pah," Gwyn said. "You're worth every penny of the very few pennies I pay you."

"But you're a fighter, Tristan?"

Tristan shook his head. "I'm a linguist."

"A soldier linguist? Speak any Irish?"

He shook his head. "Arabic mainly. Some Farsi. Some Pashto."

"What about you?" Sorcha turned to Iseult.

The younger woman shrugged, caught with her mouth to her glass. There was a pause. Her expression when she looked at Sorcha wasn't friendly. She put the glass down. "I'm Gwyn's wife."

"Surely, you're not just a wife? That's letting the sisterhood down!" Sorcha chuckled. "Isn't it, Claire?"

Claire looked surprised as if she'd been miles away. "Sorry?"

"The sisterhood?"

The older woman looked puzzled. She frowned, her expression reminiscent of a small rodent.

Sorcha smiled indulgently then turned back to Iseult. "You were saying?"

Iseult drained her glass. "I wasn't really."

Gwyn leaned over and filled it again. "She's our hostess," he said. "She leads the guests round with Claire, tells them the tales, and makes sure they're happy. And she's good at it."

"I'm sure she is. So, Claire, you're the psychic?"

Claire nodded.

"And do you sense much here?"

Claire muttered, "Many spirits."

Sorcha seemed pleased. "Yes, the place is full of spirits."

"There are some strong ones."

Sorcha talked as if she were asking casual questions, but her tone was intense. "How old are they? Which is the oldest?"

Claire looked confused. "I don't know what you mean."

"I mean, how far do your senses reach back? Can you sense very ancient ghosts here?"

At that moment, Dudley came in with the main course.

Sorcha gave a flourish of her hands. "Roast pheasant with potatoes, carrots, peas and red wine gravy. Not very sophisticated, but I did make it all myself."

Tristan tucked in, the day's travel had made him hungry.

"I'm a Christian," Claire announced to Sorcha, holding her knife and fork straight up from the table.

"As is young Iseult, I think," Sorcha said.

Iseult shook her head, but fingered the gold cross around her neck. "This was my grandmother's."

"You were close?"

"She was the only one of my family I loved."

Claire blurted, "I'm the only true Christian here."

Sorcha smiled. "Well, I'm no Christian, true or otherwise."

Claire said, "One of these spirits hates you very much: a woman with a hard face."

Sorcha shrugged. "I'm not frightened of any ghost. But, I'm curious, Claire— isn't speaking to the dead forbidden by your religion?"

"I'm a Christian spiritualist. Anyway, I don't seek them; they come to find me. They crowd around me with their messages. I've always seen them, ever since I was a girl, but then I didn't know what they were. My mother used to beat me when I told her what they said. She took me to the vicar, but he wasn't interested. Then they sent me to the doctor, but he told me I wasn't mad. I asked him for a certificate."

"To say you weren't mad?" Sorcha said.

Claire nodded. "But he wouldn't give me one."

"I bet," muttered Tristan, just loud enough for Iseult and Gwyn to hear. Iseult spluttered with laughter and put her hand over her mouth. Claire didn't notice.

Claire said to Sorcha. "I recognise you."

Sorcha smiled.

"Were you in the movies?" Claire said.

Sorcha shrugged, still smiling. "One or two, but I was younger then."

"You were in *Loving Mr Janson*."

"I was."

"I thought you were wonderful."

"Thank you, Claire. Those days are long gone, but I did manage to earn enough to buy this place."

"And you were in..." Claire sucked her lip. "Was it..."

Sorcha looked uncomfortable.

Claire stuck up her knife to command silence. "Don't tell me. It's on the tip of my tongue." Then she whirled her head round and said, "*Only The Brave*—set in the American Civil War. You were Miss Elaine."

Sorcha laughed. "Modesty forbids, but I was well-reviewed."

"I thought you were beautiful."

"Were?" Gwyn said.

"Are, is." Claire snapped. "Is beautiful." Claire cocked her head and simpered. "You are very beautiful, Lady Sorcha."

"Very kind." Sorcha looked fixedly at Claire. "Returning to our previous conversation, I am interested in messages from the old ones. The ones who've been here for thousands of years. If you sense them, I'd like to ask them a few things."

Claire nodded. She seemed pleased that Sorcha took her gift seriously. Shyly she asked, "If you aren't a Christian, what are you?"

"I'm a pagan." Sorcha narrowed her eyes, looking around as if seeking any hint of disapproval or mockery.

Tristan kept his face deadpan.

Sorcha continued, "I worship the old Irish gods."

Claire's said hurriedly, "But you believe in the spirits? You believe I can talk to them?"

Sorcha reached over and grasped Claire's hand. Claire let her do it. She even smiled. Sorcha said, "Yes, I do, Claire. I do indeed."

Tristan wiped his mouth with his handkerchief. "I don't believe in ghosts."

Sorcha took back her hand from Claire. Studying Tristan, her expression curious but confident, she said, "You said. You're wrong."

Claire nodded. "Pride goeth before destruction, and an haughty spirit before a fall."

"Prove they exist. Here in this castle, prove there are ghosts."

Sorcha smiled. "I shall. Let's see if your courage holds out."

THE BANSHEE CALLS

After dinner, Tristan strolled through to the library with his wine glass and sat by the fire. Claire had disappeared to her room, and Gwyn and Iseult were still talking to Sorcha in the so-called Room of Blood. Getting comfortable, he read about Tullabeg Castle's history.

It seemed Sir Robert Morton built the first Tullabeg Castle on a patch of drier land in the bog, and his descendants kept the lordship for centuries afterwards.

The book rambled on in a fancy Victorian way about the flora and fauna, and he learned that the locals shot the last wolf in 1784.

Tristan sipped the wine while reading about the druids who had been the first inhabitants of the Tullabeg area. In those days it had been a crannóg —a village built in the swamp, raised up on stilts above the waterlogged surface. Even after the castle was built, even after the coming of Christianity, the pagans lingered in the area of Tullabeg until Sir Robert Morton massacred them in the twelfth century. Tristan got to chapter three and closed the book.

He had also found Sorcha's book recommendation: *Of Gods and Fighting Men* by Lady Augusta Gregory. He flipped through it, found the story: *The Pursuit of Diarmuid and Gráinne*. Fionn Mac Cumhaill was a great Irish hero who had his headquarters not far from Tullabeg on the Hill of Allen. There were lots of stories about him, one of the most famous being *The Pursuit of Diarmuid and Gráinne*, but Tristan didn't read it.

Instead, book lying on the table, he finished his wine and gazed around him. The room had warmed up, and he didn't feel even a hint of an uncanny atmosphere. He wondered if Sorcha took her ghosts as gospel. She certainly talked as if she thought they were real, but if she thought she could frighten him with such talk she was wrong, and if she fancied a battle of wits, she was welcome to try.

He studied the portraits of the Mortons that hung on the walls in their faded gilt frames. They were an ugly lot. He stood, stretched his arms, and wandered around, looking at them as they hung in an order representing past centuries. A picture of Sir Robert Morton hung in pride of place. Sir Robert founded the castle, but the painting dated from some centuries after his day. Tristan guessed a later Morton commissioned it in honour of the long-deceased head of the family. The other Mortons fat and thin, old and young, glared down at him. Then he got to the cruel-faced woman. He screwed up his eyes to decipher the name at the bottom of the portrait, but the hand was old-fashioned, and he couldn't read it.

He stared at her for a minute. "You sure are an evil-looking bird."

Leaving the library, Tristan hoped he'd remember the way back to his room.

⁂

Tristan left the library and wandering in a labyrinth of darkened hallways, got lost. In his search for the way to his room, he came across parts of the castle that seemed uninhabited. Even though they were unlived in, people visited these parts from time to time judging from the footmarks that came and went in the dust. The feet of rats and mice had made their mark too, and from a set of paw marks, someone had a dog. Eventually, he found the hall with the red and black tiles and followed it to the dark staircase.

He mounted the staircase and found the hallway with the bronze bust of the unhappy man. His room was ahead, and a light came out from under Claire's door.

Tristan opened his door but stood there on the threshold without switching the light on. It felt odd inside the room. Unexpected excitement sizzled through him. He didn't believe in ghosts, but what if he caught one? He flicked the switch and found nothing unusual.

With a chuckle, he stepped inside, and with that step, the temperature dropped. In the electric light, his breath billowed out like he'd entered a fridge. Tristan frowned, backed out onto the corridor and exhaled. His breath was invisible here. He put out his hand and turned it in the air. It was definitely warmer in the hall outside, then he stepped back into his room, frowning. Yes, much colder. His breath came in clouds. He felt chill on his skin. But there was no ball of light or any other supernatural manifestation.

Tristan pulled back the heavy floral curtains and turned the handle on the window. It was secure, no gaps, no holes. He peered through the uneven glass panes, but as far as he could see not even a pinprick of light pierced the darkness. They were a long way from home, a long way in fact from anything other than Tullabeg Castle. He let the curtain drop. He could still see his breath in the air. But it was an old building made of stones that had drunk in the damp for century upon century. It was also very quiet. There wasn't even a wind.

On an impulse, he tapped on the adjoining door to Claire's room. "You okay in there, Claire?"

Her voice came back, "Yes, thank you."

He said. "I'm considering turning in. We've a lot to do tomorrow."

She didn't reply. He was sure she didn't care. He glanced at his watch. It was ten-thirty. They'd had a long day. He laughed to himself and looked around; he was sure he'd sleep even in this ghost-infested castle. This was no nexus of the uncanny; all it was was somewhere set up for tricks and misdirections. He was king of the technical tricks, cameras, lights and hidden speakers. You can't trick a tricker. He would catch Sorcha out—sure he would.

THEN, WHOLLY UNEXPECTEDLY THE HANDLE OF THE CONNECTING door between his room and Claire's turned.

A crack of light appeared, and Tristan pushed himself back against the bed's headboard.

But it was no ghost. Claire peeped round the door. She was like a female thrush, her eyes bright with life and animal insight, but no real intelligence, at least not a human one. That's what you got from spending most of your time seeing things that weren't there.

She said, "I don't blame you, Tristan."

He hesitated. "What?"

"I know you mean to be loyal. But she..." She shook her head as if she was attempting to be diplomatic. " She..." She gave a false laugh. "... Don't misunderstand me, she's a lovely girl. A beautiful girl. She'd drive the sense out of any man, I see that. But she's damaged. There are things about her you don't know. Things you can't understand."

Tristan stared. "And you can?"

"I see into her. She wants someone to properly love her, Tristan. Gwyn can't love her like that. He—" She cocked her head to one side. "He's more a protector and benefactor. Oh, she longs for romance, but she has a void inside her. I think she wants children, but he doesn't. He can't."

He paused, studying her, trying to work out whether she was for real. He needed someone to confide in. Back in Wales, people came to have their fortunes told by Claire, lots of them. Maybe she was wise, maybe she did know things. And this unspoken longing churned him up. He cleared his throat. "Tell me, Claire, you advise people on things like this?"

"I do. I do."

"Do you really know things? Have insights?"

"Of course I do. I am an honest woman. I would not lie."

He studied her. He sighed. He rubbed his face. This was stupid.

"Speak, son. Unburden yourself."

He shook his head. "I don't know."

She tilted her head. "You want to know which is most important— loyalty or love. I'm right, aren't I?"

He stared at her.

She smiled. "I know that's your question. You are torn between the two."

He shrugged as if humouring her. "Well, what would be your view on that?"

She gave a hollow laugh. "Love? People come to me, hearts full of love, broken by love, made crazy by love, and they do wild things for love; they sacrifice lives and children and careers for it. But me, I've never felt it."

"And loyalty—my husband should have been loyal, but he threw me out because he said I was a witch." She watched him. "You know, Tristan, I'm no witch. I do what I do because I can't help it. I see what I see and I have as much choice in that as you seeing what you see. I have a gift, and with that gift, I want to help people. And the dead. I want to help the dead too. I simply wish to help the spirits get to the light."

Her gaze had wandered, but now she snapped back to him. "But if I have to choose between loyalty and love, I'd say loyalty. How does that suit you?"

He said, "Funny, I thought you were going to say love."

"Duty is very important to me."

He bowed his head, pinched his brow and gave a laugh. "But in the women's magazines, the agony aunts say that if you love someone very much, you should be with them. They say that love comes above everything. I thought you'd say that too."

Claire said, "I don't know what kind of magazines you read, Tristan. But I'm not an agony aunt. I'm a truth teller."

"So it's not true that love trumps everything else?"

She cocked her head and glanced at him with her bright bird eyes. "Are you asking me to condone a sin, Tristan?"

He grimaced. "Of course not."

"You have a decision to make."

He exhaled.

Claire continued. "I can't make your decisions for you, son."

He rubbed his eyes. When he glanced up, Claire was still staring, like she was trying to read his mind. Eventually, realising the conversation was over, she nodded, retreated and pulled the door shut behind her.

She pretended to be kind, but he didn't trust her an inch.

⟡

Claire's door closed, but there was still noise outside on the corridor. He saw his bedroom door was open a chink. He thought he'd closed it. He mustn't have pushed it home so he got out of his bed and went to close it. As he stood there, he heard another door open onto the corridor. He made out Gwyn's voice and caught the final."—she needs to pay me,"

Then Iseult said, "You're too easy-going with them. You're fearless with other things, but you don't like people not to like you."

"I'll go then."

"Go."

"I will."

"Do."

"I'm not weak, Iseult, if that's what you're saying."

"I'm not saying that. I've never said that, never thought it even."

"I will ask her. And if she doesn't say yes, then we'll leave. Right now."

"Absolutely. Though, the car..."

"We can get a taxi. The car's a heap of junk, anyway."

"Whatever you say, Gwyn. I'll do what you say."

"Fine. I won't be long."

Tristan listened to the sound of Gwyn's feet descending the stairs.

Tristan stepped out onto the corridor as if to say goodnight to them both. Iseult stood outside their door in a t-shirt and pyjama pants.

"Oh, sorry," he said.

"I'm about to go to bed," she said.

"I can see." Neither of them moved into their rooms.

"I heard Gwyn."

"Yeah, he's riled up—about money. He always gets riled up about money."

"Has he gone to see her?"

"Yeah."

"This late?"

She made a face. "He wants Sorcha to pay him everything upfront. He's got it into his head that she'll trick him." She sighed. "He's been drinking."

"Why would she trick him?"

"You know what he's like. Especially about money."

"He's always been generous to me."

She said, "I didn't mean he's not generous. He's just paranoid about it. The business isn't doing so well, and..."

"He's a great guy."

"He is."

Tristan said, "I owe him a lot."

She nodded. "Me too."

He stopped. "He really was fearless."

"Yes. You've told me before."

"He never mentioned any of those times?"

"In the desert? No, that's not his style."

Tristan stared into her bedroom over her shoulder. "Ah, yes."

She looked puzzled. "What?"

He pointed into the room. "In the same Gothic style, candles, four posters. She must have spent a fortune on the decor for this place."

She smiled. "You think she's rich?"

He smiled back. "Yeah. I bet she is."

"If that's true, she can pay Gwyn what she owes us."

"I'm sure she will."

She reached out and touched his forearm with her fingertips. "I can't stop thinking about you."

He didn't pull his arm back from hers. Instead, he relished the feel of her fingertips. He was near to her. Her hair was luminous in the electric light. He felt full of sunshine being near her.

Her hand was on his arm still.

Sunshine and storm clouds all mixed up inside. He said, "You know it's wrong."

She shook her head. "We've never talked about it."

"We shouldn't talk about it. We should pretend it isn't happening."

"I can't pretend. It's eating me up."

"We've got to be strong."

"Then why did you come out of your room then when you knew Gwyn had gone?"

He blushed. "Got me there," he said.

She pulled him to her. "Just hold me. Just for a minute."

"What if he comes back?"

"We're not in the bedroom. We're only talking. It's innocent."

"It's not innocent." He didn't move away. "And if I have my arms around you?"

"I don't know. I can say I was scared—that we heard something?"

He stared. "I can't deceive him."

She began to cry. "And I can't live without you."

He put his hand out and stroked her cheek, brushing away her tears with his fingertips. The pain in his heart was a deep toothache pain, knit with the sharp stab of a broken bone, the fiery throb of a burn, the insistent pulse of a fever. He folded around her like it was a friendly thing he did, a caress of compassion only, seeking like a brother or a good friend merely to comfort some sudden unfounded fear, as if fear was the cause of her crying, as if it wasn't love.

Whatever she thought—however she had weighed up her debt to her husband, she came to her lover. They had never made love with their bodies, but he loved her and she him, so they were truly lovers and their love was a twisted, fractured thing that brought more pain than bliss. He smelled her, and it was the smell he'd longed for all his life: her youth, the summer that love brings, the soft stars and the promise of an imaginary marriage in a made-up orange grove and never-to-be children around their feet.

And she wasn't his. And that was all this love would ever be: nothing.

He broke off the embrace. And he stepped back, hanging his head.

AN EAR-SPLITTING WAIL RANG THROUGH THE CASTLE. THE SOUND rose up from the deepest cellars to the highest towers. Tristan's heart flipped, and he snapped round every way to see where the wail came from. Iseult grabbed his arm, her eyes wide with terror. The cry echoed on, rolling and lingering round all the dark corridors and rooms, howling with despair and horror, resounding with pain and death. A damned soul cried out here, Tristan thought: it was either a damned soul or a deliberate lie.

Iseult's hand went to her mouth. "What is that?"

Claire ran out of her room, now wearing her nylon nightdress and an old dressing gown, her eyes bright with excitement. "Where did that come from?"

Tristan said, "It must be a speaker system. It's Sorcha trying to scare us."

Iseult squeezed his hand. "She's doing a good job,"

Tristan's own palm was sweaty, and his heart speeded up, but he told it to calm down. By being scared, he was only playing into Sorcha's stupid tricks. This was a con. He wouldn't let Sorcha roll him over like some rube.

Claire pointed along the corridor in a direction they'd never explored. "It's coming from down there." She strode towards the source of the wail.

"Claire!" Tristan yelled. "Where are you going?"

Claire turned, a huge smile on her face. "I'm going to find the banshee!"

The wail stopped.

"It's gone," he said.

"But I sense her. Come!" She beckoned with a bony finger. "It's this way. Come on."

Claire marched off.

Tristan had to follow her; he couldn't let the crazy old dame wander down these dark corridors and break her neck. And more than that, he wouldn't let Sorcha get away with these corny tricks.

He hurried to catch Claire up, and Iseult came tagging along, reaching and squeezing his hand again.

They reached the end of the passage that was closed off by a door.

Claire pulled it open and revealed a stone spiral staircase going both up and down.

Claire clambered up the steps. "Upwards!"

Tristan saw his breath billow out. That gave him pause for a second, but it was definitely colder here: no trickery needed.

After a few steps, Tristan realised that the refurbishment of the castle was far from uniform. He remembered the sight of the ruined tower from outside. Some parts of this place were dangerous to walk. They needed to take care.

But Claire had already disappeared around the ascending spiral.

He called, "Easy, Claire. Watch your step," but if she heard him, she didn't slow down. He listened to her flat, bare feet pattering up each stone step.

Iseult giggled, now the first fright had passed.

Tristan said, "You wait here. I'll go up with that crazy woman."

Iseult shook her head. "I'm made of sterner stuff than that, my friend. I want to see the banshee too."

"There'll be nothing there, Issy. Nothing except a huge PA system."

She laughed. "Come on. Let's catch up with her."

They climbed the tower behind Claire and after ten turns of the spiral, emerged onto a dusty corridor that ran parallel with theirs below. Claire stared into the darkness, limp hand in front of her, finger curled like a pointer dog's paw.

Claire said, "It's ahead."

Iseult clutched her arms. "I'm freezing."

Claire said, "It's ahead."

Tristan pointed at the floor. "Look at all this dust,"

Iseult said, "Tristan, do you have a light?"

"I've got my phone." He switched on the white light, and it illuminated a part of the castle that seemed hardly visited. Old footmarks trailed across the floor but recent falls of dust almost wholly disguised them. "Where?"

"Come!" Claire said. "I can sense her. She's close."

Iseult grabbed Tristan's arm. Even though he knew it was nonsense, Claire's certainty and Iseult's nervousness unsettled him. Iseult gripped him tight. She was trembling

"I thought you said you were made of sterner stuff?" he whispered.

"I was exaggerating," Iseult replied — at least she was smiling.

They stalked like Scooby-Doo and Shaggy along the abandoned corridor. As they got closer to its end, the phone light lit up an ancient door. It blocked their progress and was warped and mildewed. The the door was old, it was secured with a new padlock. Claire ran up and banged on the door with the heel of her hand.

The hammering noise shattered the ancient silence of the empty tower, and Iseult let out an involuntary yelp.

Claire hammered three slow blows on the wooden door. Then stepping back, she intoned, "I call thee, spirit of this place. What message hast thou for us pilgrims?"

Iseult brought her hand to her mouth to stifle her laughter. "Pilgrims? Us?"

"This is a circus," Tristan said, loud enough for Claire to hear.

Claire waited five minutes but then, blowing air from the side of her mouth, turned on her heel. She grumbled."She's in there, but the door's locked."

As she got close to Iseult, she leaned in. "Some of us are pilgrims, even if you revel in your sin."

Iseult's eyes narrowed. Claire walked off. Isuelt yelled at Claire's back, "What do you mean by that?"

Claire didn't turn, and Iseult let the sentence drift away as if she already knew the answer and didn't want to hear it.

❧

THEY DESCENDED TO THE INHABITED PART OF THE CASTLE. ISEULT had let go of Tristan and was behind him, lost in her own thoughts. He stopped to wait for her.

They arrived at their own corridor and saw Gwyn standing with Dudley. Iseult walked forward to greet him like a dutiful wife, and he put his arms around her. He seemed half drunk.

Gwyn looked from Claire to Iseult to Tristan. "Where did you go?"

Tristan nodded at Claire. "We went looking for the banshee."

"You what?"

Tristan said to Dudley, "Great sound system by the way."

Dudley stood impassive.

"What are you talking about?" Gwyn said.

"You must have heard that wail," Iseult said. "Come on. It was loud enough for them to hear in Dublin."

"I have no idea what you're going on about. What wail?"

Then Dudley nodded, a look of understanding forming on his face. He said, "You've heard the banshee."

"Like you don't know," Tristan snapped.

Dudley shrugged. "I heard nothing. Honest. But if you did, it means someone will die before the week's out."

"Oh, God," Iseult said, burying her face in his hands.

Gwyn shook his head. "I heard nothing. I came back to find everyone gone."

In a stage whisper to Tristan, Dudley said, "You need to be careful wandering around the castle. It's not safe."

"This is such bullshit," Tristan muttered.

Dudley pointed his wavering finger. "The banshee cries three times." He paused for effect and looked each one of them in the eye. "And when she cries for the last time, someone will die."

Tristan stared at him and made a pfft sound.

"Okay, we're all tired," Gwyn said, "I'm turning in. I suggest you do the same."

Even taking the drink into account, Tristan thought Gwyn seemed more relaxed. He was even smiling. The conversation with Sorcha about money must have gone well.

Dudley strolled away without another word, and Gwyn and Iseult went into their bedroom. Tristan stood alone in the passage. Iseult threw him a lingering look over her shoulder before Gwyn reached over her to pull the door closed behind them.

Tristan ran his hand across his face. He was going to have to get a grip of himself. Now he bitterly regretted letting Iseult hold him, though then it had been all he wanted. He couldn't let this go any further. If they had never to see each other again, then so be it. If that was what maintaining his loyalty to Gwyn cost, then so be it.

But they had this whole charade to go through first: a ghost hunt where paying guests shelled out their cash in return for getting scared to death. It was all lies. They were lying to the punters, though the punters welcomed the lies. Sorcha was lying to them all for some reason of her own. Iseult and he were lying to Gwyn to spare his feelings. And he was lying to himself if he hoped he would ever be with her.

❧ 6 ☙

SOMETHING IN THE LOFT

Tristan became aware of sunlight. He must have left the curtain open the previous night because sweet autumn sunshine spilled into the bedroom. He lay there for a second, trying to remember where he was. Then he did: Tullabeg Castle. He'd expected nightmares but didn't remember his dreams at all, then noticed the sheets were twisted and half off the bed.

He swung his legs out from under the quilt, landing with the soles of his feet one on the cool wooden floorboards, the other on the antique rug.

Tristan stood by the four-poster bed. He yanked the curtains wide — no one was out in the Bog of Allen to see his nakedness, no one and nothing apart from a few clouds drifting by, and they didn't care. The bogland stretched low and flooded far away. He took in the rushes and sedges clumped together with the moss in a patchwork of greens. Some places had been worked for peat, and there were trenches in the middle distance and stacked turfs beside.

The sky was half-covered with white clouds, but there was enough sun to break through and wash the marsh in the light of a golden October. The land rose eastwards to meet the low autumn sun. That must be the Hill of Allen he could see— hideout of Fionn Mac Cumhail and his Fíanna. That was from his brief look at the book that Sorcha recommended. Such stories interested him, and he would pick it up again if he got time.

The sheer size of the bog impressed him. Anyone trying to escape from the castle that way—and the swamp was all ways—would flounder knee-deep until exhaustion drained their spirit and they drowned.

Tristan washed in the sink, dressed and wondered where the shower was, or at least a bath. There must be one. He promised himself a soak later.

Opening the door to the hall, he found Gwyn and Iseult coming out of their room.

Gwyn said, "Did you hear that row last night?"

"The wail? Sure." Tristan frowned. "I thought you hadn't heard it?"

"No, not that. Much later. Around 2 a.m."

"No, I was dead to the world."

"Iseult heard it. Didn't you Issy?"

"Yes, it was people having a quarrel."

Gwyn walked toward the stairs. "I thought some guests had turned up late and rooms weren't ready or something. It came from down below." Gwyn shook his head. "They kept on at it for about an hour, and I got up and went downstairs."

Tristan caught up with them. "Who was it?"

Gwyn shook his head "That's it. There was nobody. The house was in darkness."

Tristan laughed. "More ghosts?"

"I'm not joking Tristan. It was real. I heard it."

"Sure, let's go get breakfast."

Gwyn glowered at him. Tristan could tell he'd annoyed Gwyn by not accepting his story. As they walked downstairs, Tristan said, "It's just Sorcha messing with us."

Iseult frowned. "Why, though? I don't see what she's got to gain."

"To make us believe in her ghosts, of course."

Iseult said, "Why would she do that? We're not her paying guests. Sorcha doesn't have to convince us of anything."

Tristan said, "She likes messing with people. She strikes me as that type."

They got to the foot of the stairs. Gwyn scratched his scalp. "You know the way to the kitchen?"

Tristan grinned. "Nope. But let's go find Dudley. Where Dudley is, there lies breakfast."

They hadn't got as far as the library when they ran into Dudley.

The Irishman beamed. "Sleep well?"

Gwyn grunted. "Not really. Who were all those people downstairs at about 2 a.m.? Sounded like they were having an argument."

Dudley shook his head, his grey hair swinging across his cheeks. "No one here but us."

"I heard them," Gwyn said.

Iseult said, "I heard them too."

Tristan said, "Not me, though."

"Strange things happen here. There are visitations," Dudley said, opening the door to the kitchen.

Claire was already sitting at the long farmhouse table. She looked to be eating porridge and wore the same outfit as the previous day. Once again, she had her Bible with her. She glanced up. "Good morning."

They all sat and helped themselves to fresh toast with salted Irish butter. Soda bread and a glass jug of fresh orange juice stood on the table. Dudley offered coffee or tea.

Gwyn lit a cigarette without asking if anyone minded.

Tristan buttered his toast. "So, it's Halloween tomorrow. The gates to the Otherworld are open!"

Iseult smiled at him. "Spooky!"

"It better be spooky," Gwyn said. He looked up at Dudley. "What time are the guests due today? If some arrive today, we can give a mini-tour, then tomorrow scare them shitless."

Dudley was frying eggs and bacon. The aroma filled the kitchen. He wasn't paying attention.

"Dudley," Gwyn repeated. "What time we expecting the customers?"

Dudley turned and shrugged. "When they get here."

Gwyn took a long drag on his cigarette. "Very helpful." He lifted his coffee mug and went over to the window. "God, it's a wild place here."

Dudley kept on cooking.

Gwyn walked over the Welsh Dresser and turned over the plates. "My grandmother had some like this. Not the exact same. Similar."

Iseult smiled. "He always jabbers when he's nervous."

Gwyn twisted round. "I'm not nervous. But I do need to get everything right. You know me: piss poor planning delivers piss poor performance."

Tristan said, "You already said that."

Gwyn lifted a finger. "And did I already say that bullshit baffles brains. And bullshit is your department with your sounds and lights."

"Too true," Tristan said.

"It'll be right," Iseult said.

Dudley said, "You're going to do the old Celtic mist stuff: the pagan druids, curses, ghosts, banshees, death?"

Gwyn nodded. "You bet. We've got our technical effects courtesy of Tristan. We've got some stories, courtesy of me, pyschicness from Claire and charm and beauty via the lovely Isuelt."

Gwyn sat down again with his coffee. Tristan didn't remember him ever being so wound up before a gig. Something must be eating him. Sorcha had promised to pay, so it wasn't that. Thinking of other reasons Gwyn might be on edge made Tristan too uncomfortable. He tapped the table. "Nice old table, you've got here."

"We've got nice old everything here," Dudley said.

Gwyn turned. "Tristan, you've got places to put the speakers?"

Tristan glanced up. I've seen a few. I'll go have a scout around this morning. I'll set up the projector too."

Gwyn played some intricate drum rhythm on his juice glass. "Oh, yeah, that's good."

Tristan had invented a trick that involved a projector wired up to his laptop. He suspended a sheet of muslin in a place the guests couldn't get to and projected a sepia image of a black and white monk. It gave the effect of the monk appearing in mid-air and fluttering in the breeze.

Dudley came with the bacon and eggs plated up. Tristan wasn't massively hungry, but he couldn't resist the smell of the bacon.

Claire shot up from her seat. "I will sit in the Library and try to contact the spirits."

Gwyn blew smoke. "Sure, I'll come and get you when I need you." Then he said, "Dudley, is Sorcha around?" He hadn't touched his food.

"She's in her office."

"Can you show us?"

Dudley nodded. "She said she wanted to speak to you." He wiped his hands on his apron, took it off and hung it on the back of a chair. Gwyn followed Dudley to the door, Tristan got up to go after him. Dudley raised a finger. "Not you. She only wants to speak to your boss."

Tristan shrugged and dropped back into his chair.

Iseult sat, drinking her juice.

Gwyn stuck his head back around the door. "Apparently you too, Issy."

Iseult glanced at Tristan, then said, "Sure." She got up and followed her husband out of the room.

❧

TRISTAN WAS NOW ALONE IN THE KITCHEN. WHEN HE FINISHED HIS bacon and eggs, he put his plate in the sink and went out to find his room. He remembered the way, more or less, but still took a wrong turn down a dismal corridor and when he realised he was going wrong, had to retrace his steps. He saw no one and heard no one. The only sound was that of his own purposeful footsteps. He fetched the bag that contained his electronic gear and his laptop from his room and carried it back to the library.

Tristan dumped the bag on the oak table. The grandfather clock ticked from the corner. He hadn't noticed the ticking the previous night when the fire was hissing. But the fire was grey and dead, and the staccato ticks boomed out. The logs were now black skeletons sitting in cold piles of ash. From all around the walls, the portraits watched him.

Trying to focus on his work, Tristan busied himself, laying the technology on the table. He held up a small speaker that he would control via BlueTooth and beam horror noises from the laptop. He chose the portrait of the cruel-faced woman. He took out a tube of adhesive and glued the tiny device to the back of the picture, then lowered it back to the wall, the speaker now out of sight.

He debated putting another speaker here in the library, but that might be overkill. Then he remembered the suit of armour at the top of the main staircase coming in. That was iconic. He took his glue and speakers and went to the entrance hall. The sound of his footsteps echoed on the wooden floor. As he trotted up the stairs, he stopped and spun around, sensing someone behind him, but there was no one there. At least no one he could see. He was being silly, imagining shit. Every time he got spooked here was a victory for Sorcha. He looked around from halfway up the staircase. There was no sign of life, not even a mouse scurrying, but he still shuddered. The place had an atmosphere—and not a pleasant atmosphere either. He had thought his nerves were better.

He reached the landing. He had work to do.

The suit of armour was about five foot eight inches high. He ran his fingers over the cool iron. Someone had polished the metal, and it was worn, so it might be authentic, but the leather was a replacement.

Tristan lifted the visor and placed the speaker inside. He had voice clips that would utter terrifying words of warning from the suit of armour to freak the guests out. Tristan chuckled to himself. He must have a sadistic side after all.

❧

BACK IN THE LIBRARY, HE WAS ABOUT TO SLING THE EQUIPMENT BAG on his back and go looking for other speaker spots. As he turned to leave, he noticed the spine of the history book he'd read the night before jutting out from the shelf. He must have forgotten to put it back, and the inharmonious sight of it sticking out offended his OCD tendencies. He went to put it straight, but, on a whim, pulled it out again, riffling through the pages until he saw a reproduction of the portrait of the cruel faced woman. Tristan stopped flicking and put his finger on it. Then he laid the book on the table. The text said the portrait was of Lady Amelia Morton who died in 1788.

He read the brief biographic section about her. They called her the Bloody Countess. She was sister to the lord and, according to the book, flirted with black magic. In her search for eternal youth, she enticed young women from the neighbourhood into her service, killed them, and drank their blood. When her murderous acts came to light, the local Irish stormed the castle. They said they had no quarrel with the Mortons, but they demanded revenge for their daughter's and sisters' deaths. Lord Morton was away, but his wife handed Lady Amelia over to the locals. They flayed her alive in revenge for the deaths she had caused. The leader of the natives was a man called Éamonn O'Connor. There was mention of Lady Amelia being a "thrice-damned woman."

Tristan looked up at Lady Amelia, who stared at him with her cold eyes. "Now I know why you look such a bitch." Funny Sorcha still kept the picture hanging here. Or then again, maybe not.

Tristan pushed the book back in its place and left the library, walking along the red corridor. This would be an excellent route to take the guests with its claustrophobic closed doors. Somehow the rows of locked doors created unease. It couldn't be long before the first guests arrived. He wanted to be finished placing his speakers by then.

At the end of the hall, stairs led up towards their bedrooms. Tristan noticed an entrance to a corridor on the right. He hadn't been down there before. He turned down it.

The feeling of someone watching him grew. He even stopped and turned on his heel to surprise the watcher, but there was no one. The long hallway stretching away, the locked doors to the unknown rooms that flanked it, the gloom, the silence here, the loneliness, all served to unnerve him.

The passage veered left, then opened into a big hall. This hall was about forty feet long. He had a vague recollection that Sorcha had spoken of a Baronial Hall. The floor was dark wood and old; faded heraldic banners hung from the walls. Stained glass windows ran along the walls above head height. The windows looked to be Victorian copies of original medieval ones.

Tristan noticed an opening in the far wall. He could see stairs going up, perhaps to a minstrel's gallery. That would be a great place to put a speaker; it would boom out over the guests below when Iseult brought them into the hall to do a narration.

Tristan mounted the stairs to the minstrel's gallery and looked out over the empty hall. He imagined the feasts and parties that must have been held there: from knights and damsels in the Middle Ages to flappers and gentlemen in the 1920s. They were all gone, all dead now.

He heard the wind blowing outside. Through the window, he saw the sky had clouded over again, and the daylight was grey.

He unpacked his equipment, checking each item before placing it down. He had them in a row in front of him. He would need a booster here for the Wifi, but he knew he had a battery-powered one in his bag. He selected three speakers—one of them could put out a hundred decibels. Tristan looked about him for a site. There was a half-ledge, not ideal, but workable. He was about to place it when he saw that the wooden panel at the end of the minstrel's gallery had a scratch. This scratch disappeared behind another panel.

That was odd.

He pressed the panel, then tapped it, and his knocking echoed back. The board sounded hollow. Tristan peered at a little carved dog's head — maybe it was a wolf — on the woodwork. He grasped it, and it turned, and there was a click as the panel came open.

"Oh my God!" he said out loud. His face broke into a grin. Wait till he told Gwyn and Iseult. There was a secret panel. Tullabeg was the real deal.

⁂

Tristan pushed at the panel, and it swung open. He took out his phone from his jeans pocket. Even though he had no signal, he had charged it the night before, and the flashlight was bright. He saw a passage wide enough for a man to walk down. The gap led between the wood panelling and the thick stone exterior wall. He would expect it to be strung with cobwebs, but it wasn't.

Because he was tall, he had to stoop. The passage went on level for a while then descended a few steps. With one hand on the rough stone, he bent forward. He was concentrating. The daylight and the door were way behind him now, and if he hadn't had his phone he couldn't see his way.

The stone wall was damp to the touch, and he smelled the bog everywhere. The passage twisted left. He was going further into it than he had intended, but he was too excited with his discovery to turn back before finding out where it led. Tristan groped forward, pressing one hand against the wall, stooping to avoid banging his head against the rough stones of the passage ceiling, cursing when he did.

The passage twisted right. He could see grey shafts of light from holes in the wood panelling. That was pretty odd too.

When he got close, there was a horizontal pair of holes, about two inches apart. He laughed again. He had to squat a little but confirmed they were eye holes. This was insane. He wondered if Sorcha had created these passages, or whether they went back to Lady Amelia's time or even before. Tristan peered through the eyeholes into the library. There was no one there. Then to the right, he saw another catch. It was a hidden door. You could get from the library to the minstrel's gallery without being seen.

But the passage went on further. He followed it and found another door into the kitchen, with accompanying spy holes. From there the tunnel led between stone walls with no wooden panelling.

There was a flight of wood-wormed stairs that took him up to the castle's first floor. He came to a barrier of wooden panelling and saw there were more spy holes. Looking through, he saw it was the corridor outside their rooms.

The passage at the top of the stairs led left and right. Tristan turned right and saw another catch. He could exit the passage here, but then he saw a set of ladders ahead. They looked rickety. He shone his light and saw they led up to a loft space. After a minute's hesitation, he climbed the ladder. The old wood creaked under his tread, but they held.

Tristan dragged himself off the ladder into the loft using his elbows, covering himself with dust and grime. The loft was a huge space, running above the passageway further than he could see, vanishing into the gloom both ways. Then he saw that there were spy holes in the floor. He stepped gingerly over to them.

He groaned. The holes on the left looked down into his room. He guessed the plaster moulding of the ceiling disguised the observation point from below.

He took a peek into Claire's room. There she was sitting at her dressing table, reading the Bible. He didn't want to spy on the old bird, so he stepped away. With a churning in his stomach, he looked over at the hole in the floor that must peer down into Gwyn and Iseult's room.

Bending down, he crawled up to it. He shouldn't look. He wouldn't look. There were things he didn't want to see, so he turned back toward the ladder.

If there had been other footmarks in the dust that might show Sorcha or Dudley had spied on them, his own climbing had wiped out any traces. But there were non-human marks: mouse prints, or rat tracks, but paw marks larger than any rat's too.

What the hell could have made those? They looked almost dog-like.

A scratching noise made him spin round. Something scuffled down there in the dark.

He stared. This loft was long and low. The noise came from way back, past the holes to Claire's room. It came again. He listened. There was the sound of breathing. It was definitely there. But maybe it was the wind. The mind plays tricks in old places like this.

Tristan shrugged; he'd seen all he had to see up here. He'd uncovered evidence of Sorcha's skulduggery. It was time to leave. He grasped the top of the ladder and swung a foot onto a rung.

He heard a clattering of claws. If it was a rat, it was a bloody giant rat, the size of a dog by the sound. Its feet clicked and came towards him. Tristan fought the urge to run. He strained to see in the darkness.

Something was definitely down there.

He used the flashlight. He had to know.

Tristan played the beam down the passage. It was hard to make out what was down there. The uneven stonework warped the shadows and made things stutter and shift. He couldn't tell the difference between shadows and imagination.

He swallowed. There was something, something that didn't want to show itself. Something that waited there in the dark.

Tristan's breath stopped in his throat. He shone the beam. It was maybe a heap of clothes. It didn't move.

He should really go up and check. He could just kick it and prove to himself it was a heap of clothes, not something hiding in the dark.

Then it moved. It seemed it moved.

The shaped lifted from where it had been watching, and came at him.

Tristan backed away to the ladder, feeling for it with his feet. The thing moved fast. All at once, some primitive part of his mind took over. He got his feet on the ladder, and dropped. Then he pulled the ladder away.

Tristan stood at the bottom, looking up at the hole above, expecting something to show its face. A minute went past and everything was quiet. No more breathing, no more clattering of claws.

It was just imagination. It had freaked him, but he knew how panic bites when it gets hold. Fear bites into you and drives out sense.

There were no such things as monsters. Or more correctly, no monsters that weren't men. And there were no men here. Just the wind blowing through cracks in the wainscotting of an old building. Just old leaves rattling down an old loft. That's all it was: perfectly rational, nothing to worry about.

Tristan stepped back from the ladder, back into the secret passage. Then he found the exit door, slipped out of the passage into the hallway where his bedroom was and clicked the door closed behind him. No one could have told it was there at all. But his main worry wasn't that someone should find the secret door, it was that whatever was inside would climb down the ladder, creep into the passage and push its way out into the castle.

Tristan saw a plinth with a stone vase on it. He hurried over, removed the vase, placed it on the floor and dragged the plinth, the few feet to block off the door. Then he collected the vase and, with both hands, placed it on top of the plinth for extra weight.

He stood for some minutes watching and listening, but all was silent. It was stupid, but he felt better now he'd blocked the door. He stood, looking at it, trying to smile at his stupidity. Finally, he turned and left.

7

SEDUCTION

Tristan went into his bedroom and changed from his grimy jeans and t-shirt. He put on a woollen jumper and a pair of black jeans and debated whether he'd reveal the secret of the passage to Gwyn. He sucked his teeth. After all, what had he actually seen? And even though his reason told him he'd seen nothing, a small niggling fear didn't want Iseult to think it was a great adventure and sneak into those passages, maybe on her own. It was dangerous in there, old and dark and broken. No, he'd keep it to himself for a while.

About noon, Tristan wandered to the kitchen. Sorcha was in there making sandwiches for lunch. She wore jeans and a tight blue pullover. Her black hair tumbled down her back. She turned when she caught sight of him. "Hey, Tristan." She beamed. The preceding night's Gothic dress and theatrical speech were gone. She was an all-American girl again. "Sleep well?"

"Yeah, but I've been exploring since breakfast."

"Really? Find anything interesting?"

"Lots. Great place you've got here. All kinds of interesting nooks and crannies."

She turned from cutting cheese. "What kinds of nooks and crannies have you been delving into?"

"Unexpected ones."

She smiled. "Sounds mysterious. I hope you haven't been uncovering our secrets." She hesitated as if she'd say more, then instead, she asked him, "You want ham or cheese?"

"Both?"

"Mustard?"

"English."

She winked. "The hot kind. I guessed as much."

He smiled despite himself and sat down at the long wooden table. Sorcha reached up into the cupboard to get the mustard, and he watched her stretch as she did so. She looked like she put effort into keeping her figure. She fetched the mustard, turned and dipped the knife in the mustard pot and brought out a curl of yellow on its tip. "Enough?"

"A bit more."

"Tough guy, huh?"

Despite himself, he laughed. He knew Sorcha was flirting, but today she seemed nice, fun even. She opened up the sandwich and slathered on the mustard, then handed him the plate. She was close enough so he could smell her perfume: something expensive and floral. Funny, he would have guessed she'd go for musk and dark chocolate. Her hair waved and shimmered as she moved back and stood staring at him, hands on hips.

He threw up his hands. "What?"

She laughed. "Eat!"

He saw there was a plate covered in crumbs at the place next to his.

She saw his gaze. "Claire was here before. She's gone off for a wander around."

"Well, that's Claire for you."

Sorcha cocked her head. "Don't you guys get on?"

"Sure, professionally. I wouldn't invite her to any parties, though."

Sorcha laughed. "Do you go to many parties, Tristan? A young, good-looking man like you, I guess you'd be in demand from the ladies." She stopped. "Unless you're gay." She looked embarrassed. "I shouldn't have presumed."

"No, I'm not. Anyway, when are the guests coming?" Tristan bit into the sandwich. Everything was good. The cheese was strong, and the mustard set his mouth on fire and went up his nose.

She turned her back to him to get the coffee pot. "Want coffee?"

"Tea if possible."

"Sure. Tea. Very English."

"I'm Cornish. The Cornish claim not to be English."

"I know. Celts like us. And Gwyn and Iseult are Welsh?"

"Welsh, yes."

"A real gathering of the clans then."

He laughed. "But when are they guests coming? Just so I know when to be ready."

She shrugged. "When they come."

"You seem very relaxed about it."

"They're old friends. It's not a paid event."

"A private party?"

"Absolutely."

He watched her move about the kitchen. "Is it true about you being pagan?"

"Uh-huh. I'm a witch."

Tristan sat back, his expression hovering between amusement and scepticism. "What does that mean exactly?"

She didn't turn round. "I do magic."

"You were saying. But really?"

"No, I do."

"So, spells?"

"Yes. Love spells. Hate spells."

"Hate spells?" He shook his head. "I don't believe you."

"You don't believe I'm capable of hate?"

"No, the whole magic thing. You're a clever woman. You can't believe it either."

She turned to face him. "Believe what you want, Tristan. It's still true."

He shrugged and bit his sandwich. "What's a thrice-damned woman?"

There was the slightest flinch, then a smile. She stepped forward. "Wait."

"Sorry?"

She came right up and brushed her finger with its glossy red nail down the side of his mouth. "You had a crumb."

She lingered close. That perfume again mixed with her warmth. Desire stirred in him. Then she stepped back.

⁂

Gwyn entered with Iseult.

Tristan shot a glance at Iseult, but she wasn't looking. Sorcha walked back to the counter where the cheese and ham sat beside the bread.

Tristan flushed. "We were talking about magic charms."

There was a pause.

Gwyn said, "Oh, okay. Just saying, Sorcha, thanks for the cheque."

"No problem. You want a sandwich?"

Iseult stared at Tristan, and he felt the heat in his cheeks.

Sorcha coughed to get her attention. "Iseult, did I say how much I love your name? Do you want ham or cheese?"

Iseult's gaze darted between Tristan and Sorcha. "I'm not hungry."

Gwyn said, "She's got pre-performance nerves." He reached over to the plate before Sorcha finished making the sandwich. He snatched some loose ham with his fingers and dropped it into his mouth. "Any of the guests arrived yet?"

Sorcha shook her head.

Iseult gazed towards the window. "The fog's come down again. It's grown pretty thick."

"The fog will delay them," Tristan said.

"Just as long as they turn up," Iseult said.

Gwyn grinned. "Don't care. Been paid anyway. Got anything to drink, Sorcha?"

Iseult frowned. "It's too early."

Sorcha shrugged. "I've got some Bushmills if you want."

"Sure," Gwyn's smile widened. "Fill 'er up."

Tristan finished his sandwich and licked his fingers. "You're in a good mood, Gwyn."

"Why shouldn't I be?"

Sorcha went out to get the whiskey.

"Don't know." Tristan was about to tell them about the secret passage, but that would lead to what he thought he saw in the loft. And now, sitting in the kitchen, doubted it himself. It had been merely shadows and frayed nerves making him jittery. So instead, they sat in silence.

Munching his sandwich, Gwyn seemed lost in some happy thought. Iseult played a game on her phone. She obviously didn't need internet for that.

Sorcha came back with a glass of whiskey for Gwyn. As she walked past, she gave Tristan a sideways look and a half-smile.

Gwyn took the glass out of her hand. "Good. The day is going well." He stared at the clock and sipped the whiskey.

"Sorcha..." Tristan said.

She turned her head. Iseult watched her. "What?"

"What's a thrice-damned woman—?"

Coming back from his reverie, Gwyn looked over. "Where's Claire?"

Iseult said, "I saw her in the baronial hall..."

Tristan guessed that was the place he'd been earlier with the minstrel's gallery, where the panel led to the secret passage.

"... She was having a conversation with some invisible woman."

"Naturally," Tristan said.

Iseult snapped at him. "She has a good heart."

"Maybe," Tristan said. Iseult's attack made him frown.

Gwyn downed his whiskey. "Let's go rehearse."

No one moved. Gwyn stood and clapped. "Come on, people! The show must go on!"

Iseult and Tristan stood and followed Gwyn out of the door. Tristan turned as he was leaving, and Sorcha smiled.

THEY REHEARSED ALL AFTERNOON. ISEULT WENT OVER HER ROUTE, practising the tales she would tell the guests while Tristan sent sounds to the hidden speakers, and Gwyn clapped with delight. "That is fucking tidy, boy."

Tristan grinned. "Cool, isn't it?"

Tristan wanted to show them the fluttering monk projected onto muslin. He'd set it up at the far end of a passage that led to the broken tower. Tristan didn't tell them what he would do until he'd taken them along the corridor and then, with a click of the remote, lit the image up.

The monk materialised. Iseult jumped and put her hand to her mouth. Gwyn laughed out loud. "It's fantastic, Trist." Then he paused. "All we need now is the punters."

Because of the fog, it grew dark by four o'clockm but still no guests had arrived.

After Tristan changed, he went to the main entrance and stood, watching the castle's drive disappear into the mist. He was perhaps looking out for the arriving guests, or perhaps planning his escape. Seeing Gwyn and Iseult together as man and wife cut him like a knife. He had no right to be jealous, and he didn't want to love her, but he couldn't stand being close to her and not having her. He owed Gwyn a lot, his life even, and Iseult was Gwyn's wife. He would leave and never see them again.

But there would be no way out until the show was over until everything was done and they rolled off the ferry at the far end.

That was in the future. Now the carriage lamps were lit on both sides of the castle door like twin lighthouses beckoning into the fog. Twin beacons to lure whatever would come from the Bog of Allen right up to their door and usher the unwary into this house of hell. Then he laughed at himself. He turned into the entrance hall. The stairs loomed up in front of him and at the top was the suit of armour with its hidden microphone.

Halfwa across the entrance hall, Tristan stopped. He was getting that feeling again. He spun around and stared at the door, half expecting it to open on its own. Then he shook his head and hurried through to the library.

Claire was sitting chatting to Iseult.

Iseult glanced up. "Dinner's about ready."

"Where are the guests?"

"I don't know. The fog?" She shrugged. "I wish they'd arrive. I want it over, or at least begun."

"Yeah."

She walked away, out of Claire's earshot. He followed her. She said, "You coming through?" Her tone was frosty.

"Is? "

She stepped away. His fingers reached but didn't touch. "What?"

"I know what you think."

"About what?" She was cold.

"About Sorcha and me." Why was he even talking about this?

Her face was mask-like. "I don't think anything."

"I saw you look. She was just wiping a crumb. She's a flirt."

"What's it to do with me?"

He sighed.

Then Dudley appeared. He had his tweed suit on again. "We're in the Room of Dreams tonight."

Claire got up.

Tristan's face was flushed. Dudley's entrace allowed him to wash it away with a crooked grin. "I suppose that's the benefit of owning your own castle. You can call the rooms what you like."

❧

THE ROOM OF DREAMS WAS IN ANOTHER CORNER OF THE CASTLE, and the maze-like route to get there confused them all. Without Dudley leading, they might have got lost.

As Tristan walked through the open door, he saw a room painted cream with white pilasters flanking the doorway. Crystal chandeliers sparkled from on high. Once again, a fire blazed, and candlelight glinted off the crystal glasses. Around the walls, mysterious paintings of mythological women gazed down with empty eyes — eyes so empty that passing spirits could come and fill them. At least if they knew about the secret passage behind the walls.

Even though he knew all this atmosphere was fake, conjured as deliberately by Sorcha as he conjured a haunted house with his gadgets and sounds. But still, a strange foreboding came over him, and he avoided the eyes of the women in the portraits.

Dinner came, roast pork with vegetables served by the grinning Dudley. And every time Tristan looked up, Sorcha was smiling at him. Tonight, she wore a blood-red dress, and her fingers were heavy with silver rings, twisted in Celtic whorls and spirals.

The fire shone through the decanter of red wine, making it glow. Without waiting for Sorcha's invitation, Gwyn leaned over, grabbed the decanter and filled his glass. The air smelled of sweet wood-smoke and roast meat.

Tristan took more wine himself and drank it with a reckless abandon. If he couldn't solve the dilemma, he would dissolve it with drink. But the more he drank, the more haunted the room became. And as it turned, he seemed to sense the spirits around him, the weight of ages, the heavy sins of those who had lived in this castle: Tullabeg, whose walls were rooted in the dark earth and whose blood was the water of the peat.

The meal went on. When their plates were empty but not cleared away, Sorcha began, "So the druids founded this place..."

"Ah the druids," laughed Gwyn, raising his glass to his mouth. "They get everywhere. Wales is full of druids."

"So the druids..." Sorcha lifted her crystal goblet to her mouth. Her crimson lipstick stained the rim. She continued, undistracted. "They lived here first before there was a castle. And it is said..." she paused for dramatic effect and Tristan realised that she was drunk too.

"... It is said, they had the secret of eternal life." She observed her audience, Dudley standing behind her shoulder like a faithful dog.

"Who cares?" Iseult's blonde hair was thrown back. Her face challenged Sorcha.

Sorcha smiled. "We'd all want the secret of eternal life."

Iseult shrugged. "Would we?"

Sorcha twisted her lip. "You're young. Wait until your youth has run like sand through your fingers—then you'll want it."

Iseult muttered. "I doubt it."

Sorcha held the glass out to Dudley for more wine. He filled it dutifully, and she gulped down the blood-red liquid.

Tristan placed his empty glass on the table. "So, what happened to the druids?"

Sorcha slurred, "You Christians murdered them."

Tristan said, "Me Christians? I wasn't even here. And who says I'm a Christian?"

Claire, who had been quiet, speared her meat with a silver fork. "The enemies of God must be punished."

Tristan rolled his eyes. "Yeah, right, Claire, go back to sleep."

The psychic shot him a glance and winked.

Tristan waved at Sorcha. "Go on about the druids."

The chatelaine toyed with the locks of her dark hair. "There's little to say: they had the secret of eternal life. I want it. Simple."

"It's made up," Tristan said.

Iseult giggled.

Sorcha grunted and ran her finger along the stem of her glass. "We shall see."

An uneasy quiet settled on the room. The Room of Dreams echoed to the scraping of knives and forks on plates and the sipping of wine. After several minutes, Sorcha turned to Dudley. "Put some music on."

Dudley nodded and stalked over to the record player. He put on David Bowie's *Heroes*, then gestured to the floor. There was plenty of space to dance. Sorcha stood. The dress clung to her, and her eyes were full of fire. She reached out her hands. "Tristan, you're a single man. Dance with me?"

He blushed. "I don't dance."

"He dances." Gwyn sighted along his finger like he was pointing a pistol. "Tristan dances all right."

Sorcha looked Tristan up and then down again. "You have the build of a sportsman."

Gwyn slurred his words. "He was company middleweight boxing champion. He took up boxing to prove something to someone." Gwyn beamed at his audience. "Not that anyone cared."

Everyone was drunk. Everyone except Claire with her bird bright blinks and Dudley, watching with yellow teeth and quick eyes.

The room whirled a little.

Gwyn said, "Remember that time in Syria?"

Tristan shook his head. "Don't."

Iseult said, "Not now."

Gwyn laughed. "Yeah, but I like to tell war stories."

Iseult stared at the table. Tristan studied the silver handle of his knife.

Gwyn went on. "We had a job to go in hard and snatch the Islamic State fighters. We appeared from the desert and grabbed them—Moroccans and Libyans and fucks from Germany and England. We were supporting the Kurds. By God, the Kurds were ferocious, protecting their homeland from these invading fanatics. But we'd pull them, and Tristan would make them talk. He'd make them sing like sweet birds, and they'd tell us where the IEDs were and where the suicide bombers would be. And how they used the blind and the mentally infirm as their martyrs. And we saved lives." His voice shook with emotion, and he was gripping his glass hard.

Tristan said, "Gwyn, enough."

Gwyn shrugged and drank more wine. "They need to know about. We saved people."

Tristan grew serious. "You were the bravest."

"It was the job."

Tristan was drunker than he should be. For a second, the suspicion that Sorcha had doped the wine flashed through his mind. His voice faltering with emotion and drink, he said to Gwyn, "You saved my life."

Gwyn winked. "Somebody had to."

Sorcha came close. Bowie was still singing *Heroes*. She pulled Tristan up from his seat with both hands and wrapped her arms around him. They danced while Iseult watched them and pretended not to. Dudley appeared uninterested in what his wife was up to, turning to poke the logs as his wife clung on to Tristan.

Sorcha stroked the side of Tristan's face and whispered in his ear. "You're very attractive."

"Hmm," he said.

Iseult couldn't take her eyes off them.

Bowie sang, "'Cause we're lovers, and that is a fact. Yes, we're lovers, and that is that."

Sorcha whispered, "Come outside." She held out her hand, and

Tristan took it. The room span. She dragged him with her out of the Room of Dreams and down a dark corridor until they emerged into the hallway. The silence of the entrance hall spun around him, and Sorcha flung open the heavy doors, and let the darkness in.

They stared into the whirling night where the fog clung and wreathed and conspired. With her arm round him, Sorcha pointed into the darkness, and she said, "Out there is death," and she paused and looked at him and whispered in his ear, her lips lingering, "If you run from me, Tristan, the bog will take you and nobody will ever find your bones."

Fuddled, he still held her hand. He knew it was wrong, but the wine had him. She pressed herself against him, and he felt her hips, and as she turned, the in-curve of her belly. She put her arm around him and turned her head. He felt her wine-sodden breath on his neck. He turned towards her and met her lips. They were hot and soft. Her mouth opened. He found his hands twining in her hair. They stumbled back as a pair back until his shoulders felt the rough stone wall, and they kissed, and he reached to touch her breasts that she pressed against him.

She bit his ear. "Let's go to bed."

"But Dudley?"

"He doesn't care. He knows what I'm like."

⬥

Sorcha's bedroom was hers alone: there was no sign of any other personality. Around the walls, hung long red satin curtains. The bed was huge, made of dark wood with midnight blue drapes on the rail that ran all around it. The bed covers were thrown back, and the white linen sheets welcomed them.

On the table, by the side of the bed was a Tiffany lamp and under it a black key that looked as if it came out of a Dickens novel. Next to the key was an ancient-looking golden amulet decorated with Celtic spirals.

Sorcha stood in front of Tristran and removed her dress. The fabric was the colour of arterial blood. Discarded, she flung it over the back of the Louis XIV style chair that fronted her dressing table. Then she was in black lingerie. Fixing her eyes on his, she reached behind to unclasp her bra.

Her breasts spilled free, white as milk, crowned by nipples the colour of raspberries. Tristan's loins stiffened, and he bowed his head. Even with the wine coursing through his mind, making him stupid, his conscience fought his desire. "Dudley," he said.

"I told you. He doesn't mind." She hooked a thumb behind her to catch the elastic of her panties. She pulled them down and stepped out, standing naked in front of him. The hair between her legs was black and trimmed. She stood, thighs apart.

His eyes tracked up from her pubis up her soft belly to her full breasts, then travelled to her white throat and into blue eyes under raven-black brows.

"I'm yours, Tristan. If you want me." She spoke with assurance — as if all men fell under her spell.

"Don't you and Dudley...?"

She shook her head, her lustrous hair shifting over the bones of her shoulder. Her lips were open, her pale cheeks flushed pink with passion. "Dudley and I don't. There is a certain incompatibility. I take my pleasure from delivery boys and electricians." She grinned. "And when they aren't around, and I'm in heat, I go to the bars in Dublin. The men there think themselves lucky."

"Of course. You're beautiful."

"Come to bed." She turned and lay on the bed, her black hair fanning out, one knee raised, beckoning him with red-painted fingernails.

He shook his head. "I can't."

A frown appeared on her brow. "I'm not sure I follow. We're both adults. We're both free. You're single, aren't you?" There was something in her voice, not annoyance exactly, more like she was playing a game, the rules of which at this time, with his thinking this confused, he couldn't fathom.

He nodded. "Yes, I'm single."

"You're not a virgin, are you?"

"Of course not."

"Or shy?" She smiled. "I see. You're shy. That's it. Well, Tristan, there's no need to be frightened of me. If you give me what I need, anyway." She parted her legs further.

He was sobering up. "I should go." He turned then he heard a click. The door closed of its own accord.

He stepped back. "How did you...?"

"Close the door? How or why? Why is easy—I don't want you to leave."

Tristan stepped to the door and put his hand on the cold doorknob. He turned it and pulled, but she'd locked it. He blinked, not under-standing how this could be.

She sat up on the bed. Her teasing, wanton expression had altered. She pretended to be angry. "I'm not used to men turning me down."

"Of course not. Who would?"

"You."

"Listen, it's not you — it's me."

She threw back her head and laughed. "You're damn right, it's you." She got up from the bed, reached into the armoire and pulled out a silk nightdress in gold with a Chinese design that she put on with a graceful flourish. She fixed him with a thoughtful gaze and paused. Then she said, as if she had been waiting for her cue, "Is there someone else?"

He hesitated. She beamed with delight. "The boy's in love."

He didn't respond.

"But you're single... so..." Her face lit up. She was toying with him. "So, it's someone you can't have." She put her finger to her lip. "Maybe someone else's wife?"

His cheeks flushed.

"Oh, Diarmuid, how you keep running after Gráinne, story after story, but Fionn won't let you have her, and we all know how it turns out in the end."

There was a click behind him. He turned and reached to find the door was unlocked.

She gave a light laugh. "Now I have power over you." Her beautiful face hardened. "You can leave now, but remember true love obeys no laws. When you're brave enough, that is."

He hesitated, and she made a shooing motion with her hand.

Tristan stepped out into the cold corridor, sobering and cursing himself as a double fool. He was a fool first for entering Sorcha's room at all, and a fool second for letting him guess his secret. She was right. She did have power over him.

He made his way to his room. He stripped and threw his clothes onto the floor. Getting into bed, he pulled the cover to his chin, but he didn't sleep.

8

ISEULT'S DESIRE

seult was already in the kitchen the next morning when Tristan came down. Gwyn was sitting next to her drinking black coffee. "Man, my head hurts."

Iseult darted a glance at Tristan as he rooted around for breakfast. Jealousy gripped her like an evil spirit. Her emotions were all mixed up, and she struggled to stop shaking with rage and hurt inside.

Tristan went over to get toast and filled a glass with orange juice from the jug.

Iseult didn't speak or even look up at him.

"No guests still?" he asked.

"No," Gwyn said. "Not a one."

"Think they'll still come? It's Halloween today."

"They could still come."

Tristan sat. There was silence as he ate the dry toast.

"You got lucky last night," Gwyn said.

Iseult tried not to listen, but despite herself, she waited for his answer.

Tristan didn't respond.

Gwyn sniggered, sipping his coffee. "What was she like?"

Iseult frowned. "Don't be so vulgar."

Gwyn winked at Tristan. "I bet she was wild."

Tristan mumbled. "Nothing happened."

Nothing happened.

Gwyn echoed her thoughts. "Like hell. I saw you go out hand in hand."

Tristan shrugged. Anger flashed across his face. "Doesn't matter what you think you saw. It didn't happen."

Relief filled her like a dawn sun rising. Maybe he was telling the truth; perhaps he was true to her, but then the truth bit back. True to whom? He wasn't hers; she had no right to ask him not to sleep with other women.

Gwyn knocked back the dregs of his coffee and stood to get a refill from the pot. He shrugged. "If you're concerned about Dudley, I wouldn't be. I don't think they're like that, you know? Dudley's a kind of handyman. He's more like a pet dog to her. Anyway, you should take what you want. There are no rules in love."

Tristan rubbed his face. She thought he looked troubled.

Gwyn said, "You're single. I don't get the problem. I mean, I wouldn't have kicked her out of bed." He winced and turned to Iseult, "Sorry, babe. You know you're the only one for me."

She shook her head. What an ignorant boor her husband was. And then she thought of Tristan, thoughtful, intelligent, and up until now, uncorrupted like all the other men she'd met. Stupid thoughts, they made her feel like a kid. Idolising your boyfriend was what teenage girls did.

Tristan stood. "I'm going out for a walk."

Gwyn raised an eyebrow. "What? In the fog?"

As Tristan went out of the kitchen, Gwyn muttered. "I never took him for the sensitive type." Then he grinned. "Oh, yeah. That's right: I did."

ISEULT WAITED UNTIL TRISTAN LEFT THE KITCHEN THEN SHE GOT UP, pulling on her leather jacket. "I'm going for a wander around."

Gwyn stretched out his shoulders. "What? Someone else going to walk in the fog?"

"I'm not going outside," she snapped. "I'm going to find Claire."

"Sorry I spoke." Gwyn watched her leave, muttering at her back, "Everyone's so touchy this morning."

Iseult hurried through the cold corridors. The dark wood panelling showed faces and eyes in the patterns and whorls. As she hurried, bits of the castle shifted around her, creaking like old bones. She ran up the wide stairs. She wanted to weep and had to stop at the top for a second to compose herself. Pressing her forehead against the wooden panelling of the hallway, she hissed, "I am so stupid."

A sound rattled from way off to the left. Iseult jerked her head and peered down the ill-lit passage. Something had moved down there. She strained to see through shadows that lurked even at ten in the morning. Her eyes disentangled the shades of grey and black until she convinced herself it was merely a trick of the light, though just a second before, she could have sworn it was an animal.

She brushed her hair from her face with her fingers and stepped over to Claire's door. She hesitated, then knocked.

"Who is it?" came the older woman's sharp voice.

"Iseult."

A pause.

"What do you want?"

"I want to talk to you."

A further hesitation, then, "Come in."

Iseult opened the door to Claire's bedroom. Claire's suitcase was open on the floor, revealing a tousled mess of things: a hairbrush, and some brown shoes, an old copy of the TV Times. Clothes were strewn around the room — the charity shop clothes she wore every day. Claire glanced up, her face approximately smiling. Lips drawn back, teeth showing like standing stones on pale pink gums, Claire pointed to the wooden chair. "Sit down, Iseult. I wondered when you'd come."

Tubes and bottles of make-up covered the dressing table, and an open sachet of hair dye oozed its remains onto the tabletop.

Claire's inquisitive gaze fastened on the girl. "How can I help?"

Iseult sat. "Claire, you know things. You see things."

Claire nodded rapidly. "Yes, I do."

Iseult spread her hands over the table. "I wonder: can you tell me what will happen to me?"

"Tell your fortune?"

Iseult grimaced. "Well, that sounds cheesy... I mean, what should I do?"

"About what?"

"I have a dilemma."

"A dilemma? Hmm." Claire's eyes closed. She appeared to be gazing somewhere far away behind her eyelids. There was a long pause, and the silence grew heavy.

Claire smiled. "You don't love your husband." It wasn't a question.

Iseult tugged at the ends of her hair. "I do love him. I care for him very much."

Claire tutted. "Caring for someone isn't the same as loving them. Not as a wife should love her husband."

Iseult bowed her head. "I owe him so very much. He found me and helped me when I had nothing."

Claire's bird stare darted around Iseult's face.

Iseult's eyes filled with tears. "It's so painful. My heart's ripped in two."

Claire said, "Tell me everything. Remember that a truth unspoken becomes a poison."

Iseult sighed.

Claire cocked her head. "When did you get married?"

"Two years ago, but I've known him for five. I was nineteen when we met. I was a barmaid. He looked after me."

"How much older is he than you?"

"Fifteen years."

"That's a lot." Claire blinked. "But things went well?"

"Yes. Only, he doesn't want kids. Says he's too old." She paused. "I did want children. I'm not so sure now." Iseult sighed and brushed her eyes with the back of her hand to wipe away the tears. She stammered, "I owe him a debt of loyalty."

Claire stood and placed her hand on Iseult's, and Iseult allowed it. She stared at the table, unable to meet Claire's piercing gaze.

"I am sensitive," Claire said. "I know things others don't."

Iseult glanced up. "So what should I do?"

Claire assumed a concerned expression. At the window, the grey fog rubbed its face against the uneven panes.

Claire said, "Your choice is between loyalty and love." Without looking at the young woman, she stroked Iseult's hand. She whispered, "But Tristan is not trustworthy."

An ice-cold pain transfixed Iseult, from her lips to her belly it was as if she'd been cut open. She blurted out, "Did he sleep with her? I've got no right to complain, I only want to know."

Claire shook her head. "You can't rely on that young man. You must denounce him."

"So he did?"

Claire smiled and remained quiet.

"Okay, I just didn't know if I could believe him. I guess not."

Iseult's bowed her head, She stood. "I'm sorry, Claire. Thank you for the advice. I've got to go." She hurried from the room. In the hallway outside, she smoothed her eyes dry. She would not let this get to her. But for now, she needed to walk.

❦

Iseult walked without heeding where she was going, her fingers twisted the gold cross around her neck over and over. She turned down passages she'd never been before. The castle was huge. She left the well-trodden hallways and came to corridors where floorboards were missing and the walls were damp with mildew.

She wandered through rooms that were empty apart from broken things: a stack of ruined chairs, a damaged book — face down on the floor, against the wall, a mirror whose silvering was spotted black and in whose face her reflection emerged, smeared and tearful.

Through rooms and passages, through window after window, she saw how the fog wrapped the castle tight. Even inside, its presence intruded, dampening sounds and made her hollow steps echo. It was quiet in the bowels of the great building, only her breathing and her feet, tap-tapping as she walked.

And maybe something else—half heard.

It crept up on her, this sound. At first she didn't even hear it. For a time, she was not even aware she was being followed.

Instead her mind hammered on the same familiar tracks. Iseult knew it was wrong to want Tristan. She married Gwyn after all. Her brain knew it all, but couldn't tell her heart what to do. She remembered all the nights she had lain awake beside her sleeping husband wishing she'd never seen Tristan's face.

And it was Gwyn's fault. Why had he brought Tristan to work with him? He'd said Tristan was out of work since leaving the Army and couldn't get anything else. She'd told Gwyn that the company couldn't afford to pay another wage; they were struggling as it was. Then, in the first week, she knew she had feelings for Tristan. She tried to choke them off, but they grew. She tried to avoid him, but her mind kept returning to the image of his face and the sound of his laugh. He was funnier than Gwyn. He was cleverer than Gwyn. He was more handsome than Gwyn, and of course, he was younger than Gwyn, closer to her own age.

She was married to Gwyn, but surely, marriage should free love, not chain it up?

Iseult looked around, and her breathing caught in her chest. The gloom of the decayed corridors oppressed her. Her unmindful wandering had got her lost.

Wood creaked behind her. It was the sound of someone, but not hurrying, wanting to remain unseen. She spun round, but saw no one.

Iseult panicked, imagining someone out of sight. She hurried and half-ran until she came to a room where footprints tracked across the dust of the floor. Unlike the other neglected rooms, someone had been there recently.

The footprints led to a door painted matte black with a lock that looked well-used against the room's dusty surroundings. Iseult tried the handle, but the door wouldn't budge. She saw the keyhole, large and old.

Something flitted behind her. She turned and it was instantly gone. The room was empty, from the dark door to the mullioned window that peered out onto greyness. What she'd seen was nothing, merely an illusion brought on by the dim light, the decay, the dust and the murmurings of the old house.

Still, her heart wouldn't settle. She hurried back from the locked door the way she had come and saw a turn she'd missed. The corridor here didn't look as damp. She strode along it, then up a small flight of steps and saw she was back in the inhabited part of the castle. Strange how so little separated the two sides. Sorcha's theatrics stood next to the abandoned memories of the long-dead Mortons.

⚜

AHEAD WAS ANOTHER DOOR, PLAIN-LOOKING, AND IT WASN'T locked. Iseult pushed on it and it gave way. She felt relief to step into a furnished room. There were leather sofas and an unlit fire in the back wall and picture windows that looked out onto the broad expanse of the Bog of Allen. In today's weather, after only a few feet, the low waterlogged landscape disappeared into the grey drizzle.

Sorcha looked up. Iseult hadn't seen her. She was sitting in an armchair reading a copy of The Tatler and drinking coffee from a porcelain cup. The smell of the coffee was very appealing. "Hello," she said. "How did you find your way here?"

Iseult said, "I didn't find my way here. I got lost, and I came across it by chance." She looked around. "But it's a nice room."

There were landscape pictures on the walls and tall potted plants in corners. The sofas and chairs sat arranged around the oriental rugs.

"This is my personal room," Sorcha said. "It's the morning room. I come here for peace and quiet, and to catch up on my reading." She smiled and put down *The Tatler* with its society photoshoots of the minor aristocracy and classier celebrities. "Would you like a coffee?"

"Love one," Iseult sat on the armchair and sank into the cushion. Then she remembered about Sorcha and Tristan. She flushed.

Sorcha rang a bell push in the wall. The tinkling sound ran off into silence. Sorcha frowned at Iseult. "I didn't know."

Iseult blushed deeper. "Know what?"

"About Tristan and you."

Iseult sighed. Were her secrets open to everyone like her knickers on the washing line? The redness in her cheeks couldn't be hidden. "There's nothing to know."

Sorcha continued to look at her. "We didn't, you know."

Untold, Iseult's heart blossomed.

Sorcha continued, "He wouldn't…"

Iseult looked at the older woman, relief but also anger flooded her. "Maybe he didn't fancy you?"

Sorcha smiled. "That's spiteful, Iseult. I'm older than you are, but people tell me I've retained my charms. Men tell me, I mean." Her gaze was steady, not angry; if anything it was sympathetic.

"Sorry. I don't care about him anyway."

"Really?"

Iseult shrugged. "I shouldn't even talk to you about it." She paused. "What did he say about him and me? You obviously know so he must have said something."

"He didn't mention your name. I guessed."

Iseult nodded. He hadn't even mentioned her name.

Dudley entered. Sorcha said, "Another cup, please."

Dudley nodded, his yellow eyes watching Iseult as he turned and left.

Sorcha took a sip of her coffee. "He'll only be a minute." She put the cup down. "Why aren't you with Tristan, anyway? He's more your age."

Iseult couldn't speak.

Sorcha continued, "What is it you owe Gwyn?"

"Everything." Iseult felt tears begin. "He gave me a job."

Sorcha laughed. "A job? Men have given me jobs before, but I didn't think I needed to marry them."

"You wouldn't understand."

"Oh?"

"You're not like me."

"Aren't I?"

"No."

"At least give me a chance to understand."

Iseult shook her head.

Dudley returned with the cup and vanished again. Sorcha filled the cup from the silver coffee pot. Then she lifted the silver jug. "Cream?"

"Please."

She waited until Iseult had taken a sip. Iseult sat feeling uneasy. She couldn't ever reveal the real reason for her gratitude to Gwyn. The cream tempered the bitter taste of the coffee. She hoped Sorcha would change the subject.

The older woman stared at her. "I am very curious why you'd stay with a man fifteen years older than you, whose business, if you don't mind me saying, is in real trouble."

"He's a very kind man." Iseult challenged Sorcha with her eyes. "He helps people. He gives people breaks when they're in trouble."

"So what trouble were you in?"

"I don't want to talk about it."

Sorcha shrugged. "I'll leave you with your secrets. But what are you going to do about Tristan?"

"Nothing."

"Don't you believe in love?"

"No." She paused. "Well, I believe it exists, but I don't believe it's the meaning of life."

Sorcha said, "Love is our true destiny."

Iseult snorted. "I find it hard to credit that you believe that. You come across as cold and self-possessed."

Sorcha shook her head. "No. You can run from love, but it will always catch you up. My advice to you is to follow your heart."

Iseult paused. Looking at the carpet, she said, "Even if it means hurting someone else?"

"Love is the law."

"Who said that? Some romantic who didn't live in the real world?"

"Aleister Crowley. But the witches say it too."

"Wasn't he a black magician?"

"He was a magician. Like me."

"So you're a magician?" Iseult examined Sorcha to see whether she was being serious. The chatelaine wore her day clothes—jeans, ankle boots, and Norwegian woollen jumper. She didn't look very magical today. But Sorcha's gaze was unblinking. She nodded.

Iseult said, "What kind of magic do you do?"

"All sorts. Love magic."

"Love magic?" Iseult ran her hand through her hair. "I don't believe in magic."

"It works."

Iseult leaned over her coffee. "And what does it do?"

"It can make someone choose you. Someone you love."

Iseult gazed out of the window at the fog.

Sorcha reached and stroked Iseult's hand. "Magic can make him love you."

Iseult laughed. "This is crazy. How can it be true?"

"Try it."

Then Iseult grew serious. "But what about Gwyn?"

"He's too old for you. You can't give away your chance at true love out of loyalty to someone who helped you once, who you then thought you ought to marry as a reward for his good deed. Men don't own us, Iseult. They just think they do."

Iseult was quiet. Her heart ached for Tristan. She thought about him every minute she was awake and all through her dreams. She wanted him more than life, and she knew life without him was the same as death, wasting all her young years looking after an old man, a man who would sicken and die while she was still youthful and, when he was gone, she'd be like a faded rose, her beauty vanished, her years spent with nothing bought. Iseult said, "So it's as simple as that? You actually believe magic works?"

Sorcha nodded. "I know it does. This is Ireland. The druids built this castle on holy ground, wove spells, and foretold the future. Their magic was so strong they didn't die but lived from life to life served by the Faelchon."

"The Faelchon?" She struggled to say the name. "Who are they?"

"They were the Wolf Tribe—a pagan tribe that held the wolf sacred."

"And you think their magic worked?" Iseult said the words and let them linger in her mouth, half wanting to believe them.

"I know it did."

Iseult laughed and sipped her coffee.

Sorcha stood. "Come with me, and I'll show you something."

"Come with you now?"

"We need to go down into the tunnels."

"Tunnels? There are tunnels? This place gets weirder."

Sorcha nodded. "Extensive tunnels run under the castle. There's a secret stair."

❦

ISEULT FOLLOWED SORCHA AS THEY LEFT THE MORNING ROOM AND went along a half-familiar corridor. Sorcha stopped by an unremarkable section of the wall. A small table stood there with a stub of candle in a pewter candle holder. The smell of burned wick lingered.

Sorcha moved the table and Iseult recognised a keyhole like the one to the locked door she'd seen earlier. Sorcha put her hand to her throat and reached down into her pullover, tugging out a silver chain. On the thick silver chain was a heavy black key that looked as old as the castle. Sorcha turned it in the lock, and the door snapped open.

"Wow!" Iseult exclaimed.

Sorcha grinned. She reached into the back pocket of her jeans and pulled out her iPhone. Iseult saw it was picking up a Wifi network. Sorcha switched on the torch and beckoned. "Come."

They entered the secret passage. The damp air bathed Iseult's face, and she smelled the cold stone. "How extensive are these passages?"

Sorcha smiled enigmatically but didn't answer. "Watch your step. Follow." Sorcha reached up and flicked an old brass switch. A string of dim electric light bulbs flicked on.

They walked down the corridor and came to a junction. Sorcha went straight over, and soon they were descending further steps, older and more worn than the previous ones. Iseult's steps echoed, and her breath issued forth in a vague cloud. This place looked like it pre-dated the castle above.

At one point, Sorcha reached up to take Iseult's hand to help her over some broken stones. Dark water glinted in the electric light where the bog seeped in.

The tunnel broadened. Rusty metal tools lay heaped against the wall. Then the man-made stonework ended, and they came to a huge black door made of wood banded in iron. Nothing would get through that door. Sorcha drew the same black key from inside her blouse. She turned the key in the lock and dragged the heavy door back with a scraping creak to reveal a cavern hollowed out of the natural limestone.

Traceries of limed water ran across the ceiling and fashioned stalactites with sparkling drips hanging their ends.

"Here," Sorcha said, finally.

She shone the light and Iseult saw a rough stone carving. It was about three feet high and shaped from the local stone. It looked ancient. The carving wasn't realistic—the man had wide lenticular eyes and a slit for a mouth. The mouth hole was wide enough to place something in. The nose was a straight dagger-cut in the middle of its face. It was primitive, and Iseult shuddered.

Sorcha pointed. "That is Crom Cruach. The druids worshipped him in this very cave—a cave that kept dry, despite the surrounding bog."

"I suppose the fact it kept dry was proof it was magic to them?" Iseult said.

"It is a sacred place. A place holy to my ancestors."

Sorcha reached over and scooped something up from an alcove in the wall to the right. "Here," she said.

Iseult took it. It was damp, claggy salt. She raised her eyebrows.

Sorcha busied herself lighting candles in the alcoves with her sliver lighter. In the flickering glow, Crom Cruach's face shifted as if it was alive.

A thrill of fear rushed through Iseult's blood. What was she about to do? Her father would be screaming at her now, calling her an idolatress. That was a good enough reason to do it.

Sorcha stared at her.

Iseult held out the salt. "What do I do with this?"

"Offer it to him. So close to Halloween, the Gaelic Samhain, offerings are auspicious."

"Why salt?"

"Because salt is a symbol of the bitterness of human life, and Crom

Cruach is merciful. He will take the bitterness from you and give you what you ask him for."

Iseult hesitated. The salt was damp on her fingers. "I don't know what to ask him for."

Sorcha whispered, "You know what you want to ask him for."

Iseult nodded but didn't move.

"Do it."

"It feels wrong."

"Wrong to get what you yearn for?"

"Wrong to worship a pagan idol." Her finger went up to the cross around her neck once again.

Sorcha's mouth twisted. "Much good that trinket has done you. You can change your fate if you're brave enough to try. Kneel."

Iseult gazed at Sorcha. She didn't move. She looked at the salt on her fingers. It was all so foolish. But maybe this would be her miracle. Perhaps this small act would end her dilemma. She didn't know how it could. But something had to end this pain of longing.

Sorcha's expression in the flickering light was unreadable.

Iseult sighed. What harm could it do? How could it work anyway?

Sorcha kept staring, expectant.

It couldn't hurt, and it would keep Sorcha happy. She kneeled. The damp of the ground seeped through to her knees.

"Give him the salt."

Still she hesitated. All that Bible reading as a girl must still linger.

Sorcha said, "Duty and love come from different places. Duty comes from the world of man, but love from the realm of gods and angels."

Feeling foolish, using her fingers, Iseult stuffed the salt into the god's hard stone mouth. She packed it in with her finger-ends.

"Good," Sorcha said. "Now beg him."

"Beg him?"

The cross round Iseult's neck glinted in the candlelight. She would do it then they would leave. Iseult bowed her head.

"Good," Sorcha said.

Iseult nodded, her fingers holding the salt in the god's mouth. Then, with her eyes closed, she asked Crom Cruach to give her Tristan.

9

WHISKEY AND GHOSTS

Tristan avoided everyone the next day. He spent the time checking his equipment, though it all seemed futile now. If any guests arrived during the day, he didn't see them, and he didn't care much either. He wanted to leave Tullabeg.

As evening fell, he knew he'd have to face up to the others. No one had mentioned any big dinner. After all, there were supposed to be guests; there was supposed to be an event.

But he was glad there was no fancy dinner. He couldn't face one anyway. After a brief supper, he told them all he was turning in early, went to his room and flicked through his books.

He thought back on Sorcha's attempt at seducing him. Something about it didn't add up. There were hints, more than hints, that Sorcha already knew about Iseult and his feelings for each other, and the conflict that it created. It wasn't beyond belief that she'd engineered the whole thing, got him drunk and dragged him off just to make Iseult jealous.

He even wondered why Sorcha had found their company and hired them, bringing them over the sea from Wales. Surely some closer people could do a similar job, especially for guests who never turned up.

There was much more to this than met the eye. Dudley wasn't what he seemed either. Then there were secret passages with observation holes. For all, he knew they could be watching him now. Just in case, he stuck a finger up at the ceiling.

Tullabeg was undoubtedly full of tricks. The big question was why? Why go to all this trouble? As long as they stayed there, Tristan would make it his mission to find out.

Despite his ruminations, he eventually slept.

It was dark as pitch and he woke before he knew what had dragged him from sleep. He lay listening to the silence while his eyes made sense of the blacks and greys of the room. Some premonition of trouble came to him, and then a woman's cry split the darkness.

He jerked bolt upright. At first, he didn't know who it was, but in his half-dream state, his heart cried that it was Iseult.

❦

TRISTAN SPRANG TO HIS FEET, SHOVING THE QUILT OUT OF THE WAY and dashing to the door, entangling his feet and almost tripping in his haste. His hand was on the handle of the door as the scream came again. Relief hit him like a punch, then guilt because knowing it was only Claire felt like a relief. Tristan stopped at the door, hand on the doorknob, his heart slowing back to a normal rhythm.

His conscience told him he should really check how Claire was— the noise she'd made was heart-stopping. He moved to the connecting door but hung back. What if she was undressed? It was probably only a nightmare that made her cry out, but she had sounded truly terrified.

With a sigh, he twisted the doorknob and pushed into Claire's room. She had turned on the bedside light and was squatting on the antique bed with her knees pressed up to her chest, and her nylon dressing gown wrapped around her thin body, tied with its narrow cord. Claire's eyes were wide with fright, and she blinked like a baby bird. She stared with such hate that he thought she might scream and accuse him of taking advantage of her. Instead, her voice quaked as she said, "She was here."

Tristan frowned. "Who?"

"She was here," Claire's eyes darted around the room, searching the ceiling and the angles of the room until with a trembling finger she pointed towards a space to his left. She hissed, "She's still here."

The hairs pricked on the back of Tristan's neck. Claire's fear was infectious. The hairs pricked on the back of Tristan's neck, and he spun around, but after a second shook his head. "I don't see her. Who?"

"The woman. I saw her."

"The woman? That doesn't tell me much."

At that instant, there came a rap on the door of Claire's room. Without thinking, Tristan said, "Come in." He glanced at Claire, ready to apologise for asking someone into her room, but the psychic was still peering into space. Iseult opened the door. Her hair was tousled, and she wore a blue kimono with silver fish drawn in the Japanese style. Her feet were bare. She rubbed the sleep from her eyes. Looking concerned, she stroked Claire's shoulder. "You okay?"

Tristan watched Iseult. There was something different about her, but he couldn't say what it was. He saw she wasn't wearing the gold cross her grandmother had given her. Iseult stroked Claire and assumed a worried look as if the older woman was a beloved aunt losing her marbles.

Claire's pointy chin quivered. "The woman was here."

"Which woman?"

Tristan wandered to the window. Claire's blinds were open, and the silver glow from the almost-full moon washed the wide boglands in white light. The pools glimmered like mercury among soft morasses. Wreaths of white fog were strung over the bog like Halloween decorations. He gazed out of the window and then stole a glance at Iseult who leaned over Claire, comforting her. She had a kind heart.

A flickering blue light way out over the bog caught his eye. It flared up and flickered before burning out and vanishing. For a second he believed he'd seen a ghost, but then realised it was a will-o'-the-wisp.

Iseult turned to him, her eyes liquid with sleep. She was looking amused. She whispered, "Claire says she saw a bad woman. Did you see anything?"

"As if."

Iseult was lovely in any light, but in this faithless moonlight, she was ethereal, bewitching. He wanted to brush wisps of hair from Iseult's cheek.

"We must have a séance!" yelled Claire from her bed. "To discover her intent."

They both turned. "What? Now?" Tristan yawned. The terror over, he wanted his bed.

Claire's eyes gleamed with excitement. "Yes, now. While she is still close."

Tristan rubbed his eyes with the back of his hand. "It's like..." He checked the chunky watch with its many dials that glowed like dead fish. "... Nearly midnight."

"I insist." The older woman's face was stern and petulant. "I am the psychic. You hired me for my skills."

"Gwyn hired you..." Tristan muttered.

"You hired me for my skills!" she repeated. Her fingers clawed tight into the bedsheet. "The spirits come when they will. Never mind if it's three in the morning or four in the afternoon." She spat the words at him.

Tristan turned to Iseult with a wry smile. "She doesn't like me. Get Gwyn? He'll talk her out of it."

Iseult grimaced. "Gwyn had a heavy night. Not sure anyone will wake him until morning."

"Heavy night?"

She nodded. "He 'borrowed' some of Sorcha's whiskey to take to bed with him."

Tristan pursed his lips. "I didn't know he was back on the sauce so heavily."

She sighed. "Yeah, well."

"He said he'd cut down."

She shrugged. "He's a great guy, but not a perfect being."

Tristan didn't meet her gaze. "After all, who is?"

Iseult leaned in. "But the upshot is there's just you and me and Claire available for the séance."

Claire stared at them. "We shall start."

❧

Tristan dragged the chair from under the dressing table in Claire's room and positioned it so Iseult could sit. She smiled and thanked him. Their hands touched on the top of the chair back. She let her hand linger, but he drew his away. There was a smaller chair in the corner of the room. He got it. They pulled the chairs close together to Claire's bed, so they could sit in a triangle.

Claire looked even more birdlike in the electric lamplight. "Hold hands," she commanded. Tristan reached out and took Iseult's fingers in his. She grasped his fingers. In a seance, people held hands.

He fixed his gaze on Claire, trying to work out her state of mind from her actions.

Claire reached and took his other hand. Her grip was bony and tight where Iseult's was soft and light. He felt the dampness of Claire's soft palms as her hand clenched around his. Claire bowed her head. He noticed grey at her roots. No one spoke.

Minutes went by with no one speaking, and Tristan found his mind wandering to Iseult. She had her eyes closed, taking it seriously. He pressed her fingers as a joke. She pressed his back. Instantly, he regretted it.

Claire stiffened. She lifted her chin and said, "Welcome."

Tristan's attention snapped back to her. The psychic's eyes were shut, but he could see them moving under the eyelids, as if darting around the room, as if she watched some scene invisible to the rest of them. He shook his head; she was crazy, but still, he didn't break the circle. Iseult squeezed his hand tight.

Claire spoke. "What do you want with us, foul spirit?"

Answering herself, Claire's voice took on a different timbre and rhythm. No longer did Claire speak like a middle-aged, lower-class woman from some ex-industrial town in England. Instead, she talked in the tones of something like the eighteenth century: countrified and archaic sounding. Her lips worked then she hissed. "Irish peasants murdered me here long ago."

More theatrics. Tristan struggled to stop laughing. He said, "Who are you, oh murdered lady?"

Claire jerked her head, and her eyes flicked open like a lizard's.

Tristan sat back despite himself. Feeling him pull away, Iseult gripped his fingers tight and pulled him back.

Claire stared blankly at him with bloodshot eyes. Tristan had the strangest impression that it wasn't Claire was looking through them. A shiver ran up his spine, and he forced a laugh to recover his nerve. He turned to Iseult, raised his eyebrows and grinned. Her eyes were open, watching Claire, and she didn't grin back.

Claire's new voice declared, "I am Amelia. They flayed me and left me to die. They called me the the thrice-damned woman. How such as they dare lay hands on one of noble birth? The Thrice Damned Woman, indeed." A pause, a weird laugh.

That phrase again.

A pause, a weird laugh from Claire. She stared at him. "I will have my revenge."

Iseult squeezed his fingers harder.

Claire's eyes were blank. It was as if she wasn't there behind them. The older voice came through her mouth. "Two lovers are come, just like in the old stories. But their love cannot be proclaimed. The old king will not allow it."

Tristan looked at Iseult who was staring at Claire.

The voice went on, "Beware the Witch. She seeks your damnation."

Tristan said, "What does this even mean?"

Iseult hissed at him to be quiet.

Claire's own voice stuttered, "I see blood. Oceans of blood. Baths of blood."

There was a sensation like when someone leaves the room, and Claire shook her head as if to clear it of cobwebs. She muttered, "She is gone."

Tristan snorted. "Convenient."

Iseult gave a nervous smile. He was about to let go of both their hands and break the circle when Claire muttered, "There's something else." Her voice trailed off. She turned her head around, eyes closed as if searching for something in the land of visions.

Iseult's voice had a slight tremor. "What?"

"Deep below. Under this place."

"Oh, come on," Tristan heard the annoyance in his voice. This charade was pitiful.

"Beasts. Beasts with yellow eyes and sharp teeth."

Tristan shook his head. "Please."

Claire pointed at him with her bony finger. "They're coming for you." She sneered. "Coming for you, man of no courage." She pulled her hand away from his and smirked. "Oh yes, the beasts will devour you."

Iseult sat up straight, dropped Claire's hand but kept hold of Tristan's. She shook her now-free hand, the one squeezed bloodless by Claire, and winced. But she took Claire seriously. "What beasts? Please tell us, Claire."

Claire wore a knowing smile. "Wolves of course; wolves haunt this castle." She turned to Tristan. "But you knew that, didn't you? You've already seen one."

⚜

"Wolves?" They all three **pivoted** to see Sorcha standing at the door. She wore the gold nightdress he remembered.

"They are in this Castle." Claire poked her index finger at the floor. "Down below, waiting."

Sorcha laughed, musical, amused. "What were you doing?"

Tristan found himself angry at Sorcha. "Claire wanted us to have a séance." His anger was half due to his resentment at how Sorcha had mocked him the other night, and half due to her blatant attempts to trick them.

"A séance?" Sorcha twisted the ends of her black hair between her fingers. "And you didn't invite me?" The same smile flickered around her mouth.

Claire stared at Sorcha almost longingly. "I wish I'd thought to invite you, my lady."

Iseult and Tristan still remained on their seats while Claire was on the bed. Tristan frowned and scrutinized both Claire and Sorcha. Claire was gazing at Sorcha in adoration. What had gone between them away from the others? How had Sorcha won the twisted old woman round?

Sorcha stepped over until she stood between Tristan and Claire. She caressed Claire's shiny forehead like she was a child. "I'm not a Lady, Claire."

Claire simpered up at her. As Sorcha stood close, Tristan was aware of the pressure of her thigh against his bare arm. He guessed she knew her leg was touching him, and she didn't move away, so he drew back, and held himself away from her.

"What's this about the wolves?" Iseult whispered.

"I don't know."

"She said you'd seen one."

Tristan remembered the thing in the loft. If it was a wolf, it wasn't a natural one. "I don't know what she's talking about. She's insane."

Sorcha turned as if noticing that Iseult was there for the first time.

"You know they called the ancient tribe that inhabited this area Tuatha na bhFaelchon: The Wolf People. Their beliefs lingered around of Tullabeg and were never wiped out."

Claire jerked her head up. "That's it!"

"What's it?" Tristan **said**, unable to keep the dislike out of his voice.

"The name," Claire **said**. "The woman who was thrice damned: the flayed spirit. Her name is Morton."

Sorcha nodded. "So, she was here."

Iseult turned to Sorcha. "You talk like she's an old friend."

Sorcha shook her head. "She's no friend of mine. She hates me, but she's powerless to harm me. She's Lady Amelia Morton."

"She believes you have usurped her place." Claire's eyes narrowed. "She hates you."

Sorcha cursed in Irish.

"What?"

Sorcha smiled. "Go dtachta an diabhal í—may the devil choke her."

"Your Irish sounds authentic," Iseult **said**.

"Thank you."

"You are an accomplished, actress, My Lady," Claire **said**.

Sorcha's smile flickered, then firmed, as if she'd decided Claire was complimenting her. She turned back to Iseult. "I began learning it in Boston, it's true. But from a native speaker." She winked. "I learned it, so I can read out magic spells and speak to the ghosts of the dead druids." She reached out and stroked Claire's hair. "Whenever this lovely psychic brings them through for me."

Iseult frowned. "Why is she thrice-damned? This Lady Amelia?"

"Well, she committed three serious sins. She was an idolatress: They allege she paid homage to the devil to get him to preserve her youth. And she was an adulteress, so-called because she liked the attention of lots of handsome young men. But who can blame her for that?" Sorcha's eyes alighted on Tristan, but he was still looking at Claire. "And she was a murderess because she killed the maids and servant girls for their blood."

"Sounds like you approve of her." Tristan **said**.

Sorcha shook her head. "It was for these crimes that my ancestor Éamonn O'Connor flayed her alive."

"Ah, that's why she doesn't like you. She bears grudges." Tristan glanced at her, his eyes hard.

Sorcha leaned over and stroked Tristan's cheek. "Funny boy." He flinched away, and she chuckled. "You're talking like you believe in the ghosts now, Tristan. I didn't think it would be so easy to convince you."

His eyes hardened "I was humouring you."

"Do you want to see where she lives?" Sorcha **said**.

"Who Amelia?" Tristan saw Iseult shudder. "No, thanks."

Claire stood from the bed, the sheet still clutched in her hands. "Yes, please," She waited like an impatient little girl.

Tristan looked at the psychic. Something about this whole thing unnerved him, but he wouldn't have Sorcha thinking he was afraid of any ghost. There was no ghost, anyhow. "Sure," he **said**.

Iseult grabbed his arm. "No. I don't want to."

"Now? Can we go?" Claire **said**. "Please."

Sorcha nodded. "Of course, Claire."

"Not now," Iseult **said**. "It's night. Maybe in the morning."

Tristan could tell she was curious but frightened.

"Now", Claire said. "While the night lingers, and she is still strong."

Sorcha moved to the door, and Claire followed. Iseult stood from her chair but didn't move. "I'll stay here."

Tristan didn't move. In the doorway, Sorcha turned. "Are you coming, Tristan? Or are you chicken?"

Tristan glanced at Iseult. "I'll stay here."

Sorcha laughed. "Oh, yes. I should have guessed that. You two, like two little turtle-doves."

Hot anger rushed through Tristan like a geyser. "Careful what you say."

Sorcha gave a smirk.

Iseult put out her hand to stop him stepping forward to confront Sorcha. But Sorcha was looking at Iseult. "This one believes," she **said**, pointing. She turned to Tristan. "And I think you do too, Tristan. Coming?"

He shook his head.

Sorcha shrugged. "I didn't take you for a coward. A fool maybe, but not a coward. I must have been wrong." Without looking back, she and Claire left the room.

❧

TRISTAN STOOD THERE. SORCHA CALLING HIM AN COWARD MADE HIM want to run after her, dare anything, just to prove her wrong. But Iseult was here, and the gravity of her presence drew him to stay with her.

From the corridor, he heard Claire's loud voice. "Yes, he's a little man. He doesn't believe."

He grunted and made to set off after them. Iseult grabbed at his hand and held on to his fingers.

He stopped and sighed. "I can't put up with this bullshit, Is. We'll go to the tower, and there will be fuck all there, then we'll come back. I won't have the mad old bitch make fun of me in front of you."

Iseult said, "Don't take her so seriously. She's no threat to you. Let it be. Men are so silly about things like this."

"I won't be long."

Iseult forced a smile. "Well, I'm not staying here alone."

He reached out and took her hand. "Then come. Don't be scared. There's no such thing as ghosts."

She smiled but looked unconvinced. Finally she said, "Let's go and meet the Thrice Damned Woman."

Tristan walked with Iseult, her fingers twined around his. It was dark, but if anyone saw, he had already thought he would say he was holding her hand to steady her nerves.

Ahead of them, Claire was beside Sorcha, her arm looped through that of the witch.

They walked in darkness away from the improved parts of the castle and into the ruins. Decay infiltrated the place from wallpaper to scratched bricks, from polished wood to spider webs, from dead moths stuck to windows to dead beetles squashed against the floor. Sorcha led the way, candelabra in hand. She strode on, and the candle flames conjured shadows in nooks and crannies and threw gleaming reflections on polished wood and bright glass. As the flames flickered, the hallway bent and danced in their light.

The two women's talk drifted back. "I am committed to driving out malevolent spirits, Lady Sorcha," Claire twittered.

The shadows emphasised Sorcha's cheekbones and turned her silver-blue eyes coal black. "I'm not a Lady. I told you that."

Claire bowed. "Yes, yes, my lady. But you are a Lady to me. You are an aristocrat of the spirit." She forced the back of her hand against her teeth to stifle her mirth.

Paces behind them, Iseult shook her head. "This is crazy, but fun," she whispered. Tristan squeezed her fingers tight. He laughed.

She said, "I don't know why the hell I'm walking along a half-ruined passageway in a haunted Irish castle in the early hours of the morning."

Tristan smiled at her. "For the crack as the Irish say?"

She laughed. "It's nuts."

Claire pulled her arm and Sorcha halted. Finger held aloft, Claire hissed. "There's something else here!"

Sorcha lifted the candelabra to reveal the corridor's bare stonework and the unvarnished boards of the floor. A cracked window loomed to the side. The painted window frames were rotten, and the wind fretted around the fractured glass, seeking a way in.

"Who walks here?" Claire yelled.

Iseult shook her head. "Now it's crazier."

Tristan giggled. He tried to stifle it, but Claire span round. She spat, "Young woman, sin is crouching at your door. It desires to have you. But you must master it!"

"What?" Tristan said. "What are you talking about?"

"It's from Genesis, about Cain and Abel," Iseult said. "My dad used to read it to me."

Claire stared at them, as was Sorcha but instead of Claire's unblinking stare, she had an air of quiet amusement. Tristan ignored them both. "I didn't know you were religious," he said to Iseult.

Iseult's face twisted. "My father made me read the Bible. I wasn't allowed kids' books. He told me they corrupted the heart and let sin in."

"He sounds a fun guy," Tristan said.

"He was religious, my father — evil, but religious. I got away from him in the end."

"Thanks to Gwyn?"

"Thanks to the man that Gwyn later saved me from."

Sorcha tugged Claire round and away. "Come on, sweet lady. Let's get to the tower. Tell me what you feel."

Claire threw up her hands and, staring at Iseult, declaimed. "And behold! A woman comes to meet him, dressed as a harlot and cunning of heart."

Tristan whispered, "They should commit that woman to a lunatic asylum."

Iseult said, "She's harmless."

Tristan frowned. "She's not."

The passage grew more ruinous until holes grinned in the walls and the night air chilled their faces, coming through the walls so they smelled the great dampness of the surrounding bogland and heard the birds' bubbling cries across the empty miles of marsh. The wind tugged at Iseult's nightdress. She shivered.

"The castle fell down here." Tristan pointed out where the roof had collapsed long ago.

Sorcha's candles blew out, and Claire gasped.

Tristan sighed. "It's the wind, Claire. That's all."

It was dark. The candles were out and a cloud hid the moon. Tristan made out the silhouettes of the psychic and the witch standing ahead of him. Iseult pressed herself into him as if because of the cold, and he let her, as if he was only doing it to warm her. He told himself it was innocent, but even he didn't believe his own lie.

All the others before he met Iseult were merely her shadows: ghosts and prefigurings. Not one was like she was.

And here and now, he could be close to her in this place, in this dark, on this night for this instant but hardly longer. And here and now, it seemed enough.

In the dark behind, something moved. He whipped round his head and stared.

Iseult said, "What?"

He exhaled. "Nothing, I just thought I saw someone."

And as he stared, he saw. Back the way they had come was a shadow. It was dark there, but this shadow was thicker than the rest. He peered. And then it moved again. It was someone. He stepped back.

"Dudley?" Iseult said.

Tristan shook his head. The shadow moved back through the far door, and as it did, it was briefly more visible. It wasn't Dudley, it was a woman. It was like the woman they'd seen on the road before Gwyn crashed.

"Who else is in this castle?" he asked.

Sorcha said, "We four, then Dudley, and of course Gwyn."

"It was a woman," Tristan said. "I saw her."

"There is no woman in the castle other than the three standing here," Sorcha said.

Tristan frowned. What were all these tricks for?

Iseult stroked his arm. "Maybe it was Dudley."

Sorcha heard her. "Or your husband coming to check what you're up to."

Iseult said, "Gwyn's asleep."

Sorcha laughed. "The wonders of *uisce beatha*, eh? Such gifts it brings."

Tristan felt Iseult stiffen. But Sorcha was tired of this interruption. It seemed she wanted to get on with her drama. Sorcha gestured. "The tower is a short way ahead. But the ground is broken, and it's dangerous underfoot without light. I should have realised the candles would blow out once we were outside."

"Why didn't you bring an electric torch?" Though he hadn't brought his phone.

Sorcha laughed. "The candles were for effect. I'm all showbiz. You know that Tristan."

"I'm realising it."

The moon came out from behind a cloud, spilling silver across the ruined hallway. The ivory glow flew high above, lighting their way for a second.

Sorcha raised her hands. "Ah, thank you, my mother, the Moon."

"If the moon's your mother," Iseult said, "who's your father?"

Sorcha said archly, "My father, dear girl, is a wolf."

Tristan shuddered. Whether it was the setting in a ruined passage in an ancient castle, the moon high above, the dark, the damp, or the lateness of the hour and his nerves stretched by fatigue and constant thinking, whether it was any of these, or all of them, he felt uneasy, and to cover his unease, he whispered, "She's so full of shit, but I almost think she believes this crap."

"Maybe it's true," Iseult said. "Maybe she actually is a witch, daughter of Sister Moon and Brother Wolf."

"Yeah, right. And I'm Charlie Chaplin." He shook his head. "She's a fraud. No more, no less."

Sorcha intoned, "You see that door..."

Tristan and Iseult looked where Sorcha pointed.

A tower, inkier than the charcoal sky stood in front of them, rising like a ruler, broken at the top. Tristan craned his neck and saw the empty sockets of windows. The tower was old and ruined and looked unsafe. But despite the age of the masonry around it, the warped and mildewed wooden door had a modern lock and a shiny hasp that blocked their entry.

This was the tower Claire had brought them to the time before, where she'd sensed the ghost. Claire hadn't know that story then. And he thought that maybe she wasn't a fraud after all, then dismissed the thought.

A strange fear gripped him. He couldn't say what triggered it, but his mouth was dry and his palms sweaty.

Sorcha continued, "They murdered Amelia Morton in there."

"I sense her." Claire's voice was dreamy.

Tristan cleared his throat. "Are we going in?" His hands trembled. He hoped Iseult didn't realise he was frightened.

In the pale moonlight, Sorcha's eyes were black pools. "No." Her expression was unreadable. She said, "It's said that anyone who climbs the tower is dead by morning."

His mouth was dry. He said, "So, you've never climbed your own tower?"

Sorcha said, "I've been in but never to the top."

"Dead by morning, eh?" Tristan stepped forward. He wouldn't let her see he was scared of this.

"Are you brave enough, little boy?" Sorcha said. "After all, you don't believe any of this."

He nodded. "I'll climb it—if only to show you what bullshit this all is."

Iseult held him by the crook of his elbow. "No, don't."

He stopped, locking gaze with Sorcha. Her eyes were dark-blue and unfathomable.

"I think you're more valuable to Iseult alive, Tristan," the witch said. "Besides, I don't have the key. Dudley keeps it."

Iseult asked, "Why is it padlocked? It's just an old ruin."

Sorcha said, "For safety reasons."

She pivoted and strode back the way they had come. Tristan and Iseult turned to go back with her. After a few paces, yelped.

Tristan stopped."You okay? What's up?"

"I cut myself on a piece of glass."

A jagged shard stuck out from a shattered window frame that had collapsed against the stone wall. He yelled after Sorcha. "You could get sued for that. This place is a death trap."

"It's not Disneyworld, that's for sure", Sorcha called. She waited until they caught up and ran her finger along the cut on Iseult's forearm. She put the tip of her finger to her lips and licked the fresh blood. "Salty."

"Gross," Tristan said."I mean totally freakish."

"It's only blood," Sorcha said. "I didn't think a soldier would be scared of a little blood. And the blood of the Thrice Damned Woman is a powerful elixir. That's why they killed Amelia - for her blood."

Iseult frowned. "But I'm not a Thrice Damned Woman."

Sorcha smiled. "Not so far, anyway."

❦

TRISTAN AND ISEULT PARTED AT HIS DOOR. HE COULD HEAR GWYN'S heavy snores issuing from their room along the passage.

Iseult said, "What's going on here? I didn't believe her about locking the tower for safety reasons. She's got secrets."

Tristan said, "Why are we even here?"

Iseult shrugged.

Tristan said, "I'm going to find out what's in that tower."

Iseult touched his arm. "Don't, Tristan. It's dangerous. We'll be leaving soon. It doesn't matter."

"It does matter. I won't have her call me a coward."

"You're not a coward. I've never thought that."

He almost reached out to her, but didn't.

She hesitated. "I should go."

He nodded. "It's late."

"See you in the morning." She smiled.

"Sure."

She still didn't leave.

"Why aren't you wearing your gold cross?" Tristan asked.

Iseult's hand darted to her throat. She shrugged. "I just took it off."

He gazed at her. In the dim electric chandelier light on the corridor, she shone like moonlight and spindrift, aglow with youth and beauty.

"Is it a sin?" she said.

"Is what a sin?"

"That I love you."

Tristan sighed. "The sin isn't in falling in love, it's what you do about it"

"It feels fated."

"I never believed in fate. And, even if it is fate, does that excuse us?"

"I'm ripped in two, Tristan."

"We can't betray Gwyn," he said.

She put her finger to his lips to stop him speaking. "I know." Her eyes filmed with tears, and she stepped away backwards, never taking her gaze from him, until she turned and walked quickly away.

Tristan went back and into his room. He turned off the room light, pulled back the covers and rolled into bed. He was exhausted.

Lying there, he heard a scrabbling noise outside. He waited. It came again. There was something in the passage.

Quietly, he got up from his bed. He padded to the door and stood there, hand on the doorknob. The noise came again.

Was this more Sorcha?

But when he opened the door, he heard it again. It was pitch black out there. He listened.

Nothing for a long time, then when he was about to go back into his room. He heard it. The noise came from behind the secret door he'd found. Whatever had been lurking in the loft space, had come down and was now in the passage behind the walls. The heavy stone plinth with its vase on top still blocked the exit, but something was closer. Something was behind that flimsy door.

He went back into his room, and turned the key in the door. He hoped Iseult had locked hers.

10

NAMES AND POWERS

Tristan lay staring at stared at the bedroom door and watched and listened until, against his will, he fell asleep.

Jerking awake with a start, he sat up and peered at his watch. It was 6 a.m. He got out of bed, dragged back the curtain and viewed the bogland empty and ghostlike under wreaths of morning mist. It was still not fully light.

Tristan stood and pulled on his t-shirt and jeans. Then he picked up the heavy green pullover that lay in a heap beside the bed and dragged it over his head. There were a jug and ewer on the side, and he washed with the cold water, when he'd finished, poured water into a glass and used it to clean his teeth. He laced his shoes and hurried out of the room. The corridor was deathly quiet except for Claire snoring from next door, and Gwyn further down the passage. With Claire and Gwyn together, it was like some kind of devilish chorus.

He checked the plinth and the vase, but they still guarded the secret door. There was no sign anything had got into the hallway.

His head pounded. Tristan calculated he'd had around three hours sleep. He ran his hand through his hair. He could do with a shower, but so far hadn't seen one.

He strode on, way turning right then straight along, then around all the twists and turns that took him to the back stairs. He hurried down the stairs and made his way through the library with a sideways glance at the portrait of Lady Amelia. Was it her he'd seen in the shadows the night before?

His shoed feet clip-clopped on the stone floor. It was cold here, and the damp got into his bones, but he knew where he was going.

He half expected to run into Dudley on the ground floor, but there was no one about. He hurried through the library past the turn for the kitchen until he arrived at the main entrance hall. The grand stairs swept up to his right, and the suit of armour with the hidden microphone stood on the top landing like a guard.

Tristan threw back the bolt of the main doors, and the heavy rattle echoed through the entrance hall. He waited a second for any sound coming in response, any distant footsteps, any sign that someone was alerted.

Then he yanked on the main door handle, which juddered open. The smell of the moss hit him and tendrils of fog drifted into the room. He went out into the morning. Even in the last ten minutes, it had got lighter, but not light: The clouds were down, and a slow drizzle pitter-pattered. It wouldn't be properly light all day.

The patch of lawn stretched in front of the building and the retaining wall struggled to keep the bog at bay, but moss grew on it and infiltrated the old stone. A paved drive bent round to the right, and he followed it. His footsteps were duller and damper now.

Gwyn's car emerged from the mist, grey like an old photograph. Tristan went up to it and tried the boot. It wasn't locked. He hadn't expected it to be. After all, it didn't work and there was no one around here to steal anything. Lifting the boot lid, he saw the bag of tools that Gwyn kept there. There was a short saw, some screwdrivers, a wrench and a lump hammer. God alone knows why Gwyn felt he needed a lump hammer in his car, but Tristan had seen it before and knew it was there.

He pulled out the hammer, feeling its reassuring weight. Now, he had something to defend himself with. He'd seen some strange things in the castle. Without doubt, they were tricks, but he was glad of the hammer in his hand.

Tristan slammed the boot and turned to go back to the castle door. He was halfway back when he heard a noise. He spun round and it came again—a low growl, like a big dog might make. He saw nothing through the mist and called, "Who's there?"

No answer came.

After one long look around, Tristan grunted and walked back to the castle door. He was about to step through it when he heard the noise again. This time, there was the clatter of claws on the stone flags behind. He twisted, fingers squeezing the shaft of the hammer. His palms were sweaty and his mouth dry as he stared out into the fog. There was a shape there. What was it? As he watched, the shape moved, almost flowed. It sought the cover of a wall. It wasn't man-shaped. It didn't move like a man either, it was lower and quicker—some kind of animal? His breath billowed out. He narrowed his eyes—what beast was this?

Tristan waited but saw nothing more. The mist billowed and the light drizzled pattered down. He stood a minute, maybe three. What he'd taken for an animal must be was a wall or the gatepost, their edges obscured by mist. He peered harder. No, there was nothing.

And yet. He wasn't sure until it moved again, shifting position, hunkering down. The shape lurked by the wall, and now it moved again. This time faster, this time heading for him. It covered the ground quickly, loping, moving like a nightmare across the ground.

Tristan turned and ran. Breath gasping, heart hammering, he got to the castle door without looking back, and jumped into the foyer, one hand on the door-handle, the other squeezing the shaft of the hammer. The shape was a breath away. He held his breath. He lifted the hammer to strike. Then Dudley emerged from the fog.

The Irishman grinned. "Did I scare you?"

"You didn't scare me." Tristan paused. "Was that you out there?"

"Sure. Only me."

"But you moved fast."

"What of it?"

Tristan shook his head. "But it wasn't as tall as you. It was lower down."

Dudley winked. "Like it was running on four legs?"

Tristan's brow furrowed. His mouth was dry and his heart still beat faster than it should. "Yes, like that."

Dudley said, "You know, Mr Gifford, the fog makes you think you see things. People see all sort of things at Tullabeg, but I thought you were more rational than that. You're a man ruled by his head, not his emotions, surely?"

"I did see something."

"That's it: something. Somthing that was me. Like I say, people think they see all sorts of things here, but mostly it's just me."

"What were you doing out there?"

"You'd be surprised what I get up to." Dudley chuckled. "You've been out for a walk, I see." He nodded at the hammer in Tristan's hand. "You could do some damage with that."

"I need it to fix a microphone in the wall."

"You be careful of our walls. They're ancient."

"Hmm."

"You'll be coming for breakfast now then? I haven't started cooking. Thought no one would be up yet." Dudley's long yellow teeth showed as the Irishman pulled his lips into a smile.

"I'm just going back upstairs. I'll be down in half an hour."

"Keen. Admirable to be active so early."

Tristan frowned.

"All the work and all. Keeping yourself busy while your boss and his lovely wife share that beautiful goose-down bed."

Tristan muttered, "Like I said, I'll be down later."

Dudley gave Tristan a lingering look. He smiled like he knew something Tristan didn't. Sorcha had that smile too.

Tristan turned and climbed the main stairs, feeling Dudley's eyes bore into his back all the way. He shrugged his shoulders to shake the feeling off and pushed Dudley from his mind. He had things to do.

He figured he was getting at last an idea of the layout of the castle. He guessed that if he went up to the first landing and turned right, he would arrive on the corridor where his bedroom was.

At the top of the stairs, by the suit of armour, he stopped and looked back. Dudley wasn't there.

THE SUIT OF ARMOUR CAUGHT HIS EYE AGAIN. HIS GAZE LINGERED on the sword in the scabbard. He had the strangest feeling he needed to protect himself. After a moment's hesitation, he pulled the sword from its sheath. It was big and bulky, too big to carry around. Then he saw the dagger. That would be smaller and easier to use, not as fearsome, but a reassurance against whatever foe he imagined he might meet. He drew the dagger from its brown leather scabbard and saw it was blunt. The blade hardly held an edge. He scrutinised it. It wasn't even made of iron or steel. In fact, it looked like it was made of silver. It must be an ornamental weapon, not meant for any real fighting. He put it back. Then he shook his head. What was he thinking of? This place must be getting to him. He didn't need a sword or a dagger. The castle was full of lies and tricks, of echoes and mirages, all of these, but no real threat. Not really. It was all just psychological, set up by Sorcha for no other reason than she liked playing with peoples' minds.

TRISTAN TURNED AND STRODE OFF TOWARDS HIS BEDROOM. HIS sense of direction had been right and he found it without difficulty, but he didn't go in. He walked past his door and made his way along the passageway that Sorcha had taken them down the previous night.

He could see much better now in the early morning light how the passageway came to a ruinous end. The roof was off, and moss and ferns had colonised the broken stone. The floor looked dodgy, and he avoided weak-looking floorboards. There in front of him was the shattered tower, with its warped door. The padlock on the door was intact. Tristan gazed up, taking in its height. The windows were holes, and the top was fractured, blackened and broken.

Jackdaws squawked and crows lifted from the tower's top as Tristan stopped in front of the door. He twisted the padlock. It didn't give. This was a kind of burglary, and he knew it was wrong, but Sorcha had infuriated him. She'd challenged his courage, and now he wanted to know himself if he was brave enough to face the dread that seized him when he'd stood there the previous night. Though Dudley had been mocking him, he'd been right. Tristan was a man of reason, ruled by his head. He didn't trust emotions, they unmanned him.

He lifted the lump hammer and smashed it against the padlock, causing it to buckle but not break. The blow clanged among the stones. He raised the hammer again, and with all his strength brought it down. This time the clasp broke. The lock hung, so he put down the hammer and twisted it free, dropping it with a clunk onto the stone steps. With the lock off, the door creaked open, and a smell like a watery grave hit his nostrils.

Now he could find what Sorcha had wanted kept secret.

The door was stiff, but he dragged it so he could squeeze through.

The light inside the tower was poor, but he saw the floor was shattered. Tristan stepped forward the the edge and peered down where it plunged into a cave about forty feet below.

Then he looked up to see the stair winding around in a spiral. No guard rail protected the climber from a fall on the inward side, but the steps were wide enough to allow him to mount them, at least here at the bottom.

With the hammer in his hand, he stepped up. He mounted first one step, then another. About twenty feet up, he faltered. He had never suffered from vertigo, but the lack of anything to hold onto and the drop to his right filled his mind with chattering voices of danger.

He kept on going up. At first, all was well. He used his left hand to support himself against the outer wall, but the tower got narrower, and the steps thinner and more slanted. Halfway up, he paused to gather his courage. He didn't look down.

He remembered in the desert, on the night op, when he'd lost it. He'd killed his prisoner. He hadn't intended to but the guy suddenly died when he was there, a weak heart or something. Tristan had never killed a man. He was a linguist. He went to bits, way out there, with only the guys of his patrol.

Gwyn saved him, slapped his face, sobered him enough so they could complete the mission. Gwyn said it was always like that, one or two died. You can't make a cheescake without broken biscuits.

The rest of the troop said he'd bottled it, that he wasn't one of them. He was Int. Corps, not SAS. But Gwyn told them to shut it, and Tristan vowed he would never lose his nerve again.

This was what that was all about. Tristan hated emotions that came from nowhere, or rather somewhere deep inside, but somewhere outside his control and direction. Tristed trusted knowledge and thinking. Fear and love: they were the enemy. But such strong enemies. They made you do things you never intended.

Tristan told himself that if he climbed to the top of the tower and found nothing, that would prove that the banshee was only Sorcha trying to scare them. There was no ghost. There was nothing in this castle that she hadn't created by her stories.

He began again, climbing another higher spiral of stairs. After only a few steps, he was breathing fast, but not from exertion. He looked for a crevice in the wall to dig his fingers into, but the stones were too smooth. There was no anchor. He would have to rely on his balance alone.

He went slower now, more careful about where he placed his feet. Two more steps and a scattering of rotten stone fell away under his right boot. That made him stop.

He was very high. He couldn't swallow. Sweat filmed his forehead. He said out loud, 'Fear is just a feeling.'

And a thought came back in echo: love is just a feeling, but that's got you beat too.

Tristan looked up to see how far he had to go. Daylight filtered down and from the lip of a broken floor way above, ravens watched. They sat black-hooded like a trio of hanging judges, blinking their bright eyes. They did not fly away; he was too far beneath them.

A wave of dizziness made him teeter. He lurched, pressing his shoulder and face against damp render and breathing in gasps. He needed a second. Just a second, and he mustn't look down. If he looked down, his fear would paralyze him and he'd be stuck, neither up nor down.

The stairs were only two feet wide now, still safe if he was careful and watched his feet and kept his balance.

He trod with care, hand against the wall. Three more steps, and a gap came into view where one step had fallen away. He would have to jump.

Stinging sweat dripped from Tristan's brow, running into his eye, stinging with salt. He glanced up. He was almost there, and above was part of a floor still intact. If it would bear his weight. But he had to focus, first thing was the gap. Then the floor. He laughed. He might never get as far as the floor, so no need to worry about that yet.

He wiped the sweat from his top lip, got ready, tensed, but waited.

Who would know if he didn't go all the way up? He was doing only doing this to prove his courage. He'd had some idea that Sorcha kept something in here, but now he saw that no one climbed this far up. No one.

If he turned and went down now, his failed nerves would be his secret. But Sorcha would look at him with those mocking eyes that seemed to see through to every weakness and every sin. She would know his fear had beaten him.

And he would know.

Then he heard the door below open. Tristan froze. Who the hell was this? First, he thought the wind had blown it, but there was no wind. Something had definitely entered down there at the tower's entrance.

He pressed himself into the wall. He was out of sight of the door, but if someone, or something, climbed the stairs, he had nowhere to hide. They would see him, frozen by fear, and he couldn't escape.

He had to move. He sized up the gap, muttered, and leapt. But as he landed, he slipped, and pitched forward, tottering, loosing balance, until, lurching his shoulder to the left and throwing his centre of gravity away from the terrible drop, he scrabbled at the wall, his fingers grasping at a hole. Steadying himself, he pulled himself in and breathed.

He slumped there and his heartbeat slowed. He was safe, but he'd made a noise. Whoever was down there must have heard him. The heavy steps of someone thudded up the stone staircase. If the guy came, there would be a confrontation. Tristan gripped the hammer, but knew to fight on this broken staircase would be suicide.

But the tower had been locked. Dudley and Sorcha didn't want him here: they wanted this place to stay secret. It was like there was some-thing important hidden here. But what would they do if they found him snooping?

Whoever it was, got closer. Breathing fast, Tristan jumped his way up the remaining steps. When he got to the top, he would at least be on the floor, if it would hold him. And if it would hold him, he could turn and defend himself.

He couldn't see the person coming up behind him, but he heard him. Whoever it was, was climbing up faster than he had. Then the sound of rapid footsteps stopped suddenly. Tristan guessed they'd arrived at the gap.

Tristan could go down and face the intruder. He could wait where he was. He could go up further. He only had a short way to go to the broken floor above, but he waited, holding his breath, straining to hear the sound of his pursuer. Whoever was coming up would need to leap the gap. A minute went by, then another, but no one jumped. Then he heard the crunch of a boot heel twisted round and the footsteps went down and away.

The door at the bottom scraped shut. Tristan listened for the click of a replacement padlock, but none came. That made sense. They hadn't been expecting him to smash the padlock so wouldn't have a new one with them.

But they could fetch one.

Tristan considered turning back and hurrying down. That would be the sensible thing to do. But he was so close to the top now. He had to see what was up there. Once he'd looked he would descend.

He took the final few steps in haste. When he reached the top, he saw no speaker system, no set of electrical tricks set up by Sorcha to broadcast the banshee's scream over the castle. There was only the damp air here, the watching ravens, and a heap of sticks. Or it seemed they were sticks.

Twigs had fallen from the birds' nests across the stones of the floor. But there was something else lay there too, brown, brittle, and old, sprawled in an untidy heap. He tested the floor with each step to make sure it didn't give way under him. When he got close to the heap, he picked up the sticks, disentangling them from what lay below. Beneath the broken branches were bones.

At first, he thought birds of prey brought them there, remains of their meals, the splintered bones of lambs or rabbits. But the bones were much bigger than that.

Once he had pulled off all the sticks, it was unmistakable what they were. They were human bones. Tristan recognised the pelvis and the shattered rib cage. And there, some feet away, cracked and rolled on its side was a skull. Some of its teeth were missing, and the eye holes gaped dry and empty. Someone had severed the skull from the spine on purpose, with one harsh blow by the look of it. If it was only the skeleton of someone who had got up here but couldn't get back down, why was the head cut off?

He remembered they cut the heads off vampires so they couldn't rise again. Then he sighed: a few more days in this castle, and he'd be certifiable. The simple explanation was the skull had rolled away from the spine when a raven picking at its flesh had pushed it long ago. That's all it was: The skeleton of a man who'd come up and couldn't get down, or a woman, but not a vampire, not a banshee, merely a tragedy. The bones were old. They might date from the days before Sorcha bought the castle and began its restoration. She might have told the truth for once and she may never have been up here at all. It took some nerve to climb those steps, and his pursuer hadn't been able to muster the courage to jump the gap in teh broken stairs.

Maybe Sorcha really kept the tower closed because it was dangerous but she used that fact as a prop to increase the mystery of the place. Once again, she was proved a fake—not a solitary witch, just a simple fraud.

Tristan felt better. He looked at the hammer in his hand and felt foolish that he had it. This place made you scared. It made you imagine things.

He allowed himself a smile. Time to descend.

IT WAS STILL EARLY WHEN TRISTAN GOT BACK TO HIS ROOM. HE found the door flung open and, rushing to look inside, he saw someone had ransacked the room. The quilt was dragged from the bed, and the sheets and all his possessions were hurled across the room.

He stepped in and saw his hold-all was upended and its contents scattered. Tristan went on his hands and knees and retrieved his shaving brush and spare belt from the floor. The electrical equipment was all deployed, so there wasn't much left in the room a vandal could break, but his earphones were squashed into the floor, mashed as if by a heavy boot and he picked them up and groaned. He shook his head; whoever had been there was looking for something, but what secrets did they think they'd find?

Tristan put his ear to the connecting door that led through to Claire's room. Her snores seeped out like a buzz saw. Whoever pillaged his room hadn't disturbed the psychic, though they couldn't have been quiet, and whoever it was knew he'd got up early. They'd been watching him. Tristan bent to retrieve his books.

Someone was standing at the door. He spun around and saw Dudley. The tall Irishman was observing him. Anger sparked in Tristan. "Did you do this? What were you looking for?"

Dudley held his tongue.

Tristan went to the door and squared up to the Irishman who stood a head taller than him. "I know you did it. You knew I was out of the room, so you came in and pulled everything apart."

Dudley leered. "Why would I do that?"

"I don't know. I've got nothing to hide."

Dudley winked. "If you've got nothing to hide, why hide it?"

Tristan's hands made fists. "I've hidden nothing."

Dudley grinned. "Clean conscience, eh? Excellent. But you'll be wanting another room."

Tristan narrowed his eyes. "Why? I can pull this one straight."

"No, but there's a better one. Come, I'll show you."

The Irishman strode off, and Tristan followed.

What was going on here?

Dudley mounted the stairs ahead of him, going fast. The staircase twisted round, and Tristan realised they were ascending another tower.

He remembered he'd seen three towers that first evening, from outside on the road. The central one was solid, the ruined tower was to the left and this must be the other small one on the right. Dudley stopped at a brown-painted door and threw it open with a flourish.

Tristan climbed the last steps behind Dudley and looked in. The room was beautiful--far better than the one he had on the floor below. It was circular and had a stone fireplace laid with peat turfs and screws of paper ready to light. The bed looked better too, and the view over the castle roofs was impressive. Crows scratched about above the ceiling.

"I don't get it," he said.

"What's to get?"

"Why now? What are you up to?"

"This is a better room. One of the best. Why complain?"

"Because I don't know what your scheme is."

Dudley chuckled. "Why don't you accept your luck? Or your fate?"

"What do you mean, fate?"

"What you're here for, what you're destined to do."

"What are you talking about my fate? I'm not destined to do anything."

Dudley laughed. "Ah, free will is it? There may be fate and there may be free will—but how do you know the difference when every path takes you to the same ending? "

Tristan was tired of Dudley's meaningless utterences. "Why didn't you put me in here to start off with?"

Dudley scratched the back of his head. "Lady Sorcha said to offer you the room now."

"Lady Sorcha?"

"She's a lady to me."

"And why did you search my room below?"

"Who says I did it?"

"Who else would?"

Dudley shrugged. "I think other people may be interested in your secrets, Mr Gifford. They might have been looking for incriminating evidence?"

"Bullshit," Tristan said, but instantly thought of Gwyn.

Dudley wagged his finger. "See you at breakfast. Don't be late."

As Dudley left, Tristan looked around him and wondered again why on earth Sorcha wanted to offer him this better room now?

And surely it was Dudley who'd ransacked his room. They were trying to unnerve him. They wanted him to think it was Gwyn. But even if Gwyn had been searching his room for evidence of something going on between him and Iseult, why would that prompt Sorcha to provide him with this new room? Unless she wanted to separate him from the rest of the group. And then he thought: unless she wanted to come to him without the others knowing.

And all that shit about fate. He glanced at his watch. Breakfast would be in an hour. He lay down on the bed to wait and gazed out of the window at the scudding clouds.

⚜

NOT MEANING TO, TRISTAN FELL INTO A DEEP SLEEP IN HIS TOWER room. He failed to get up for breakfast and woke an hour and a half later, jumping off the bed, cursing and splashing water on his face from the pot ewer, then hurrying down the spiral staircase.

Outside Gwyn and Iseult's door, he hesitated a minute, then knocked.

Gwyn opened it. He was brushing his teeth. "Hey man," Gwyn said through the white foam.

Tristan took in the three-quarters empty whiskey bottle. "Where's Iseult?"

He thought Gwyn reacted oddly to his question. He couldn't say how - there was no pause, no edge to his reply, but something.

Gwyn gestured with the toothbrush. "Dunno. I sort of remember her getting up." He winced. "I was a bit hungover." His face brightened, toothbrush back in mouth, "But now it's lunchtime. Morning is boring. The guests should arrive soon, and that's what we're here for."

"To be honest, I'll be glad to be finished with it and we can leave," Tristan said. He didn't mention about his room change.

Gwyn put the toothpaste down on the table beside the jug full of water. "I hope that bloody mechanic comes today. I need the car fixed." He rubbed his eyes.

Gwyn followed Tristan down the corridor towards the kitchen. Once again, he looked at the portrait of Lady Amelia. Halfway through the empty library, feet slapping on the floorboards, he was gripped by the sense of being watched. He stared at the picture, but her painted face looked like it always did. Tristan shook his head. "This is a weird place."

Gwyn grinned. "Good. Weird is good. I need a smoke more than an eat. Want to come with me to the door?"

Tristan's remembered the dog shape in the mist. Going to the door where he'd seen it would help exorcise the stupid nerves it had given him. "Yeah, sure."

He followed his boss to the door.

"Sorcha's full of tricks. But she did pay you though?" Tristan watched Gwyn light up, the Welshman cupping his hand to nurture the flame. He sucked at the cigarette until, with a look of satisfaction, he saw the fire had caught. He took a drag and said, "Sorry?"

"She's paid you—Sorcha?"

Gwyn nodded. "Good as. Got a cheque, but not cashed it yet. No banks in the Bog of Allen." He grinned. "This is a wild place." He gestured with his cigarette to the flat and empty wetland. "Imagine building a castle here. Why? Who did it?"

"Finn McCool, apparently."

"I heard Normans and Druids."

Tristan laughed. "Some such. History wasn't my strong point."

"Thought you were pretty academic."

"I'm good with words. Languages. Grammar. I can remember shit like that."

"You should learn Gaelic so we can understand what's going on between Sorcha and Dudley."

Tristan shrugged. He was cold. The early dawn mist had vanished, but the air was chill. "Yeah, I'll get to it."

Gwyn smiled. "And quick." He flicked his cigarette away into the marsh. "To lunch. Or is it breakfast?"

Turning, looking down the long road that led to civilisation, Tristan scratched his head. "I don't get how nobody's come yet — guests."

Gwyn turned as he walked. "Soon they will. You ready for it?"

"Sure, all the electronics are in place."

"I wonder where Iseult is?" Gwyn looked concerned.

Tristan volunteered, "With Claire?"

Gwyn made a pfft noise and disappeared into the castle. Tristan followed him.

They were at the kitchen when Tristan said, "I am grateful, you know."

Gwyn seemed preoccupied. "Grateful? What for?"

"You know."

Gwyn waved away his concern. "Ah, the Syrian desert again. We should leave that shit behind us now. Memories of that place are bad juju. Anyway, I was doing the job. I would have done it for anyone."

Tristan stared at Gwyn. "I know. But I messed up. I lost my nerve. You saved my life."

Gwyn gave a big toothy grin and slapped Tristan on the back. "I saved lots of peoples' lives. Anybody who says he wasn't scared shitless is a liar. It's not being scared, it's being scared but still doing your job."

"And I didn't."

"Come on, it was a lapse. We all have lapses."

"Did you ever?"

Gwyn grimaced. "What?"

"Lapse, break."

"Listen, I was plenty frightened at times."

"But you didn't ever actually break. I never saw it."

Gwyn exhaled. "I'm just the same as anybody else."

Tristan thought he wasn't the same as anybody else. He'd never met anyone like him. Gwyn was drunken, angry, often wrong, but still when push came to shove—a hero. And that's what made it so hard.

If Gwyn had been a shit, it would have been like rescuing Iseult, almost virtuous. But Gwyn's innate decency made Tristan's feelings for Iseult wicked. He never wanted to fall in love with Iseult, but each time he saw her again desire caught like a flame to paper. She struck at him and lodged in his heart like a golden knife. Maybe that's what Dudley meant by fate.

Gwyn was watching him. Tristan hoped his thoughts weren't plain on his face. And then he thought Gwyn knew anyway and forgave him all the same. But that was wrong. Gwyn was a hero, and he wouldn't wear the cuckold's crown without a fight.

❧❧❧

THEY ENTERED THE KITCHEN AND FOUND SORCHA SEATED, WEARING a crisp white shirt, hair pulled back in a ponytail, her face scrubbed clean, gleaming silver rings on her fingers. She looked up as they entered. "Arthur and Lancelot."

Gwyn frowned. "What?"

"A literary allusion, my dear. Are you well?"

"Yeah, I'm good," Gwyn's South Wales accent made the Americanism sound odd. "You seen Is?"

"Iseult?" Sorcha shook her head. "Not today."

Gwyn sat. "She won't be far. Get me a coffee, Trist?"

Tristan nodded and went over to the range upon which the coffee pot sat steaming. Dudley stood beside him. The Irishman whispered, "I forgot to ask, did you have fun this morning?"

"Fun?"

"Exploring. Breaking."

"I put some speakers up. I was getting things ready for tonight. I couldn't sleep for thinking of what I had to do, so I got up early." He poured out two mugs full. "You have fun?" he asked Dudley.

"Fun?"

"Entering. Breaking."

Dudley laughed. He said something in Irish.

"That's a bad habit," Tristan said, taking the coffee to Gwyn.

"What? Speaking my own language in my own country?"

"No, being a dick."

Sorcha laughed, the musical sound ringing in the kitchen. Dudley scowled, glanced at his mistress.

"You're funny, Tristan," Sorcha said. He avoided her eye.

Gwyn sipped his coffee. "When are the guests coming?"

Instead of answering, Sorcha said, "I did a bit of research."

"Oh yeah?" Gwyn said. "By the way, what's for lunch? I missed breakfast."

She nodded over to the range where there were covered plates. "Gammon, eggs, and boiled potatoes."

Gwyn stood up to get them. "Want one, Trist?"

Tristan nodded. He was watching Sorcha. She was like a snake, scheming something.

Gwyn handed him a plate. Tristan pulled off the silver paper and took the knife and fork. He ate while Gwyn talked.

"Research, then?"

She nodded. "Your company isn't doing too well."

Gwyn frowned but said between mouthfuls. "And that's news to who?"

She shrugged. "I booked you because I thought you could use the work."

"Well, that's no lie. Thank you anyway."

"I looked you up on the Internet. I thought it would be fun to have you here, but less fun to have guests scuttling around my house." She studied her nails. "And your name amused me."

"My name's funny?"

She glanced up. "It's the Welsh equivalent of the Irish Fionn. Gwyn, Fionn—means holy or sacred."

"White, it means too. I take it to refer to my hair after years of worrying where the next gig's coming from."

"So, I hired you."

"Because of my name?" Gwyn shook his head. "Weird. But you've paid, so that's fine."

Sorcha said, "Things have resonance: names, places. This area was the abode of Fionn Mac Cumhail."

Tristan said, "Finn McCool. Yeah, I heard."

Sorcha smiled and reached across the table and stroked Tristan's muscular forearm. He pulled away. She pointed. "And here we have our fine young Tristan. Whose name means sadness if I'm not mistaken."

"More names," Gwyn said.

Sorcha studied him. "Names are magic: 'By names and images are all powers awakened and reawakened'."

"If you say so. Anyway, what about the guests?"

She looked down like a method actor preparing to deliver a line.

Gwyn paused. "So? Something's up."

She shrugged. "Nothing's up."

Tristan butted in. "But where are the guests? I thought they'd be here by now."

Gwyn's eyes narrowed. "Yeah. Me too."

"They're not coming," she said.

Gwyn flinched and took a bite of his gammon.

Tristan leaned forward. "Why not?"

She seemed nonchalant. "Because I never invited them."

Gwyn's waved his fork. "I don't get this."

She didn't answer.

Gwyn said, "So you're paying me — us — to be here, but you've got no income coming in to cover the costs. You make no money out of it?"

"I don't need money."

Tristan said, "So what did you hire us for?"

She looked at him. "For the pleasure of your company?"

Gwyn shrugged. "I don't care as long as you pay me."

But Tristan was unhappy. "I don't like this."

"What's not to like?" said Gwyn. "A fee with no work."

"I don't like people fucking with me."

"She's not fucking with you. You work for me. You get paid. What's the beef?"

"There's much more to this, Gwyn," Tristan said.

Sorcha laughed again. "Boys, boys. Enjoy being here."

Tristan ignored her. He said to Gwyn, "Both of them have been smiling from the start as if they know something we don't."

Gwyn lit another cigarette. "Take it easy, tiger. What could they know? It's an ordinary job. Don't let the castle spook you."

Anger flashed through Tristan. "I'm not spooked." He sat back, staring at Sorcha who wore an air of faint amusement. He asked, "What do you really want, Sorcha? From us being here?"

She toyed with her hair. "Listen to Gwyn, Tristan. Don't let the castle spook you. It's heavy with memories — with injustices and cruelty. It has a way of changing people."

"It won't change me."

She met his gaze. "The castle remembers, it if we try to forget, it will not let us. Things can be done here because of what happened long ago—things that couldn't be accomplished elsewhere."

Tristan snorted. "I don't even know what you're talking about."

Gwyn said, "So maybe we should leave? If we have no show, I mean. What's the point staying?"

Dudley said, "Your car doesn't work."

Gwyn said, "I thought you'd rung the mechanic."

"I did."

"And?"

"He's busy. Maybe tomorrow."

Tristan said, "Why don't we just leave. Hitch a lift and go."

"Because my car," Gwyn said. "Besides, free food and lodge."

Sorcha smiled. "Yes, please stay. You might as well enjoy your mini vacation. Dudley and I will be at your service." She stood. "Anyway, I must do a little errand." She gave a wave as she left them, Dudley trailing after her.

Tristan turned to Gwyn, "This feels like a trap."

Gwyn shook his head, "You're overreacting. As usual."

DUTY AND PASSION

Earlier, Iseult woke, groggy from lack of sleep. Gwyn lay to her left, his arm splayed across her chest. He was snoring. She looked at him, the unshaven chin, the stubble now more grey than black, the hair sticking up and needing a wash. She watched him for minutes, observing the rise and fall of his chest, listening to the soft buzz of his breathing. On her dressing table was a bottle of whiskey, but only about half an inch of the yellow brown liquor was left. A glass sat beside it, drained and covered in greasy marks of fingers and lips.

Iseult slipped out of the bed and fetched her clothes. The varnished wood was smooth and chill under her soles. Then her feet found the warmer rug, and she stood on that while she took and fastened her bra. She pulled on her panties and found a shirt, jeans and a sweater. She had to find a shower; she loathed to feel so unclean.

"Gwyn." He didn't stir. "Gwyn," she said again, reaching out her hand and stroking his cheek. His skin was waxy and his slumber was deep. She stepped back. He was killing himself with drink. She'd tried to speak to him about it but he didn't want to acknowledge his problem. All he said was that it helped him relax, then grew angry, and she changed the subject. She hoped it wasn't her that drove him to drink.

She tried to be kind and be a supportive wife to him; she owed him that.

Iseult closed the bedroom door behind her as quietly as she could. Out in the corridor, the reality of where she was hit her: a haunted Irish castle on Halloween. She smiled, childishly delighted. Then she looked over her shoulder at Tristan's room. She imagined him sleeping there. She imagined being with him, but then shook the thought off. Still she hesitated, thinking she could knock, and ask him down to breakfast, but knew that, whatever she told herself, that if she knocked on his door, it wasn't because she wanted to remind him about breakfast. Guilt grew like a rank weed and she hurried down the corridor toward the kitchen. She paused at the top of the landing. There was a weird smell—damp and organic, like old peat. She looked at the wooden floor and saw a trail of water along it. What the hell was that all about?

۞

IN THE KITCHEN, ONLY CLAIRE SAT AT THE LONG WOODEN TABLE. IT was set for four but the plates and cutlery were unused except Claire's. "Hi," she said.

Claire blinked and nodded. She had a slice of toast up to her mouth and a smear of butter on her sharp chin. "Hello," she replied with her mouth full.

Iseult walked over to the old fashioned range and got the coffee pot. "Coffee, Claire?"

Claire bit off more toast. She shook her head and pointed at her teacup, still half full.

Iseult poured her own coffee and cut a slice from the fresh loaf with the mother-of-pearl handled bread knife. She put the bread in the toaster, and while she was waiting, observed Claire. The psychic finished the toast and licked her fingers clean of butter, still leaving the smear on her chin. Iseult noticed that Claire wore a cheap mood ring, the sort you buy from the One Pound Shop or get at a funfair. Maybe she'd always worn it, but Iseult had never taken enough notice of her before.

Claire twisted her head round. "More toast for me."

Iseult shrugged. "Sure," but she frowned despite herself—manners would be nice.

As if guessing what she was thinking, or reading her mind, Claire added, "Please."

Iseult cut another slice. Her toast was done now and while Claire's bread browned, she buttered her toast with the salted Irish butter. "No one else around?" she asked Claire.

"No,"

"Not even Dudley? I thought he'd be here."

"No. No one."

Iseult said quickly, "You haven't seen Tristan?"

Instead of answering that question, Claire said, "Where's your husband?"

"Asleep. I'll take him some tea and toast up."

Claire cackled. "He'd prefer whiskey, I think."

"Hmm." Iseult frowned.

When Claire's toast was ready, Iseult buttered that and handed it to her, then sat herself down. They ate in silence except for Claire's loud munching. Iseult took a sip of coffee. It was bitter. She ate more toast.

Claire cocked her head and blinked. "You're sad."

Iseult felt the weight in her heart. "Am I?" she replied without meeting Claire's bright eyes.

There was a pause while Claire ate more toast. "I know, you know," she said finally.

"Know what?"

"About you and Tristan."

Iseult started as if someone had just given her a death sentence. How could her innermost secret be so easily known? And if Claire knew, Gwyn might.

Iseult didn't respond. She kept her head down, eyes focused on the plate but seeing nothing. The toast was dry and tasteless as she forced herself to chew. If she stayed quiet, it might go away, Claire might go away, as if the words were never voiced and the thoughts never thought.

The psychic stared, bright-eyed. "I know you want him."

Anger surged through Iseult. "It's not like that," she snapped, but inside she knew it was.

Claire stood up. For a crazy second, Iseult thought she was going to go and tell Gwyn. Then the psychic said, "You want more coffee?" Her grating accent made the question all the more absurd.

"No." Iseult put the toast on the plate. She didn't want it. She couldn't meet the woman's eyes.

Claire said conversationally. "You can't help loving someone. The heart wants what it wants."

Iseult said in a flat voice, "I love my husband."

Claire sat again. She cradled the mug in her hand. She was a clever woman, thought Iseult. Clever like a polecat is clever - feral, conniving, ever seeking mischief. She imagined Claire like a magpie finding some shiny trinket, some secret or lie, and turning it over with her beak, regarding it as a treasure.

Claire blinked. She had found cheese from somewhere. She bit into it. "There are different kinds of love, Iseult. There's love that comes from duty. And love that comes from lust."

Claire stepped over and took Iseult's fingers in her bony hand. Iseult shuddered and went to pull away, but she knew she had to be careful of this woman, so she let her hand lie and endured her touch.

"You love Gwyn from duty, and Tristan from passion." Claire spoke in a sing-song rhythm, like she was talking to a toddler. Even if her words were a trick, she said them like she had sympathy. Maybe she was sympathetic. Iseult reached out for someone to forgive her. She muttered, "I owe Gwyn such a lot."

"What do you owe him?" Claire cocked her head on the other side.

Iseult's eyes filled with hot tears. She hated herself for crying and she wiped the tears with her arm then shrugged. "He found me when I was nothing—in a bar. I was in a terrifying relationship with a violent man. Gwyn sorted that out."

The psychic cocked her head again. "Sorted it out?"

"Dealt with it. It was so bad I thought it would end my life, but Gwyn threw me a lifeline."

"How?"

Iseult didn't look up. "Doesn't matter."

There was a long pause. Claire watched her then said, "So it's a question of duty versus love?"

Iseult knew Claire was fishing. Probably just for her own gossipy satisfaction, but she was wary. She cleared her throat. "I don't see it like that."

"Don't you?" Claire nibbled on the cheese, now more like a rat than a magpie. She reached over across Iseult's arms and took the butter dish. "Mind if I get the butter?"

You've already done it, thought Iseult.

Claire put extra butter on the half slice of toast that was left. Iseult considered leaving.

Claire blurted, "So what will you do about it?"

Iseult met her gaze now. "Do about what?"

"About Tristan."

Iseult remembered what she had done with Sorcha in front of that strange idol. She reached for the gold cross around her throat, but it was gone. She'd taken it off and put it away. The whole episode seemed so odd now, and nothing was resolved, nothing was further forward. She wondered how she'd thought at the time that magic would solve all her problems. She'd been like a little girl, wanting what she wanted with no heed of the consequences. Iseult sighed. She regretted kneeling down before the thing now. It was so stupid and childish. It had demeaned her. Asking for Tristan when she owed Gwyn her freedom and maybe her life. She hung her head.

"He's no good you know," Claire said.

"Who?" Iseult had been thinking of Gwyn, lying drunk in the bed, but she knew Claire meant Tristan.

"He's a false prophet — an unbeliever. He denies the messages of the spirits."

This sudden demonstration of Claire's child-like mind gave Iseult relief. A smile came but she concealed it and looked up and met Claire's eyes. "You mean because he doesn't believe in the banshee?"

Claire's claw like hands, all sinews and bones, gripped the table. She nodded rapidly. "Someone will die here. The banshee has cried and it must be so."

Iseult exhaled and sat back. The spell was broken. Her guilt dissipated. It would come back, but Claire's ridiculousness had evaporated it for now. Iseult slapped her palms on the table. "I'm not sure I believe that."

Claire leaned in conspiratorially. "That's because he has poisoned your mind. Beware of false prophets, which come to you in sheep's clothing, but inwardly they are ravening wolves. Ye shall know them by their fruits. Do men gather grapes of thorns, or figs of thistles? Even so every good tree bringeth forth good fruit; but a corrupt tree bringeth forth evil fruit." She paused then added, "Matthew 7:15," in case Iseult hadn't recognised the quotation.

She had.

Claire snatched at Iseult's wrist but Iseult dragged it away and sprang up, regarding Claire with fear and wonder. The woman was insane.

Claire blinked at her. "Sin is real, Iseult." Then a smirk. "Have you done anything with him yet?"

"No!" she blurted. Then quieter, but still firm, "Of course not. No." The thought of Tristan conjured his image. She thought of him silhouetted at her front door. Her tone speaking to Claire was indignant but inside, her heart responded to his name with yearning. It was true: she hadn't slept with him, but in her heart, she knew she wanted to; she wanted to feel his hands on her body and his weight on her and the hardness of his muscle.

Claire seemed satisfied with her response. "Good," she clucked. "Because once sin gets a foothold, it breeds, once, twice, even thrice."

Iseult's conversation with Claire left her stomach churning. She needed to unburden herself, talk to someone sympathetic. It was unthinkable she could speak of these feelings to Gwyn, or Tristan, or God forbid, Dudley. That left only Sorcha.

❧

ISEULT FOUND THE CHATELAINE IN THE THE MORNING ROOM WITH the picture windows. She was sitting there drinking coffee, flicking through the Irish Times. Iseult wondered whether it was today's copy as she'd heard no car leaving the castle to fetch it nor anyone arriving to bring it. There was no sign that the mechanic had arrived to fix the car so they could get out of there either.

The marsh stretched away through the window in front of them, the rushes and remaining heads of bog cotton looking cold and wild. Iseult shivered and was glad the bog couldn't get in.

"Iseult," Sorcha said, smiling as if Iseult was her best friend. "Sit." She patted the sofa beside her.

Iseult sat obediently.

"I'll get Dudley to bring you some coffee." Sorcha reached for the silver bell but Iseult put her hand on it. "No, I don't want any."

Sorcha raised a dark eyebrow and regarded the young woman. The morning gathered around them. Iseult was quiet. Sorcha reached out and pushed Iseult's hair away from her brow. "You're sad," Sorcha said. It was a statement, not a question. Claire had said the very same thing.

Iseult laughed, but the sound was hollow. She stared through the window. "The days are so short at this time of year. It's like we're wrapped in darkness."

"It's the beginning of the Celtic winter; they would sacrifice the beasts they couldn't feed through the cold months and the ones they kept, they led between two bonfires to purify them. They called it Samhain, summer's end."

"You know lots of things about Celtic history."

Sorcha shrugged. "It's been my everlasting interest. Ireland always drew me. It was like a magnet. And to this place too - Tullabeg, the home of my ancestors."

Iseult tugged at her hair. "I envy you your sense of roots."

"Roots are important."

"To some people. To others not so much."

"I guess." A pause, until Sorcha said, "Did it work?"

At first Iseult pretended not to know what she meant. She was embarrassed about kneeling to the idol of Crom Cruach. Sorcha preserved the silence until finally Iseult muttered, "Of course not."

Sorcha leaned forward, attentive. "Maybe you didn't want it to work that much."

Iseult gave a heavy sigh. "I'm so torn." Her eyes filled up. "I'm like the sea; the tide comes in and goes out. Sometimes I think I should go with my love for Tristan but then I'm pulled back by what I owe Gwyn."

"What do you owe Gwyn?" Sorcha said quietly.

"My life."

"He saved your life?"

Iseult's hand went for the missing gold cross. "No, but figuratively. The life I have now, I owe to him: my house, any money I have, my freedom."

"Freedom? That's a strange thing to say."

"I mean that literally."

There was quiet. Iseult noticed the ticking of the grandfather clock. She hadn't even seen it was there. That rhythmic sound and the restless wind outside made her feel outside herself. Sorcha took Iseult's hand. She stroked it. "You can tell me all about it." She sat back suddenly. "But now I'm prying."

Iseult gave a thin smile. "I don't think you mind prying, Sorcha."

Sorcha's eyes narrowed but, as if after a second's inner debate on how to react to the comment, she smiled. "Really my dear, I only want what's best for you."

"You do? Why?"

Sorcha shrugged as if bemused. "Because people want to help people?"

"Do they?" Iseult studied Sorcha as if waiting for an expression or look that would help her decide what she thought about the witch.

Sorcha clasped both hands around Iseult's hand and squeezed. Iseult didn't pull away from her. Iseult's eyes, blue as spring flowers, searched Sorcha's eyes azure like an Irish lake.

Sorcha said, "I think you're very unhappy Iseult."

Iseult grimaced. "No, I'm not very unhappy. I can't have what I want. I'm like a petulant teen."

Sorcha shook her head. "Take what you want, Iseult. Life's too short. Take what you want. It will only be offered once."

"Did you?"

Sorcha's gaze was fierce. "Oh yes. I always did."

Iseult looked away. "We're different."

"Yes, I deal with my problems but you wait for someone else to come and fix them for you."

The older woman's words stung Iseult. A sudden burst of mixed emotions shook her like a crack of thunder across the sky — shame, guilt, fear and she dragged her hands free of Sorcha's grip. "Fuck you."

Sorcha threw back her head and laughed.

Iseult's flush deepened.

Sorcha said, "It's nice to finally see some spirit."

Iseult's anger subsided as suddenly as it had come and the feeling of impotence almost drowned her.

Sorcha added, "I'm not unhappy. That's another difference between us."

"Neither am I." Iseult's words sounded hollow even to herself. She picked at her throat. "I don't think Tristan will break his debt of honour to Gwyn. I admire him for that, even though I want him with every bone in my body."

"So both of you owe Gwyn something? You and Tristan too?" Sorcha seemed interested.

Iseult said, "Gwyn saved his life. Something went wrong."

"Tristan lost his nerve. That's what happened."

Iseult's anger rose again. "There are things about Tristan you don't know. He's a gentle person, thoughtful, but he has a tremendous sense of right and wrong. He'll do anything for a cause he believes in."

Sorcha didn't meet Iseult's gaze. She examined her elegant fingers. "But he's too cowardly to take you, even though he loves you."

"He loves me?" A thrill ran through Iseult when she heard the words as if she never quite believed it until Sorcha confirmed it for her.

"Of course. I've seen his eyes follow you and the look on his face like a soft boy."

"It's doesn't do anything about it, not because he's a coward but because he's too honourable."

"Honour can be a good excuse if you don't have the guts to do something dishonourable."

Iseult's eyes flashed. "You're making me angry now. It's because he's a good man."

"Then that leaves you with a problem."

"No problem. I'll just endure."

"Will you?"

Iseult stood. "You don't mind upsetting people do you?"

"Not if it's in their best interests."

"Or yours perhaps." Iseult didn't know why she said it. How could it be in Sorcha's interest for her to leave Gwyn? Sorcha ignored her comment anyway. She wandered over to an antique chest of drawers that nestled against the back wall. Papers lay on it. Sorcha took a key and unlocked it. She pulled out a little crystal bottle.

"What the hell is that?" Iseult raised her eyebrows. "Poitín?" She laughed, suddenly nervous and put her hand to her mouth, unsure how to react.

"No."

"I'm not drinking it."

"It's not for you to drink."

"Then what's it for?"

"It's for Tristan to drink."

Realisation dawned on Iseult's face. She laughed. "A love potion? You're having me on."

It was almost dark outside despite it being early. Sorcha walked over to the standard lamp and switched it on. Then she came to Iseult and handed her the small glass bottle. Iseult studied it like Sorcha had given her a weapon. She hesitated standing there gazing at the thing, glancing at the table top, thinking she would leave it there, but instead her hand curled around the phial and she placed it in the pocket of her jacket.

Sorcha smiled. "Come on. Let's go and find the others."

12

DOGS AND BITCHES

Tristan said, "And you're taking it too well."

Gwyn sighed. "Chill your box, man. Let's finish eating." Gwyn tucked into the remains of his lunch, nodding and saying with his mouth full, "This is good. You don't know what you're missing."

Tristan picked at the food with his fork until Sorcha and Iseult came in. Iseult entered the room, and Tristan's attention snapped to her. He noticed how she appeared more friendly with Sorcha. He guessed they'd been spending time together and now knew each other better. That was bad. He was about to ask Iseult where they'd been, but she wouldn't meet his gaze.

He stood. "I'm going for some fresh air."

There was a muttering of "Sure", "Okay, see you in a minute" around the table. Nobody looked up to watch him leave. He guessed he'd pissed Gwyn off by talking about his suspicions when Gwyn preferred to take the easy way and let things be. Tristan couldn't get away from the feeling that something terrible was on its way. But Gwyn couldn't be told. That was his problem. He'd always been that way. Gwyn was your best friend as long as you deferred to his authority and, most of the time, Tristan did that. But now his boss seemed blind to Sorcha's machinations. Tristan didn't trust a single bone in her body.

⁂

Without looking back, Tristan left the kitchen and took a corridor he didn't remember walking down before. He took scant notice of his environment as he walked. At times, he'd break out of his reverie and see the dust, the ripped wallpaper, and spiders in old webs by the ceiling. More than once, he watched as a mouse scurried ahead of him across his path, but he cared little for anything.

He saw a door ahead with a pane of Victorian stained glass. When he got up to it, it opened to a courtyard of bleached grass and rushes. He drew the door open and cold air blew past him, but he welcomed its chill to bring him back to the reality of his situation, to allay this malady of love.

The courtyard area was surrounded by grey castle walls that seemed to reach up halfway to the sky. He stepped out and waded through the rank grass up to his calf. A ruined structure stood in the courtyard's middle. When he got to it, he stood with one hand on the wet stone.

The stones looked hundreds of years old. Some had fallen, and lichen covered what remained, making it the structure look almost natural as if the rocks had grown from the ground beneath the castle.

Behind the wall, Tristan saw a staircase leading down. At the bottom was a dark door. The door was much newer than the stone, and there was a shiny chain and padlock on it. All these padlocked doors hiding secrets, but this one wasn't fastened.

As Tristan stared, he had the irrational feeling that something ominous lurked down there. Half to dismiss his ridiculous fear, he stepped over the broken wall and lowered himself onto the steps. The stones were slippery from the recent rain, and as he descended, he pressed his hand hand on the wall. The stairwell stank of earth and rain. He reached the the door, pushed it and it swung ajar with hardly a sound.

The opening revealed more stairs going down. There was one flight, and then a stone-flagged tunnel disappearing into the ground.

Low grey light came down from the overcast sky behind, and by it, he descended to the tunnel floor. Water puddled from the surrounding walls on the stone. He wondered how the whole castle hadn't sunk down and disappeared centuries before. Unless the castle was an upgrowth of hell itself, erupting from the underworld like a fang into the grey Irish skies.

He walked on. And then came — not a noise, not a vision — only a feeling: a presentiment. He ransacked his mind for what triggered his unease. The place had all the elements necessary for a scene in a horror movie: the damp, the underground stink, the claustrophobic passage that stretched away in front. Anyone would feel unsettled here.

He knew how easy it was to play tricks on a man's mind to bring about fear. He'd done it himself in Syria: blindfold them, play white noise at them, never let them know what's going on. That way you fuel their paranoia until you become their only friend and they're glad to tell you about the next attack, the next suicide bomb. Sharpen his fear and man's minds is malleable. Fear disembowels your reason. Fear is a weapon. Sorcha knew that.

Tristan took out his phone and switched on the flashlight. Its white beam lit very little here. The darkness of centuries was too thick. Down here were ancient shadows and dreams of things that sucked light and brought nightmare.

He bit his lip and stepped further into the tunnel. And there among centuries-old stone he found a modern light switch and turned it on. Up on the ceiling, stretching down the passage on a wire, a string of light bulbs flicked alight. Tristan saw his breath.

He inched forward until he reached a junction in the passage. Ahead he could see steps descending further. How deep did this go?

A tunnel disappeared into the dark to his left, but a strange airlessness hung that way. To the right was a different feeling; something was alive down there. It had an animal stink, sour with musk. Whatever lurked there was famished and unappeased.

Tristan chose the left way, stepping forward and slipping in the thin mud. The floor was wet under foot, the walls damp under fingers. He was deep under the bog, and water oozed through the walls.

After he'd gone about thirty yards, he realised the tunnel continued on much further. An intuition struck him that this passage connected with the steps he'd seen at the chapel by the road where they'd stopped on the first day. And if it was true, that was a long walk there and a long walk back.

But it was a way out. But he was not ready to leave, he still had to find out what secrets Sorcha hid down here in the tunnels.

So he turned back and picked his way over the smooth flagstones until he reached the junction.

The right pathway smelled of animals. He walked down it a way, illuminated by the inadequate light bulbs. He got so far when the smell spooked him. It was like his uncle's old German Shepherd but wilder and more primal. Who would keep dogs down here in the dark?

He heard movement: legs, a jostling, a noticing and a hunger, ears pricked, snouts lifted, sniffing him out.

He imagined the red gleam of their eyes. The thudding beat of his heart rose into his throat. He could go on to prove he wasn't scared, but bravado isn't brave, it's brainless. To run into a pack of dogs down here would be suicide. The dogs were protecting something, he was sure of that. He turned and strode back to the steps.

When he got to the wooden door, he threw a backward glance, as if he might see them behind him, conjured from the darkness like spirit hounds, but there was was nothing. He passed through the door, closed the door behind him, went up the steps and breathed.

STANDING THERE, LOOKING DOWN AT HIM WAS DUDLEY.

Tristan spat. "Jesus, you scared the shit out of me."

Dudley said, "Jesus doesn't live here. He never felt welcome." Then, "You're quite the explorer, aren't you, Mr Tristan Gifford?" Dudley grinned his lopsided grin and swept back his shaggy grey hair from where it hung over his left cheek. He wore the same amused smile as Sorcha: the smiles of people who know something.

Tristan said, "What are you doing here?"

"Me? I live here. What's your excuse?"

"I was just exploring. I've got nothing else to do. The door was open."

Dudley said, "You're a foolish little man, aren't you?"

"And you're an ugly big one."

"Wander where you want, but you can't escape your fate, Mr Gifford."

"Maybe I dont want to."

"Now, there's a thing. Maybe you're finally seeing sense."

Tristan hurried up the slippery steps and pushed past Dudley, glad even to be in the dismal courtyard with its dying weeds. The walls surrounding the courtyard were like prison walls — blank and punctuated by windows like watching eyes. Above the castle, the sky rolled: grey on grey on grey.

From behind him now, Dudley called. "Be careful, though, when you're wandering around. We wouldn't want you coming to an untimely end."

❧

Tristan found a door back into the castle, though it wasn't the one he'd taken before. Inside, he hesitated and stepped behind the door, watching Dudley, who loitered the ruined wall in the courtyard's middle. The Irishman checked around him, as if seeing if Tristan had left, then descended the steps.

After a minute, Dudley appeared again, glanced over his shoulder and sauntered into the castle. After a second, Tristan followed him. Dudley seemed relaxed. He walked on without looking back. As he went, he whistled an old folk tune, and Tristan followed the music along corridors, keeping back as they went up the narrow stairs.

Dudley strode through rooms filled with boxes of broken dolls, a piano, and a rolled-up carpet. Tristan was always in earshot but out of sight. He followed through another corridor, the whistling leading him on. All the rooms were unfamiliar, but Tristan made a note of the route so he could find the way back. Tristan heard Dudley mounting more steps, still whistling.

The stairs creaked under Dudley's heavy tread, and a door groaned opened. Tristan slowed up, feeling his way forward with his fingers to find himself in a room that must have been the corner of the castle. The walls here were heavy stone blocks, like a colossal bastion and a window overlooked the drowned plain. It was dim. Tristan backed into a darker corner, hardly breathing. He didn't follow Dudley because if Dudley turned back, he would have nowhere to hide.

As the minutes went by, Tristan almost thought better of his plan, and considered retreating to find the others. But he didn't. A curiosity to know Dudley's inner workings possessed him — to find out the things Dudley didn't want him to know. Up to now, Sorcha and Dudley held all the cards, but by uncovering their secrets one by one, Tristan could reclaim the advantage.

After ten minutes, Tristan's patience was rewarded as he heard Dudley descending the stairs. He listened to the whistling again. This time it was another tune - *From Bantry Bay to Derry Quay*. Then the sound faded. He waited a while in case Dudley knew he was there and lurking to turn round and find him, but the Irishman didn't return.

Tristan hurried up the narrow twisting tower staircase. At the top, there was a door in need of re-painting. An old fashioned latch secured it. He tried it and found it wasn't locked. Dudley felt so safe in his own place that he left his room unlocked.

Tristan entered Dudley's chambers. There wasn't much furniture, only a long narrow bed, a plain wooden table with a wooden chair and an old book on the table. Tristan picked it up. It was in Irish, printed in the old fashioned Gaelic script.

There was a window, above head height, as if designed to watch the sky, not the land. The clever eyes of a hooded crow blinked at him through it. The bird perched on the stone around the slit window, gazing at him. Tristan had the ridiculous idea that it was one of Sorcha's spies.

Better leave. Then he noticed that smell again — the stench of dog. The stink was strong here. Maybe Dudley kept a dog, though he'd never seen it and it wasn't here now.

A quick glance around showed him there was nothing else in the room, so Tristan turned and left.

Tristan returned to the library and found it empty. He sat trying to read, but couldn't concentrate, and kept looking at the door. He knew he was waiting for Iseult, but she didn't come.

While he sat, Claire entered the room and sat, motionless, staring into space, looking at nothing — like a cow or a sheep might.

After half an hour, Gwyn came in with Dudley and sat down to smoke. Dudley brought him an old glass ashtray with Harp Lager written on it in orange letters. Gwyn's cigarette smoke curled up, and a draught near the ceiling caught it and twisted it away. In his right hand, Gwyn clenched a drained whiskey glass. Dudley must have given it to him.

"Still no mechanic!" Gwyn said. "If I was a suspicious man, I'd think you never called him, Dud."

"Would I lie to you?" Dudley grinned.

"Yep."

Too bloody true, Tristan thought. They wanted to keep them here still. The game still wasn't played out, whatever it was.

And then Iseult entered like a young queen, and Tristan's heart turned over. He glancedd up, and she met his eyes and smiled. Tristan saw Gwyn glance at her then follow her eyes back to Tristan. Iseult put her smile away.

They sat in the library in silence. Gloom gathered. They'd frittered the day away, and it was dark again. What were they even doing lingering here now they knew Sorcha hadn't invited any guests? They could have abandoned the car and got a lift out of here. But no one had moved.

Gwyn ground the cigarette into the ashtray. He said to Iseult, "Where've you been?"

Iseult turned and pointed. "With Sorcha. Girl talk, you know?" She smiled, but the attempt at a light mood fell flat.

Sorcha came in after her. The company was now assembled. Sorcha stopped at the door then turned to eye the lights in the chandelier above. They flickered and dimmed. "I think the generator is playing up," she said. "We'd better get candles." She turned to Dudley and asked him something in Irish. He nodded and disappeared.

"I thought we could play a game before dinner," Sorcha said.

Gwyn leered. "Gin Rummy or Strip Poker?"

Claire pulled a sour face. She flicked through her Bible's thin paper pages without looking up. Gwyn was in a provoking mood. He reached over and pulled the Bible down so he could see her face. "Like to see young Tristan here naked? Let me tell you, he looks good in the buff." He winked at Tristan. "Remember the communal showers in Tikrit?"

Tristan forced a laugh. "How could I forget? I saw things there I've never forgotten. Though I tried pretty hard."

Iseult was between him and Gwyn. He felt her presence like a magnet drawing the iron in his blood.

Gwyn reached drunkenly and pulled Iseult close to him in the crook of his left arm, but did it too roughly, still smiling like it was a joke. He aimed for her lips, but she turned her face away at the last instant, and he slobbered a kiss on her cheek. She pulled a face. Tristan thought the kiss must stink of whiskey. He felt a wave of anger and an instinct to protect her, but for the thousandth time, reminded himself she wasn't his to protect. Still, if Gwyn went too far in his boozy resentful humour, he would say something. There were limits to the way you treated a woman, even if she was your wife.

"I was thinking Bridge," Sorcha said.

"I can't play," Tristan said, glad to be distracted. "My mother tried to teach me once, but it seemed to me they designed it to be complicated."

"I'll teach you, Tristan." Sorcha reached over and tickled his hand. He yanked it away, and she put on a mock hurt look.

Iseult was watching.

"Why don't you get Tristan a drink, Iseult?" Sorcha said.

"Why should she get him one?" Gwyn snapped.

"I don't mind." Iseult stood.

Gwyn dragged her down again. "He can get his own drink. Isn't that so, Trist?"

"Sure. But I don't want one."

"You don't want one?" Gwyn said. "What kind of soldier are you? A soldier never turns down a drink."

"I'm not a soldier any more."

"I'll have another, Sorcha," Gwyn said. "But you'll need more Bushmills. I finished what was left in the bottle." Gwyn turned to Tristan and mock-punched him on the shoulder. "I always wondered about you, Tristan. You read too many books. You think too much."

"Do I?" Tristan sighed. This was a re-run of old stuff. It was Gwyn drinking too much and his nasty side coming out. Tristan thought maybe Sorcha would see it and refuse to get more whiskey, but she didn't. She fetched a fresh bottle. Gwyn chuckled and licked his lips as she poured him a large measure. This would be fuel on the fire.

"Yeah, like I was saying...," Gwyn continued.

Tristan groaned.

"... It wasn't real soldiering what you did."

"No."

"I mean, breaking a man to make him talk. But not by hitting him. I mean, I can understand violence. But by getting inside his head and making him think you were his friend. That's sneaky. Immoral." From the grin on his face, Gwyn appeared to be teasing, like it was a joke.

Tristan looked at his hands. "I thought a lot about that."

Gwyn guffawed. "I bet you did. That's my point — too much thinking."

Iseult said, "Can you think too much?"

Gwyn sneered. "Sure as shit you can."

Tristan flushed. "I thought about how to stop terrorists."

Gwyn's grin fell away and revealed the mood that lurked underneath. He sneered. "You're so fucking pious. Mr High and Mighty. Mr Butter Wouldn't Melt. I bet your shit doesn't stink either."

Tristan's jaw clenched. He knew it was because Gwyn was drunk, but it was also about Iseult.

Gwyn opened his mouth to begin another tirade, but Iseult snapped, "Enough!"

Gwyn leered. "Taking his side, eh?"

"What about that drink now, Tristan?" Sorcha said, smiling.

"Yeah, I think I will."

Iseult said, "Tristan, I'm not sure this is wise."

He tightened his mouth. "Neither am I."

Sorcha got him a glass and poured Tristan a measure of whiskey.

Gwyn scratched his cheek."You know, Is. If I didn't know better, I'd say you liked young Tristan there."

"Shut up, Gwyn. You're drunk."

"Not half as drunk as I will be soon." He gulped his whiskey and reached for the bottle Sorcha had put down. Sorcha was paying rapt attention to the interchange between Gwyn and Tristan. Claire was also listening to every word while pretending to read the Bible. Iseult looked like she would cry.

Dudley came back with fresh candles, and then the lights went out.

"Well-timed," Gwyn said as they sat in the sudden dark.

Dudley lit the candles, and their faces appeared around the table, summoned by the unsteady flames.

Claire turned her head from side to side, peering into the gloom like an excited magpie. "The Banshee is close. Great sins will soon be committed."

Gwyn laughed and raised his glass. The whiskey shone on his lips in the candlelight. "I hope they're going to be between my missus and me. They've been rarer than I'd like recently."

"For Christ's sake, Gwyn. You're going too far." Iseult stood and stepped away from the table. She was trembling.

"Fine," Gwyn shrugged. "Leave me. Sit next to your boyfriend."

"I'm going to sit next to Sorcha. How long before we eat?" Iseult walked round the table.

Tristan stood too. "Need a hand with the generator, Dudley?"

"No," the Irishman said.

"I know about generators," Tristan said. "Let me look."

Dudley gave a non-committal shrug. "I don't need you."

Tristan downed his whiskey. "I'm coming, anyway." He followed Dudley down the passage. Dudley had an electric torch in his hand. Tristan was glad to get away from Gwyn. In the morning, Gwyn wouldn't remember half of what he'd said or done, and he'd be everyone's friend again. But for the next few hours, he would be insufferable.

❦

DUDLEY STALKED AHEAD.

"Where's the generator?" Tristan said from behind.

"This way."

Tristan realised they were walking past the door to the courtyard where he'd found the steps going down. He hurried to keep up with Dudley who strode on, not waiting. "What type of generator is it?" he said.

"Petrol."

"Run out of fuel?"

"No."

They walked down the steps. Then along the tunnel. Tristan had no idea of where he was or how he would get back if Dudley left him. But he could get back, even in the dark. The place was big, but it wasn't infinite.

Then Dudley stopped. "In there." He pointed to a closed door.

Tristan regarded it. "Okay," he said finally.

"Go in," Dudley said.

"What? On my own?"

"You said you know about generators. You go in, and I'll hold the light."

After a pause, Tristan stepped forward. He reached and turned the door handle and went in. The room smelled of petrol and static electricity. The generator sat against the wall and Dudley played his torch beam over it. There were five or six jerrycans that Tristan guessed were full of petrol. The generator was a model that Tristan had seen before. He took about three minutes to realise that the fuse had tripped, something as simple as that. He guessed the castle wiring was dodgy. He checked the switches and was about to put it back on when he saw steps leading down from the corner of this room.

Dudley saw him looking. "They lead down to the tunnels. There are lots of tunnels under the castle, lots of ways in, but few ways out. A bit like your predicament."

Tristan ignored whatever innuendo was meant. He said, "Do you still use the tunnels?"

"Sure. We keep things in them."

Tristan remembered the dog smell. "What kind of things?"

Dudley chuckled softly. "Things we don't want people to see. That's where we take our prisoners."

Hairs prickled on the back of Tristan's neck. "Okay," he said. Dudley loomed behind him. He was about three inches taller but didn't carry the muscle that Tristan did. Tristan's throat tightened. He could smell the Irishman's rank odour. He swallowed. "Animals?"

"Animals?" Dudley laughed. "Yes. Did you see them?"

"No. But I knew they were there. What kind of animals? Dogs?"

"Sons of the Land: a sort of dog, yes; you're right. They were the totem beast of the tribe that lived here. My people."

Tristan found replacement fuses. "Okay, I think I've got this. Do you want me to switch it on?"

"Why did you come with me if you're scared of me?" Dudley said.

Tristan's hands were sweaty. "I'm not scared of you." Dudley stood close. Tristan said, "I'm going to put the genny back on." Tristan tripped the switch, and the light flickered and steadied — a bare electric bulb hung from a dirty wire. The light reduced the room to plain ordinariness. He felt Dudley staring at the back of his head. Tristan twisted. Dudley was there, but the light diminished his threat. Tristan glanced at the stairs that led down. There was no door to keep the dogs from coming up.

Dudley scratched his scalp through his long hair. "I think you came to get away from Gwyn. Maybe it's him you're scared of?"

Tristan said, "I'm not scared of Gwyn either. I respect him — when he's sober at least. But I'm not scared of him."

"Maybe you should be. He knows you want his wife." The Irishman winked. "And I don't think he likes that."

13

THE WARM SWEET BREATH
OF LOVE

Tristan and Dudley had not returned. The candles burned in the centre of the table, casting a flickering, eerie light. The atmosphere in the room was awkward. Iseult was upset.

Gwyn slurred his words. "Damn this power cut."

Iseult turned and stalked away. "I'm going to bed."

"I'll come upstairs with you," Claire called from behind her. She got up and scurried after Iseult out of the library.

Sorcha and Gwyn were left alone. Sorcha smiled and lifted her glass to her lips. Crimson lipstick left a pattern on the glass in the shape of a red kiss. "Everyone's gone. And I made *salmon-en-croute*."

Gwyn poured more whiskey. "Yeah, well. So what?"

"So what I made *salon-en-croute*?"

He shook his head. "Nah. So fucking what."

Sorcha tilted her head. "You're upset."

Gwyn shrugged. "Me? No. Why should I be upset?"

"You're drinking."

"I always drink. I drink whether I'm upset or whether I'm happy. Drinking lubricates the mind."

"You don't care that no guests are coming?"

"You're still paying me."

"You don't wonder why?"

Gwyn lifted the cut glass beaker to his lips. He sipped, savoured, and then downed the whiskey. "Wonder why what?" he said.

"You're not a very inquisitive man, Gwyn." Sorcha paused. She languidly filled his glass then hers, his with Irish whiskey, hers with French wine. "Where did you meet Iseult?"

He looked at her as if considering whether to answer, then he said, "I met her in a bar."

"Ah." Sorcha laughed. "That sounds sordid."

He shook his head. "It wasn't. I was manager. She worked there. It was in Haverfordwest: The White Ox. You know it?"

"Of course not."

He bowed his head. The night pressed in all around. He drank more whiskey. "She was going out with this guy. He was a first-class tool. How the fuck she ever thought he was a romantic prospect is beyond me." He paused. "She's a bit younger than me."

"I noticed."

"If she doesn't care about the age difference then I don't. I'm getting the better half of the deal, right?" He laughed to himself.

Sorcha watched with rapt attention. "Go on."

"So, this guy she was with. He took drugs. Gareth, his name was. He rode a motorcycle. He played in a band. You get the picture?"

"Yes, we see."

"What?"

"*The Leader of the Pack.*"

"Oh yeah. Well. He thought he was the bee's knees. So did she I guess, at first."

"What went wrong?"

Gwyn grimaced. "He used to kick the shit out of her. She worked for me. She turned up with bruises, and I'd send her home. I told her to leave him. But she didn't."

"Weak."

Gwyn twirled his glass. "She's soft. She's an idealist. She had this idea about fixing him."

"I never wanted to fix anyone."

"I bet."

Sorcha ignored him. "But she couldn't fix him?"

"Of course fucking not." Gwyn's words slurred. He had the glass in his hand, held up to his eye, peering at the candle through a prism of amber whiskey. "You can't fix cunts."

Sorcha was quiet, but her eyes studied him like a buzzard circles above a rabbit. She had not drunk from her glass. "So what did you do?"

He tapped the edge of his nose with his finger. "That's for me to know and you to find out."

She didn't smile.

He said, "Anyway, Sorcha. You're a beautiful woman. Just saying."

"You think so?"

"Hmm."

"But you love your wife?"

"Sure. Of course. She's my world."

"Do you think you're a good husband?"

"That's a personal question."

"Yes, but answer it."

"I might tell you to fuck off."

"You might."

Gwyn stared up at the ceiling. "I'm a fuck up. The things I've seen. Fuck yes. Even the things I've done." He narrowed his eyes to squint at Sorcha. "You know? So, no. Probably." His head dropped. "It's not like I mean to be an arse. It just happens."

"I can only guess the terrible things you've seen. You seem a very brave man." She stretched out her hand on the table close enough to hers so he could take it if he wanted. She whispered, "We could sleep together if you'd like."

Gwyn sat back and stared at her. Then he threw back his head and laughed. "Why eat out on mutton when I've got steak at home?"

Sorcha snatched back her hand. Her voice was icy. "But make sure she's still home when you get back."

The lights came on as Tristan fixed the generator on the other side of the castle. Sorcha drained her glass and left Gwyn to drink alone.

DUDLEY LEFT TRISTAN TO FIND HIS WAY BACK TO THE LIBRARY. Tristan entered and found Gwyn alone, staring into the fire. "Penny for your thoughts."

Gwyn eyed his whiskey. "You don't want to know my thoughts."

"I got the generator fixed."

Gwyn pointed at the light. "Yeah, I guessed."

Tristan looked around the room. Lady Amelia Morton glared back at him from her portrait. "Where's everyone else?"

"Fucked off."

Gwyn took a gulp of whiskey then reached for the bottle to refill his glass.

"Go easy on that stuff," Tristan said.

"I don't care."

"Hey man, what's up?" Tristan sat on the chair next to Gwyn, but Gwyn didn't turn round. He kept looking into the fire as if its flames held answers to whatever questions were going through his mind.

"As you said, we're still getting paid," Tristan gestured. "So..."

Gwyn twisted round. "You don't know what's bothering me?"

Tristan's guts heaved. "No."

Gwyn put the glass to his lips, drank then put it down. He wiped his mouth with the back of his hand. "You," he said.

"Me? What've I done?" The worm of guilt gnawed at Tristan's guts. Gwyn couldn't read his mind and his desires, but Sorcha had guessed, so did Gwyn suspect too? He tensed up. Nothing had happened between him and Iseult. There was nothing to confess, nothing substantial, nothing physical.

Gwyn's eyes narrowed. "I don't know. What have you done?" His pale blue eyes were watery and the conjunctiva pale and pink.

Tristan's mouth narrowed. "Nothing."

Gwyn turned back to the fire. "Okay, then. Nothing to worry about."

Tristan changed the subject. "What's the plans for tomorrow? We leaving?"

"I guess. Not too early. Need the car fixed."

"We could just leave."

"We could. Probably should. I've got the cheque. I can go to the town and get the mechanic sent back. Don't think they've really rung for one, anyway."

"Why not? What are they playing at?"

"Don't care. Honestly do not give a shit."

Tristan sighed. "And dinner tonight?"

"Fucked up. Sorcha went off in a huff because no one turned up to eat her salmon."

Tristan stood. "Okay. I'll leave you to it."

Without watching him go, Gwyn said, "And don't do anything I wouldn't."

Tristan shook his head.

Gwyn stood up from the kitchen table and put out a hand to steady himself. Damn, that whiskey had gone straight to his head. He turned and the room turned with him. He would have to lay off this stuff. He knew it was killing him day by day, but even one day without a drink was hard on his nerves. If not for each morning's eye opener from the secret bottle he kept in his backpack, his nerves would jangle and his hands would shake. The alcohol turned down emotions and put worries on mute, for a while, for just the short while it coursed through his veins, and when it was gone, he had to top it up again to get the same effect.

He took a step. The floor swayed. That was okay. The old banshee bitch portrait glared at him and he gave it the finger.

He needed to find Iseult. The feeling in his gut and the tension in his shoulders told him she was upset, and the vague malaise of guilt told him it was his fault. He knew he wasn't much of a husband. He could hardly count himself a success at much. Gwyn James Productions Ltd: They struggled for money; they had an old beat up car — recently driven by him into a swamp. That was sort of funny. He grinned as he made his way to the stairs. Not fixed either. Their house was rented, not owned. But Iseult was young and beautiful. She could do better, he knew. She must know too, but why she stuck with him was a mystery.

Almost a mystery. A mystery until he remembered that he knew it wasn't, but pretended it was because it suited him. He got her free from that biker fucker Gareth after all and told her he would have done it for anyone, which wasn't true, and that his part in her liberation brought no obligations, and he meant it too. But she couldn't help but feel obliged and that, though unasked for, suited him. She was young and beautiful and she lit up his grey and dying life.

Gwyn left the kitchen. The stairs loomed up out of the dark. He took a breath as if that would clear his head. If he could just find her and smooth things out. He remembered her face and soft sentimental love filled him. There on the stairs, leaning on the banninster, his head bowed and tears in his eyes, he wept as he thought of Iseult. But that wouldn't do. He couldn't let anyone see the old soldier crying. S A Fucking S. He remembered passing selection. He was so proud. He put his hand to the wall to steady himself, breathed in. Yes, all was good.

Time to find Iseult.

He climbed one step at a time, planting each foot, regarding them as if he'd never seen feet before, then losing focus as his mind drifted off on the river of alcohol. Up again, step by step by step until he was at the corridor where his bedroom was. There was their door. His and hers. Standing on tiptoes, he knocked at the door as if he needed permission to enter. Once a warrior, now a whiskey-addled fool, he was a shy stable lad awaiting entrance to the chamber of a princess.

No answer came.

He cleared his throat. "Iseult? Issy?" He knocked again, his knuckles rapping on the wood, but gentle still. "Iseult?" He spoke louder. Then, quiet as Christmas morning, he opened the door. The empty bed tangled his mind like a puzzle.

His brow furrowed. "Oh," he said, hand to the door's edge as the whiskey lurched and threatened to derail him. "I wonder where she is?" he said aloud, his words sounding slurred even to himself.

He butted his head against the door frame, almost hard enough to knock sense in. He looked at his watch. Though his eyes saw the numbers, their meaning swam away from him. It was late and she should be here.

New emotions emerged.

He couldn't reflect on them; he'd always been bad at looking at his feelings before they ended up in actions, but it was worse now. Besides sentimental affection, resentment and now jealousy ripped him up. His mouth tightened. His lips were wet.

Gwyn turned his head toward the stairs that led up to Tristan's tower room. Dudley showed him Tristan's new room. There was something about his old room being trashed. He didn't know why Dudley had taken him up there, but Dudley had shown him Tristan's new room. He knew where Tristan would be. And Tristan would know where Iseult was.

Oh, yes.

Gwyn's mouth set and his hands balled into fists. He walked towards the stairs before even deciding to do so. Then he had to piss and turning and finding an empty vase on a heavy stone plinth that stood in the passage, he peed into it. Dribbling, he put himself away, stumbled and knocked the thing over. "Fucking hell," he muttered. He booted the plinth, hurt his toes, and plinth and vase thumped onto the wooden floor.

Remembering his mission, Gwyn turned and faced those twisting stairs. Tristan would know where Iseult was. After all, the two were such good friends. "Friends," he spat the word.

He smiled, poor little Tristan — clever troubled Tristan. He remembered one night around a fire with the desert stars like a mouthful of diamonds spat into the sky overhead. The dry aromatic wood smoke tainted their desert combat clothes. There had been vodka. Not whiskey like tonight. Cheap vodka one of the guys had brought with him from camp. They were three days out. Tristan had made one thin little guy — some kind of commissar — sing and tell them enemy dispositions. The man died; this happens with broken birds, and so far out in the desert, who would know? Who would care?

But Tristan cared, he'd fucking lost his shit and gone running out alerting every raghead in the fucking desert. A short firefight. The enemy weren't much. Idiot kids really. Gwyn sorted it. That night, after the death, he put his arm around Tristan's shoulders and squeezed. "You can't make an cheesecake without breaking biscuits." Tristan had looked at him. He explained, "Broken biscuits for the base — yummy."

Gwyn had seen other blokes break. But they'd killed too many. They were like the guys who work in slaughterhouses. One day they've just killed too many cows, and they put the bolt gun to their own head.

"Maybe we were a little too rough," Gwyn consoled him. This happened, regrettable, but proportionate in the face of the threat.

Tristan took up boxing. He wanted to live up to his dad. His dad had been a major in the Light Infantry. The kid adored him, but wanted to be a professor, not a soldier. He went to university, then Tristan's dad died, and out of some sense of being the dutiful son, he joined up.

But he wasn't cut out for aggression, so he became a linguist then an interrogator, which was a fancy name for a torturer. Tristan told him once that he thought his dad would be ashamed of what he did.

Gwyn could understand torture. It was necessary to save lives. He didn't understand the mind that ate up languages and grammar and read books that had too many words. In fact all books had too many words; Gwyn liked manuals. With a manual you get what you need, except the pages in German and Dutch and Italian — you don't need them. They should get their own manuals and keep out of the English ones.

His rumination made him forget why he was there until he remembered Iseult. A sudden pang of lust. She was a fine thing — worth climbing stairs for. Up he went. He thought he was steadier. But the twisting spiral staircase in damp stone foxed him like a fairground puzzle room, a hall of stone mirrors that unsettled his head. He took more steps. He was out of breath so he stopped. What the hell was he going up here for, anyway? Tristan would be asleep. Iseult was probably with Claire talking ghost shit. But he was halfway up so he'd go up to the top. ask Tristan then go down.

Unless she was with him.

Yes. What about that? That little fucking bitch. After all he'd fucking done for her. He knew she had a soft spot for Tristan. He was young and cute. Gwyn got that. But loyalty was loyalty and marriage was marriage. Himself, when he made a vow he stuck to it – to Queen and Country, to mother, father and wife.

If Iseult was in there with him, Gwyn would kill them both.

He knew it. He vowed it. No one made a cuckold of him. Gwyn James was nobody's fool. He stomped up the remaining steps and saw the door was ajar, but the room was dark apart from the flickering light of a fire out of sight. They were in there fucking. He knew it. He screwed his fists and rage drove him like a red wave. He drew back his foot to kick in the door.

A scream split the air.

The noise was like a brick through a window. He whipped his head round and down. A woman's shriek came from below — a cry of terror. He knew it was Iseult and so, his anger melting like ice in vodka, he rushed down the stairs to save his wife.

❦

CLAIRE WAS READING THE STORY OF BOAZ AND RUTH BEFORE SHE fell asleep. She approved of the older man marrying the beautiful Ruth to protect her. As she dozed off she smiled.

The unlit light buzzed while Claire snored. Then minutes, a quarter of an hour, twenty minutes and the odour of burned engine oil washed under the door, causing her to sniff and stir in sleep. The curtains at her window lifted as if something sought entrance; they tug-tug-tugged in an unfelt breeze. Claire snuffled. The light buzzed again; the smell wove itself into a shadow.

Something brushed her ear. Claire scratched. Claire coughed, sat, and wiped her forearm across her wet lips. Not awake yet, she moved her legs out of the bed, dragging her feet, pulling sheets with her. Realisation shocked her awake: a cold spirit came through — a ghost of something flayed.

The psychic leapt out of bed, soles smacking the cold wooden boards. She yanked the counterpane in her bony hands to hold up like a shield. A presence intruded - something cold and wicked that meant her ill.

Claire scrabbled for the Bible on her bedside table. The Holy Book would protect her. Her claw fingers tightened on it and, with the counterpane like a shield and the Bible thrust out like a sword, she shrieked, "Sinful woman — thou shalt not pass!"

She saw it standing by the door, old, evil, flayed and fluorescent black: like the light tubes in the horror side show where she worked before God found her. The creature was taller than her but Claire rushed it like a cat at a bear. She shoved the Bible into its unholy face. "Get thee gone! In the name of the Lord, I command thee!"

But the thing remained.

Claire was used to seeing spirits; ever since she was a little girl they'd coiled around her, whispering messages, muttering threats. They kept her awake at night and when she told her father, he beat her first for being a liar, then took her to a doctor. The doctor saw the bruises but asked about the voices, someone else who didn't care.

The shape bent towards her like a column of smoke in a winter wind. She reeled back, afraid but her faith steadied. No creature of darkness like this could defeat her or her Lord. She shoved the Bible at the banshee thing and the black-backed book pushed through roiling cloud. She saw its woman face with white eyes and a jagged mouth like those that children cut in pumpkins.

It wanted to hurt her; she knew it. Its voice entered her mind and talked to her of sin and tempted her with imaginings of Tristan's body. She saw his naked chest and his thing, swinging there between his legs. The sweet excitement of lust warmed her loins as his face swam before her. Young, pretty Tristan with his strong eyes and his smile always for Iseult and never for her.

The ghost's voice was the echoes and the calls of owls from old towers, but it told her she deserved more — that she'd always deserved more. When she was at school with her spots and the kids calling her weird and witch and putting a dead rat in her locker. The pretty girls always got the boys she wanted and so she'd turned from boys and found love in Jesus. Images of the pale, sacrificed God mingled with those of Tristan's naked torso and she saw the thing clearer now — the thing between his legs, coiling like a serpent.

She shrieked at the banshee, "Temptress! I will not befoul my Faith. You will not drag me down to your hell of sex and lust!"

Gwyn barged open the door of her room. He reeled forward, almost stumbled and put his hand on the frame to steady himself. "Iseult!" he yelled. "Where is she?"

Claire's face contorted, and she screamed at the banshee. "Get ye behind me!" She sobbed and clutched the Bible between her white fingers.

Gwyn stared at her, his eyes swimming. "Where's Iseult?"

He yelled like he couldn't see the banshee. She turned her head toward him and sneered — another one obsessed with the blonde slut. At least he had the excuse of being her husband. Could he not see that she, Claire, was being attacked by the banshee? Her eyes flooded. No one cared — no knight on his charger would ever come to rescue, thin, bird-bodied Claire.

But Gwyn came at her and placed his hand on her shoulder as if to shake her, not in rescue but in reprimand. And then as if his presence had banished it, the banshee departed. Claire shook off Gwyn's grip.

He thrust his drink-drowned eyes in her face. "Iseult — have you seen her?"

He wept. A wave of revulsion sickened Claire. She scoffed, "No. I haven't," and under her breath she hissed, "Cuckold."

◈

Claire and Gwyn were sitting on Claire's bed. Close together but vacant in expression, their minds miles away. Claire stared at the ceiling, her eyes on some distant point. She pressed her Bible to her chest with her right hand, her left buried itself in the sheet, winding the linen between her fingers and pulling at it as if it was an anchor, fastening her to the earth.

Gwyn's head was down, tilted left. A line of drool dangling towards the floor. His cheeks were red as if he'd been crying. Neither spoke when Sorcha and Dudley entered.

Dudley muttered to Sorcha in Irish. She nodded but didn't smile.

At the sound of Dudley's whisper, Claire and Gwyn awoke from their separate dreams. Claire lowered her chin and her eyes flew to Dudley before fixing on Sorcha. Her mouth worked as if preparing to speak.

Gwyn lifted his face from the floor. His bleary eyes focused on

Sorcha, ignoring Dudley, and he wiped the drool from his lips with the back of his hand. He spoke first. "Sorcha, have you seen Iseult?"

Claire looked at him furiously and, before Sorcha could reply, she blurted, "The Banshee was here."

Sorcha said, "We must destroy her. Once and forever."

Claire nodded rapidly. "Yes. I will drive her out. With my Faith, I will drive her out."

Gwyn stared sadly at Sorcha. He looked puzzled, adrift, and still drunk. Sorcha ignored him. She went up to Claire and stroked her hair. Dudley looked on, standing like an undertaker at someone's funeral.

"Claire," Sorcha squeezed the psychic's thin hand. "Faith isn't enough."

Claire's mouth tightened as if Sorcha had spoken the most repulsive and unbelievable curse. "Faith isn't enough?"

As if to forestall Claire's anger, Sorcha ran her hand down the woman's grey cheek and cupped her bony chin. "No."

Claire dropped her head. "Then what?"

"A way exists." Sorcha stood back and brought her fingers thoughtfully to her lips. She wandered to the window. The night was silent outside, the wind and rain gone away. Sorcha gazed over the benighted Bog of Allen.

"What?" Claire stood and shuffled to the chatelaine. Looking up at the taller woman, she peered like an inquisitive jackdaw, blinking and curious. Gwyn stared dumbly. The reek of his sour breath polluted the room.

Claire was insistent. "What, Lady Sorcha? How?"

Sorcha turned like an actress on a stage. She delivered her line with a turn of her head. "We want blood."

"Blood? Ordinary blood?"

Sorcha shook her head. "No, special blood."

"Tell me how, Lady."

A small sad look came over Sorcha's face. She shrugged as if it might be impossible.

Claire stroked Sorcha's arm with ungainly strokes. Sorcha allowed her touch until she put her hand on Claire's, stopping the caress. She gave a sad sympathetic smile. "I don't know if you're up to it, Claire."

"But my Faith is strong!"

"I said: faith is not enough."

Claire shook her head in a rage, like a small child infuriated by mother's teasing. "My blood is good enough."

Sorcha smiled sadly. "But it's not your blood we need."

"Then whose?"

"The blood of a thrice-damned woman."

"Thrice damned?"

Gwyn sighed. "She's talked about this before — murderess, idolatress..."

"... Adulteress," Sorcha finished it for him.

"In what way an idolatress?" Claire said.

"Someone who has worshipped an idol."

Claire nodded. "Yes. Of course. Yes. But who?"

"Someone close," Sorcha said. "Close to being all three."

"A murderess?" Claire's voice sounded incredulous. "Here?"

"Have you seen Iseult?" Gwyn asked plaintively.

Sorcha considered him.

"I saw her talking to Tristan," Dudley piped up from the corner of the room. He stood in shadow and his face was hard to read. "But that was much earlier. Before we went to bed."

❦

AFTER HE'D LEFT GWYN IN THE KITCHEN, TRISTAN WENT UP TO HIS room. He heard the rain hammer on the windows as he walked up the stairs. He wanted to leave this place — this castle, this country, and be far from Sorcha and her twisted manservant, or husband, or whatever he was.

Tristan got to the landing. At least Dudley had told him there was a bath at the end of the corridor. He climbed the stairs to his tower, wondering again how come he'd been lucky to get this circular room. He made a fire from crumpled up pages of the *Irish Times* and chopped kindling wood then broke up a peat turf into three and arranged it round the wigwam of wood. Tristan got the long kitchen matches and set fire to the paper, watching the fire catch and being glad as the heat flared on his face.

Then he placed the metal-mesh fire guard in front of the dancing fire, took his towel from the bed and left the circular room to descend in search of the bath.

He passed the stone plinth and the vase and saw it was still in place. He'd found the bathroom on his wanderings down this corridor.

He had a solitary bath in lukewarm water. It was his first for days and the water carried the dirt of his body away. He watched it going down the plughole as he dried himself on the rough towel. It was too cold to linger, and he pulled on his shirt while his back was still damp. He made his way along the passage back to the stairs that led up to the tower. There was no sound but the low moan of the wind and the drumming of the rain in the darkness outside.

Up in his circular room the fire had done its work, and he warmed his hands. He picked up coals from the bucket with his fingers and placed them around the heart of the fire, between the glowing peats. He regarded the smuts from the coal on his finger ends and, with a shrug, wiped them on his jeans, and then he went to the window and stared out. The pane, irregular because of its age, gave a rain-smeared view of a darkened world. As he watched, droplets gathered and ran and on the glass and the wind-blown showers pounded them away.

Someone knocked on his door. He started and turned his head to look. He cleared his throat. "Come in."

Iseult pushed the door open. In each hand she held a goblet of wine. She was pale in the orange firelight and didn't enter the room, instead she lingered at the door, frowning, seeking his gaze and approval, gold cross still missing, looking like she'd made a decision.

Tension and emotion woke in his stomach and rose through his solar plexus to his throat. He sat back on the bed. "Iseult."

She smiled, but it was unconvincing. She was nervous. "Who did you think it was going to be? The Easter Bunny?"

"How did you know about my new room? I didn't mention it."

"Dudley told me."

"Really? Why would he do that?"

She shrugged. "I don't know. He just did."

Tristan thought: almost like he was setting it up: her and me.

He looked at her and she was beautiful and he struggled with his words and they wouldn't come as she stood in his room alone with him. She paused on the threshold, frowned again. "Can I come in?"

He noticed her hands shook. He stood up from the bed. "Yes, of course."

"Nice room," she said, stepping in, holding out a the silver goblet of white wine. He took the wine, looked at it and drained half. The crispness of it soured his tongue. His eyes were down; he couldn't look at her. She reached round and pushed the door closed. He heard it click, but then it came slightly open. She looked at the door move. "Must be a ghost."

He gave a gentle laugh.

She pointed. "You got the fire going."

"Yeah." He stared at the dancing flames. He felt their heat so close in that narrow room.

She looked around like a tourist. "It's got lots of character."

"The room? Yeah. I lucked out getting this one. Not much space though. My old room was trashed." He paused. "Iseult, did Gwyn get up early and go to my old room?"

She shook her head. "No, he was dead to the world."

"You sure?"

She frowned at him. "I would have heard him get up. Why?"

"Someone was looking for something."

"Who would do that? Dudley?"

"I don't know," he said. "I can't see why. They want something from us."

"I don't trust Dudley," Iseult said.

"Nor Sorcha."

"I don't know about her. I'm in two minds. Sometimes she seems kind."

He said quickly. "No she's not. She's a rat. She means us ill."

"We'll be leaving tomorrow, anyway. Can I sit down?"

They stood in the middle of the small circular room, close enough to touch but not touching. He turned and stepped away, the back of his legs against the bed. "There's no other chair," he said.

"I can sit next to you on the bed."

He kept standing. "That wine had a funny taste. What's yours like?"

She sat on the bed anyway, looked up at him. "It's fine. Don't worry."

He rubbed his forehead and sat next to her. Their legs touched. The heat from her thigh burned into his like the element of an electric fire.

"What about Gwyn?" he said. The glass was in his hand. She looked down. Excitement like fire ran through his belly. A faint scent of perfume and skin: lemon blossom, ocean waves and her wrapped round his heart. He bowed his head. He couldn't speak.

He heard her hesitate. "He's being a total dick tonight."

Tristan nodded "Yep." He finished his wine and put the empty glass on the beside table. Finally, he said, "Why are you here, Iseult? In this room."

She reached out and put her hand on his forearm, her slender fingers amidst the dark hairs. He looked at her hand as if it was some shy bird.

She said, "I've decided something. We both owe him, but it doesn't mean he owns us, Tristan. One debt can't trump everything else forever."

"Two debts." He turned his head towards her.

She was close. She had inclined her forehead and without knowing he'd done it, he mirrored her until their heads were only inches apart. Outside the rain teemed down. The fire hissed and crackled.

He pulled back, struck by conscience. Pulled back — but still close enough to feel her body heat.

She muttered, "He drinks too much. He's either sentimental and cloyingly drunk, trying to paw me, or he snaps and talks like I'm dirt. I can't take the walking on eggshells. I know I owe him so much, but I can't be with him anymore."

She began to cry. He gently took his thumb to her cheeks and brushed the tears away, but more flowed.

"And so I'm your way out?" he said quietly. He realised what a dick-ish thing it was to say as soon as the words left his mouth, and he regretted it, but she hadn't taken offence. Frown lines marked her forehead.

"This is no easy way out, Tristan. He'll probably kill us, but I have to give my heart to truth."

"Truth." Tristan savoured the word with the aftertaste of the bitter wine. "And now we're deceiving him."

"We don't have to deceive him. We can tell him."

"He'll kill us," Tristan smiled wryly. "I've seen him kill."

Iseult pursed her lips as if about to blurt something out. He sensed there was a secret she hadn't shared. He listened, but she said nothing and smiled instead. He stroked the hair from where it had half fallen across her eyes. "But I'm not frightened of dying if it's with you," he said finally.

She laughed. "That's a corny line." Then she met his eyes. "I want to do this." She unbuttoned her shirt. Her fingers went to her throat, and she struggled with the button as if it was trying to save her by refusing to come undone. He reached over and undid it for her. Their eyes met; brown and blue —like the river running into the sea. Oceans and tides came from one to the other. Her lips opened. He put his hand behind her head and cupped it there.

"I love you," he said.

"I know." She laughed.

"It's wrong though," he said.

"Love versus duty. Truth versus deceit." Her mouth tightened into a wry smile. "Someone should write a play about us."

Then he kissed her. The kiss at first was tentative and searching, but as they each became more confident that the other returned their desire, it grew voracious. They undid her shirt in a rush, and she pulled it over her shoulder. He looked at her scalloped salmon pink bra and saw that the breasts hardly moved when they were free. They were small and round and tipped with rosebuds. He thought how he'd loved her so long but never seen her naked breasts before. She smiled nervously and undid her belt. She pulled her way out of the tight jeans and as she threw them on the floor a small crystal bottle came from her pocket and rolled under the bed. Tristan saw it; a tiny empty crystal bottle but then she took his face in her hands and they kissed again.

They made love and while he entered her and she held onto him like a gift. The door to his room stood ajar, because she had forgotten to close it after the spirit blew it open.

Sorcha's silver goblets rolled on the floor.

14

THE PUPPET MISTRESS

Iseult crept back to the bedroom she shared with Gwyn. She opened the door as quietly as she could, but Gwyn was snoring heavily, and the alcohol from his breath permeated the room like sour perfume. She stripped off her blouse and slipped down her jeans, then felt a flush of panic and stopped. There was no shower here to wash Tristan's smell from her, so she had no choice but to go on.

Without looking at her husband, she slipped under the covers and had to push Gwyn's arm away to make space. The limb was heavy, and she was as delicate as she could be in moving it. He groaned and moved, and his snoring stopped for a few seconds before resuming. The room was dark, and the air had a deadened feel to it. All around, she sensed the castle watching her as if it was alive. The ghosts within its walls huddled in shadows and observed her and her husband. For an hour or more, Iseult lay awake beside Gwyn, staring into the darkness and wishing she was lying with Tristan.

As she drifted into sleep, she dreamed about the thrice-damned woman, Lady Amelia Morton: idolatress, adulteress and murderess. Sorcha's ancestor flayed her for her sins. No wonder her ghost hung around the place looking for revenge. Iseult's mind grew hazy, and she dreamed.

Gwyn woke before her. He had been down to the kitchen and brought her a mug of coffee. She awakened as he came into the room and sat up on her elbows.

"Here, babe. Dudley's finest."

The coffee smelled good, but she couldn't look at him. She took the mug.

He winced. "Sorry, if I was a bit of an arsehole last night..." He stunk of alcohol, and his salt and pepper stubble made him look dirty.

She didn't respond.

He shrugged. "I know. It's the drink. I'm not a nice guy when I've had too much." He leaned in for a kiss, and she pushed him away. She guessed he'd think his drunken behaviour had pissed her off, but she couldn't kiss him while guilt pulsed in her chest like a another heart.

"Did you help me to bed?" His voice had a puzzled, fuddled tone.

She shook her head.

"Ah yeah," he said. "I remember." He raised his eyebrows and rubbed his brow. He went over to stare out of the window into the grey weather. "Fuck, Claire was screeching about something. Ghosts." He snorted. "Silly cow."

"There are no such things as ghosts," Iseult said.

"Of course not." He smiled. "Though you remember that gig at Chillingham Castle? That was weird."

Iseult cut him off. "When are we leaving?"

"Today, I think. If I can get the car to start."

"I don't think they ever called a mechanic."

Gwyn said, "You're as paranoid as Tristan. Of course they did. Why would they want us to stay here?"

She said, "I don't know. I just want to leave soon."

He shrugged. "Of course. There's nothing to keep us here now." He came over to the bed. He reached out to touch her. She flinched, but she let his hand rest on her arm. He said, "I feel so guilty, Is. I'm such a bastard to you, and I don't mean to be."

She looked up to him, forcing a smile. Her lips narrowed. "You've nothing to feel guilty about."

"Good," he said slowly. Then he gave a wan smile. "Love you, Is. I don't deserve you."

ISEULT HAD FALLEN BACK TO SLEEP. GWYN GAZED AT HER LOVELY face and thought she must be tired. He got up slowly. It was late-ish now. The cup of coffee he'd fetched earlier was stone cold. He stroked the hair of his lady-love where it lay on the pillow. He knew he'd pissed Iseult off, so he let her lie. He pulled on his pants and shirt and went down for breakfast.

Sorcha was there in her jeans. Dudley was in the corner cutting carrots. Gwyn grunted, and Sorcha pointed at the coffee pot. He poured himself a mug of thick, black Joe, and she indicated a bacon sandwich she'd laid with its plate on the heavy wood kitchen table. He grunted again, sat and bit into the bacon.

She grinned. "Bad head?"

He cleared his throat and chewed at his sandwich. "Sorta. Good sandwich—bacon's full of sodium."

"Sodium?"

"Good for hangovers."

"Ah, yes. So they say. And water. You'll be dehydrated." She paused. "Do you remember much of last night?"

"Some. I think I upset people."

She nodded. "I think so."

"Tristan?"

"Earlier. Yes."

"And Iseult?"

"Yes. I think so..."

"Maybe Claire?"

"Maybe."

He squinted. "And you?"

Sorcha shook her head. She pulled her dark hair into a ponytail, wound the hairband around it to keep it in place and sat opposite him. She chuckled. "Oh, no. Not me."

"That's one then. Good."

"You're welcome."

He drank his coffee in one slug and pushed the empty mug towards her. "More?"

She sighed. "You're a real gent, Gwyn." But she got up and filled his mug for him.

He seized it from her hand, "thanks," and took a mouthful. "So, I didn't upset you?"

"No."

He said, "I remember being on my own towards the end of the night—just before I blacked out. What happened to you lot?"

"Who lot?"

He brought his hand to his face and stroked his forehead with his blunt fingers. "You know. You, Iseult et cetera."

Sorcha smiled. "I went to bed."

He looked puzzled. "I thought Iseult was with you."

"No, not with me." She studied her nails.

He said, "I upset her. I was a jerk."

Sorcha leaned against the kitchen counter. "Yeah, but I'm sure she upset you too."

He cocked his head and half-closed an eye as if the grey Irish morning light was blinding. "Upset me? How?"

Sorcha cleared her throat. "I don't know if I should be the one to tell you this..."

An edge of suspicion came into his voice. "What are you going on about?"

"Look, Gwyn." She dragged his hand towards her in a motherly fashion. He let her take it. She held it like he was very dear to her.

His bloodshot eyes fixed her. "What?"

"Iseult went with Tristan last night."

He tilted his head. "Went?"

"You know what I mean."

"What the fuck." Gwyn rocketed to his feet. He rubbed his face with both hands and snapped his head up to stare at her. "What?" He looked like a dazed bear.

She was mock-apologetic. "I'm sorry. Maybe I shouldn't have said anything."

"What the fuck? Went with Tristan? What the fuck?" His head swayed from side to side, and sobs like an ocean wracked him, bowing his shoulders like waves.

She said tenderly, "I'm sorry."

Gwyn slammed his fist down on the kitchen table. "Went with fucking Tristan? Like what? Fucked him?"

Sorcha spread her hands apart in sympathy. Her face was like an dark angel's, framed in sorrow, her azure eyes were planets of ill omen.

"I don't know what to say."

He straightened. "Have you got a drink?"

She nodded, fetched the Bushmills from the cupboard, and poured him a measure into a chipped glass.

He necked it and held out the glass. "More."

"Sure, but go easy," she said but still refilled his glass while watching him.

He swallowed the whiskey in one gulp and wiped his mouth with the back of his hand. His eyes narrowed like slits in grey snow. "No way. This isn't true. You're fucking with me."

"No."

"No, no. You're fucking shitting me. Why would you fucking say this?"

She gave him an open, regretful smile. "Because it's true, Gwyn."

He spun around like she'd slapped him and roared. He bayed at the ceiling like a wounded animal. With a snarl, Gwyn hurled his glass against the wall where it shattered into a thousand shards. "Bastard!"

Sorcha nodded to Dudley, who went to clear up the pieces.

Gwyn pulled at his hair. His mouth sagged. He turned to the witch. "What should I do?"

"You'd better work it out with them."

"Fucking work it out with them? I'll fucking kill them." His face flushed beetroot red. He brought his fist to his teeth and bit his knuckles. "I'll fucking kill them."

Dudley entered the kitchen as if on cue. Sorcha flashed him a conspiratorial glance. The Irishman stood at the door watching, his grey hair hanging lank.

Gwyn made to leave the kitchen, stomping to the door, growling like an angry dog. Dudley put out his hand to fend him off. Gwyn stopped and drew back his fist. "Get out of my fucking way."

"Easy, tiger," Dudley said. "Listen to what the lady has to say."

Gwyn spun round.

Sorcha stood behind him. "I understand why you're angry."

Gwyn gave a bitter laugh.

She said, "I understand that you want to hurt them."

"Him." Confusion flashed across his face. "Him. I wouldn't hurt a woman."

"Yes. Of course."

Gwyn stepped toward the door, but Dudley held up his hand again and flashed a warning stare. Gwyn snarled at him then pivoted to address Sorcha. "Say your say, then let me do what I want."

"I can make it easier for you."

He shook his head, puzzled. "How?"

"This is a big place," she said.

"Very big." Dudley winked. "You wouldn't find him. Not if he wanted to hide from you."

"And he would hide from you," Sorcha purred. "He'd be frightened."

Gwyn bowed his head. Tears ran through his fingers and dropped to the stone floor like melting stars. From behind his hands, he whispered, "I'll fucking kill him. After all I did for that cunt."

Sorcha stroked his back.

"We'll get him for you," Dudley said.

Gwyn dropped his hands and stared at the Irishman. "How?"

Dudley smiled. "We'll keep him someplace. Then tell you where he is. That's the easiest way."

Sorcha was playing with a button at the throat of her shirt. She nodded. "That's easiest."

"But why would you do that for me?"

"We don't like betrayal." Dudley's yellow teeth showed as he grinned. "Do we, Sorcha?"

She shook her head. "Not at all." She caressed then gripped Gwyn's shoulder. "We're on your side. Go and sit. I'll come back and tell you when we're ready for you. Then we'll take him to you and justice will be done."

Gwyn turned, head still bowed. He went meek as a lamb and sat at the table. Looking plaintively up, he said, "Got another whiskey?"

"Sure, sure," Dudley fetched the bottle.

"I'll be right back," Sorcha said and closed the kitchen door behind her.

⚜

TRISTAN SAT IN THE LIBRARY LEAFING THROUGH THE BOOK ABOUT Tullabeg, but he wasn't taking it in. Iseult had left him in the night. After that, he hadn't slept. He got up in the grey morning light, packed and brought his bag down, ready to leave, but instead of going into the kitchen, where he guessed he'd run into Gwyn, he'd come to the library.

As they had lain in each other's arms all that long night, Iseult and he had decided they would tell Gwyn - they owed him that, but not here and not now. They wanted to wait until they were back over the sea, home in Wales.

He wouldn't take it well.

Sorcha entered the library. "Ah, Tristan here you are. Sleep well?"

He heard the wickedness in her voice, but she couldn't know — that was just his paranoia. "Sure. I'm ready to be off now, though."

"Not hungry?"

"Hungry?"

She pointed toward where the kitchen would be.

He shook his head.

Sorcha approached him, twisting her dark hair between her fingers. "I know you don't believe in magic or spirits—"

He cut her off. "No."

"Or anything supernatural."

"No. You're right. I don't."

"But Iseult does."

He shook his head. "Not really. She might get frightened when people talk about these things." He looked at Sorcha pointedly. "Especially when people are deliberately trying to make her scared."

Sorcha nodded patronisingly. "You're right. That must be it." She turned. "Sure you don't want breakfast? Gwyn's waiting for you in the kitchen." Sorcha sauntered away. He leapt up, reached out and grabbed her shoulder.

She put her hand on his. "Tristan!" She grinned in mock alarm. "How strong you are!"

"What do you mean—'that must be it?' Is something wrong with Iseult? Where is she?"

Sorcha grinned. "Well, I don't know what you two got up to last night." She paused and waited for his reaction.

He was sharp. "Just get on with it. Where is she?"

Sorcha sighed theatrically. "That's not very kind to speak to me like that, Tristan. Not kind at all."

His jaw tightened.

Sorcha cocked her head. "You see, she's frightened."

"Frightened? What of?"

"She wouldn't say. But she won't come out of her room."

He was dazed. "What? I don't get it."

"Something has scared her. Come on, I'll take you to her."

Bewildered, he followed Sorcha to the library door and part way down the passage when she stopped. "Of course, we'll have to go through the kitchen."

He scowled at her. "Yeah, so?"

She sucked her teeth. "Gwyn's in the kitchen. He seems in a bad mood."

Tristan paused. What if she knew, and she'd told Gwyn? He didn't want to get into a fight with Gwyn before he'd ensured Iseult was okay. He exhaled. "Is there another way?"

"You don't want to bump into Gwyn?" She smiled.

"Not yet. Show me the other way."

Sorcha looked puzzled. She was putting it on.

"What games are you playing, Sorcha?"

She arched her brows. "Me? No games. What games are you playing, Tristan? You and little Iseult."

"Are you implying something?"

"I'm not implying anything. You left your door open. I was just walking around my own castle, and I heard these sounds. Unmistakable sounds. Wasn't sure you had it in you after our little embarrassment the other night. But I took a little peek through the door, and it seems you do have it in you." She leered wickedly. "Or maybe Iseult had it in her, yes?"

He held himself back from slapping her. She would have loved that. "Does Gwyn know?" he said quietly.

Sorcha chuckled. "Who knows what Gwyn knows? He's so befuddled by drink all the time." She leaned in. "To tell the truth, I don't blame her. You're by far the better catch."

"Take me to her."

Sorcha turned and beckoned. He followed her back through the library, and he realised she was heading to her own bedroom.

"Where are we going? I don't get it."

"Well, since you don't want to bump into Gwyn, we'll have to go up this way."

He shook his head but followed her. They hurried up the stairs.

Near the top, Sorcha frowned. "She's in grave danger here, you know, Tristan."

"Iseult is?"

Sorcha nodded. He was behind her. He watched her ponytail bob as she climbed the stairs.

"Yes. Someone here wants her dead."

He frowned. "Gwyn?"

She shrugged. "I don't know who exactly."

"Then what are you talking about?"

"I was reading her cards, you know? Just by myself, curious about her fate, and it seems the old story will see itself played out yet again."

They were now on the landing. She made to go on, but he grabbed her arm and didn't let go. "Which story?"

She stared at him. "Arthur and Guinevere, with the ever-so dashing Lancelot. Diarmuid and Gráinne with the jealous Fionn Mac Cumhail. And of course Tristan and Isolde on the run from old King Mark. Didn't you think the names were a tremendous coincidence?"

"The names?"

"Tristan and Iseult, and Gwyn, who is, of course, Fionn. There's no such thing as a coincidence, and because the names are the same, the story is the same. It doesn't end well for Iseult, I'm afraid."

Tristan flinched as if she'd hit him. "This is bullshit." He spat the words. "Absolute nonsense."

"Feel free to go and work it out with Fionn." She put a hand to her mouth as if she were terribly amused. "I mean Gwyn."

He said, "Just show me where Iseult is."

⚜

"SURE. UP THIS WAY." SHE WALKED OFF TOWARD HER BEDROOM. Tristan hurried after her. At the door, he paused. "This is your room."

She nodded. "There's a secret way."

Tristan remembered the passages behind the walls. He followed her into her bedroom. He remembered it too well. The long satin drapes around the walls, the four-poster bed, the table beside the bed with the antique golden amulet and the black key. Except now there was no black key.

Sorcha went to the wall and touched the wood panel at a specific place, and it opened, revealing a passage. She beckoned. "Come."

Tristan entered behind her. The stone walls radiated cold, and the smell of old wood filled his nostrils.

Sorcha produced a silver petrol lighter from her pocket. She rasped her thumb on the wheel, and a blue and yellow flame sprung up. "Follow. Be careful, the ground is uneven."

He had to stoop as he made his way behind Sorcha down the narrow passage. They came to some stone steps. "Up there." She pointed. "You go first."

"Me go first? Why?"

She took the lighter flame close to illuminate her face as if she was a monster. "Scared of ghosts, Tristan?" She laughed.

"There's no such things as ghosts," he snapped.

She twisted her mouth — mocking him. "Not so sure about that, buddy. But here's your chance to prove your courage to Iseult. Up the stairs and onto the roof. Over the slates and there she is — and all without bumping into cross old Gwyn."

Tristan barged past her. She pointed the lighter over his shoulder, but already he could see the grey of natural light ahead. He stopped and looked over his shoulder. "This leads to the roof?"

"Yeah, yeah." She winked. "I'll be right behind you, my brave soldier boy."

He ignored her tone, turned and rushed up the stairs. At the top of the stairs, he entered an attic room. He looked up and saw a skylight in the form of a glass cupola reinforced with Victorian cast iron ribs. He pointed at it. "Through here to the roof?"

Sorcha nodded. She was below him on the stairs. He paused. Something was wrong.

He hadn't paid attention. Sorcha grabbed the trapdoor and slammed it shut to imprison him in the attic. A metal bar grated as she locked the trapdoor against him. He roared in anger and stamped on the floor, thumping his heel into the wooden trapdoor that shuddered but didn't budge. He got on his hands and knees, looking for a hand-hold to drag it open but his fingers found none. He banged again and again with his fist, the pain shooting up his arms. And then he stopped.

As he stood in the grey daylight, his mind ran back to what Sorcha had said — someone wanted Iseult dead. He banged his forehead against the crumbling plaster of the wall. Someone wanted Iseult dead, and he remembered what Iseult had told him - that if Gwyn found out, he would kill them both. That's who wanted her dead. He threw back his head and roared.

❦

"COME WITH ME, CLAIRE," SORCHA SAID, REACHING BACK TO TAKE the psychic's thin hand. Claire was puzzled. She hadn't been up long, but at least she'd had a good sleep while all the others were carrying on drinking. The spirits had been quite troubled, but then one like a blackbird came and sang in her ear lulling her to the land of Nod. She smiled as she remembered.

"Claire? Come on." Sorcha was smiling. "Or are you tired? It was a busy night in the castle last night."

"No, milady, I dreamed of blackbirds." She had also dreamed of bare men, but she wasn't going to admit that.

"You haven't seen Tristan this morning?"

"No, milady."

"He was busy." A wicked smile played on Sorcha's lips. "With Iseult."

"With Iseult?" That blonde whore. Claire brought her hand to her mouth as she realised what milady had meant. "Really?"

Sorcha nodded.

"Doing it?"

"Yes. I heard them."

Claire thought about hearing them, and it made her feel tingly in her lower tummy. Then she pushed the tingles away. They were un-Christian. She burst into staccato, hysterical laughter. Doing it. With his thing. She couldn't stop the laughter. She laughed so much, her chest hurt, and she couldn't breathe.

"Come on, Claire," Milady Sorcha said. She was frowning. Claire stopped laughing. Then she started again: with his thing. Doing it.

"Claire, we need to go."

Milady was cross with her now, she could tell. She didn't want to upset her. She was so nice and kind.

Sorcha walked off. Claire tripped off after the lady of the castle as she took her down passages and upstairs until they arrived at a delightful room. A four-poster bed sat in the middle with long satin drapes hanging around the walls. Very pleasant. Sorcha reached over to the table beside the bed and picked up an old-looking golden amulet on a chain. She handed it to Claire. "Do you get any feelings from this?"

Claire's fingers touched the amulet, and she got an electric shock and pushed it back to Sorcha.

"It's that powerful?" Sorcha's eyes widened. "Take it and tell me if you feel anyone's presence in it."

With trepidation, Claire reached out and touched it. She got the same electrical shock but not so strong. She closed her eyes and imagined herself in a grove of trees. Looking up, she saw the stars like pointed crowns, and in the middle of the clearing was a leaping fire. She heard the cracking of the wood as it burned. She stood with others wearing robes of green. They talked an old talk she didn't know, except it sounded like the jabber-jabber that Dudley said to Lady Sorcha sometimes.

"What do you see?" Lady Sorcha was interested. Claire described what she'd seen.

"Druids. I have waited so long for someone with enough power to reach back so far." She came and stroked Claire's arm. "And you are here, you lovely lady."

Claire beamed. She had a warm feeling in her tummy. She weighed the gold amulet in her hand. "This is very old."

Sorcha nodded. "Come through into my ritual room."

Claire didn't like the sound of that — it sounded un-Christian, but Sorcha had opened a door and led through to another room. This room was painted black and had magical symbols daubed on it in red. Claire recognised a pentagram. A circle was drawn in white on the floor with words in ancient lettering she couldn't read. In the centre of the room was a black box and on the box, a silver cup, a dagger, a dish and wand with a tip of quartz.

Magic power buzzed through the room. Claire heard it humming out of sight, out of sound. She heard it with her inner ears, the ones the ghosts spoke through. She saw golden figures dancing — small people with shining hair and silver wings. In the shadows in the angles were misty things, dark and lupine with faces like long dogs. They were old, and they watched. Lady Sorcha couldn't see them — only her, Claire.

Sorcha reached and got a cloak from a peg. She handed it to Claire. It was lovely and soft.

"Put it on."

Claire slipped it over her head. It had a hood. She put the hood up. She wondered what Jesus would think of this, then she supposed he wouldn't mind: he loved her after all.

Sorcha had put on a cloak too. She looked beautiful. She stood before the black altar and burned incense. Then she spoke in Irish.

"Is this correct?" Claire blinked. "This place and this thing we're doing."

Sorcha smiled but didn't stop talking Irish.

Claire watched her. She wished she had her Bible so she could consult Leviticus to check whether this was lawful. Leviticus wasn't always accurate for modern times, though. It didn't allow Christian Psychics, for example, and she was one.

"Claire?"

Claire brought her thoughts back to the room. The fairies danced around her feet and the wolf-men watched from the corners. "Yes, my lady?"

"Hold the amulet again."

Claire nodded and gathered up the golden thing from Sorcha's grasp. It shimmered and whirred in her hand. It felt alive now as if Sorcha's words had charged it up. There was someone in it. She peered at the smooth gold. Someone moved inside it. It trapped his face with its pretty shine.

"Lady Sorcha, who—." She began, but then she knew. It was one of the green men from the oak grove. Claire knew a Christian like her had put him in here long ago and he couldn't leave.

"What does he say?" Sorcha asked.

Claire concentrated, but she only heard whispers. She saw his face a little. He looked pained.

"What does he say?"

Claire frowned. She shook her head. "He's too far away," she said finally.

Sorcha sighed. "No matter. I thought that would be the case."

"He's here inside the amulet," Claire said. "Stuck."

Sorcha nodded and pulled off her cloak.

Claire snatched at hers. "Can I keep this on? It's lovely."

"Of course, Claire. You can keep everything you want. You're my special friend."

"When do we destroy the banshee? That is my true mission here, not druids."

"Soon. Go to her Tower and watch her with your psychic eyes. Tell me what she's doing."

❦

WHEN SORCHA DIDN'T ARRIVE WITH TRISTAN, GWYN BARGED PAST Dudley and out of the kitchen. The Irishman watched him go. When he knew Dudley could no longer see him, Gwyn let the tears flow down his cheeks and ran sobbing along the darkened corridors and up the stairs. Halfway up, he stopped, held the bannister and doubled up in paroxysms of grief. After a minute, he straightened, composed himself and hurried up the remaining steps until he reached the landing. Their bedroom door was closed against him. He approached it and stood, hand raised as if to knock, then, changing his mind, he turned the handle and entered.

Iseult lay drowsy under the sheets, her blonde hair was unkempt. She rubbed her eyes. "Sorry, I was going to get up. I fell back asleep."

The room lurched from his hangover. "You'll be tired I guess," he said. His hand shook as he gripped the metal knob of the bedstead.

She rolled to the bed edge and stood. She wore the nightdress he'd bought her in Paris. He couldn't bring himself to admire her figure because when he did the thought of Tristan's hands on her took over his mind. He swallowed and wiped his lips. Their room was en-suite, and she wandered through to the bathroom, studying herself in the mirror and sighing. She grabbed her toothbrush and brushed her teeth, her back to him.

He put his fist to his mouth, then pulled it away to give him air to speak. "I know," he said finally.

Her eyes, blue as Delft porcelain, flicked to him in the mirror. She continued to brush her teeth.

He leaned against the door frame. His stomach acid sloshed and burned. He cleared his throat. "I know."

She stopped brushing. Still meeting his eyes only through the mirror, she said, "Know what?"

An alchemy of emotions began in his gut: grief, terror and anger like a red fountain pumping in time with his enraged heart. He gripped the door frame and stuttered, "Don't fucking deny it."

Iseult turned. Her eye twitched, and she held the toothbrush across her breast like a feeble shield.

Gwyn slapped the edge of his fist against the door frame. He was almost doubled up. "Don't fucking deny it."

She was shaking. "Deny what?"

Gwyn doubled like he'd been punched. He brought both hands up and grabbed his hair. "You did it with Tristan. You fucked my friend." Spit dribbled from his mouth. He clenched his eyes then they snapped open, bloodshot and fierce.

She spread out her hands as if she didn't know what he meant.

He shook his head. "Please, don't playact with me. After all I've done for you. You would have gone to jail if I hadn't helped you."

He'd never said that before — never mentioned what he'd saved her from. He'd never wanted to, but now she'd twisted a knife in his gut, and it burned like white-hot iron. He collapsed back against the door. He couldn't look at her.

"I want to get dressed," she said and skirted past him. He stared into the mirror that revealed half her back as she snapped on her bra, pulled on a top then snatched her jeans and stepped into them.

He couldn't believe it. "You have nothing to say?"

She threw things in her bag. "It's true I do owe you so much. I was going to tell you."

"Tell me when? When you were back home, and you could both do a runner in the middle of the night and get safe from me?"

She spun around. "Get safe from you?" Her eyes hardened. "A second ago, you reminded me of all that I owed you. You helped me get out of a violent relationship that nearly killed me. You made me safe, and I will always be grateful to you for that." She wiped the palms of her hands on her jeans. Her voice shook. "But now you're threatening me?"

Gwyn's guilt rushed over him like a mountain river. His emotions changed again. "I would never hurt you, Iseult. I didn't mean that." He stepped forward, and she flinched back.

Her eyes widened. Gwyn saw her chest rising as she breathed fast. "But you'd hurt Tristan?" She moved towards the door. The knife in his guts twisted again. He gave a sardonic smile. "I get it. You want to go warn your lover boy." He stepped closer to her.

She trembled as she backed away. Her hand was on the bedroom door handle. Her eyes were wild, and she studied every move he made.

He balled his fist. "He's gonna get what's coming to him. He's betrayed me, and he owes me everything too."

Iseult dashed to the door, but he kicked it, and it slammed closed. He moved to stand between her and escape.

Iseult's eyes darted around the room as if she was looking for a weapon. She was a cornered beast. He knew that look. He'd seen it so many times in his Special Forces days — just before he was going to kill a man, and the man knew. How could he hurt her? He loved her. He stammered, "Just tell me you love me. Tell me it was all a mistake. You were drunk. It happens. As long as he goes, we can be together and happy again."

She shook her head. Tears ran down her cheeks.

He wiped his mouth. "Just say it. Say you love me."

She cleared her throat and wiped her tears away.

His fists clenched. "Say you love me."

Finally, she muttered, "I care about you deeply. I owe you so much."

He began to weep. As he sobbed, he ran his hand through his greying hair. The hangover jangled his nerves, and he couldn't think straight.

She stepped forward, reaching a hand to touch his arm. He let her.

"I care so deeply about you," she repeated.

He studied her fingers on his arm. "Say that last night was a mistake."

She didn't reply.

He took her hand in his. He squeezed it. "Last night was a mistake." For every second she didn't reply, he squeezed harder.

She yelped and tried to draw her hand away, but he had it fast. "Or maybe it wasn't a mistake?" His voice was threatening. "Maybe you'd been planning on fucking him for a long time. Is that it?" He was hurting her, and he knew it. He twisted her fingers back, and she shouted out. He knew how to hurt people. That had been his business.

Tears flowed down her face. "Let go of my hand, Gwyn."

He gripped her slender fingers hard as a vice. "Tell me first."

Through teeth gritted from pain, she said, "I love him."

Gwyn took his other hand and slapped her face. She reeled away, and he let her go free. She staggered back and brought her hand to her cheek. Her eyes were wide in shock at what he'd done.

Horror and shame replaced anger. "I didn't mean it." He was desperate.

She moved to the door and opened it. He screwed his hands tight. He didn't know what to do. At the door she turned, hand still at her cheek. Her voice was cold. "Another man once did that to me. I vowed he would never do it again. You will never do it again, either."

He watched her leave the room then he turned and punched the door so hard he thought he'd broken his knuckles. Bringing his injured fist to his eyes, he howled like a wolf then smeared his fingers against his face to wipe off the tears.

He was alone. The sound of the wind fretted at the windows, but otherwise, all was silence. He remembered the vodka. He had a quarter bottle stashed in his case for emergencies, so he rushed across the room, dragging out his clothes and throwing them until he saw the gleaming bottle then he grabbed it, twisted the tin top and clashed the glass neck against his teeth. He glugged the vodka down, and it burned. Coming up for air, he wiped the spirit from his mouth with the back of his hand and in his grief. It was Tristan who'd seduced her into this betrayal. He would kill him for his treachery.

15

THE KNIFE

Iseult entered the kitchen and saw Sorcha. The witch was scrubbed and clean. She looked up. "The island is full of noises..." Her eyes suddenly widened in concern. "You've been hit — your cheek."

Iseult sat. "Yeah, get me a coffee, can you?"

"Sure. I seem to be doing a lot of that this morning." Sorcha stood and fetched the coffee pot. She poured it into a mug that said *World's Best Gardener* and pushed it to Iseult. The china scraped over the wood and clouds of steam rose into the cold kitchen air.

Iseult took a gulp. "Have you seen Tristan?"

Sorcha shook her head. "Not this morning."

"He must still be in his room."

Sorcha pointed at the redness already promising a deep bruise. "Gwyn did this?"

Iseult nodded.

Sorcha muttered, "Bastard."

Iseult grunted.

The older woman leaned and stroked Iseult's arm. "Men are such bastards."

Iseult didn't meet her eyes. "I'm not without guilt."

"There's no excuse for violence. None."

"No, I know."

Sorcha hesitated, ran her finger around the rim of her coffee mug, then said tentatively, "Were you in a violent relationship before?"

Iseult glanced up. Her head felt far away. "Before what?"

"Before Gwyn."

The younger woman's eyes narrowed. "I'm not a serial victim if that's what you mean."

Sorcha's hand left the mug, and she studied it. "No, it's just, I've had friends who ended up with another guy—"

"—who hit them?"

"Yeah, kinda."

Iseult spoke quietly. "He beat me badly. I ended up in hospital. The man who did it before — he never did it again."

"Did you go back to him?"

"Yep. But I knew what I was going for."

The witch was interested. "Which was?"

"Never mind."

"I'm not sure what that means."

"Doesn't matter."

"Okay." Sorcha stood. "You drank that fast. More coffee?"

Iseult placed her hand on top of her mug. "I'm good thanks."

Sorcha sat again. She seemed on edge. "It was because of you and Tristan - why Gwyn hit you?"

Iseult sighed deeply. She eyed Sorcha. "You knew?"

Sorcha gave a soft laugh. "I'm not blind. I just noticed who was where when last night. It was only a matter of time."

Iseult didn't reply.

Sorcha pushed her questions further. "But you want to be with him?"

The younger woman nodded. Tears glistened in her blue eyes.

"Well then, what's the problem?"

"Gwyn, of course."

"I mean of course he's sore now—heartbroken—but that is always true in these situations."

Iseult hesitated a long time. She rubbed her hand across her eyes.

Looking down, she said, "Last night things were different. I thought I could be brave. I thought that true love made everything okay and would ride out any storm."

"But that's changed?"

"The cold light of day and all. I love Tristan but I must stay with Gwyn."

"Because you're afraid of Gwyn."

Iseult shook her head. "No, well yes, but not in the way you think."

"I hear he can be pretty violent."

"Yes, and I want Tristan to be safe."

"But why can't you two get away and be together?"

Iseult gazed out of the kitchen window. "Gwyn knows something about me. It means I can never be with Tristan." She gave a sour smile. "Something serious. He's never mentioned it to anyone."

Sorcha spoke slowly as if thinking hard. "It's a pretty serious secret he knows if you have to stay with a man who beats you."

"He doesn't beat me."

Sorcha pointed to Iseult's damaged face.

"Just once."

"That's how it starts, honey - with the the first time." Sorcha sat closer. "But what's this secret?"

"It's serious."

"Want to tell me?"

Iseult laughed bitterly. "No. Then you'd have power over me too."

Sorcha narrowed her eyes. "Intriguing. But I want to help."

"We need to send Tristan away. Can you call a taxi for him?"

"Sure. If that's what you want. But I think you should go with him."

"That's kind. But it can't happen." She wiped tears away with her finger-ends. "Silly cow. Anyway, if Tristan knew my little secret, he'd never want to see me again."

"So, Tristan doesn't know either?"

"No."

Sorcha took Iseult's hand again and massaged it gently. "Listen, we've all done things that seem terrible to us, but with perspective, they're quite minor."

"This wasn't minor."

"But you won't tell me what it was?"

Iseult shook her head. "I need you to get a taxi for Tristan. I'll go and find him and somehow get him out before Gwyn gets hold of him." She looked up. "Could you do me a favour and occupy Gwyn?"

"Of course. You think they'll fight?"

"Oh, yes. Gwyn's lived a life of extreme violence. He was in Special Forces in Syria."

"I know. He said."

Iseult's gaze was steady. "Violence solves every problem, he says."

"So they'll fight, and it'll be serious."

"More than that. Gwyn will kill him. Tristan won't want to leave me, but I'll be okay. Gwyn hit me, and it shocked him. It's not in his code to hit women. He won't hurt me again. He'll take it all out on Tristan. And he'll be drunk."

"Where will he get drink? I'll lock it all away."

"He has secret stashes. All alcoholics do." Iseult stood. "Please will you call a taxi? I'll find Tristan. You go talk to Gwyn and keep him busy. Let me know when the taxi comes. Or send Dudley. I need to keep Tristan safe."

"It'll be a while. We're a fair way away from town."

"But ring now, please." At the door, Iseult paused. "I know we're not exactly friends..."

Sorcha smiled. "I like to think we're friends."

Iseult shrugged. "But I will owe you so much if you can help me keep Tristan away from Gwyn."

"Of course. You go now and find him. I'll ring for a taxi."

Iseult turned and hurried out of the kitchen.

☙❧

Iseult rushed up the stairs, her heart thumping. She paused at the top. Her and Gwyn's bedroom door was ajar, but she could hear no sound. She wondered what he was doing and guessed he was still in there feeling sorry for himself and drinking. She didn't want to see him, so she inched her way to the bottom of the staircase that led up to Tristan's tower. It had a strange mythical ring to it:

Tristan's Tower, as if their story belonged to the castle and always had.

This staircase was narrower. She remembered climbing it the night before, goblet in hand and the silly love potion already in the wine. She'd been so confident then. So sure there was a solution to the problem that tortured her heart. She would be with Tristan and choose love over duty. The magic of the night before was the ash of the morning after.

In the light of day, she knew the hold Gwyn had over her was hard as iron. The power of love, whatever that meant, held no sway over the kingdom of guilt that possessed her.

But she had to see him safely out of this trap she'd lured him into. She hadn't meant it. It was like she herself had taken the love potion as soon as she walked through the castle doors, and it had driven all sense from her head and intoxicated her with the feelings in her heart.

But sense had now returned.

She stood, heart in mouth, outside the heavy wooden door to Tristan's circular room. Tentatively, she knocked, sheepish for what they had done, but also with a thrill like electricity that she would see him again. But the knocking fell flat. No one answered. She twisted the knob and stepped inside. She could smell Tristan — not the sour smell of stale whiskey — but aftershave and soap and the smell of his skin and hair.

The room was empty. Where the hell was he?

Panic flashed through her. What if Gwyn had caught him already? She turned and rushed down the stairs, almost tripping in her haste and having to grab the rail to stop her fall. She caught her breath and tried to still her heart. Gwyn hadn't got him. She would have heard them fighting, or at least the sound of angry voices. She stopped outside Gwyn's room. The door was still ajar. Silence reigned there too.

Sorcha came up the stairs like this was a play, and she had waited there for her cue.

"Where's Gwyn?" asked Iseult.

Sorcha smiled reassuringly. She jerked her thumb behind her. "With Dudley in the kitchen."

"Why? How come I didn't bump into him?" Her mind tumbled over itself. "Did you ring the taxi?"

Sorcha held up her hand. "So many questions. Why - he thinks he's waiting for Tristan. How come you didn't bump into him? I led him by a shortcut. Did I ring the taxi - yes."

"How long till it comes? Where's Tristan?"

"More questions. About a half-hour. Don't know."

"I need to find him. He must be somewhere. You must know where he is."

"I don't."

"Then I'll look for him." Iseult glanced down the corridor that led past Claire's door. The stone vase had been knocked off its plinth. Then she looked down the stairs past Sorcha. Dudley was coming up. "I thought you said Dudley was with Gwyn."

Sorcha looked over her shoulder and saw Dudley. Dudley spoke in Irish.

"Where's Gwyn?" Iseult stammered. "Has he found Tristan?" Her palms were sweating again, and her mouth dry.

Sorcha spoke again to Dudley. The Irishman shrugged his shoulders.

"Speak English!" Iseult snapped. "I can't understand you."

Sorcha sighed. "He says Gwyn's gone looking for Tristan and he couldn't stop him. He took a weapon."

"A weapon? Call the police," Iseult stammered. The room spun, and she put her hand to the wall.

"It'll take a long time for the Gardaí to get here," Dudley said. "They'll ask what crime was committed. And so far, there hasn't been one." He showed his teeth, grinning like a dog.

"I need to find Tristan." Iseult rubbed her face. She didn't want to cry in front of them. She beseeched them, "Do you have any idea where he is?"

Sorcha stepped closer and put her left hand onto Iseult's arm in a gesture of comfort. She had something clasped in her right hand, out of sight.

"I'm going to find Tristan." Iseult made to walk off down the corridor.

Sorcha gripped her arm tight and wouldn't let her go. "Be careful," the older woman said.

"Careful? Me? Why?" Iseult felt confused. Her head wasn't working right.

"In case you run into Gwyn."

"Gwyn won't hurt me." Instinctively her hand came to her cheek. It was sore, the bruise coming out now. "Not again."

Dudley shook his head sadly. "He said he will kill you."

It was like a hammer hit her. She reeled back. "Kill me? No, that's not right."

Dudley shrugged. He stared at her, his eyes were convex lenses of ebony, embedded in amber. "That's what he said."

"Here." Sorcha offered her something. She couldn't make out what it was at first. Iseult stared at Sorcha's right hand and watched as the palm unfolded to reveal a knife. It was about eight inches long with a wicked serrated blade. Iseult looked at Sorcha, then back at the knife. "What?"

"Take it," Sorcha said. "For defence."

"A knife?"

Sorcha nodded. "Dudley's hunting knife. Gwyn's much stronger than you. He'll kill you."

Iseult shook her head. She stammered, "I don't need a knife."

Sorcha studied her. She cocked her head. "Not even to protect Tristan?" It was almost a smile.

Anxiety flooded Iseult. She felt unwell. She remembered the time before and turned and yanked herself free of Sorcha's grip. Sorcha let her go. Iseult walked a half dozen paces down the passage then stopped and looked back. "I don't need a knife," she repeated.

Sorcha smiled like she was Iseult's best friend. "I think you should take it. For Tristan — to save him from Gwyn."

Iseult swallowed. It was true. She walked back to Sorcha and took the hunting knife from her hand. She gazed at in her hand like it was an alien flower, gripped it, felt the weight. It was a killing thing. It could gut a man as easy as it could gut a fish. She nodded, turned and fled down the passage.

ISEULT HURRIED, KNIFE IN HAND, DOWN THE PASSAGE THAT GOT more dilapidated the further she went from the inhabited area. She didn't know where she was going, but she ran, frantic to find Tristan. She remembered that he had been so keen to go into the Banshee Tower — the place they'd walked to that night with Claire and Sorcha when Sorcha's candles blew out and they claimed the banshee was locked in the tower. That was out of the way. Maybe Tristan was there keeping out of Gwyn's way.

She half-remembered the route, getting lost and turning back until she saw the place where she'd cut her arm. Dried blood still smeared the glass shard. Holes lurked in the wall here and in the greying daylight, she saw how unsafe the floor was. She hadn't noticed the rotten floorboards in the dark. They were lucky they hadn't fallen through.

But Tristan wasn't there. The door to the tower was padlocked. The lock looked brand new. She grunted and spun around, stepping over debris and holes in the floor to make her way back.

A figure in a cloak stood at the intersection of passages in front of her.

Iseult stopped cold. Iseult gripped the knife hard. "Who's that?"

The figure threw back her hood. It was Claire.

Iseult shook her head and stepped forward. She muttered, "Where did you get that ridiculous cloak?"

Claire stared at her. "From Lady Sorcha. She appreciates me."

Iseult exhaled. "Have you seen Tristan?"

Claire's mouth twitched. "He'll have run away. Now he's done the deed, he's got had what he wanted. Cowards like him always run."

"Done the deed?" Iseult snapped her head around. "What do you mean?"

Claire glanced at the knife in Iseult's hand, but she didn't seem scared. "Milady Sorcha told me."

"Sorcha told you what?" There was Sorcha pretending to be her friend and all the while tittle-tattling behind her back. She'd been right not to trust the bitch.

Claire held her hand to her mouth and snickered. "That you and he had, you know — done it." She broke out laughing.

Iseult shook her head. "You sure are a crazy cow, Claire."

Claire blinked. "It's good he's gone. Now you can be true to your husband. Not that he's much better, the drunken oaf. I never liked them— men and their cocky things, but loyalty's what counts." She smiled. "Sorcha and I are going to destroy the banshee." She pointed at the tower. "She lives in there."

Iseult thought of saying something, but the old woman wasn't worth her breath. Tristan wasn't in the tower. She turned and hurried back into the main body of the castle. She glanced behind to see Claire lost in thought, staring at the Banshee Tower.

DESPERATE TO FIND TRISTAN, ISEULT WANDERED LOST FROM DISUSED room to disused room. She didn't know this floor at all and every passage looked the same. It smelled of mildew, and the wind moaned as it entered through holes in windows and walls. She looked at her watch: one o'clock. Her wrist shook as she gripped the knife, and the hilt was damp with sweat. She was wasting so much time wandering around. Gwyn must have found Tristan by now.

She determined to go back the way she had come. If she could find where she had seen Claire and turn right, she'd get back to the landing where their bedrooms were. She walked down a corridor where the carpet stunk from rain that had come in and was tacky under her feet. She stepped over the decayed corpse of a crow. Something thumped to her right, and she spun, thrusting the knife out. Only shadows and echoes. No one was there, but the sense of being watched lingered in the air. She called, "Who is it?"

The wind grieved and the castle groaned, shifting its ancient bulk.

"Who's there?" Her voice echoed flatly against the damp wood and old stone. The castle moved again in its sleep. "I know there's someone there." The knife tip trembled. She coughed. "Come out." It was maybe Dudley watching her — he was enough of a freak to do that.

Then she dropped the knife to her side and shook her head. Her fear for Tristan was unseating her mind.

She saw stairs ahead leading down to the right. She ran over to them and down. They creaked and gave, and she thought she might go through the wood, but she reached the bottom and was down on the ground floor again. She half recognised where she was and tried to make her way to the front entrance.

Tristan might be there, watching outside. Or he might have run through the bogland and away. He might have left her behind, just like Claire said he would. She halted and sagged against the damp wall.

She had to go back to Gwyn because Gwyn knew her secret and if he told the police, then she'd go to jail, and she wouldn't ever have Tristan.

Hopelessness cut her like a cold wind.

But there was a way out. The bog was immense. It would suck down sins and bury them out of sight. She shook her head to clear it. She wouldn't do that. She was a fighter and always had been.

Iseult stared at the knife in her hand.

Gwyn was the only one who knew her secret. The only one.

Her heart flipped over. Ahead was a familiar corridor that led to the kitchen. The door was open, but she couldn't see anyone. She couldn't see them, but she heard someone moving. It could be Tristan, or it could be Gwyn. She looked at the knife again and gripped it hard. Slowly, she walked toward the kitchen door. Either way, she was ready.

Gwyn stood looking out of the window, a tumbler of whiskey in his hand. Iseult stepped through the door.

He spun around and saw her. "Iseult," he said, his voice a broken whisper. His eyes moved to her cheek. The bruise must be noticeable now. She shifted the knife behind her back so he wouldn't see it.

He put his whiskey down on the table and came towards her. He inclined his head but didn't touch her. Tears streamed over grizzled cheeks. "I'm so sorry I hit you, Iseult. You know I never would."

She was cold. "But you did."

He shook his head. "It's not me. It wasn't me. It was the drink. It was my anger."

Hate for him blossomed in her. She repeated. "It wasn't me, it was my anger: where have I heard that before? Oh yeah, from every scumbag man who wants to dodge responsibility for his violence." She pointed to the whiskey. "Where did you get that?"

He looked puzzled, glanced back, saw what she meant. "That? Sorcha got me it."

"I told her to keep drink away from you."

He wasn't listening. "I'm just so sorry. Can you forgive me?" He couldn't meet her eyes.

Her hand tightened on the knife. "What have you done with Tristan?"

He looked up, surprised. "Nothing. Yet." His mouth tightened. "Where is he?"

"I wouldn't tell you if I knew."

He sneered. "So that's how it is. He's your preference, of course." He noticed her arm hiding behind her back. "What have you got there?"

She showed him. His eyes widened. "Jesus." He shook his head. "And who were you going to use that on?"

"No one. It was for defence."

"Defence from whom?"

Her mouth tightened.

Quick as a viper, he snatched her arm, twisted it and deadened her wrist with his strong fingers, so the knife fell with a clatter on the stone floor. She shrieked. He kicked the blade across the floor away from her and spat, "Plenty of people tried to kill me, Iseult. None of them made it. Just a little warning."

She was wringing the pain out of her hand and fell back away from him, stammering "I wouldn't have..."

But she knew she would.

He was cold now. "Sure, you wouldn't." He levelled his finger at her. "Just remember that I know something about you. Something I bet you haven't even told Tristan."

She glanced away, unable to hold his burning gaze.

He smiled a cruel smile. "No, you haven't told him." He laughed bitterly. "Well, I guess I always was a fool with women. Should have realised by now you can't trust them." He looked back at her and shook his head. "But I thought you were different. Just goes to show how wrong you can be."

It was her turn to be sorry. Though she had pain in her face and hand caused by him, she also had the sting of guilt from her adultery. Her eyes strayed to the knife where it lay on the stone flags.

He saw her looking. "Don't even think about it. Now fuck off back to your boyfriend and tell him I'm gonna cut his fucking throat. With that."

As she left the kitchen, she heard the rasping sound of Gwyn grabbing his whiskey glass from the kitchen table behind her. The whiskey — his only real friend.

⁂

Sorcha was lingering outside the kitchen in the corridor. She'd heard the whole thing.

Iseult hissed, "You gave him whiskey."

Sorcha looked apologetic. She whispered. "He was insistent. I was frightened of him."

Iseult didn't know whether to believe her or not.

Sorcha put her finger to her lips. She motioned for them to move away from the kitchen door. Iseult could hear Gwyn cursing into his whiskey. She thought she heard the scrape of metal on stone as if he'd picked up the knife. Her heart fell; she'd handed over the weapon to him herself — a weapon he could now use on Tristan. Tristan wouldn't be expecting it; he'd be defenceless. How foolish and weak she was when all came to all.

Sorcha reached out and took her wrist, the one Gwyn had twisted. Iseult yelped and jerked it away.

Sorcha frowned. "He hurt you again?"

Iseult shook her head.

Sorcha said, "I don't believe you."

"It doesn't matter. Where's Tristan? I really need to see him."

Sorcha beckoned her to follow, hurrying down the corridor with Iseult wide eyed with panic.

At the bottom of the stairs, Iseult pulled her to a stop. "Where is he? Is he safe?"

"Yes. Dudley's up there to show you. He'll take you to him."

"Oh, thank God."

Sorcha smiled and stroked Iseult's arm. "Don't fret. It'll all be all right. Where's the knife?"

"Gwyn took it off me."

"Okay."

"Did you call the police?"

"Yes, yes."

"How long will they be?"

Sorcha shrugged. "We're a way out of town. Twenty minutes."

"But Tristan's safe?"

"Sure. You join him. Dudley'll show you."

"What about you?"

Sorcha grimaced. "I will try to de-escalate the situation. A drunken jealous man and a hunting knife are never a good combination. I'll try to calm him down."

Not knowing what prompted her, Iseult reached out and hugged the older woman. She held Sorcha to her chest. Her bones and muscles ached as she buried her head in Sorcha's shoulder. She cried again. "Thank you."

"For what?"

"For keeping Tristan safe. I'm sorry I didn't trust you before."

Sorcha broke the embrace. "Not a problem." She grabbed both of Iseult's shoulders. "You go now. Up the stairs. Dudley's waiting for you. He'll show you were Tristan is. I'll defuse the situation."

"Why don't you leave it to the police?"

"He'll fight them and it could get bad. He'll listen to me, I know."

Dudley stood there. He beckoned Iseult with his long finger. "Come and I'll show you where Tristan is. We have him somewhere where Gwyn can't get to him."

❧ 16 ☙

ROOFTOPS AND RITUALS

Tristan paced across the floor of the restricted room. He looked up at the grey sky and thought about smashing the window but knew it would be futile because the metal grille held the glass in place. He studied the floor, seeking any points of weakness but found none. He was trapped and at Sorcha's mercy. Tristan sat with his head in his hands. How had it all come to this? He hadn't asked to love Iseult, but it happened anyway. He hadn't intended to betray Gwyn, but so it had been: The wheel spins. The dice fall. The cards turn. The players play their parts and the drama unfolds.

Last night, when Iseult came to his room, he could have told her to leave. He could blame the wine, and he could blame the weather, and he could blame the way the lock of hair fell over her cheek, but, in the end, responsibility rested in him. It lodged in his heart like an arrow.

Truth was, he was a heel, a scumbag, a betrayer. But he knew he couldn't be other. He loved her. Loving Isuelt was as much of him as the brown of his eyes, the black of his hair, the red of his blood. All his life he hadn't known it, but there it had been anyway, under the surface, waiting for the day in Pembrokeshire when she walked into the bar with Gwyn, and he said hello.

Play the part that life has given you willingly or reluctantly, but either way, you will play it: scoundrel or knave; knight or thief, you will play your role.

Tristan buried his head in his hands, and some romantic idea that love is stronger than rules ran through his thoughts. And love makes adultery okay, doesn't it? If you love a woman, truly, madly, deeply then you can cheat her husband. You can be a liar if you're a liar for love.

Tristan stood, banged his head against the wall.

Anyway, it was done, and he'd have to make the best of it. Gwyn would never forgive him, but at least he would be with Iseult.

He wiped plaster from his forehead. The walls of this attic room were old and damp.

He sat down, dejected. He had the sensation he was being observed. He stood and patrolled the room seeking any eye holes, but there were none. Still, the hair on his neck pricked up. There was someone in the room with him. Someone — or something.

Feeling stupid, he whispered, "Who are you?"

He stood still waiting for an answer, but none came, just the sound of the wind above the ceiling and the settling of old wood and ancient stone. But there was someone there, he was sure.

He spoke out loud. "Amelia Morton? Friend or foe?" Nothing, of course, nothing. But my enemy's enemy is my friend. A ghost can pass through walls, but I can't.

Time went by, and through the grid of the cupola glass, he saw grey clouds progress across the sky. The day grew old, and darkness came visiting like an old friend.

In the gloom, he stood and walked across to the plaster walls of the room. The walls were old and damp.

That was a thought: the walls were old and damp.

Tristan walked over and pressed the plaster. It crumbled and beneath his fingers. Walls this old would be made of wattle and daub, and after all these centuries would be half-rotted. He probed with his fingers and found weak points. On impulse, he pulled back his fist and knocked a hole straight through the wall.

Another room was revealed. Tristan saw pigeon droppings on the floor, so the birds could come in and out of the room. Gritting his teeth, he punched, then drew back his fist to hit again until he cracked a hole big enough for him to use both hands to rip a way through. When his hands were sore, he smashed it with his knees and his hands and shoulders. He made an unholy row.

He stopped to listen. He didn't want Sorcha and Dudley to come back now when he thought he had a way out. He listened harder. He thought he heard the sound of someone climbing stairs below him. It had been hours since Sorcha locked him in here. He waited for them to unbolt the trapdoor and them to present him with Gwyn so they could watch them slug it out like gladiators.

But no one came.

And all the time Tristan was locked in here, Iseult was out there. And God alone knew what Sorcha was planning. She was the one he was scared of, not Gwyn.

With a curse, he bashed at the wall. He smashed at it. He ripped at it, and then there was room for him to grab the hole with his fingers, pull the soft lath apart and squeeze through sideways.

❧

GASPING FOR BREATH, FILMED WITH SWEAT, BUT EXHILARATED TO BE free, Tristan stood in the new room. He glanced up and by the pale moonlight, as he had hoped, the skylight in this not secured by an iron grid. There was a hole in the glass where the pigeons got in.

A dirty old box sat in the corner. The faded writing showed that the wood and wire had once contained beer bottles from a local brewery. He dragged the box to the centre of the room and tested it with one foot to make sure it wouldn't give under his weight. He stepped on it, and the box creaked and threatened to give way, but without standing on the box, he had no way of reaching the broken window.

It held for now.

He strained his fingers to touch the rusted metal surrounds of the windowpane.

Tristan managed to push the window slightly open. Stretching further brought an ominous crack and a wobble in the box. If it gave way, he was just as trapped in here as in the room with the iron grille.

He stretched every sinew of his back and shoulder to get some purchase. His fingers pushed through to feel the cold slate of the roof. Then, using the strength built in his upper body from all those years in the army gym, he dragged himself up, straining and sweating and he pulled himself through and out onto the roof.

Squatting by the skylight, getting his bearings, Tristan waited. He was on the roof top of the castle. The castle roof looked solid in some parts but in others, it was caved in completely. The day was overcast and though still only afternoon, it was hard to see for certain where was safe. The roof was mainly pitched and slated, but there were some flat parts here and there and some ways e could descend into the castle below. If he could get there without falling through the rotten roof.

Tristan inched his way up the slippery slates to the ridge line.

He stood there up on the height, maintaining his balance with outstretched arms. From here, you could see everything. He gazed out over the vast bog of Allen and over to Fionn Mac Cumhail's hill and then over to the broken Banshee Tower.

In the ruined tower, and a woman's face appeared in a glassless window at the top. This woman stared at him with cold eyes. It was crazy anybody was up there. He knew how difficult it was to get to the top of that tower. He blinked, sure it was a woman, but when he stared harder, there was no one there.

☙❦❧

TRISTAN KNEW THAT IN THE POOR LIGHT AND SLIMY DAMP IT WOULD be dangerous to cross the roof, but the alternative was to go back to his prison and wait whatever Sorcha had planned for him.

Tristan took a step, and another. So far so good. Ten feet along and his foot slipped, throwing him off balance, taking the legs from beneath him and sending him sliding. He slithered down the pitched roof, scrabbling for a grip on the smooth slates, failing to gain purchase and careering to slip and go over the edge and drop fifty feet.

The slates slipped past. He had to slow himself, to stop himself, but he kept sliding. His fingers ripped; his nails tore and his fall acceler-ated, scraping down the tiles, ploughing through the moss, and finally catching his boot against the cast-iron gutter to stop with a clang. He lay there, cheek against the cold slate with his fingers bleeding and his heart hammering.

The guttering was a hundred years old and if it had been in any worse state of repair, he would have fallen to his death. He breathed deliberately trying to calm his imagination. He was hurt and hanging on the bottom of the roof, but he wasn't dead.

Lying there on the damp roof, he knew he couldn't afford to die. He was convinced that Gwyn wouldn't hurt Iseult. The most likely person to want Iseult dead was Sorcha. But why? It made no sense. What on earth would she want to murder Iseult for? But he'd thought it, and irrational as it was, now he feared it.

Tristan crawled on his hands and knees back to the ridge-line. Once there, he stood and balanced before going on. His fingers hurt like hell. He was too high. He had to find a safe way down. He took one step after another, placing his feet deliberately with arms out to the sides like a tightrope walker. After ten another yards, he got to a chimney stack, and hugged it like it was his saviour. From there, he saw he could lower himself to a partly flat section of the roof. A ruined wickerwork chair and an old table covered with bird droppings sat there. He guessed this was where the castle's inhabitants sat and enjoyed the view on fine summer nights: an antique roof garden.

The breeze suddenly gusted, and he wobbled. He needed to get off the roof. He knelt, got one hand on the chimney stack and dropped. From the ruined roof garden, he saw a mildewed French window that might allow him access into the castle. He wiped his wet and bloody palms on his jeans. The sticky blood might make him slip.

He peered into the room and shook his head. The room was set up as a temple for black magic rituals. Someone had painted an inverted pentagram on the walls in red and round it was strange lettering in ancient Irish script. A black altar stood in the middle of the room. On the floor round it a circle was painted and on the altar were a black dish, a dagger whose hilt was covered in letters, a wand with a crystal tip and an elegant silver goblet. He guessed this was Sorcha's secret chamber where she did her magic spells. She'd said she was a witch, and Tristan guessed now she was a witch of a particularly black kind. Where did this madness end?

The French windows were locked and he couldn't get an entry without smashing his way through. He suspected that the door from the ritual room would lead to Sorcha's bedroom.

It was too risky to go that way. He'd be safer dropping into the coutryard. He edged to what he thought might be a way down. After a few feet, a noise came up from the courtyard below. The courtyard itself was out of sight from where he stood, but he could hear things going on there.

At first, he didn't know what the noise could be, then a realization grew in his heart and his skin prickled. He went on his knees; and crawled across until he found a spot on the roof from where he could get a view of the courtyard.

He wiped sweat from his brow, and smeared blood in its place. Big grey dogs wandered the courtyard. They looked like German Shepherds except they were bigger and leaner. Without a doubt, they were wolves. And as if to confirm his suspicion, they threw back their heads, first one then the rest, and howled with a wail that conjured northern forests and wastes of ice.

It was like a dream.

The ancient human terror of wolves kindled in his heart. They were beautiful in their indolent power. Dudley said he kept them, the sons of the land, a kind of dog. He fed them and they would follow him, savage to anyone Dudley set them on. Tristan knew they would bring him down at Dudley's command, as if he was a deer. He wouldn't be going down into that way.

❧

TRISTAN MADE HIS WAY BACK TO THE FRENCH DOORS. DUDLEY AND Sorcha might hear him come in, but he couldn't stay on the roof. It was darker now, and the wind was stronger. He might not survive another walk across the slates and he could not descend into the courtyard with the wolves down there. He would have to come this way. He smashed the glass with his boot heel then reached in and undid the catch. Stepping inside, he stood in Sorcha's ritual room and started at the magic symbols. Though he didn't believe in such things, still, he shuddered.

A door led through to Sorcha's bedroom. The door was unlocked and Tristan carefully opened it, listened, heard nothing, and stepped through.

Sorcha's room was as he remembered it. The golden amulet still sat on the table by the bed but the black key that had lain beside it was now gone.

Through sheer bad luck, someone was coming up the steps. He glanced round and saw that the Gothic decor of Sorcha's bedroom lent itself to hiding. The long full length satin red drapes reached the floor all round the room, so he slipped behind those and waited.

When she entered, Sorcha was not alone. She was talking to some-one, and she was speaking English. At first that made Tristan think that it wasn't Dudley but he heard the Irishman's familiar tones. So they didn't speak Irish all the time. That was just for show: more of her trickery. There was nothing about Sorcha that he could trust.

"Is everything nearly ready?" Sorcha said.

"Yes." Dudley replied. "It's all ready. We just need to get them into position. Tristan's in the attic and Iseult is in the Tower."

"We need to get Gwyn to attack Tristan when Iseult can see, so she goes to defend Tristan..."

"... and her lovelorn heart makes her stab her husband in the back." Dudley laughed. "Then she'll be a murderess."

There was a sound of fumbling fingers near the drape. "Got it," Sorcha said. "Let's go back and get Gwyn. Time to lead him to Tristan. Then we get Iseult to see the fight and intervene."

"How are we going to dispose of the bodies?" Dudley said.

Sorcha laughed. "There are so many ways." She sounded amused. "We could feed them to the wolves, throw them into the bog, or just lock them in a room and they'd never be found. After all nobody will be looking for them. Nobody knows they're here apart from themselves."

"I hope Iseult hasn't jumped off the Banshee Tower."

Sorcha said, "She's not so brave, or desperate. Besides, she wants her Tristan. She wouldn't kill herself."

"It's not as safe as you think. She could lower herself down into the tunnels."

"Down that drop from the tower? I don't think so."

"She might risk it if she was desperate. And you don't want her dead. She's not the thrice damned woman yet," Dudley said.

"She's very close."

Dudley grunted. "Gwyn is wandering around with a knife now, and he's pretty drunk and angry."

Sorcha said, "Have you got the key for the new Tower padlock?"

Dudley muttered.

"Keep it. Time to go."

"So, lead Gwyn to Tristan?"

"Yes, just stage manage it so they're already fighting by the time she arrives with the knife."

He heard their voices diminish as they walked away. Apparently Sorcha had got what she came for and the door clicked closed.

Tristan came out from behind the drapes. He scanned the room to see what she'd come for. The golden amulet was gone.

He stood by the bed, his mind reeling. Iseult was in the ruined tower and they were on their way there. There was no way he could get in front of them, and they had the key so even if he arrived first, he couldn't let her out. The only thing in his favour was that they still thought he was locked in so they would bring Iseult to him. But they planned to bring Gwyn first. He could hang around behind and wait until they arrived with Iseult. Then somehow he'd take her and they'd get away. Somehow.

That plan didn't seem so good. They held all the cards. And then he thought: I need a weapon.

TRISTAN RACKED HIS BRAINS TO THINK OF A WEAPON THAT WOULD even the odds in his favour. The lump hammer in the boot of Gwyn's car, that was the only thing he could think of. A lump hammer versus a knife. It would be a bloody fight.

Waiting until Sorcha and Dudley's voices had disappeared, Tristan made his way out of Sorcha's bedroom and down the stairs, almost tripping in his hurry. He went stealthily, ready to duck out of sight if he spied someone, but there was no one. The place was deserted.

He arrived in the library to see a fire lit. The flames cast unsteady light across the room. The long tables with their black candles were still set out for the imaginary guests. The skull was still on the table next to the Ouija Board. He was about to hurry through the library when the portrait of Lady Amelia caught his eyes. Though she was a murdering bitch, she had no love of the O'Connors, and if Claire was to be believed, Lady Amelia hated Sorcha personally.

Who knows? Maybe it was her he'd seen in the tower window? But she was a ghost and he didn't believe in ghosts.

He aimed for the far door, planning to take the passage that led to the entrance hall and from there out of the big doors to Gwyn's car to get the hammer.

As he walked by, the planchette on the Ouija Board jerked.

There was no doubt about it. It had moved.

Tristan stopped. This must be a trick of the flickering light, but then it moved again. With his own eyes, he saw it shift and heard the scrape of the bone planchette across the card of the board.

"My God," he said. He took a step back.

He stood, hearing his heartbeat in his ears, not turning his head. This was insane. A second went by. Nothing more happened.

He reminded himself that didn't believe in this, then reminded himself that it had happened. He rubbed his eyes.

He had no time to waste. He started off, and it moved again. As he watched, the planchette jerked its way across the board.

"What the hell is happening here?" he said out loud.

Despite himself, his skin prickled and the chill in the room raised goose flesh. Automatically, he glanced at Lady Amelia's portrait, half expecting her eyes to move. The oil painting remained an oil painting — it didn't move. But the planchette on the Ouija Board did. He stood, staring at the thing. If it was spelling out a message, he had missed most of it.

The room grew cold. He stooped and looked under the table for magnets or some other mechanisms but he found nothing. He ran his fingers in a square on the table around the board, just in case there was a micro-fibre pulling the planchette. He even chopped the air above the Ouija Board with his hand and stared up at the wood panelled ceiling and the chandelier. There was no clear way the planchette could be moving, but still it moved.

His world jolted. The dreamlike feeling came over him again as when he'd seen the wolves. He was in a nightmare, struggling to wake while Fate made dead women speak and boards of wood and bone spelled out messages.

As he watched, the planchette went through the same repetitive motions. It was repeating a message. He studied it and mouthed the letters as he watched the bone triangle move to a letter, pause, then move to the next one in an abrupt jerk. He spelled it out in his head. The message was: *I am the thrice damned woman.*

This was crazy. He had to find Iseult and get out of that place. But the Ouija Board's planchette was moving. It was impossible, but.

He cleared his throat. "Can you help me save Iseult?"

The planchette scurried: *Yes.*

Feeling foolish talking to the air, Tristan said, "Who are you?"

The Thrice Damned Woman.

He sighed in irritation. This was wasting his time. He gave it one last chance. "What's your name?"

You know my name.

"No, I don't." He thought the planchette would repeat the Thrice Damned rubbish, but it spelled out: *Amelia.*

He looked at the portrait, still suspecting this was down to Sorcha.

It continued: *I am the Banshee.*

"From the Tower?"

My remains were left there to rot.

"Okay, but how does this help me now?"

I am the witch's enemy.

"Sorcha?"

The American.

Tristan wondered whether they even had Americans when Amelia was around. "So how does that help me and Iseult?"

She plans to make her the Thrice Damned Woman.

"Who? Iseult?" This was the weirdest thing he'd ever done in his life, and he was doing it when he had other urgent things to do. But what if the Banshee was real, and it wanted to aid him if only to hurt Sorcha?

The planchette moved. *She will use her blood for the ritual.*

"What?"

Summon me so I can aid you.

"How to summon you?"

And then he snarled. He'd almost believed this shit, but it was more of Sorcha's trickery. He said out loud, "Seriously, Sorcha, I thought you were subtler than that cheese ball." He snatched the bone planchette and hurled it into the dark corner of the Library.

Sorcha didn't even know he was there.

He had to get a weapon and then get Iseult. This had just delayed things.

❧

TRISTAN LEFT THE LIBRARY, HEAD DOWN, HURRYING TO GET THE hammer.

A figure wearing a long dark cloak with the hood up, face in shadows, stood in the corridor. He stepped back, paused. "Okay, who's this?"

With a scream, the figure launched itself at him. It hit him but he did not stumble back - it was light, and the hood came down revealing Claire's face twisting with hate.

Pinning her arms, he said, "Jesus, Claire? What the hell are you doing?"

She tried to rake him with her fingernails, shrieking and trying again and again to hurt him. He fended her off easily. He had one hand on each of her skinny wrists and held her kicking at him like an imprisoned fiend.

"When you get drunk on wine and lapse into lechery, do not blame the wine; the lust was in your heart before you drank the first drop!"

"Calm down, Claire. Where is Iseult? Have you seen her?"

"Adulterer, breaker of Christ's law!" She screamed.

He had to grip her tighter just to hold her in place. He muttered, "I think you'll find that Christ forgave the woman taken in adultery."

"Then my Lord can forgive what I can not." All the fight went out of her like a paper bag emptying of air. She bowed her head and began to weep. "He is so much greater than I."

Tristan shook his head. This woman truly was a nut job. He let go of her wrists and her hands fell to her side. He studied her. Where did she even get that cloak? She looked like an extra from a Dennis Wheatley movie.

"Claire..." He felt foolish saying it. "I wanted to ask you. I think I saw someone at the tower window?"

She snapped her head up and blinked. "The Banshee Tower?"

He nodded. "Have you felt anything? You know you said about Lady Amelia."

Claire cocked her head. "So now you believe? Now you've seen her, you believe. But I believed without seeing her. I had faith."

"What does she want?"

"You believe!"

"I didn't say that. But humour me."

"She knows my Lady Sorcha and I will soon summon her and defeat her. We wait for night. Then we will call her and trap her inside a magic circle and blow her out like she was a candle flame." She clicked her thumb and forefinger to emphasise her point.

What if this banshee was real? He'd seen the Ouija Board move and seen that face at the window. Lady Amelia's ghost had even promised to aid him, but what could a ghost do?

Could he trust Claire either? No, and neither could he trust Gwyn. Tristan knew it was only him who could save Iseult now.

As if reading his thoughts, Claire said, "Who's side are you on, Tristan? The banshee's or Lady Sorcha's? And mine." She smiled her weird smile.

The shock of her jumping at him wearing that cloak had driven everything from his mind, but now he urgently remembered: "Where's Iseult? Have you seen her?"

Claire gave a smug laugh. "You would want to know that, wouldn't you?" She scratched her cheek. "But I suppose it does speak for you. You've seduced her but not abandoned her. How gallant. I didn't think men really stuck with women once they'd had their way."

"Have you seen her?" He insisted.

She nodded rapidly.

He stepped forward. "Where?"

She giggled. "I shan't tell you."

"Is she in the tower?"

"I shall not tell you!"

He snatched her hand and held it. Her eyes widened in fright. "Bully!" she spat, but he had her tight.

"Tell me where Iseult is."

"No."

His hand balled into a fist.

She glanced down at it. "So you will beat it out of me, will you?"

His jaw tightened. Then he shook his head. He let go of her. Had seriously considered punching a crazy old woman? He sighed heavily.

"Penny for them," Claire said.

He wasn't going to hit her and if she wouldn't tell him, Claire would have to keep her secrets. "Never mind," he said.

Behind him, Claire called. "Sorcha's told me all about you. You can't escape your fate. The legend will have blood."

He walked away, leaving Claire standing talking to herself. Then he looked back and saw that the hem of her cloak was dirty and that it had a rip in it — a clean cut like a knife would make, or a piece of glass. He suddenly knew where she'd been: she'd been at the Banshee Tower. Maybe they'd locked Iseult in there.

But they would be waiting for him. He couldn't go unarmed. He had to get the hammer first.

❦

Tristan made his way to the Entrance Hall. The front door was barred and as cautiously as he could, he dragged back the iron bar and swung the great door inwards with a creak. It was deepest night and the dark hung heavy its sombre glory. The marsh air hit his face like the breath of a ghost.

Tristan knew where Gwyn's car was and he hurried round to where he had placed the hammer back in the boot.

He looked over his shoulder to make sure he wasn't being followed. Nothing. The wind sighed like a jilted lover. The rain fell soft and unfriendly.

The boot of the car wasn't locked but that wasn't suspicious. He hadn't locked it when he returned the hammer. Tristan yanked open the boot and looked in. All the other tools were present, just as he left them, but the lump hammer was gone, and the screwdriver, and, in fact, anything that could be used as a weapon. Either Gwyn had come and removed them — which seemed unlikely, or Dudley had followed him after he'd seen him with the hammer and retrieved the tools from Gwyn's car, stashing them somewhere.

Without the key to the tower padlock, or the hammer, Tristan would have to find some other way to open the door and save Iseult. Maybe he could find a stone, a brick or a boulder to smash the padlock.

He'd wasted too much time already. Soon Sorcha would have the story set up and the actors in place ready for Tristan to enter and play his part. He had to get there before that.

Tristan figured out the quickest way from where he was to the tower. He ran into the entrance hall. There was the armchair Iseult had sat on before things went to hell and the table with the magazine she'd read. He glanced up to the top of the stairs. The suit of armour stood there. He paused. Hanging from the belt of the suit of armour was the sword. Of course. That would be his weapon. He would play paper, scissors, rock and he would have the sword and Gwyn would have the knife. He didn't want to fight Gwyn, and maybe the sight of the sword would sober Gwyn and they could talk. If he could only make Gwyn see how they were being manipulated, there was a chance.

Tristan ran up the stairs and drew the sword from its scabbard.

Once again, he felt its weight, once again he tested its edge. It was sharp. If he carried a naked sword around, he would cut himself so he undid the belt around the suit of armour and transferred it to himself. He stood at the top of the staircase with a sword and scabbard. He felt like King Arthur, or maybe Sir Lancelot of the Lake. Also attached to the sword belt was the knife. He remembered that the knife was silver and soft and carried no edge. That would be no use.

He looked at the dagger sheath and tried to work out how to take it off the belt, but he couldn't so he took the dagger with him as well.

UNSOUND MINDS

Gwyn looked at the empty glass on the kitchen table. He gripped it, threw his head back and sucked out the last drops.

He couldn't believe what he'd done. He'd struck his wife. He'd never hit a woman. Ever. Especially one he loved so much.

Gwyn's anger turned to a throbbing grief. He'd fucked up his whole life. It was only going into the army as a youth that had kept him out of prison. When he'd come out of the military, he'd got a job managing pubs, moving as a relief manager from pub to pub. That had suited him — a cowboy, lonesome on the trail. And then he'd met Iseult, and he'd loved her long before she knew it.

It chewed him up she lived with that piece of shit. He knew that Gareth beat her. He'd thought of saying something when he was alone with her, but it was none of his business. Instead, he'd bantered and pretended his feelings didn't exist. Of course, he knew she couldn't love him. He was old and ugly, and she was so beautiful, slender and fair as a Celtic princess.

Then that night when fuck-face Gareth had come in angry and spitting. Gwyn told him to watch his mouth, but the punk had snarled, "Mind your own fucking business, grandpa." He snapped at

Iseult. "You're coming home now. My shirts are dirty and the place is a tip."

Iseult followed him out, head down. Everyone in the bar stared as they went. Gwyn waited: what business was it of his? He drummed his fingers on the bar. The staff watched him. He shouldn't go after them.

But if he didn't, the story would repeat itself, and she'd come in tomorrow, the bruises covered in concealer. Or if Gareth hit her really bad, maybe she'd take a few days off sick then come in Saturday, telling the story about how she walked into a door. Again. Laughing and saying, "Clumsy me!" Again.

Fuck it. He wasn't even supposed to love her.

Gwyn had eyed the whisky. That might help. That might take his mind off things. He pursed his lips. He blew out air. He rubbed his chin and had said to Alun, "I'm stepping out for a bit."

Alun was polishing glasses with a tea-towel. He frowned. "You okay, boss?"

"Sure. Sure. Won't be long. You okay keeping an eye here?"

"Yeah, of course. No probs."

Gwyn went out of the White Ox, round the back where his old van was parked. He got in the van and followed them home. He knew where Iseult lived. He'd given her a lift once.

Gwyn drove fast. He got there as they arrived.

Gareth pulled up his bike outside their scabby council house and dragged Iseult by the wrist. She was crying, and Gwyn saw neighbours' curtains twitch, but no one came to help, not one even shouted for Gareth to stop.

At the door, Gareth gave Iseult the back of his hand. She put her arms up to protect herself. Gareth grabbed her forearm and yanked her inside the house.

Gwyn parked outside and waited. His blood was on fire. He debated whether to go in or drive back to the White Ox because if he went in there, he would do something extreme, something fatal, something a judge wouldn't forgive. They would talk about his distinguished military record. They would mention he was protecting a woman from a man twice her size. But they'd still send him down. Because Gwyn wouldn't stop. He always finished a job.

He thought he should turn his back and leave. He was going to spend the rest of his life in jail, all because of that shitbag. The guy wouldn't kill Iseult, he'd just rough her up. For a second, Gwyn thought maybe he'd call the cops, but the cops didn't give a shit about a domestic on this council estate. They'd take their time if they came at all.

Gwyn turned off the engine and got out.

He stood looking into the windows. The lights were on downstairs. He rang the bell. No one heard it; certainly, no one answered, so he tried the door and found it open.

Threadbare carpet, cheap furniture, a huge TV, an Xbox controller, dirty clothes on the floor and chairs, empty beer cans. Iseult was there. Gareth was there.

Gareth was on the floor, sprawled, arm out. He was bleeding heavily.

He made a noise, not like talking, not like laughing, but gasping, air coming out the wrong holes. Iseult had plunged a kitchen knife into his chest. Not once or twice but again and again in a frenzy. Then she turned, blonde hair hanging down, eyes red from crying, bruises flowering on her face and collar bone, and the knife in her fist, blade reddened, blood flowing down the handle over her fingers, sticky and bright, all along her hand, dripping onto her wrist, staining her blue floral dress.

She saw Gwyn, met his eyes, and looked at Gareth's still twitching form.

Gwyn said, "We'll sort it out."

Iseult was terrified. She looked at him, face as white as a ghost. She thought he'd tell the cops, but he never would.

Gwyn had killed men who had more rights on life than that fucker, men who were good husbands and sons, just enemy. Enemy is all they were. Other times they might have done training together, might have had a laugh, might have even been friends. He felt sorry for some of those, those young men he'd slotted for Queen and Country, but he didn't spare an ounce of regret on the death of that woman-beating fuck.

Gwyn's life was not wholly law-abiding. He knew people who could do things, and he made the body vanish. Nobody came looking for Gareth. It seemed he had few friends and his family were all in jail or off their heads on drugs.

Afterwards, Iseult stuck with Gwyn. She cooked for him. They went to the pictures. At first, he thought it was out of indebtedness, but then one night she told him she loved him, and he thought he'd finally stepped from under the dark star that had cursed his life.

Just goes to show how wrong you can be.

GWYN PICKED UP THE KNIFE. HE WALKED UNHEEDING THROUGH Tullabeg castle to its main door and into the grey light of late afternoon. He strode along the low tarmac road that led through the Bog of Allen. Walls of mist rose on either side. At one point, near the ruined chapel, he sat, listening to the sucking of the marsh and the running water below the surface. Mournful birds called.

Full night came. It stole up slowly, so he hardly recognised its coming. When he could only see a few yards in front of him, he stepped out into the bog.

Gwyn went up to his calves with the first step, sloshing among the sedge. He dragged up his feet and splashed through the pools. With the next step, he went to his knees. He had planned to get far out and slice open his throat.

But the wetland would take care of everything. The bog, that ancient undertaker, would take him under as she had many before him. The wetland would hold him and preserve him, face-down, never found, a mystery, a lost man unmourned.

Iseult had who she wanted, and it wasn't him.

Gwyn needed no knife to die here. He dropped the blade, and it lay on the black surface of the mire, glinting in the moss. Another step and he was waist-deep. The cold seeped through him. He would die of hypothermia. He would drown. His breath would bubble away. If he could only fall.

The chill stole his sense, and he lapsed into a dream state. The peat held him upright, chest-deep, head lolling.

Dudley must have followed his tracks. The iron grip of the Irishman dragged him free of the sucking morass. "Oh, no," Dudley said, "You don't get to kill yourself. We have need of your death ourselves."

REVELATIONS

As Iseult was about to follow Dudley out of the kitchen, Sorcha said, "Gwyn is very drunk now, and he has a knife — the knife I gave you. That makes him very dangerous."

"Why did you give him whiskey?" Iseult said. "I agree that he's dangerous — but you've made it worse. I guess he's been drinking all day now."

Dudley said, "We need to hurry..." He looked at Iseult. "I'm guessing that you want to get out of here?"

"Only if I go with Tristan. Is he safe?"

Dudley nodded. "We've got him somewhere secure. Just come with us, and we'll take you to him, but we need to be careful not to run into Gwyn."

Iseult hesitated. She scanned both of their faces to see whether they might be lying. "And have the police arrived yet? It's been a long time since you rang them, Sorcha."

Sorcha shook her head.

Iseult said, "You didn't really call them, did you?"

Dudley interrupted. "Of course we did." Dudley was taking more of the lead now than he had before. Iseult wondered what this signified. She also realised that she had minimal choice. Every word could be a lie — it probably was, but if she argued with them, they would hide Tristan from her. So she followed.

As they walked down the black and red-tiled corridor, Sorcha said, "You never did tell me how much you owed Gwyn."

Iseult bowed her head. "What I owe Gwyn?" She laughed bitterly. "I seem to have a talent for getting into relationships with violent men. Though, I never believed Gwyn was like that. In the beginning, he was kind. In fact, up until we entered your door." She glanced around. "It's as if something in this place poisoned him."

Sorcha said, "Gwyn isn't without virtue. I understand his sense of duty — his army service."

"Do you really understand, though?" Iseult frowned. "I didn't imagine you feeling a sense of duty or obligation to anyone."

Sorcha looked thoughtful. "That's where you're wrong. I have a deep sense of obligation to my ancestors. The people who lived in this place so long ago. I would never betray them."

Iseult stopped. "What is it that you really want, Sorcha?"

"I told you when you first came."

"The gift of eternal life? I thought you were joking."

"No, I wasn't. My people were destined to live forever."

"Your people? And who exactly are they — the Irish?"

"The Irish, of course. But my true people are of the tribe who inhabited this place — the Faelchon — the Wolf People."

Dudley was watching them as they walked, taking an interest in the conversation. This again was new. Iseult always felt Dudley never listened, was never interested in anything other than what went on in his own strange head.

"My people were murdered", Sorcha said. "Murdered by those who came after them — the Christians."

"I know you hate the Christians — historically, figuratively," said Iseult. "But why have you done this to us?"

"I didn't do any of this to you. You did it to yourselves," Sorcha said. "You were fated to."

Iseult furrowed her brow. "What do you mean we were fated to?"

"You can't escape Fate — especially in a place like Tullabeg. The land has a memory. Buildings have a memory. Our ancestors knew this.

The so-called primitive people knew Fate wrote stories for them, and they played them out again and again."

Iseult said, "Knowing too much about your fate is never a good thing."

Sorcha laughed. "It depends on who you are."

They were walking quickly again. Iseult felt a sudden flash of understanding the Sorcha — sympathy even. She was a faded actress. She guessed once Sorcha had been the talk of the town, and when she was young, everyone wanted her. Her youth had faded, like everyone's youth fades, but for Sorcha, youth was the thing she couldn't live without. She was a narcissist, and her narcissism couldn't tolerate the slow collapse of age. Narcissists are dangerous, and Sorcha was capable of doing anything to stop having to look into herself and realise she had nothing left.

So she'd come here to Tullabeg in search of an illusion, some make-believe magic that would restore her beauty and make people want her again. She'd fled the land of her birth — America — and run away from everything modern to bury herself in a dream in this godforsaken place. But she had had a goal. Even though eternal youth was an illusion, Sorcha would pay any price to get it.

Iseult vowed that for her there would be no more lies. From now, what was in her heart would be visible to all. Whatever crimes she had committed, she would confess. If people would judge her, then let her be judged. She would be no Sorcha, hiding in a web of make-believe.

Iseult bowed her head. "What do I owe Gwyn? Where do I begin? It happened a long time ago in Wales. I was very young at the time. I was working in the White Ox in Haverfordwest. I was in a relationship with a horrible man. I think I was going through my bad boy phase, and boy was he a bad boy. Of course, he drank and womanised and cheated and gambled — I could take that — even expected it. My own upbringing with my father led me to think of myself as worthless and in a strange way when this guy smacked me, it felt like it was only what I deserved."

Sorcha listened, waiting.

Iseult continued. "And then Gwyn came along. He was the new manager of the bar, and he treated me like a real person. I knew he fancied me. And of course, he was older. My friend said I was looking for a father figure — but that wasn't true. Truth is, I took a while to get used to the idea someone wasn't beastly to me all the time."

"And then one night my boyfriend came into the White Ox. He was drunk, and something minor had pissed him off. I think he lost £10 at cards. He spoke to me in his usual manner – what was unusual about it was that Gwyn was there. Gwyn told him to be quiet. This guy was much younger than Gwyn and snarled and turned on him and told him to shut his mouth in mind his business."

"Then what?"

"And then the guy dragged me out of the bar. I thought I was going to get my usual beating. But what was different was that Gwyn followed."

"So Gwyn hurt him?" Sorcha asked.

Iseult shook her head. "No, not at all."

"So, what happened?"

"My boyfriend made me get on the back of his motorbike, and he drove us to the dingy flat we were renting at the time. He dragged me by my hair into the house, kicked open the door and threw me into the living room. I thought he'd beat me, then force himself on me. He'd done it before, and, as I said, this all seemed so normal to me until that night. But I think it was because of the concern in Gwyn's face in the bar. Somehow he'd inspired in me the belief I didn't deserve it. Gareth, that was his name, picked up a beer to slake his thirst before the exercise of hitting me. Then he went to the toilet upstairs, and I went to the kitchen."

Sorcha was standing still now, paying rapt attention. "So is that when Gwyn arrived?"

"No, this wasn't about Gwyn. I went into the kitchen, picked up a knife, and when Gareth came down the stairs unbuttoning his fly, I was waiting for him. He laughed at me and said I wouldn't have the courage to use the knife. And to tell the truth, I was terrified. My hand was shaking, I didn't think I would stab him. I thought me brandishing the knife would scare him — and that he would leave me alone. That's all I wanted — to be left alone."

The light of realisation was dawning in Sorcha's eyes. Quietly she said, "I don't understand why you owe Gwyn so much. I'm guessing that you actually stabbed this guy. But how does Gwyn come into this?"

Iseult's head was down. "Gareth lunged at me, he grabbed my wrist with such force that it made me drop the knife. And then he was going to beat me black and blue. He said he would, and I believed him. He'd done it before but this time I knew would be so much worse. The knife lay on the carpet in the entrance hall. I looked at it. He punched me, and I fell, but I landed near the knife. I saw red."

Iseult was shaking. She put her hand to face. All the old emotions of that night rushed back as if she were reliving the terrible experience. Sorcha put a comforting hand on her shoulder and whispered, "Don't worry, you're fine now. You're safe again."

"Safe? I don't care about being safe. I just want Tristan to get away. Then I'll go back and face Gwyn."

"How badly was he hurt — this man?" Sorcha said.

Iseult shook her head. "You don't understand. He wasn't just hurt. He was dead. I killed him. I murdered him."

"And so did you go to prison? I'm sure that any judge would look leniently on you because you were a victim of domestic violence, and the way the man treated you was abominable."

"No, I didn't go to prison. I didn't go because Gwyn arrived after I'd done it. He came in while I was plunging the knife into the body of the man who was already dead. He took the knife from me. I thought he'd tell the police — that he'd say he had to obey the law. But Gwyn has lived a different life. The things he saw in the army make him think differently to other people. For example, death— murder — whatever you'd call it; was not unusual for him. He came from an organisation where it was normal, even the right thing to do. If someone is going to kill you, you kill them first. I think he actually said that to me that night."

Sorcha nodded. "I see."

Iseult turned to look Sorcha in the eye. "And so that's what I owe Gwyn. I can never be free of him. But now, I don't care if he tells the police and I go to jail. I just want Tristan to be okay."

They stood at the place where the ruined corridor gave way to the more inhabited areas. They had stopped walking as if it was no longer necessary for them to go any further.

Dudley looked at Sorcha, and in English, he said, "She is a murderess."

Dudley said, "Follow me. I'll take you to Tristan."

TRISTAN TIGHTENED THE SWORD BELT UNTIL IT HUNG COMFORTABLY around his hips. Enemies stood between him and Iseult — wolves, Gwyn, Dudley, Sorcha and Claire, but at least now he wasn't unarmed. But, even armed, it made sense not to run into anyone on his way.

From his exploration when he was setting up his sound equipment, he knew there was an entrance into the secret passages from nearby. He moved over to the wood panelled wall and examined it with his finger ends. He rapped on it and heard the hollow noise showed him he hadn't been wrong. Feeling his way along, he came across a catch disguised as part of the light fitting at head height. It clicked as the wooden panel came open.

Tristan switched on the flashlight function of his phone as he made his way through the secret passage up the stairs until he came to a place he recognised. This was the passage that led to the corridor where their bedrooms lay. He inched his way along and saw the secret door hung open.

He stepped onto the hallway and saw the heavy plinth and the stone vase had been kicked over. Whatever had been kept inside the passage, was now out.

His hand went to his sword. He looked around. All was silent. From here it was an easy journey down the corridor until he came to the ruined part of the castle and out onto the roofless part leading to the Banshee Tower.

It was dusk and the moon was rising outside.

He remembered overhearing Dudley and Sorcha. They wanted the blood of the Thrice-Damned-Woman. The three sins were idolatry, and he didn't think Iseult would do that. Adultery, which she was now guilty of and murder. She wasn't a murderess. She was safe until they got her to kill someone. Tristan knew they had planned to get her to stab Gwyn to defend him. But that hadn't happened yet.

Until it happened, Iseult's blood was no good to them. There were two sins yet to commit, though Dudley and Sorcha would be doing their damnedest to bring them about.

Where would they get her to worship an idol? He thought of Sorcha's ritual room, the one he'd got into from the roof.

The moon rode among the clouds. Tristan looked up and saw it was full. He peered down to his left, got onto the slates and tested them with his feet before he inched his way forward.

It was fully dark. Clouds churned above him. In the damp gloom, he found his way to a part of the roof that overlooked the central courtyard. It was vaguely illuminated by lights from the surrounding corridors. He saw the dark shapes of wolves waiting patiently.

Tristan was about to walk further along to the flat roof that gave entrance to Sorcha's Room of Rituals, when he saw movement at the cellar entrance. The wolves flocked to the new shape that climbed up the stairs and howled and snickered in welcome. The figure was taller than a wolf.

It was Dudley.

Tristan dropped as low as he could and waited. He saw the Irishman come out into the grassy courtyard. Dudley did a strange thing — he removed his jacket and his shirt and his trousers until he stood there naked. The light was faint, but Tristan could not be mistaken about what he saw. Dudley was a well muscled man for his age. Tristan never have guessed that someone who looked so shabby and unkempt would be so fit and healthy without his clothes. Dudley threw back his head to stare into the sky right at the full moon. He cried out. A dark covering sprouted over his body and Tristan realised it was hair, not hair — fur. Fur grew on Dudley's back his arms. His fingers, which had always been tipped with those claw-like nails elongated until his arms resembled dogs' forepaws. Dudley fell forward onto his hands and knees. Tristan watched as grey fur covered him completely, his years sharpened and his muscles grew into those of a wolf. And then there was no more man—only a beast.

If Tristan had not seen this with his own eyes, he would never have believed it possible. Everything he'd believed before was unreliable. These things might not be possible in bright city streets in places filled with science and commerce, but in out-of-the-way places like Tullabeg, in places that had never forgotten the old ways, things older than roads and houses held sway.

Tristan felt a nightmare held him, or a psychosis, but he wasn't sleeping, and he wasn't crazy, and the woman he loved was in danger in the power of these people. Horror mounted as he realised the threat these things posed to him and Iseult — to Gwyn and Claire too. When Dudley asked Sorcha how they would dispose of the bodies, he'd been serious. Tristan gripped his sword hilt.

If he couldn't trust rationality and science any more he would have to use Sorcha's own methods against them. Maybe, in this upside down world of witchcraft and werewolves, he really could call the banshee to help him.

DUDLEY WALKED OFF AHEAD. ISEULT HESITATED. COULD SHE TRUST Dudley? But then what choice did she have. Sorcha and Dudley were in charge here. Maybe they really did have Tristan safe. "Where is he?"

"In the tower."

"The Banshee Tower?"

Dudley sniggered. "So called."

"Why there?"

Dudley paused. He rubbed his head as if trying to remember the explanation. "Well, Sorcha said..." Then he winked.

"I don't understand you. Just show me."

Dudley gestured. "Of course, my princess."

Iseult's heart banged. "Cut the quips. I'm not in the mood, Dudley. Just show me where he is."

"You've been there before."

She nodded.

His smile grew broader. "Then let's go." He swept his hand in a gesture she should proceed. They left Sorcha and went down the dilapidated corridor, she hurrying, he strolling. She looked back. "Please, hurry."

The Irishman gave a lopsided grin. "You don't need me, fair Iseult. You know the way to your tryst. I'll be behind right you."

Iseult got to the tower door and saw again the shiny new padlock securing the door. It was afternoon but it hadn't been properly light all day because of the weather.

Dudley was ten paces behind. "You locked him in?" she said.

Dudley nodded. "For his own safety. Obviously."

Iseult frowned. It made sense, but still, to lock him in. "Does he have a key?"

Dudley shook his head. He fumbled in the pocket of his tweed trousers. He dragged out the key like the little boy producing a plum. "I have the key." He waggled it.

"Open the lock please."

Dudley was by her shoulder now. She cleared her throat to yell for Tristan, but Dudley laid his long hand on her back. "Don't be yelling. We wouldn't want to draw attention to where we are. You never know who's listening."

Iseult guessed she meant Gwyn. Or maybe Claire. She'd been hanging round here. Maybe she had seen them bringing Tristan here and had already reported back to Gwyn. With her Christian morals and the Ten Commandments, she probably saw it as her duty. A pang of fear rose from Iseult's stomach to her throat: Gwyn with a knife. The door wouldn't hold him back until the police came. She wasn't worried about herself, but Tristan. She trembled. "Okay."

Dudley took his time opening the lock. He fiddled with the key. Tension ate her up. He sniggered, "Little keys, not good for my big hands." He looked at her and smirked.

Iseult stared at his hands. His fingers were strangely long, and the nails were yellow and hard like an old man's toes, or a beast's claws. "Hurry," she said.

"Just a second now."

"Are you sure he's in here?"

"Of course. Would I lie to you?" He was really close to her. He stank. He must never wash. He had the aroma of a wet dog. She didn't know how Sorcha could let him into bed with her, then she remembered that she didn't.

With a click the padlock came open. Taking his time, Dudley unclasped it. He dragged the door open with a scraping noise.

The abandoned smell of the place attacked her. It stunk of pigeon shit and rot. She heard the flutter high above as birds flew off. She took a step inside into the gloom. It was five degrees cooler than the outside. "Tristan?" She said quietly, not wanting to draw attention — not wanting Gwyn to hear them. She couldn't see him.

Dudley was shaking his head looking at the scrape marks on the floor. "Need to take a quarter inch off the bottom of that door."

It was silent in the tower. Was he really here? She peered up but her eyes weren't used to the dark. She saw the grey sky through the broken roof. Nothing moved. She hung back. "Tristan?" she called up in a half whisper. She didn't believe Tristan was there. She turned round questioningly.

Dudley was at her shoulder. "He's up there, near the top."

Still she lingered at the threshold. Something was wrong. Uncertainty grew in her like a vine. Was he asleep? Was he injured? The first seemed impossible.

She felt Dudley's breath on her neck. She stepped away from him in distaste and she was inside the door. With his long hands, Dudley shoved her and slammed the door shut.

❧ 19 ☙

A BONE

laire stood outside the Banshee Tower that now held both Iseult and the evil Lady Amelia. It was still afternoon.

Amelia and Iseult were well suited in their sins.

Claire had stood out of sight when Dudley pushed Iseult in and locked the door. It was none of her business what they did with that little sinner. She was here to defeat the banshee.

She waited lost in reverie and didn't hear Sorcha until the witch was upon her. Claire jumped, startled, then her face broke into a beaming smile.

"My Lady," she said genuflecting.

"Stand straight, Claire." Sorcha narrowed her eyes. "Listen carefully, it's almost time."

Claire cocked her head in what she thought was a pleasing way. She'd done that with her mother. Mummy always rewarded her with a pat or stroke and sometimes a biscuit. She simpered, "How may I help?" Her heart swelled with love for this lady with her blue eyes and black eye shadow — a little too heavily applied for Claire's taste, though she could forgive anything of Sorcha. Sorcha was the only one who'd ever believed in her. The warmth of Sorcha's regard made her swoon and put out her hand to the wall.

Sorcha frowned. "Are you all right, Claire?"

Claire nodded. "Yes, my lady."

Sorcha shook her head, and Claire thought she would tell her off again for calling her "My Lady," but she was indeed a lady. After doctors and vicars and husbands — well, only one husband — had doubted her, called her crazy. Called her— Claire — crazy when she was the most clear-sighted of them all. She was a Christian Psychic who saw through the veil between this life and the next like an astronaut sees through space dust. She was worth something. Sorcha saw that. Lady Sorcha, the only one who ever had.

Sorcha cleared her throat. "Claire."

Her own name came as if from miles away. Claire's head had got noisier since coming to the castle. Also, since she stopped taking that nasty clozapine. Claire strained to sweep away stray thoughts that clung like cobwebs around the memories of the dead. Many poor lost spirits haunted here: in Sorcha's magic room the druids, the greenwood men with their old Irish words. So old. And the bones of the grey wolves. Of course, like she'd told Tristan. Her mouth wrinkled at the name. That finely muscled man wouldn't even look at her, not even if she took her clothes off. She had wanted to take her clothes off in front of him and point between her legs and say, "Here — a real woman!" Not that thin little bitch he lusted after that he had fucked. Oops. That was a bad word. She didn't show Tristan her lady space because she knew he would humiliate her by refusing her like they all did. She spat on the ground.

"Claire?" Sorcha's azure eyes filled with concern.

"A Christian Psychic. Yes." Claire nodded. She needed to please. Priests and doctors and husbands and naked young men with their hard muscles — they had all rejected her, but not My Lady Sorcha. She believed.

"So, you are a Christian Psychic, and what do you want most in the world?"

Claire thought. She wouldn't say that.

Sorcha peered at her.

"To lead all lost souls to the light," she volunteered.

"And?" Sorcha was patient. She loved her for it. She reached out and stroked her arm, and Sorcha let her do it.

"And?" Claire forced a smile. She struggled to understand. Something was wanting.

"What else do you want?"

Aha! It dawned on her. She slitted her eyes and tightened her mouth. "To drive out evil spirits."

"Yes, and if I summon the banshee, the most evil of all of them, you will finish her? You will do your part?"

"Oh yes, My Lady Sorcha."

"And how can we destroy her?"

"With blood?" It was half a question, but Sorcha's smile told her she'd got the answer right. She almost clapped.

"Whose blood?"

"The Blood of the Thrice Damned Woman." The name was a charm, a magic spell. The words made her feel dreamy.

Lady Amelia shifted into sight through the Tower wall. She watched them from the spirit world. Claire knew her now. She waggled her finger at the ghost in warning. Her time would soon be up.

Sorcha sighed. "That's right Claire." Following Claire's gaze, she said, "Who are you smiling at?"

"Her." Claire pointed. "Her."

Sorcha nodded like she understood. "And we must kill her."

"Well, drive her out. She's already dead. Sorry to correct you, Lady Sorcha."

"Drive her out, yes."

Claire worried that Sorcha was growing cross with her. She often made people cross. She put her finger hard to her lip to signal Lady Amelia to be quiet. Stop babbling, bitch!

Sorcha said, "Come with me now."

"And leave the Tower? What if she gets out?"

"Who?"

"The banshee."

Sorcha shook her head and sighed. "She won't get out. Come with me to the tunnels."

Claire's heart fluttered. She tightened her fingers. "But wolves hunt there, and now something bigger than a wolf — something that follows her." She pointed at the pale moon, visible in daytime between the vaporous clouds, flying full and high behind the Banshee Tower, waiting for the night and her time to shine.

"No, Claire. He follows me. And don't worry about the wolves. They won't hurt you while you do what I say."

"Do what you say?"

"No need to repeat what I say, Claire, you're not a parrot."

"Not a parr—." Claire clamped her lips before they finished the sentence.

Sorcha reached and stroked Claire's shoulder. Claire wanted to purr like a cat. Sorcha's affection made her warm inside. No one had ever been kind to her before like this. Not since mummy and then she'd died.

"Claire, before we kill the banshee, I need you to help me with something else."

Claire's eyes were bright. "What?"

"Remember the druid in the amulet?"

"Yes, but he was too far away to talk."

Sorcha smiled. "You are the most talented psychic I've met. You are the only one who can reach him — speak to him and ask him."

"Ask them what?"

"He has the secret I want, what I've always wanted, but I must shed the blood of the Thrice Damned Woman. That is the only material base strong enough because he is so attenuated, so far in the past."

Claire blinked.

Sorcha said, "Do you know what a material base is?"

"No."

"When I evoke a spirit, it needs a substance from which to materialise. Sometimes incense is enough, but for the druids who are so old and so far removed from us, I need the strongest material possible. I stumbled across the power of the Thrice Damned Woman when I was researching into Amelia Morton."

"With whom the kings of the earth have committed fornication, and the inhabitants of the earth have been made drunk with the wine of her fornication."

"Just so."

"Revelations 17:2."

"Claire, it's essential you do what I say. You will be my scryer. I will conduct the invocation, but until he materialises, only you will know he's there. You must report what he's saying and help me out with some other things."

"Like getting the blood of the Thrice Damned Woman?"

"Yes."

"With a knife?"

"With a ritual athame — a knife, yes."

"Lots of blood?"

Sorcha pursed her lips.

Claire said, "And then we'll summon the banshee because she is evil and that is my true role. I will help you with this druid, Lady Sorcha, but then we must destroy the banshee and all evil spirits in this place."

"That's fine. But first I need you to fetch Iseult to where I'm going to show you." Sorcha studied Claire. The psychic's face gleamed with sweat. She didn't feel well. It was all the excitement of being believed.

Sorcha gently took her hand. "I will show you the place you need to bring Iseult. Yes?"

Claire nodded. "Yes."

"Let's go."

As they walked, Claire said, "But I won't kill her. I won't break the Sixth Commandment."

"No," Sorcha said. "Of course not."

❧

CLAIRE FOLLOWED SORCHA DOWN THROUGH THE CASTLE. THEY entered the Courtyard, and anxiety gripped Claire's tiny heart. Beasts were there; wolves, eight or nine of them. They stood up when Sorcha entered. Claire gasped and put her hand to her mouth. Sorcha reached back and snatched her wrist, yanking her along. "They won't hurt you while you're with me."

But there was something else here. Claire sensed it. Something big.

It was Dudley but not as a man. He was close in the shadows, but she couldn't see him.

Sorcha led her to the Generator Room. The noisy machine pumped out a stink of smoke and petroleum. There was a set of stairs in the corner, leading down.

"Down there?" Claire said.

Sorcha nodded. Claire held back. Sorcha grasped her wrist and dragged her down into the tunnels. They were dimly lit with electric bulbs. The ground was muddy and was spoiling the shoes she bought in British Home Stores. But Sorcha didn't let go. "Remember the route, Claire. Through the generator room. Down the steps, left-hand tunnel. It's important."

Claire looked around the tunnel. She saw clumps of vegetation here, a mark on the wall that looked like cheese there, and a big stone she tripped over that had a line of quartz running through it. She would remember the way.

Then Sorcha came to a big old door. She took out her black key and turned it in the lock.

The power of the room hit Claire like an ocean wave. It was ancient and un-Christian. She stared with horror at the stone god that sat in the centre of the cave. He came from before Jesus. He knew nothing about Jesus. He sat there in stone, waiting to be fed salt and fire. She hesitated at the cave entrance, one hand on the old door.

"Come in, Claire." Sorcha's tone was sharp.

Claire shuffled forward. This place frightened her.

"Do you remember the way from here to the Banshee Tower?"

Claire bowed her head. "Yes, milady."

"And can I trust you to bring Iseult here, when it's time?"

"Yes, milady."

Sorcha placed the golden amulet that held the druid's spirit in an alcove, then she turned. "Let's go back."

Claire was pleased to leave that place. In the Courtyard amid the knee-high grass, the wolf-man bared his teeth from the shadows, and Claire hurried into the castle snatching at Lady Sorcha's dress for comfort and safety.

TRISTAN STOOD ON THE ROOF WATCHING THE WOLF DUDLEY ACCEPT the greeting of his pack in the Courtyard. The wolves reared up to lick the werewolf's muzzle and wove around his legs as if he was their father.

His only hope was to escape with Iseult and avoid running into the werewolf and his pack. Tristan still thought Iseult was in the Banshee Tower. The problem was getting there safely. He had the sword, but there was no point running into people he could avoid. He could get into the secret passages through the French windows that led to the Ritual Room.

Tristan made his way over the roof to the French windows he'd broken before and let himself into the Room of Rituals.

The air of sorcery was heavy on the room.

He closed his eyes. "Lady Amelia, I don't believe in you, but I could sure use your help right now."

It was night. The only light came from the full moon outside. The room felt drenched in all the magic Sorcha had conjured there over the years and arcane symbols glared at him from the walls, made uncanny by the baleful moonlight. Ritual implements lay on the top of the black altar: wand, dagger, bowl and cup —more craziness. Crazier that he almost believed it.

The odour of the cloying scent of flowers came from nowhere.

The air chilled and his breath was suddenly visible. He shivered. Something supernatural was happening. He looked to his left and, in the moonlight, saw a shape materialise. The face and limbs were of wreathing smoke.

The smoke took on a woman's shape. Its eyes were holes and its mouth a jagged line. The mouth opened, and it screamed. The howl echoed through his mind, penetrating every room, every tower, every attic, every dungeon of the Castle. Tristan put his hands over his ears and stepped back in horror. The howl of the banshee.

The thing did not move. He half expected it to attack him, but it didn't. And then it beckoned him to come closer. He looked at it and studied its face and saw it bore a resemblance to Lady Amelia Morton's portrait. Something was happening — her power was growing. Before she'd only been able to move a Ouija Board, now she could appear before him.

The banshee spoke in a murmur like whispers of grass in the wind. He heard its voice half in his mind and half through his ears. He listened to it like a voice in a dream. The Banshee told him that Sorcha was planning a ritual and that Iseult was in great danger.

The banshee's voice came again, "If you wish to save your love – you must summon me."

"But how do I do that?"

The figure writhed in silence. He realised it was struggling to stay as if it had nearly used all its power to remain for as long as it had.

"How do I do that?" He repeated.

The banshee's figure grew harder to see.

"How?"

He heard its fading answer, "Beckon me with my finger bone."

"What does that mean?"

But the banshee had vanished.

☙❧

GWYN SAT IN THE LIBRARY BY THE FIRE. DUDLEY HAD BROUGHT HIM some dry clothes after he pulled him out of the bog. The flames warmed his face. Dudley had also given him the hunting knife back, and it sat on the mahogany table beside the armchair. Gwyn took a slug of the whiskey Dudley had also provided. Dudley then left on some errand of his own.

"I'm being treated like a prince," Gwyn muttered to the air. "Wonder what they want?"

Gwyn looked at the long wooden table upon which still lay the black candles, the old skull and the Ouija Board. He noticed the bone planchette was missing and located it with a glance to the corner of the room. He raised a glass to the portrait of Lady Amelia Morton. "Did you do that, you old bitch? In a fit of rage because no one was listening to you?" He took another deep draught of whiskey, and the liquid seared his throat. Gwyn wiped his mouth with the back of his hand. You'd think I'd be used to whiskey after so many years of practice.

He coughed. His chest felt wheezy. He might be coming down with double pneumonia, but so what? Without Iseult, he wanted to die anyway. He would have done it before in the bog if Dudley hadn't rescued him.

Dudley never struck him as the merciful kind so he must need him for something. Gwyn studied his fingers wrapped around the tumbler while the whiskey reflected a thousand flames in its golden heart. Dudley had saved him because Dudley wanted him to kill Tristan. Gwyn laughed bitterly — that seemed to be the only time anyone wanted him: when there was a killing to be done.

He swirled the glass. But why the fuck did Dudley want Tristan dead? Then it dawned on him. Dudley wanted Tristan dead because Tristan had fucked Sorcha. That's what it all boils down to. He laughed out loud.

We're jealous little monkeys and all our motivations are the same as our jungle ancestors. Dress it up with civilization but the only things that motivate us are lust, jealousy and terror.

Gwyn put down the whiskey glass and took up the dagger: a fine hunting knife. He rubbed his thumb gently along the edge. It was sharp.

If he couldn't manage to cut his own throat, he'd have to cut someone else's.

Someone came in. Gwyn thought it would be Dudley, but it was Sorcha.

"Where's your husband?" he said.

"Dudley?"

"You got more than one?"

She gave a fake laugh. "No. Dudley's otherwise occupied."

"Sounds serious."

She sat down. "Listen, Gwyn." She glanced at the knife.

"I'm listening."

"Want more whiskey?"

He shook his head. "I think I've had enough. Specially if I'm going to have a rumble with my wife's boyfriend. You said you knew where he was."

She studied her hands. "I knew. But he's got out. We locked him in somewhere so you could go get him."

"Very kind of you." He gave her an even stare.

"But he's resourceful."

"Yeah. Tricky. Turns out he's trickier than any of us thought."

"He got out. But I think I know where he'll be."

"Oh yeah? Do tell." Gwyn cocked his head and made to listen.

"I think he'll go to the ruined tower."

"The Banshee Tower?"

"As you call it. Yes."

"Why would he do that?"

"Because Iseult's there."

"This gets curiouser and curiouser." Gwyn shook his head. "And why the fuck would Iseult be in the Banshee Tower?" He turned the knife hilt over in his hand.

Sorcha pushed her chair back. He saw her glance at the door. She was scared of him and the knife. Good. "So?" he said.

"I wanted to keep her safe from you."

Gwyn stared at her. Maybe what she said was true; then suspicion: his old soldier sense told him he shouldn't trust a word this sly bitch said. "You're such a generous and kind soul, Sorcha. Who would have guessed?"

She frowned.

"If you wanted to keep Iseult safe from me, how come you just told me where she is?"

Sorcha waved down Gwyn's anger. "Gwyn, things changed. I didn't think he'd get out. Now, I'm worried he'll hurt Iseult. You have to stop him."

"The only person you're worried about Sorcha is you." He stood. "But, anyway," he said. "Looks like I've got an appointment."

He reached out and picked up the hunting knife from the table. It was a lovely sharp weapon. It would do nicely.

❦

Tristan pondered the banshee's words: *beckon me with my finger bone*. What the hell did that mean? Was it a riddle? Did it symbolise something? A flash of insight hit him. It wasn't a riddle at all. He needed to get the banshee's finger bone to summon her. And the bones at the top of the Banshee Tower were those of Lady Amelia Morton. From the rip in Claire's cloak, he guessed that Iseult was in the tower too.

He took the secret passage from Sorcha's room. He risked turning his phone on to give light. He reached the library and through the secret eyeholes, saw Gwyn sitting by the fire twisting a whiskey glass in his hand. A knife lay on the table. Gwyn must be waiting for Iseult, and because he had the knife, Tristan feared the worst. He hadn't thought Gwyn would ever harm her. But he was so drunk now — so unpredictable.

The only hopeful thing was that Gwyn was still sitting there and, for their own reasons, Sorcha and Dudley were keeping Iseult from him.

He got up to the bedroom floor via the secret passage and then came out into the corridor outside Claire's room. The vase and plinth still lay knocked over on the wooden floor. There was no sign of anything or anybody.

Tristan hurried along the hallway and where it turned to lead to the roofless passage with its dirt and broken glass, drew the sword from his scabbard.

It was dark, but the moon gave enough light so he could see Claire standing by the door, still in her cloak. She looked up when she saw him approach.

"Get away from me, adulterer!" When the moonlight gleamed on the blade, she screamed like a stuck pig. "Help! Help! He plans to murder me!"

She shrunk back from him and pressed herself against the tower door. Tristan covered the ground between them, and he stood in front of her sword in hand. She was still screaming, hands to her face, "Murderer! Help! Lady Sorcha, help!"

The noise pierced his head. "Shut up, Claire. Please shut up."

She didn't.

Above the din of Claire's shrieks, he heard hammering on the door. "Tristan, is that you?" It was Iseult's voice.

He stared at the mildewed door. It was closed. And it now had a new padlock.

Claire stood between him and Iseult. All he needed was to smash the lock with the sword then they'd be free. Then they could escape from this cursed, hellish castle. Claire didn't budge. "Claire get out the way, or I swear to God..."

She sneered. "That you'll hurt me. Well, go on then! I will be a martyr to my God!" She put her hands together in prayer and stared at the sky. The crazy cow was doing his head in. He seized her as gently as he could and made to move her aside, but she stood firm. "You will not get to her. Lady Sorcha has given me the mission of keeping her here until she calls for her."

"In the name of all that is holy, Claire, get out of my way."

Claire stood there, defiant, her face twisted in a snarl, her hands still held forward in prayer.

Tristan yanked her sideways so he could get to the lock. Through gritted teeth, he said, "Iseult, wait a second. I'll smash this lock." Once he did that, he would go up the stairs, dangerous in this dark, but he had to. He'd get the finger bone, but he didn't have a clue what to do with it. He sighed. He had to have faith that the spirit hated Sorcha enough to help them.

Spirits and magic. He remembered Sorcha's trick with the lights and the way she'd closed her bedroom door without touching it that night she'd tried to seduce him. Maybe she really did have magic powers.

The world was turned upside down.

Tristan got the pommel of the sword and reversed it so he could crunch the padlock open. Claire snatched at him with her bony hands, but he pushed her off.

Someone else was running along the corridor towards them. From behind, Tristan heard a roar and pivoted to see Gwyn hurtling down the ruined hall with a knife in his hand.

He glanced at the lock. One blow with the pommel might break it, possibly two.

Gwyn's feet pounded on the wooden floorboards behind.

Claire pushed herself in the way of the padlock. Tristan gritted his teeth and shoved her. He turned. Gwyn was nearly on him.

Claire grabbed the padlock, standing to block him getting to it.

Tristan snarled. With his free hand he went to prise her off, but Gwyn was only feet away. There was no time. With a sigh, he turned.

He hefted the sword into a fighting position, and said, "Gwyn, I don't want to hurt you."

Gwyn stopped. He looked at the sword and then at the knife he held. "Got a bigger one than me then? Maybe that's the attraction."

"Gwyn, Iseult's in here. We need to get her out of here. Sorcha wants her dead, to take her blood for some magic ritual. Dudley has turned into a wolf. We've got to work together."

Gwyn said, "You've lost your mind. Maybe all that sinning has sent you daft." He turned to the psychic who glowered at him. "What do you think, Claire?"

Claire remained silent.

"Please, Gwyn. If you want to fight me afterwards, then fine. But let's get Iseult out of here before they harm her."

Gwyn paused as if studying Tristan and considering his offer. "Nah. I'm going to kill you first. Tell you what though, if you aren't a total coward, why don't you throw down the sword and I'll put this down." He nodded at the hunting knife. "Then we can settle it man to man."

Tristan's grip on the sword was sweaty. He didn't want to hurt Gwyn. He'd done too much to him already taking Iseult from him.

Gwyn's mouth tightened. He slurred his words. "I see. Once a coward, always a coward. Let's do it then." He lunged at Tristan with the hunting knife.

Tristan sidestepped, and the two men circled.

Gwyn lunged again and Tristan levelled the sword. He had a far longer reach with the sword than Gwyn and the knife. There was no way Gwyn could get inside his guard without getting skewered.

But Tristan held back. "Put the knife down, Gwyn. Let's just get Iseult."

Gwyn didn't speak. He jabbed and Tristan fell back.

He lunged and Tristan went back another pace. "Gwyn, I really don't want to hurt you."

"I don't think you can, so rest easy on that score."

Gwyn came forward snarling. This time Tristan nicked him with the sword. It was a light touch, deliberately so. There was no way Gwyn could get close enough to do any harm.

Then Claire leapt forward and shoved Tristan, sending him unbalanced towards Gwyn.

Gwyn looked as surprised as Tristan at Claire's intervention, but he shifted his knife to a stabbing grip and swung down. Tristan lost his balance, and Gwyn, still drunk, missed.

Tristan stumbled and went flat on his face.

Gwuyn gave a roar of triumph.

Tristan turned over and the floor gave way. The rotten floorboards collapsed into the tunnels below. Tristan tumbled down along with the broken wood and and his sword went with him, leaving Gwyn standing at the edge of the hole, staring down.

Gwyn called down as Tristan fell, "I'll give it to you — that's a dramatic way to chicken out of a fight."

20

THE THRICE DAMNED WOMAN

Sorcha appeared from behind them. "What happened?"

Claire turned her head, pleased milady was there. "Tristan came, and he fought Gwyn, but he fell." Claire pointed. She giggled. "I pushed him." She didn't know whether that would please Lady Sorcha or not, but she'd had to do it — she hated him so much.

Gwyn stared down into the hole. Claire saw sweat dripping from his nose. What a dirty beast. And he smelled of whiskey.

Gwyn said, "I hope he's dead." He glanced at Sorcha. "I want to take my wife and leave." He jerked his thumb at the Tower behind. "I believe you've locked her up safe for me." His eyes swam with whiskey. His tone was disrespectful of My Lady. Claire hoped she'd punish him.

Claire shook her head. "Not for you."

Gwyn spun round, his eyes bleary. "Who asked you?"

Claire shook her head again. She stamped her foot. "No! You can't take her."

Gwyn pushed past Claire. "You fucking head case, get out of my way."

Claire rushed to the door and stood with her back against it, her hands behind her back gripping the padlock.

Gwyn sighed. "Get out of the way before I punch you. I don't normally hit women—"

They all say that, Claire thought. Then there would be a <u>but.</u>

"But, I want to get my wife."

Claire laughed. "But!"

He shook his head. "What?"

"You said, but. I knew you would. And you can't have her because we need her blood." Then she realised she shouldn't have said that because Lady Sorcha flashed an angry stare.

Claire put her hand to her mouth. "Oops," she said.

Gwyn took Claire by the shoulders and wrenched her out of the way. She went tottering almost to the big hole Tristan had fallen down. "Sorry," she mouthed at Sorcha as she righted herself, but Sorcha didn't smile. She was angry because Claire had mentioned the blood. Gwyn wasn't supposed to know about that.

Gwyn put the knife blade in the padlock hasp and twisted, trying to break it. It didn't look like he could get enough leverage to snap the lock with the knife blade. He turned to Sorcha. "Do you have the key?"

"Dudley has it."

"Get him to open it."

"She doesn't have to." Claire spat the words. Sorcha put up a hand to silence her. Claire stood abashed and quiet.

"Gwyn," Sorcha shook her head. "She doesn't want to go with you. She's not calling out for you. She knows you're here, but she's not asked for you."

"She asked for Tristan," Claire blurted.

"Exactly," Sorcha said. "She asked for Tristan. She doesn't want to go with you. I want what's best for her."

Gwyn raised an eyebrow. "Now you care about her welfare?" His eyes swam.

"Yes."

"What's this mad bitch saying about blood?" He pointed at Claire in a very rude manner.

"I don't need you now Gwyn. I thought I did, but your wife's revelation made things different. And then I thought you'd be useful to get rid of Tristan, but it seems that Claire did that already by pushing him down the hole."

Claire grinned and clapped. Sorcha was pleased with her. She shouldn't have killed a man, that was against the Commandments, but technically, it was the fall that killed him, not her. She hadn't meant him to go crashing down through the hole, she'd only meant to push him onto Gwyn's knife. Claire shrugged. Maybe the Commandments should be updated, and anyway, what was important was that someone loved her. Jesus had never been very good at listening and comforting her, and she had My Lady Sorcha now. She would swap Jesus for Sorcha.

"Give me the key, Sorcha." Gwyn held his left hand out. In his right he had the knife. His tone was threatening. Little squiggles of anxiety ran up Claire's fingers and made her bird heart flip-flop. Milady was in danger.

Sorcha shook her head.

Gwyn presented the tip of the blade towards Sorcha. "This is how this will work — you're going to get that lock open and let my wife out so we can leave."

"Or?"

He studied her. "Or I'll cut you, woman or not."

"How dare you speak to Lady Sorcha—" Claire began, but Sorcha motioned for her silence.

Sorcha did not look fazed at all. "You don't believe in magic do you, Gwyn?"

"Not magic. Conjuring tricks, sure. Young Tristan was right on that score at least. You're a fraud."

Sorcha continued. "I need the Druid's help with the big magics, but the little ones I can manage on my own."

Gwyn stood defiant. "More bullshit". Claire thought he was going to stab Lady Sorcha. She looked to her left. A piece of masonry the size of a brick lay close by.

"So, you're going to magic me?" Gwyn sneered. "Try it. Then I'll gut you and your lapdog Dudley and take the key."

Lady Sorcha began to say something but Claire stooped, picked up the stone.

Gwyn was too busy sneering at Lady Sorcha that he didn't notice that Claire had raised a big rock up high. He didn't notice her because he never noticed her.

This time he should have.

She smacked hit Gwyn across the back of his head with the masory. The Welshman stumbled forward then crumpled to the ground, blood pouring from his scalp. He made a funny noise and then lay still.

Claire put her hand to her mouth. "Do you think I've killed him?" She blinked rapidly.

Sorcha knelt by Gwyn's unmoving form and took a pulse at his neck. "No," she said.

Claire shrugged. "Well, it wouldn't matter if I had, because he smoked too much anyway and he would have died of that."

"What are we going to do with his body?" Claire whispered pointing at the door. "We don't want her to see. She might not agree to come with us into the tunnels so we can cut her for her blood."

"Normally, I'd ask Dudley."

"But he's with the wolves now."

"Yes."

"We could both move him," Claire volunteered. "Drag him to the hole and throw him in. I'm sure we could manage it between us."

Sorcha laughed. "You really are a wicked old woman."

"No, milady. Good. A Christian Psychic." But she wondered whether she was really still a Christian now she worshipped Lady Sorcha rather than Jesus.

Sorcha moved towards Gwyn's body. "I believe you said that already. Take his legs."

Both women heaved and dragged Gwyn to the hole. Breathing heavily, they rolled his unconscious body into the darkness below.

He hit the floor below with a dull thump. The same spot Tristan had landed minutes before.

Rubbing her hands to clean them of the dirt, Sorcha said, "Claire would you go and make me a coffee?"

"Yes, milady." She was glad of any chance to serve her mistress. "And take it to the morning room? I want to move Iseult there just in case her lovers have survived and come back to try and gallantly save her."

⁂

ISEULT WAS STANDING JUST INSIDE THE TOWER DOOR WHEN SOMEONE opened it. Framed in the moonlight, she saw Sorcha.

"Where's Tristan?" She stammered. "I heard Gwyn's voice. Did Gwyn harm him?"

Sorcha screwed up her face. "It got difficult. They met. We had trouble keeping them apart."

"But you did? Tristan was here. He was going to open the door then I heard Gwyn..."

"Yes, they're both fine. But if Gwyn gets hold of Tristan, then..."

"Where are they?"

"Safe."

"So you separated them?"

Sorcha shrugged. "Yes. Dudley took Gwyn off for a drink, to discuss the wickedness of women, man to man."

Iseult narrowed her eyes. "I don't know whether to believe you."

"Don't worry, my dear. They're both safe."

"Where did Tristan go? I can't believe you persuaded him to leave me. It's not like him."

"It's Gwyn; he was frightened of Gwyn."

"No, that's not right. He's not a coward. He might avoid a fight because it was the sensible thing to do, but not out of cowardice."

"You maybe don't know him as well as you think."

It just wasn't true. Sorcha was still playing games. She feared for Tristan. "Take me to him."

Sorcha said, "I will, but we have to be cautious that Gwyn doesn't find out where he is."

Iseult's lips trembled. "I suppose. I just want him safe. Where is he?"

"I'll show you."

Sorcha must have sensed her distress because she squeezed her fingers. She whispered, "The other guy. The one you hurt. For what it's worth, I would have done the same."

Iseult ignored her. "Was Claire here?"

Sorcha nodded. "She took Tristan off to where I told her."

"And Tristan went with her and left me?"

"Yes."

That didn't seem right. But one thing was clear, she could do nothing while locked in that tower. She decided to play along. "Okay. What do I do now?"

"Follow me. Let's begin to sort this mess out."

⁂

ISEULT WALKED WITH SORCHA TO THE MORNING ROOM; THE pleasant space with the long windows where they'd had coffee the day before. The curtains were drawn, keeping the night out. A cup of coffee stood steaming on the table by the sofa. Iseult said, "He's not here? Where is he?"

"I told you — with Claire. We're just waiting for the word from Dudley that Gwyn is out of the way, then we can take you to Tristan."

"Okay," Iseult said quietly. The standard lamps around the Morning Room were on and made the place look cosy and domesticated. The domesticity jarred with the events that were unfolding. The tasteful cushions and classical furniture were jarring. At least she was no longer in the tower.

She had to try and get one step ahead of Sorcha. Sorcha's motivations were obscure. What could she want with her? Maybe Dudley really had put her in the Tower to keep her safe from Gwyn, but whatever Sorcha had planned, she felt more confident that she could escape from here than from where she'd been locked up.

Sorcha waved with a smile. "Forget the coffee." She pointed at a table where there were various drinks bottles. "I've got some nice Chablis. It's not chilled."

Iseult shrugged and smiled. "Beggars can't be choosers."

Sorcha got two glasses and poured herself one, then Iseult.

Iseult stared out of the side window. "It's a dark night."

Sorcha said, "Yes, the day has deserted us. I'm glad you told me about that man. It made things so much easier."

Iseult sipped her wine, then put the glass down. She kneaded her brow with her slender fingers.

"It must feel like a relief. Telling someone other than Gwyn," Sorcha continued.

Iseult sat back and studied Sorcha. "You're not going to tell the police about me, are you?"

"Me? Tell the police?" I don't think so. "I've always been a bit anti-establishment. We girls can't go running to the man with all our secrets, can we?"

It suited Iseult to pretend that Sorcha's charm was working. "I'm so grateful you've kept Tristan safe," she said. "I just want to see him."

Sorcha nodded. "If you stay here, I'll get Claire to fetch you when we know Gwyn is not going to run into you. Don't you worry."

"And then what?"

Sorcha shrugged. "Then you leave of course."

"With Gwyn too?"

"No, not with Gwyn. Gwyn will stay here."

Iseult stared at the older woman. "What do you mean?"

Sorcha threw back her head and laughed. She looked genuinely amused.

"What? Don't make fun of me, Sorcha."

Sorcha controlled her laughter. "You thought we were going to kill him, didn't you?"

"No."

Sorcha burst out laughing again. "You so did." She took a sip of wine. "No, it's been a long day. Sorry about locking you in that tower by the way. I just wanted you to be safe, and Gwyn was angry."

Iseult frowned. "So what's different?"

"Dudley had a long talk with him."

Iseult grunted, drank more wine. "Go on."

"Dudley said you weren't worth it."

"When did you speak to Dudley?"

Sorcha smiled. "Dudley and I communicate through magick."

Iseult raised an eyebrow. "Really? I thought you spoke Irish." This was so much bullshit.

"Oh, Iseult, when will you finally believe in me?"

"Oh, I believe in you, Sorcha."

Sorcha tilted her head, studying Iseult, but Iseult knew that narcissists believe all flattery, no matter how absurd. She said, "So Gwyn thinks I'm not worth it now?"

"Sorry. It's just a thing men say."

"But Gwyn said that?"

Sorcha nodded. "Sure."

Iseult shook her head. "I don't buy it."

Sorcha looked at her. "I think that's vanity talking. You've hurt him. He's been hurt before. It doesn't take much to convince him that all women are treacherous bitches."

Iseult studied her hands. Maybe it was true. Maybe Gwyn could shake her off like an old coat. A couple of drinks with Dudley, maybe that's all it took. She had no right to feel the hurt she did. But that was good. If he could get over her so easily then good. If he could get over her, then that was better for him.

As if reading her thoughts, Sorcha said, "But he still wants to kill Tristan."

Iseult said, "Really kill him?"

Sorcha shrugged. "It won't come to that."

"So you and Dudley are going to spirit me and Tristan out of this castle out of the goodness of your heart?"

Sorcha nodded.

Iseult said, "Why?"

"Because we're nice people? And..."

"And what?"

"Because in the story, Diarmuid and Gráinne escape the wrathful Fionn."

Iseult shrugged. "I don't know the story."

Sorcha smiled. "You know how I like my legends."

"I don't know the story of Diarmuid and Gráinne, but I can't help but think there's something more going on."

"No that's it. We just want to help."

Iseult muttered, "Yeah, right."

"No, honest injun. Pinkie swear."

Iseult looked at the night that swirled outside the window. "So what now?"

"Well, we need to get you and Tristan together and get you out via the tunnel."

"The tunnel?"

Sorcha nodded. "The one that leads under the bog. It comes out by the ruined chapel."

Iseult remembered. "That passage really comes all the way to the castle?"

"Sure does."

Sorcha stood. Iseult stood too. Sorcha waved her down. "No, you sit."

"You'll bring Tristan to me?"

The witch shook her head. "No, you're not listening. Claire will come and fetch you."

"Not Dudley?"

"No, Dudley's busy. It will be Claire."

Now it seemed Claire had become part of Sorcha's staff.

Sorcha stood at the door. "Claire and Gwyn will stay here after you and Tristan leave. We can use the help. Anyway, enjoy your wine, and sit tight. I'll send for you when it's safe."

☙❦❧

ISEULT'S STOMACH WAS KNOTTED. SHE PACED THE MORNING ROOM after Sorcha left. It seemed ages until Claire arrived.

Claire still wore the theatrical cloak. "Hello, Iseult," she said.

"Claire," Iseult ran towards her. "Where's Tristan?"

"I don't know. He ran off. That's not important."

"I thought he went with you. Sorcha said..."

Claire gulped then grew crafty. "Ah, yes. He did. But he ran off."

"Will you take me to him?"

Claire looked puzzled. "No, I'm to take you to Lady Sorcha."

"She said you would take me to Tristan. This doesn't make sense. It's not what she said."

"Lady Sorcha's waiting for you." Claire held out her hand. "Come on."

Iseult took her hand automatically. Maybe Tristan was now with Sorcha.

The psychic's palm was clammy with sweat. "You know Gwyn wants to kill you?" she said as they walked.

Iseult's stomach turned over. She walked faster. "Let's get to Tristan."

Claire shook her head. "No. Lady Sorcha."

"So, they're not together?"

"Erm. Lady Sorcha knows where he is."

Iseult saw she would get nowhere with Claire. "Okay, her first, then she can explain what's changed."

They walked further on. Conversationally, Claire said. "When we go through the courtyard, don't look at the wolves, just hold my hand tight and ignore them."

"Wolves?" Iseult wondered how deep Claire was slipping into her psychosis. It seemed she was now hallucinating wolves.

"They won't hurt me, Lady Sorcha says, but they might hurt you." She glanced at Iseult, appraising her like she was a joint of beef. "We don't want the wolves to get you and drink all your blood."

"Claire, please, let's just hurry."

Claire led Iseult to the door that opened into the Courtyard. Though it was dark, the moonlight gave enough illumination so she could see the grey stone stairs that led down below the castle. "Down there?"

"There's a quicker way to where we're going. Follow."

Claire led her to the generator room. The generator gave a mechanical whine and the lights on it flickered. The place stunk of fuel. There was a flight of stairs leading down.

"Down there?"

"Yes, yes."

Iseult swallowed. This did not look good. On an impulse, she reached into her pocket. She had her gold cross there. After she'd given the salt to Crom Cruach, it hadn't felt right to wear it, but she'd kept it safe. With a quick movement, she plucked it from her pocket, and let it drop to the ground. Claire didn't see.

Iseult said, "Please can we hurry, Claire? Show me where she is."

Claire pointed to the stairs. "Come on then."

Iseult ran toward the steps. Claire followed her, grinning inanely.

At the bottom of the steps the tunnel forked. "Which way?" Iseult stammered.

"Down."

Iseult said, "Show me. Please."

Claire said, "Down here." She indicated into the dark.

"That way?"

Claire nodded. "Lady Sorcha told me to tell you that if you want to live, you should follow me."

Iseult had never wanted to live more: she wanted to live for Tristan

21

KING ARTHUR AND SIR LANCELOT

Tristan picked himself up from his heavy fall. It was dark in the tunnel he'd landed in. But he wasn't in such as mess as he should have been given the height he'd fallen from. The rotten wood that came down with him had cushioned his fall, as had the two inches of mud in the tunnel bottom. He stood painfully and checked himself for injuries. His body hurt, but wasn't broken. The tunnel was lit by similar electric bulbs to those he'd seen before, though this wasn't the same tunnel.

He looked up at the hole he'd fallen through. He'd dropped nearly two floors. Tristan craned his neck and stared up. It was dark down here, but moonlight washed the open sky silver from where the roof was broken. Gwyn was still up there and he would now go for Iseult. It would take him very little time to break the padlock, and Claire couldn't or wouldn't stop him.

Tristan had to climb back up as fast as he could.

Tristan remembered the wolves in the Courtyard, and Dudley with them. He reached and picked up his sword from where it lay on the floor nearby. At least he had that. The belt was still round his waist. He placed the sword in the scabbard.

The odds were overwhelming, even if he neutralised Gwyn.

Tristan jogged down the passage, hoping that he wouldn't run into the wolves. There had been a lot of them in the courtyard with Dudley, but some might linger down here.

After a few wrong turns he recognised that he was in the long tunnel that led way out under the marsh. That was the wrong way. He turned back and ran down the tunnel through the cloying darkness, the weight of the sword bouncing on his hip. Tristan ran, his breath growing ragged.

He ran on maybe a hundred yards then stopped. A growl rumbled in the darkness ahead. It sounded like something big made it.

Some of the bulbs overhead were out and the light was poor. He heard the drip of water from the stones. He hesitated. He had to go that way to get back.

The growl came again, echoing on the damp walls. Tristan's hand went to the sword.

The wolf came forward from the shadows and Tristan stepped back, pulling the sword free of its scabbard. The wolf's eyes gleamed in the light. Tristan sweated despite the cold. His hand was sticky on the hilt.

The wolf snarled and leapt. Tristan swung wildly at it, but the sword didn't connect, and his wild swinging unbalanced him, but when he stumbled at least it was out of the wolf's leap.

The beast turned and came at him again. This time Tristan brought up the sword underhanded. The wolf flinched back, and the sword missed. The creature was wary of the blade.

"Look, I don't want to hurt you," Tristan said. "Just let me go on my way."

Wolves are not people. Pity does not move them. The wolf snarled and jumped. It hit Tristan's shoulder and knocked him. It snapped for his throat, but he rolled and shoved it with his left hand. His fingers gripped its warm fur and he felt the hardness of its bone and muscle. It tried to bite the hand that fended it off, fangs gleaming with saliva, but Tristan rolled around, brought up his right hand with the sword. The wolf snapped, but Tristan plunged the blade through its ribs.

It surprised him how easily the blade slipped into flesh. He knew that's what it was designed for, but, even so, the simplicity of killing something astonished him. The beast yelped and jerked as the sword impaled it. Blood flowed through its fur and onto the tunnel floor.

It lay panting, regarding him with glassy, dying eyes, and grief and sorrow overwhelmed him because of what he'd done. He'd killed a creature. In all his years in the army, he'd only killed one man, and he'd never meant to do that. He'd always thought it was because he was soft. That's what soldiers do. That's what his father did. That's what Gwyn did.

But now he realised it wasn't glorious to kill, even in self-defence, it was a gut-wrenching tragedy.

Tristan stood back, the tip of his sword red and dragging on the ground, then lifted the blade. The wolf was dead now. He felt tears in his eyes. Tristan looked at the sword. He had a weapon, but could he really use it against Gwyn — even to defend himself or Iseult? He looked at the stricken beast. Much as he despised himself for it, it seemed he could kill to protect himself, and almost certainly to protect Iseult from Sorcha, or Dudley, or even Gwyn.

He turned; first, he had to puzzle his way through this maze, get up to the Tower and save Iseult.

But he was lost.

"Damn this place."

❦

TRISTAN WALKED FURTHER INTO THE TUNNELS. HE HURRIED HIS pace. Tristan didn't know where he was. These tunnels looked familiar and that might mean he was getting close to the stairs.

There were no more wolves. For now. He broke into a run.

He saw a dark shape on the tunnel floor. It groaned. Tristan stopped a few yards short, sword in hand. He saw broken wood, rotten timbers come down from above.

This was where he had fallen. Some light leaked in from the moon above. He looked up and saw the hole. Who was this?

He warily approached the shape and when he was close there was enough light to show that it was Gwyn. Tristan sheathed his sword and went over to his ex-sergeant. Gwyn was still breathing, but unconscious.

In the poor light, he examined Gwyn. He had an injury to his scalp and blood caked his hair. Tristan shook him gently. "Gwyn."

The older man stirred and groaned. Tristan glanced back up at the gap in the ceiling. There was no way he could climb back that way. But Gwyn was here, and Iseult wasn't. What if Gwyn had tried to protect her and Dudley or Sorcha had tripped or thrown him down here?

He shook Gwyn again but couldn't rouse him. He wasn't bleeding. He was breathing. He was just unconscious. He had no open wounds or obvious major injuries and Tristan had no way of scanning him to see if he had internal damage.

The choice was simple. Stay to look after Gwyn, or go to save Iseult.

He even thought about carrying Gwyn up the stairs with him. But Gwyn was heavy. He couldn't do it.

He was wasting time. Iseult was in danger.

"I'm really sorry, mate," Tristan said. "But I've got to go."

❦

WITH ONE LAST LOOK AT GWYN, HE TURNED TO LEAVE. THE FIRST time, he'd tried to find the way up, he'd gone the wrong way, now he would try the other.

Navigating by instinct through the disused passageways, he came to a more used path. He smelled the wolves, then he heard them. He stepped back and pressed himself into an alcove, hand on his sword hilt.

The moonlight from above radiated into a chamber ahead and to his left. He recognised it as the chamber at the foot of the entry stairs. The steps there led up to the courtyard with its long grass. From there he could trace his way back to the Banshee Tower. He knew they wanted her blood. He had to hurry. They may even have cut her by now.

He hesitated. The werewolf had been in the courtyard. Fear

gripped his heart. He swallowed. He wiped his sweaty hands on his jeans, grabbed the sword hilt again, and stepped forward.

He went to climb the steps and saw movement. They were up there — lots of them. In the moonlight, the grey fur of the wolves looked to be traced with silver. He ducked down. In their midst stood a taller figure, upright on two legs. It was the wolf Dudley. Tristan had been very stealthy. It hadn't seen him. He couldn't fight that many. He had to be careful the wind didn't take his scent to them. There was no way he could go up into the courtyard.

Then they started to move. They were coming down.

Tristan crept back down the steps, gripped the sword harder and pressed himself into the stone alcove as if he hoped to merge with the rock. He heard their claws on the damp stone. He heard their breathing. They were yapping excitedly. He pushed his head back. He was out of sight, but couldn't see what they were doing, whether they were coming his way or had turned down the other passage. The sound of trotting claws got further away. He he risked a glance and peeped out like a child playing peek-a-boo.

The creatures had gone: no grey wolves, no man-wolves, no Faelchon.

❦

He he had to get moving.

Tristan mounted the ancient stone steps at a run and emerged into the moonlit courtyard. Tristan saw a smashed window with dangerous shards of glass sticking up on the far side of the courtyard. But no wolves. He exhaled in relief, sword still gripped tight.

A stone flew past his head from below.

Tristan moved and another smashed against the masonry of the castle wall behind him. Gwyn roared in anger and ran from the steps below. He stooped to pick up another rock and hurled at Tristan's head. Tristan jerked to avoid it and Gwyn rushed him like an angry bull.

Tristan yelled, "Gwyn, they've got Iseult! We need to get to her."

The older man slammed into Tristan, knocking the wind out of him and sending them both reeling. The sword went flying from Tristan's hand and he fell onto the grass.

Gwyn was on him, quick as lighting. Gwyn straddled Tristan, punching at his face. Tristan rolled sideways from under Gwyn, getting leverage and heaving up and out. He lifted Gwyn off his feet and Gwyn tumbled left, spluttering whiskey scented spit. In the moonlight, his eyes were bloodshot and his lips slobbered. Blood had run down his face from his scalp wound and made him look demonic. Tristan got up, then stepped back, putting up his hands. The sword was on the grass to his right, out of reach.

Gwyn stood in a boxing stance, swaying, breathing hard.

Tristan stood his ground. "Listen—"

Anger twisted Gwyn's face as he ran forward swinging, but Gwyn was drunk or concussed and Tristan was more nimble than him even if he had been sober.

"Gwyn, I don't have time to fight you..."

Gwyn snarled, "But I have time to fight you. Fact is I'm going to kill you. I thought you were dead before, now I'll make sure."

Tristan watched every move the older man made, waiting for him to spring drunkenly again. "I understand why you're angry about this. Of course you are. But we don't have time."

Gwyn howled like a dog, keening the words, "You don't know the meaning of angry. How could you even think you'd know how I felt? How do you think I feel about you betraying me by sleeping with my wife?"

Tristan said, "I never meant to hurt you."

"But you meant to fuck her?"

"Don't use that word."

"What? You made love, is that it? You're in love? So if you're in love that makes fucking my wife okay?"

"Gwyn, please we need to get to Iseult. We can do this later. I'll fight you later if you want."

"You hypocritical fucker. Your heart always wanted her. And your cock. You would have been an adulterer even if you'd never stuck it in her."

Tristan turned to look at the door from the courtyard. Dudley and Sorcha had Iseult at their mercy. "Gwyn, come with me. Do this later."

Gwyn rushed forward and slammed his fist into Tristan's face. Blood spurted from Tristan's mouth and he fell back. Gwyn shoved him against the wall and got one hand around his throat. He brought the other back and punched Tristan again. Tristan knew if he didn't get out of that clinch, Gwyn would pummel him to death. He couldn't afford to die.

Gwyn's face twisted. He was beyond all reason. As he pulled his fist back again, Tristan struggled to get out of its way, and failed.

Gwyn's hand was round Tristan's throat, and he was gasping now for air. Tristan twisted left and right trying to get free from Gwyn's grip, but Gwyn clutched and choked him with his left hand. With his right hand Gwyn tried to punch him again but Tristan grabbed his wrist and held it tight.

He didn't want to hurt Gwyn more than he already had, but he would have to fight back.

Tristan brought up his knee into Gwyn's groin. The older man reeled back in pain and that was all Tristan needed. He got away from the wall. He stood breathing heavily, fists up.

Gwyn's eyes were red suns of rage. Tristan was going to have to hurt Gwyn more — so much that he gave up the fight and Tristan could leave.

Gwyn ran at him again, flailing. As Gwyn went by, Tristan tripped him. Gwyn fell forward and collided with the low wall. He struggled to right himself in his dazed state, one hand pressed against the floor, mouth open and drooling, eyes unfocused. Tristan stepped forward and delivered a surgical punch to Gwyn's sternum.

Gwyn fell but attempted to get up. He still wanted to fight. Tristan punched him hard in the face. Gwyn's nose burst and blood smeared Tristan's fist. "Now lie down," he snapped.

Gwyn struggled to his knees but couldn't get to his feet. Watching this was breaking Tristan's heart. He respected the man. Gwyn had done nothing to deserve this, and Tristan knew his love for Iseult had caused it. Fate would have blood it seemed.

Gwyn slurred, "I'm going to hurt you boy." But the alcohol and cigarettes had taken their toll. His breath came heavily, and blood oozed from his nose.

"I'm really sorry about this," Tristan said and with the flat of his foot stamped Gwyn to the floor. Gwyn moved but couldn't rise again. He was beaten. "Gwyn."

Gwyn coughed as he lay on the floor. His arm flopped over his chest. His breath was ragged and his eyes closed.

"Gwyn," Tristan repeated. "This courtyard was full of wolves. They're still around."

"Eh?" Gwyn's eyes still weren't open. He brought his hand to his face, smearing blood from his nose to his mouth.

"You're in danger. Get away. Get safe."

"So fuck. I've got nothing left. You took the only good thing in my life." Gwyn spluttered blood and spit.

"I have to go to Iseult."

Gwyn was lost in his own guilt. He muttered. "I hurt her. I hit her. I never meant to. I never hurt a woman."

"Go find somewhere safe - a room. Lock yourself in."

Gwyn laughed bitterly and the laugh turned into a ragged cough. He stared at the sky. "And now I need advice from a nothing like you to make me safe? You never even killed a man—at least on purpose." Gwyn struggled to get up onto his elbow. "Fuck off and leave me. Fuck off and leave my wife alone."

Tristan turned, picked up the sword from the ground and entered the castle by the courtyard door.

꧁꧂

TRISTAN RAN THROUGH THE CASTLE, JUMPING UP THE STAIRS, AND sprinting along the corridor and finally arriving at the Banshee Tower. He was some yards short of it, but the door hung open, showing the darkness within. He stood staring. She was gone. Where had they taken her? How would he find out? He needed help, but who would help him now?

He stood at the open door he called out for Iseult. There was no answer. There was no sign of Claire nor Sorcha either.

Sorcha was taking Iseult somewhere with Claire's connivance. They were all against him now. He stared up the dark throat of the tower. Maybe there was one ally left. It had seemed like a dream, but then so did everything here. The banshee said she would aid him against Sorcha, if he summoned her, and to summon her he needed her fingerbone.

The banshee's skeleton was up on the top of this Tower. He would have to go up twice as fast as he had done before. If the way up the spiral staircase of broken stones had been dangerous in the daylight, it was trebly so now. He could use his phone for light, but if he did that robbed him of a hand and he needed both hands to balance and grip the wall. There was still the moonlight, the ivory luminescence spilt in via broken windows and the hole at the top.

He climbed the stairs, in the semi-dark, hardly knowing where to place his feet and knowing that if he misstepped, he would fall and if he fell that would be the end of him.

Everytime the moonlight shone through an empty window, he studied the steps up, remembered them and plunged into shadow again. The moon was so bright it made the shadows black as pitch. He could not see where his feet were, he had to trust to memory.

And then, breathing hard, hands shaking, he arrived at the gap. The first step was in moonlight, but after that: void.

The tower walls leaned in. The steps slanted away. He'd lost his balance in the day, but saved himself. His throat tightened. His lips were dry. He jumped

As if some supernatural force aided him, he landed even better than the first time, no tripping, no overbalancing, just standing feet planted square, heart slowing.

He had to hurry. He rushed up the remaining narrow steps into the full light of the moon on what remained of the ancient tower floor.

The banshee's skeleton was still there, the skull rolled away. But it wasn't the skull he needed. By moon-light, he scrabbled among the twigs, bird droppings and brown ancient bones until he found the brittle hand. He snatched up whole digits as the hand came apart in his grasp. He thrust three or four finger bones in his pocket. He had no idea which finger bone was wanted, perhaps any would do.

And now he had to descend. Faster than he ever thought possible, certainly faster than was safe he went down. Whether it was by the grace of God and his angels or the power of the wicked Amelia Morton, he arrived at the bottom in once piece.

But at the door of the Banshee Tower he remembered he didn't know where Iseult was. She could be anywhere in these scores of rooms, tunnels, towers or even outside in the bog. He had no idea.

22

THE SUMMONING OF THE DRUID

They were in the tunnels below the castle, and Iseult had to trust Claire to lead her to someone who might know where Tristan was. She burned to find Tristan, and she was not convinced that Sorcha had separated him from Gwyn or that Dudley had Gwyn somewhere apart. All she had to go on was Sorcha's word — and that word had been conveyed by her acolyte, the clearly unhinged Claire. A wretched sickness rose in Iseult's guts; it was the rank feeling of fear she'd felt the night she stabbed Gareth. She wanted to get away from Tullabeg, escape to somewhere peaceful where she and Tristan could live an everyday life. But if the gods wanted her to have peace, it wasn't yet.

These tunnels were a maze. Without Claire, she'd be lost.

Claire pointed down the passage. "Down there."

"Are you sure?" The smell of dogs permeated the whole place. She hadn't noticed it before when she came down with Sorcha, how could she not notice that animal stink?

Claire said, "Of course I'm sure that's the way!"

Iseult sighed. She had no choice other than to trust the woman. She had to follow where she led. They walked down the brick-built tunnel along the clay floor. This was the route she'd taken when Sorcha took her to the chamber of Crom Cruach.

Iseult grew afraid—she had no wish to end up in the room again. It was a dead-end. Why would Tristan be waiting there for her?

"I don't want to go down there, Claire." She looked over her shoulder, expecting to see Gwyn hurtling down the corridor, knife in hand.

"We have to go to meet Lady Sorcha."

Iseult felt desperate. "Sorcha told me she only wanted to let me and Tristan go. You were to stay here with Gwyn. She said she wanted Tristan and I to be safe."

Claire tittered. "Oh, I'm sure she only wants to make sure you're safe and to reunite you with Tristan." Claire seemed so amused at the comment that Iseult became unnerved. Her panic mounted as they walked farther. Iseult said, "I don't want to go deeper. We'll get lost."

"Then you won't see Tristan. And remember Gwyn's not far behind."

Iseult darted a look over her shoulder, then ahead. "Is it far?"

"Not very."

"And Tristan's there?"

"If Lady Sorcha says so."

Iseult sighed. "Very well. Let's go."

They hurried through the labyrinth where walls bent and retreated in the artificial light.

Claire seemed troubled. "Did you ever see the banshee?" Claire blurted as if the matter was a great preoccupation to her.

"No," Iseult said. "I heard the call. I'm not sure what to make of it. I don't know if I can believe there is a banshee."

Claire frowned. "Oh, yes the banshee exists, and she is a very evil spirit. She's called three times now, and that means someone will die." She looked at Iseult meaningfully. "I can't let that person be Lady Sorcha. This Lady Amelia banshee wants to have her revenge on Lady Sorcha. And you know I am sworn as part of my Christian duty to rid the earth of such evil things."

"I know you say that, Claire."

Claire nodded rapidly. "Oh, it's true. We must destroy the banshee. But my lady Sorcha has a method in mind."

"And what method is that?" Iseult humoured the old woman.

"Oh, you'll see." Claire grinned and showed her small teeth. The tone of her voice chilled Iseult's blood. She didn't want to go any further into the tunnels with this madwoman. Suddenly, she entirely disbelieved both Claire and Sorcha. Tristan wasn't down here. She stopped dead. "I'm not going any further, Claire."

"Oh, yes, you are."

"You can't make me, Claire. I'm going to turn round now and find my own way to Tristan. Whether you help me not. I want to go with him."

"But what if you run into Gwyn? He will kill you, wrapping his strong hands around your neck." Claire's eyes were wide with excitement. She almost licked her lips.

"I'll take my chances." Iseult turned her back on Claire and walked off.

With a grunt, Claire snatched at her. Iseult shrugged off the woman's assault and pushed her away. Claire fell back against the wall snarling then leapt at Iseult like a wild woman. The attack's ferocity was unexpected — Iseult couldn't believe Claire's lean frame held such strength.

Claire slammed Iseult against the wall, and Iseult stumbled and put one hand down to the clay floor but was overbalanced. And then from an inside pocket, Claire produced a length of twine. While Iseult struggled to get her balance, Claire wrapped the yarn around her wrist. Then she snatched Iseult's other arm, sending her falling on her back. Claire straddled Iseult's prone form tugged the twine around and round Iseult's wrists until she was tightly held. Then she looped it into a knot. Her pink tongue extended between her thin lips. "You're mine now, you filthy little harlot."

"Claire, what are you doing? Let me go," Iseult begged.

Claire yanked Iseult to her feet. "Follow," she barked.

ISEULT STUMBLED AND ALMOST FELL AS CLAIRE DRAGGED HER DOWN the tunnel. She remembered this way only too well. Ahead, through the open door, the light of a hundred candles flickered in Crom Cruach's cavern, and flames danced behind wreaths of incense. Sorcha stood with her back to them, dressed in a long flowing black robe with a hood like a Satanist from a 1970s horror movie.

Candles threw up pools of uncertain light from alcoves all around the stone chamber, dancing like wicked faeries. Sorcha turned when they entered and gave a broad smile. "Ah, Claire, thank you. And Iseult too." She wagged a red-nailed finger in front of the psychic, "I hope you weren't too rough with her, Claire?"

"She wouldn't come of her own accord, so I had to bind her." Claire looked at her feet, abashed. "You warned me I might."

"I did indeed Claire." Then she looked at Iseult. "I guessed you'd be reticent to meet your fate."

"I'm surprised you trusted her to bring me," Iseult said.

"Claire is loyal beyond words, and she is far more resourceful than you ever gave her credit for."

Claire beamed.

"This is illegal," Iseult spluttered. "You can't tie someone up."

"You can't kill someone, yet you did." Sorcha smiled and reached into a recess behind the statue of Crom Cruach. The idol stood in his stone glory, staring with sightless, lentil-shaped eyes. Sorcha extracted an object, and when she turned, Iseult saw it gleaming in the candle-light. It was a long, curved dagger. Iseult pulled back, but Claire yanked her close and tight, hissing, "Listen when Lady Sorcha speaks."

Iseult composed herself. Her throat constricted, but she managed to croak, "What are you going to do with that?"

The witch stared; her silver eyes the colour of a bad moon in the flickering light. "I'm going to take your blood."

"My blood?"

"The blood of the thrice-damned woman. I was going to get you to kill Gwyn, or Tristan, I didn't mind which. I made you an idolatress; you made yourself into an adulteress. I thought I was going to have to give you a push into being a murderess, but when you told me that you already were... " Sorcha's laugh echoed in the chamber. "What a gift that was — a present from my Lord."

Iseult cleared her throat. "And what will you do once you have my blood?"

Claire cocked her head. "Thou shalt not kill!" she said, looking at Iseult, and then she snapped her head to gaze at Sorcha. "Thou shalt not kill, milady?"

Iseult patted Claire's scalp. "Quite so."

The psychic continued, "That would be un-Christian."

Sorcha nodded. "But if I were to let her go at night and make her way over the bog and she drowned. I wouldn't be killing her, would I? It wouldn't be me..."

The psychic pondered. "I suppose not."

Sorcha examined her ritual knife in the flickering light. "And if she stumbled and splashed through the bog, plunging into a dark pool, going up to the knees, and then, if a wolf pack came across her and that wolf pack was hungry, that wouldn't be me killing her, would it?"

Claire put her thumb to her mouth in thought. "No," she said finally. "They couldn't hold you responsible for that."

"Because you see, Claire, Iseult knows a little too much about what goes on here now — too much for me to feel comfortable with her sharing that knowledge."

The psychic looked troubled, and then she smiled. "I've decided to give up Jesus, anyway. So I suppose the Commandments don't count any more." Her expression transformed into one of child-like eagerness. "We must destroy the banshee now. We must cleanse this place of that evil spirit."

"And what do we need for that Claire?"

"Blood."

"Whose blood?" Sorcha handed Claire the athame.

Claire's eyes fluttered. She glanced slyly at Iseult and pointed. "Hers."

Sorcha reached and brought a silver goblet from the alcove. "Cut her when I say so and let it run into the cup."

Claire nodded like a deranged blackbird.

Sorcha turned to the idol. She bowed and performed ritual movements, speaking liquid words in Irish. She looked up the ceiling, making sinuous hand gestures, and then she kneeled down before

Crom. On the drier ground in front of him, she burned herbs. "Hand me mugwort and dittany," she said over her shoulder.

Claire rustled among the herbs laid out to the right of the chamber on a low stone shelf. She picked out two of them and handed them to Sorcha. Raising her voice in evocation, Sorcha burned the herbs and filled the chamber with the sweet smell of dittany of Crete. Then she burned the mugwort. Smoke wreathed through the cavern. Sorcha stretched and took an old looking golden amulet. She gave it to Claire. The psychic gripped it, but her eyes widened like it had bitten her. She stared at it, nodding, holding it tighter. She looked at Sorcha for instructions.

Iseult glanced behind her. With them both preoccupied she could perhaps escape, she could perhaps run and hide in the dark. Iseult tensed herself. She tugged on the rope that Claire held to test it. The psychic was preoccupied with the amulet and her grip on the rope that held Iseult was loose.

Claire's eyes closed. She muttered, "He is stirring in the amulet."

Without turning, adding more herbs to the fire, Sorcha said in a low voice, "Stronger now?"

"He is old — very old. But not stronger. Still far away."

"Is the picture clearer? What does he look like?"

"He wears brown and green with a dark beard. His eyes are like stars."

"What does he say?"

"He is too far away. I can't hear him. He needs something to come closer to us — a bridge."

Sorcha nodded. "The blood. I need the Blood of the Thrice Damned Woman."

"I thought the blood was to kill the banshee?" Claire asked.

"Of course," Sorcha said. "That too."

Claire yelled to the ceiling. "It is wonderful blood indeed!"

Iseult's eyes flashed wide. "What? You're both crazy." She tugged at the rope, but Claire pulled it tight.

"Cut her."

Claire's eyes opened as her attention switched from the spirit of the druid in the golden amulet. She turned and steadied the knife in her hand. She gripped Iseult's forearm. Iseult struggled to pull it away, but the psychic held it closer to her and tight. She had to drop the rope for a second but seized Iseult's arm with fingers that felt like iron.

"Sorry, harlot," Claire said and slid the knife's sharp blade along the pale flesh of Iseult's inner wrist.

Iseult yelped in pain as the blade cut into her forearm. Blood flowed from the wound and Claire tried to catch it in the silver goblet, but she couldn't manage the goblet and the athame and to hold Iseult's wrist at the same time. The blood dripped to the floor. Claire waved the goblet under the drops, trying to catch them but missing half at least.

"Blood," snapped Sorcha. She fed myrrh and frankincense into the fire of sticks, and the fire blazed brighter in front of the idol, filling the cave with aromatic smoke.

"Sorry, milady," Claire stuttered. She stuck her tongue out as she worked with rapt attention. She gathered the blood that still ran from Iseult's wound.

Sorcha reached behind, not taking her eye from the statue of Crom Cruach and she poured the blood into the fire. The fire hissed like a snake, causing Sorcha to edge back.

"Is that enough?" Claire asked.

"Tell me if he's closer."

Claire closed her eyes. "Yes, he's close." And then, open-mouthed, she pointed.

Iseult looked at the writhing smoke and there, in the air, a figure materialised. It was the figure of an ancient-looking man in green and brown whose eyes were like stars. "My God," she said.

Sorcha focused on the ritual and held up her hands in supplication. "He's finally come through."

She gazed at the druid, a smug smile on her lips. "Master, after so long. After so many years, I finally see you."

The figure was silent.

Claire had her eyes tightly closed.

"Claire, what does he say?" Sorcha demanded.

Claire nodded as if listening to an inner voice. Iseult watched as the figure of the druid floated in the air. She had the feeling that it was neither evil nor good, but instead as neutral as if he were a beast of the field or a great oak tree. He cared nothing for their troubles. He cared nothing for Sorcha.

Sorcha bowed her head. "Ask him for the secret of how I obtain eternal youth."

Claire's eyes were still closed. She didn't reply.

Sorcha turned to Claire. "Ask him for the steps for the ritual of eternal life."

Claire nodded. She clamped her eyes tight. Minutes went by.

Sorcha snapped. "What is going on?"

Claire whispered, "He does not speak, my lady."

Sorcha's mouth narrowed. "Master, I wish to learn from you. Please do not withhold this wisdom from me."

The figure stared inscrutably. He was so ancient, so removed from them. Whatever Sorcha felt about him, hthe druid's expression held no love for the witch. It was like looking at a creature from another order of life; a plant or an animal — like a deer with quiet, empty eyes.

"He won't answer you, mistress," Claire said.

"Can't?"

Claire shook her head. "Won't. Now, he speaks. He says you are evil. You are not worthy of the secret."

Sorcha gave a grim laugh. "Evil? Not worthy? Let's see about that." She reached over and took the amulet from Claire's hands. "This is the talisman I recovered from the the druids' grove. The Christians used their own magic to entrap him in it, and so when I burn it, it hurts him. We'll see if he answers me when he feels pain."

Sorcha took a pair of tongs that lay in the alcove. She grabbed the amulet in their pincers then thrust the talisman into the heart of the flames. She turned it both sides, roasting it until it glowed cherry-red and sparks came off it. Then she pulled it out.

While the amulet was being burned, Iseult saw the figure of the druid shudder in pain.

"Ask him now?" Sorcha grinned.

Claire shook her head. "He still refuses to tell you."

Sorcha grunted and thrust the talisman in the fire again. She put in the heart of the flames, and the figure writhed. His face twisted in angony and the talisman glowed white-hot. "Will he tell us now?"

"He won't speak."

Sorcha held the talisman in the fire. Flames of blue and orange curled around it. Black smoke rose.

"Perhaps the ritual needs more blood." Sorcha placed the talisman on the ground beside the fire, and it singed and fizzled in the damp there. "Maybe more blood will persuade him to tell me."

"No, it's not more blood, he wants. He won't tell you because he says you're evil."

"Get me her blood," the witch snarled.

Claire started like a scolded schoolgirl and snatched up the athame. She was so awkward. She held it like she was frightened of it.

Sorcha snarled, "You stupid woman. Let me do it myself." She came forward and snatched the knife from Claire. Knife up, she approached Iseult. Behind her, Claire wept, tears flowing because Lady Sorcha had spoken to her so sharply.

Iseult jerked away from the knife.

Sorcha snapped, "Claire, the rope — hold her."

Claire picked up the rope and yanked it tight. Iseult strained away from the blade, but she couldn't get out of the cavern because of how tight Claire gripped her leash.

Sorcha looked into Iseult's eyes. "I may need all your blood for this."

❧ 23 ❧

WEREWOLF

Tristan stood at the bottom of the Banshee Tower. He didn't know where Iseult was so he would have to guess. If he guessed wrong, he'd never see her again. He stood, paralysed by not knowing. Then he remembered what Dudley had said. They'd been in the generator room, and Tristan saw the stairs going down. Dudley said, "That's where we take our prisoners,"

That's where they'd taken Iseult.

He knew the way to the Generator Room. He was there in minutes. And there, at the top of the stairs that led down, something glinted on the muddy floor. He stooped to pick it up. It was a gold cross: Iseult's gold cross. She was showing him where they'd taken her.

Faster now and more confident, Tristan descended into the tunnels below the castle. Footmarks led down the left-hand tunnel, and he went after them.

He heard the beasts before he saw them — the pattering of their paws, their snuffling and their snarls. The wolves were some way down the tunnel, but they had spotted him. Tristan peered into the gloom. At least the man-wolf was not with them. The beasts waited.

He guessed they were sizing him up like a pack of wolves in the wildwood sizes up a deer. Tristan considered turning and finding another way, but they were faster than he was and he wouldn't get far. Besides, there was no other way possible. He would never leave Iseult, even if it meant his death.

He looked at the sword in his hand. How could a man fight a whole pack of wolves?

It looked like he would have to find out. He tensed, preparing for their onslaught, but at first, they sidled, halting then inching forward. The lead wolf's eyes glinted like rubies in the electric light. For some reason, Tristan thought she was a bitch. The others took their lead from her, and as she became less wary, they came.

Tristan dropped into a crouch.

The bitch wolf leapt at him with a snarl. He rolled right, and she flew past, then snapped around and came at him from behind. He jumped back, but the wolf was at him before he could get out of her way. Tristan whipped the sword, and it caught her a glancing blow across her front paw. Cut, she yelped but didn't stop.

She snapped in and he felt the crunch of her jaw on his left arm, but she didn't get a grip and didn't fasten. Flesh ripped as he tore his arm free.

Behind her, the others formed a half-moon as if waiting for her order to attack. He feinted with his sword, and she snarled. Her paw was bleeding. She drew back keeping her eyes fixed on him. She was limping.

The pain shot up his arm, and blood flowed freely down his wrist and onto his fingers.

The she-wolf waited. Then she made a noise and they all moved. They snarled and leapt, and the rest of the pack were on him. Tristan swung the sword in an arc to fend them off. Some retreated, others, braver, slyer, went around the sides.

Soon they would pull him down.

They snapped at him, lips curled, fangs showing. None of them made significant contact. They stood in a circle, one darting forward, then another.

They leapt high, and he guessed that they were trying to go for his throat to take him to the floor and asphyxiate him.

All this time, Iseult was down here at Sorcha's mercy.

He jumped forward and jabbed a lead wolf between its front legs. It was a strong blow and the blade sunk in. The beast growled then rolled. Tristan dragged out the sword and the wolf lay still.

Their brother's death enraged the others, and they formed a circle, snapping and darting when they saw a chance. Tristan kept the sword level, sweeping it this way and that. One rushed and bit.

It wasn't much of a bite. But slowly and surely they were wearing him down. It wouldn't be long now before they had him.

Tristan dodged and sliced across its muzzle, cutting to the bone. It ran away yelping, maddened from pain.

"I wish I didn't have to do this," he muttered. When he killed another, it was like a switch was thrown. They weren't trying as hard. He guessed they must be like this with bears in the wild, or bulls. They try to bring them down, but when the prey makes them pay too dearly, they back off. They now saw him as a serious opponent.

They fought more until he killed two more and wounded seven others. Yelling, standing by the still-warm wolf bodies, Tristan brandished the reddened sword. They backed off further.

Panting, he watched the wolves in a half-circle around him. He saw human footprints led down the passage ahead.

She'd gone that way. He had no time. The wolves had delayed him too long. He had to get to Iseult. Tristan advanced, and the wolves fell back on the sides to let him pass.

Then he thought about Gwyn. Gwyn would be defenceless against this pack. He was old and wounded, ideal prey for the wolf pack. Gwyn lay in the courtyard above his head. He could go back for him, but that would mean abandoning Iseult.

Gwyn or Iseult? It broke his heart to leave his old sergeant. And then he thought that at least he could lead them away. That might give Gwyn a chance to recover and escape.

"Come on, you furry bastards. Come on." He taunted the wolves. They growled. They waited. "Come on. Good doggies, come on."

They gave no sign of moving so he sighed, followed Iseult's footprints in the mud. The wolves watched him go, and their lamp eyes glowed in the light of the electric bulbs.

Then they began to trot after him, snickering and snapping at each other in their frustration but afraid of the sword. They followed, dogging his steps, watching his every move.

❧

TRISTAN GOT A FEW PACES BEFORE HE SENSED IT. SOMETHING LARGE lurked in the darkness ahead. He peered, struggling to make it out, then it moved. The shadow loomed, threw back its head and bayed in worship of the unseen moon. The wolf creature that was Dudley emerged from the tunnel's depths and snarled.

Eight feet tall with muscles like ship's ropes, the werewolf came from the darkness, now visible in the poor light, hate like hot coals burning in its eyes, rushing to attack.

Tristan waved the heavy sword blade but missed. The wolf was not wary of the sword, and the swinging blade did not slow it a step. It growled, lurching forward and Tristan retreated, stumbling backward, terror of the supernatural thing shaking his hands but courage steadying them again.

The wolf pack watched, leaving the fight to their lord.

The werewolf swung but overreached, snarling and snapping, and Tristan, more nimble, stepped right. Seeing his chance, he jabbed, made the wolf go back, and then he lunged. He stuck the sword into the wolfman's shoulder and though his blade sank to the bone, the wolf did not bleed, did not howl, and did not stop. It snatched at the sword, knocking it away.

The wolf was tall and terrible, roaring and baring yellow fangs. Its eyes held both beast hate and biped wit, and it snapped its jaws in mockery at this weak man.

Tristan recoiled, puzzled. The sword had penetrated at least an inch, but there was no blood.

It came. Tristan stumbled over a rock and staggered away, righting himself, but not quick enough as wolf claws, cutthroat-sharp, raked his chest, sliced his throat, and came back to carve his flesh. Blood poured, skin split and pain numbed his mind, unfocusing it, clouding it, agony ringing out like a car alarm.

Once more his sword pierced the wolf, this time its belly, and once again it did not harm. Tristan was amazed. By rights, he had disembow-elled it, but the werewolf seemed hardly hurt, in fact not hurt at all, not stopped, nor hindered, and when Tristan snatched back the sword tip, the steel was unblemished: no blood, no gore; neither bile nor ichor stained it, and Tristan stood, blinking.

What did this mean?

The wolf creature struck, and the hammer blow smashed Tristan down. With creaking knees, he tried to stand. He thrust the sword, but again, to no avail. The steel struck but caused no damage.

Not steel.

With a smash of its mighty forepaw, the werewolf knocked the sword from Tristan's hand. The beast stood between him and Iseult, and he could not allow myth, magic or monster to stop him. He had to get through.

If he could only reach her. But he wouldn't get past it, a few paces and it would catch him, punching him down, snapping his arms, stomping his life like a broken butterfly into the bloody mud.

Even without hope, better to fight on. All he had were his fists. He raised them. He challenged it. It came.

Step by backward step he went, retreating up the tunnel until moonlight flooded the scene. There at the bottom of the courtyard stairs, the fight was almost finished. Tristan had lost, and the moon, the mother of wolves, watched and waited.

The beast that had been Dudley howled to the great ivory disk above.

Not steel, but silver.

Tristan touched the handle of the blunt-edged dagger at his belt. The Mortons had fought the wolf people: they knew what killed them. That's why the dagger was on the sword belt. The moonlight raised the wolves up, but moon-made metal, the sacred silver struck them down again.

Tristan snatched for the dagger, but the werewolf caught him a glancing blow. His feet lost their purchase in the mud, and he fell on the steps, the dagger, now half-drawn, flew from his bloody hand.

The wolf thing hit him hard, and Tristan, not fully up, collapsed into the wet ground. Blood smeared the floor, and a crimson flower bloomed through his white shirt, making his arm wet and his grip slippery. He reached for the dropped dagger, touched it, his finger-ends closing on the hilt, pulling it closer, almost getting it, and he raised himself to better reach, finally grasping the hilt, but the wolf smashed him down, and he could not stand again.

The werewolf towered above Tristan's broken body, eyes like jewels, spit-strung fangs, breath sweet with the smell of offal. The beast stamped him into the ground, once and twice and the dagger fell from Tristan's hand and lay.

His eyelids closed with pain, but he saw werewolf's eyes glittering like the stars that fell with Lucifer from Heaven. It had the victory and it would it would eat him and when it had its fill throw the rest of him to its pack.

Tristan knew he was dying.

In the last minutes of thought, he recalled there was still something to do. In the final moments of memory, he remembered what it was. Tristan reached into his pocket, teeth gritted, and dragged out Lady Amelia Morton's finger bone. Blood dripped from his wrist onto the bone, and where the blood touched, the fingerbone smoked. This smoke smelled of witch pyres and sabbats and centuries. This smoke curled and drifted and called. This smoke sent a message.

Tristan breathed fast and ragged. In the ivory gleam of the full moon, Tristan muttered, "Banshee, take my blood as a sacrifice. Come to my call."

Tristan saw his blood-covered hands and his blood-mired arms and his blood-soaked shirt stained black in the shadow, and with his failing breath, he whispered, "Save her."

In that instant, somewhere far above, the banshee cried out. The sound of its agony penetrated all the walls and the cellars of the castle. The wail rolled like an echo from the deepest dungeons to the highest towers, spreading, and swelling like a droning wave across the emptiness of the Bog of Allen, resounding, repeating and dying away.

At the banshee's call, the werewolf lifted its head. It sensed the coming of its ancient enemy, turned from Tristan, and ran. The rest of its pack, who had been watching, lifted their muzzles. They followed.

The hot breeze blew down the tunnel, setting the bulbs swinging on their wire and heralding the approach of something unseen. The werewolf hurried down the passage in the direction Iseult had already gone.

⁂

FAR ABOVE TRISTAN, IN THE BANSHEE TOWER, SOMETHING STIRRED. The dark bird feathers that overlay the dry bones of the skeleton on the top floor of the tower fluttered in the breeze, and the ravens stirred uneasily, waking from dreams of mice and weasels.

Here now, darkness clustered and whispered, and the moon's white fingers stroked the bones alive. For the moon is mistress of deceit and has no loyalty for her children.

A grey mist coalesced and gathered as if thickened from a vapour of blood. Soon, a shape leeched from Lady Amelia Morton's scattered bones until it became the recognisable form of a woman. Then the figure began to move and drifted down the tower.

At the door, it hesitated until it seeped through holes in the wood and found its way outside. It blew along the ruined hallway and entered into the castle's inhabited areas until it was at the entrance to the courtyard.

It passed Gwyn as he stirred to lift himself from the ground. It passed by the stricken Tristan unnoticed and went down into the tunnels. It drifted along the passages until it came to where the wolves turned and rushed at it. The beasts jumped and snapped, jaws sailing through its misty form. And if they couldn't hurt it, it could hurt them. With hands of fog, it dragged across their fur, ripping free their skin and baring their bones and searing their muscles beneath their pelts. The wolves howled in pain. It killed most, and the others turned to flee.

The werewolf ran ahead of the pack. When it heard the plight of its pack-mates, it almost turned to come to their aid, but its first loyalty was to its mistress, Sorcha. It had to protect her.

The banshee arrived before it at the cavern where Sorcha tortured the druid, and the banshee howled its death scream and entered in.

TRISTAN WAS BARELY CONSCIOUS. HE LAY IN THE COLD MUD. Coagulated plugs of dark blood staunched the flow from his wounds. He tried to raise his head but slumped back down again. He tried again. He had to get to his feet. He had no idea what the banshee could do to help, but now it had wailed, someone must die. He struggled to get on his elbows. By him, the silver dagger lay dirtied with mud. He reached for it and dragged it with his fingertips across the ground toward him.

He heard someone approach. If it was the werewolf, he was dead. The figure stopped. Tristan shifted his head and looked up.

Gwyn shook his head and looked down at the broken man. "Tristan, we went through a lot together, but you threw that all away. You took my wife from me and look at you now." He gave a hollow laugh. "I guess justice is served."

Tristan groaned.

Gwyn scratched his stubbly cheek. "I would kill you, but someone has done my work for me. I'm guessing it was Dudley, am I right?"

Tristan's mouth was dry. "Gwyn..." He struggled to form the words. "Dudley's—"

Gwyn drew back his foot and booted Tristan in the ribs. Tristan winced and grabbed his injured side.

"On second thoughts," Gwyn said. "I don't care who did it, as long as you die."

"Gwyn... I need to tell you..." His speech was interrupted by a bout of ragged coughing that was agony to his wounded chest.

"Can it." Gwyn stooped to pick up the sword. He weighed it in his hands. "I'll take this with me. I'd love to chat, but I think you're out of time, and I have to go and rescue my wife from big bad Dudley and take her home with me."

Gwyn turned and waved. Walking away, he called, "Chin-chin," without looking back and strode in the direction the werewolf had taken.

❧ 24 ❧

BEAN SÍDHE

Iseult saw Sorcha looking down the tunnel. She saw Sorcha's eyes flash wide in alarm. She saw Sorcha step away from the door.

What was this?

Iseult tried to twist her head so that she could see what was coming down the tunnel, but Claire gripped her leash tight, and she couldn't move.

Anyway, there was no sound, no flicker of a torch, nothing to suggest anything was about to occur. But she knew it was.

She looked back at the witch whose face had drained pale. Maybe Sorcha was having one of her witch premonitions. Iseult focused on the rope. She needed to get free.

Then the banshee wailed.

The scream was ear-splitting, and all three women turned to stare at the door. The wail, after being so loud, grew less. There were some moments of settling. For a second, maybe more, it was as if nothing had happened and Iseult had imagined the noise. But they all stood around, stupified.

And it was only for a second for next the wind came — a hot breeze like a train approaching, a rustling sound, intensifying, growing stronger. And then that feeling: a tension so great it made your skin itch and your scalp tight and your mouth dry. It was a building of awful anticipation, like something about to burst, a building crescendo of something so far unseen.

The string of cheap electric light bulbs began to shake, the bulbs flapping and bouncing on the wire. A low whistle like a kettle boiling grew louder down in the tunnel — louder and higher and closer. The door to the chamber rattled.

An ancient error rose in Iseult's throat and threatened to choke her. She struggled against the rope to get free.

Claire backed away from the door, visibly shaking, her face twisted in fright and she stammered, "Who is it that comes?"

In her terror, Claire pulled the rope tighter still. Sorcha put her fingers to her lips. She backed off.

Then the door blew open, and a creature of mist and darkness entered in.

Though it was not corporeal, Iseult saw the face of Amelia Morton. A rushing wind surrounded her and voices from long-ago chanting hung in the air. The fire's flames to rippled and fluttered.

The figure of the tortured druid reached out to the banshee. The spirits were conjoined in some way. It was as if centuries of haunting this place; they had grown used to each other's company, and Sorcha was their common enemy.

The Witch of Tullabeg stumbled back away from the banshee, falling over herself in her haste to escape. But there was no escape; the banshee filled the door like a stopper in a bottle.

Now Sorcha's focus was off the druid, the image of the ancient man flickered and was gone.

Trying to protect her mistress, but still holding the rope, Claire snatched the ritual athame. She rushed forward and sliced at the Banshee, but the blade slipped through its form. In a frenzy, Claire slashed again. Lady Amelia paid her no attention. It was as if the banshee didn't know she was there, or didn't care.

The banshee fixed its attention on Sorcha and with a voice like the west wind sighing through barley, spoke: "Sorcha O'Connor, descendant of the man who flayed me alive, I vowed revenge on all your bloodline, and it was this vow, uttered as I lay dying, that cursed me to remain here. Remain here I shall, until I kill the last of the line of my torturers. Until you die, I will never be free of Tullabeg."

Backing off, bringing her hands to her face, raking her cheeks with her blood-red nails, Sorcha yelled out in panic. She called for Dudley to save her.

But Dudley wasn't there.

With a roar like wind through mountain pines, the Banshee attacked Sorcha. With a keening like a storm over the sea, it ripped her.

Despite its incorporeal nature, when it touched Sorcha with its grey hands it burned her. The witch screamed in agony. Red welts appeared wherever the banshee grasped her flesh.

Sorcha fell back and screamed out again for aid, from Dudley — from anyone.

Iseult stood, hands still bound, and Claire stood screaming but still holding the rope.

The creature wrapped its misty form around Sorcha and fastened onto the witch like a leech, draining her life.

Sorcha's face twisted in pain, and as the banshee drank her energy, the spirit turned from grey and black to blood red.

The banshee sloughed off layers of Sorcha's skin, and the skin flapped and curled and fell and revealed red muscle and bleeding sinew. The creature flayed her alive as Sorcha's ancestor had done to it centuries before. With blood bubblng through her lips, Sorcha screamed out for Dudley.

Something ran down the tunnel.

Claire leapt at the Banshee to pull it off her mistress. She had dropped the ritual dagger, but still held the twine in her left hand. Her blows still went through it. She wailed and cried and wept.

Iseult yanked free the rope from Claire's hand and it ran through her fingers and Iseult pulled it free to retreat out of the way to undo the knot. She got her hands free, rubbed her wrists and could do nothing other than watch Sorcha's terrible fate.

Sorcha screamed out for help again, and a monstrous creature irrupted into the room with a roar.

It it was a wolf that walked on its hind legs. Iseult pressed herself against the rocky wall. She looked to the door, but couldn't get out because the werewolf was in the way. The werewolf rushed at the Banshee.

❧

As if sensing the werewolf's threat, the Banshee turned from Sorcha, and the witch collapsed bleeding onto the floor.

The banshee pulsed red with the heartbeat of Sorcha's consumed energy as it turned to face the werewolf. The man-wolf snapped at the thing's ghostly form, but its fangs passed through its red mist body. Equally, the banshee appeared unable to hurt the werewwolf. And so, the wolf and banshee were locked in fruitless combat, neither able to inflict damage on the other.

Sorcha groaned in pain, blood streaming from her stripped skin. She lay against the chamber wall, one hand dripping blood onto the stone idol of Crom Cruach. Through bleeding lips, she spat, "Claire, exorcise the banshee as we planned. Use Iseult's blood. Throw it on the fire."

Claire bent and snatched up the athame from the ground. Iseult was frantically trying to undo the knot, but Claire came at her. Iseult lifted her hands in defence, but the psychic yanked Iseult's blonde hair and dragged her toward the fire. Iseult stumbled along with the psychic. When she had her close to the flame, Claire reeled the rope in, held it tight, then grunted and jabbed Iseult in the arm with the knife. Iseult cried out as blood ran and hissed and steamed and dripped into the flames.

Claire muttered a Christian prayer of exorcism, then she turned and screamed, "The Blood of The Thrice Damned Woman curses you!"

With her first words, the banshee was less substantial.

"And casts you out into the hell reserved for you!"

The banshee faded. A strange thin keening cut the air as the spirit lost its hold on this world. After all the centuries it had lingered, it was cast out by the blood of the Thrice Damned Woman, but instead of going to the limbo it had hoped after killing Sorcha, the Blood of the Thrice Damned Woman cast it into hell.

Iseult watched as the banshee diminished until it was only a few wisps of smoke in the air. The creature that had been Amelia Morton in life was defeated, and it vanished.

Claire yelled in triumph. "And so all evil spirits will be cast out by me." Then she looked down at Sorcha. Sorcha was dying: she couldn't survive with injuries like those. Claire bent and stroked the witch's bloody face. "My lady, I will help you. I will heal you."

Sorcha tried to speak from her ruined, flayed face, but the words were lost in bubbles of blood.

The werewolf elbowed Claire aside, sending her careening into the wall. It knelt down and nestled Sorcha's head in its huge paws then threw back its head and howled.

Iseult took her chance and ran.

THE WEREWOLF TURNED, EYES FILLED WITH GRIEF. AND GRIEF turned to anger as if it blamed Iseult for the death of its mistress. Iseult fled down the corridor away from it.

Snarling, the beast ran after her. Iseult got no distance before a heavy blow landed between her shoulder blades, sending her staggering forward. The werewolf's claws ripped her dress and drew blood. Iseult coughed and stumbled forward until she fell headlong, hand scraping on the floor. She scrambled round and faced her assailant. The wolf stood above her, its teeth poised to rip out her throat, then she heard Gwyn yell. "Get away from my wife."

The wolf looked at Gwyn who was coming down the corridor and it snarled.

Gwyn said, "If you want to take anyone come and take me." He had the sword in his hand.

The wolf ran at Gwyn, snarling and roaring. Iseult climbed to her knees then stood, hand against the tunnel wall as Gwyn battled the Wolf.

Gwyn jabbed and slashed at the beast with the sword, but the steel blade did no damage. Gwyn looked at the sword, astonished it hadn't drawn blood.

Gwyn reached two-thirds up the height of the wolf. The werewolf turned to glance at his sword hand, annoyed maybe by the blade's faint sting. It growled then attacked and bit on Gwyn's forearm and severed it. Its huge jaws crunched through the bone and spat out the hand and wrist. Gwyn shrieked in agony and stumbled backwards, holding his bloody stump, blood spurting out.

The wolf leapt at him as he fell back. Gwyn pressed back against it with all his strength, and Iseult saw his sinews and the strain on his face but it all he could do was hold the wolf back, and he was weakening as the blood pumped from his severed wrist. Gwyn's good hand was at the wolf's throat, pushing so it couldn't bite him. But the wolf's muzzle drew closer, snapping jaws inching towards Gwyn's face as it bore its massive strength down on him.

⁂

"Iseult, run to me."

Iseult glanced up and saw the bloody figure of Tristan leaning against the tunnel wall. The wolf turned its muzzle from Gwyn and growled.

Tristan was badly injured and his breath was coming in gasps between clenched teeth. He was covered in blood and looked hardly able to stand, but still he held out his hand to her.

The wolf regarded him with contempt and turned its gaze back to Gwyn.

Gwyn struggled against the beast, his strength nearly gone. The werewolf pushed him down with its foot and Gwyn sprawled, bleeding in the mud. The wolf planted its foot on his back so he could not move, but still Gwyn struggled, trying to prise himself free, his breath rasped, his face pressed in the dirt. It cost the wolf no effort to keep him pushed down there.

"Leave him, monster," Tristan yelled.

Iseult stood halfway between Tristan and Gwyn. Her escape route was past Tristan, but Gwyn still lived, and she couldn't leave him to the werewolf. Tristan reached out. Iseult shook her head.

"I'll get Gwyn, Iseult, but come back behind me."

The wolf watched them.

Still Iseult didn't move.

Tristan strained towards her. His face was covered with blood, his teeth smeared with it, one eye half-closed. "Iseult! Just come to me."

And then with a snap of its jaw, the wolf jumped forward and grabbed at Iseult. She stumbled down, knocked to the floor and lay there only feet from her husband. Gwyn opened an eye. He muttered, "Go. Go with Tristan."

She scrambled to her feet, but the wolf yanked her back again, and tripped her and stood over both her and Gwyn. It held neither of them but everyone knew that it would snatch them back if they tried to crawl away.

Then Tristan ran forward with a yell and flung himself at the wolf.

With an effortless swing of its arm, the wolf slammed Tristan against the tunnel wall where he lay coughing. It regarded Gwyn and Iseult in turn, gaze switching between first one then the other, as if decided which to kill first.

Iseult wept. Her husband lay dying in the mud, a flawed man, but a man that had tried to save her when he could have left her to her fate, not once but many times.

And Tristan, who'd come back to rescue her, bloodied and broken, slumped against the wall.

Iseult's heart tore. Tristan couldn't survive his wounds. She had condemned him to death. She'd condemned both of them. If neither of them had loved her, both of them would have lived, but their love for her pinned them to this fate like moths pierced with needles and stuck on a board. All three of them were replaying an ancient tragedy, as if Fate had called them to walk this stage only to be struck down.

Gwyn was dying. And there was no way Tristan could defeat the wolf. He was half-dead already, and it was filled with anger and super-human strength.

The wolf stood to its full height and howled.

But Tristan painfully stood, roared his defiance and limped at it.

Iseult saw that Tristan gripped something in his hand — a small dagger made of silver. Tristan had put his faith in the supernatural properties of the metal of the moon.

The werewolf strode to meet Tristan, contemptuous of his challenge. But Tristan, even with his wounds, stood his ground. He stepped to the side at the last minute of the werewolf's lazy attack, and as the werewolf roared past him, he shifted his grip, and thrust the silver dagger at the wolf's back.

The wolf was moving too fast, and the dagger missed.

Tristan turned, his face twisted in pain. Maybe even this dagger would fail now.

The wolf pivoted round and came at him. It saw the silver dagger, snarled and knocked it from Tristan's grip, sending it spinning into the mud out of reach.

Iseult realised that the werewolf knew what the dagger was made of.

Tristan glanced at where the dagger had fallen, and back at the wolf. Iseult knew he couldn't cover the ground fast enough, even if he were fit, and bearing such injuries as he did, there was no hope at all he could reach the dagger before it killed him.

From behind them came the insane howl of Claire. The psychic was running up the corridor, the athame in her hand. "I'll kill you, I'll kill you! Faithless! You fornicator!" she screamed.

The wolf looked up and blinked.

Iseult realised Claire was running at Tristan. She branished the weapon and Tristan looked at her, blinked blood from his eyes, and looked back at the wolf, frowning.

Claire came raised her arm, ready to stab Tristan. Tristan was facing the wolf, paying no heed to Claire's dagger.

"You swine!" Claire shrieked. "I loved you, and you despised me. I worshipped you, but my love for you was beneath your contempt. I will punish you now."

As she stepped forward, Gwyn reached out and snatched Claire's ankle as she stepped past his stricken form. He made her fall. The wolf turned and with a lazy swipe of its forearm swept her away and sent her crashing into the stone wall of the tunnel. Her head struck a rock and lolled sideways at a sickening angle. The athame fell from her grip onto the floor, she muttered something and coughed. Blood ran from her right ear and she moved no more.

Taking Claire's dagger, Gwyn struggled to his knees. The wolf turned and planted its right paw on his forehead, forcing him down. With his last strength, Gwyn resisted, neck muscles knotting, forehead creased, eyes shut against the pressure, then like a tree finally bends and breaks under an enormous load, Gwyn shuddered to his knees and then slumped as the wolf overpowered him.

He fell, and the werewolf knocked his guarding arm aside and bit at his throat. Iseult heard the snapping of its jaw and saw the spray of her husband's blood. She put her hand to her mouth and shrieked

The wolf turned back to Tristan, but Tristan had used the distraction created by Gwyn to grab the silver dagger. He held it behind his back. The wolf snarled. It rushed and raised both arms to slice down.

Tristan stepped foward holding the dagger.

The wolf's bulk and strength smashed him to the ground, but the werewolf's own momentum drove the silver dagger into its chest.

As the magic metal entered its heart, the werewolf shrieked its death cry and rolled onto the floor, writhing in agony, the dagger like a silver pin in its heart. And then as it rolled the wolf shape fell from it and Dudley regained his human form. He lay, in death rangy and pale, now unmoving in the red mud of the tunnel floor.

"How did you manage...?" Iseult stuttered.

Tristan said weakly, "Despite what I thought, all the myths are true: Werewolves change under the full moon and silver is the only thing that can kill them."

Tristan collapsed against the wall, his chest heaving in ragged coughs. Iseult rushed to help him. His wounds were matted, and the blood dried. In some places, the scabs had split and fresh blood seeped out. He was grievously wounded. Iseult knew they were miles from a doctor and further from any hospital. His head lolled, and he wavered in and out of consciousness.

No modern medicine would save him.

Iseult held his hands between his and cried out into the air of that cursed and fated place. "If there is a God, any god, that can help me, help me now."

She nestled her head against his chest and pulled him close. She didn't care that he was bloodied. She sobbed and began to sing a lullaby. In the dark of the tunnel, a feeling flowed from the ground beneath her and the walls around her, and connected her with an ancient spring of life, the natural life of the earth that had been worshipped in this place since pagan times.

Staring down the tunnel, she saw the stone figure of Crom Cruach, the candles still fluttering round him. She sang on. The words were not ones she remembered ever learning and were in an ancient Celtic tongue that was strangely familiar as if remembered from a former life.

As she sang, she knew in her heart that her words were healing Tristan, and that was because she loved him. Wrong or right, she loved him, he was hers, and she was his for as long as they lived.

And so the legends are true: Fate called Tristan and Iseult to live their story again and be bound again by their love and their loss.

SUANTRAÍ

After he finished marvelling at the miracle of his healing, Tristan said, "This place needs to be burned down."

Iseult followed him as they went through the tunnels and Tristan led her to where the generator was.

The wolfpack had fled.

Jerrycans full of petrol sat on a shelf in the room and Tristan took them and sloshed their contents around the floor. The worst of his wounds were healed, but he still winced as he shook the heavy containers.

"Now, the castle." Tristan took the jerry cans up the stairs and into the Castle proper. He went to the Library and poured petrol around the room and on the bookshelves. He looked up at the portrait of Lady Amelia Morton who stared back with dead painted eyes. Tristan saw the silver lighter that Sorcha had left beside the black candles. He cut and inch off the top of a candle and placed it in an ashtray that he filled with petrol. "That'll be the fuse."

Iseult touched him. "Are you sure you want to do this?"

Tristan grimaced with pain as he said, "I'm scared that if we don't burn the place down, we, or people like us, will have to come here and do this all again."

He lit the candle, making very sure that the flame did not go near the petrol. And then he took Iseult by the hand and they retreated down into the cellars.

"I reckon an hour and then the whole place will go up," Tristan said.

"Which way now?"

"I know it's strange but I want to take the tunnel under the bog to the chapel."

"So no one sees us leave?"

He shook his head. "I can't explain. It will seem like we're being reborn."

She smiled. "You're weird."

"I'm not the man I pretended to be. I'm not a regular guy. I'm not a hero. I prefer languages to football. There's a lot of things about me, you might not like once you get to know me better."

"No," she said. "I like everything about you, weird or not."

They made their way along the damp tunnel. After a few yards, the electric light bulbs came to an end as if Sorcha had not ever come this way. Iseult was glad they were leaving her influence behind. They walked in darkness, having to believe that eventually the tunnel would come to an end, having faith they would emerge into daylight again. And then, they saw grey light ahead.

The emerged by the ruined chapel by the road that led away from Tullabeg. It was dawn. Iseult asked Tristan to sit and using moss from the Bog of Allen, she cleaned clotted blood from his wounds. Then they walked towards the town. When they had been walking half an hour, a local man in a plumber's van offered to give them a lift.

As they drove through the grey morning light the man asked, "Where have you been?" He gave them a strange glance and said, "Not to Tullabeg Castle I hope?" Without waiting for an answer, he added, "That's a strange spot. There are lots of legends around that place. I wouldn't go there — certainly not in the dark."

"I heard it burned down," Tristan said quietly.

"Really? I wonder what happened to old Dudley." He grinned as he drove. "They say he was a—" The man stopped himself.

"He was a what?" asked Iseult.

"Never mind," the Irishman said. "It's just a load of country talk. Things like that don't exist."

The car with its three passengers, Tristan and Iseult in the back and the owner in the front, drove out of the Bog of Allen, heading towards Dublin. As they left, the mist vanished, the clouds cleared and the sun rode high in the blue Autumn sky.

The man shook their hands, wished them well and dropped them by the main road. From there, they made their way to Dublin and from there across the sea to Wales. And there they lived as man and wife until the end of their days.

❧ 26 ❧

ISEULT AUX MAINS BLANCHES

I n those days, there were many kings and there was often war between the kingdoms of the Isle of the Mighty and the Island of Erin. And there was sometimes peace.

The story tells that King Mark of Cornwall, in an effort to foster peace, was to wed Iseult, the daughter of the King of Ireland. Mark was much older than she, but the match was a good one politically and he had heard of her beauty. Mark was an old grizzled warrior and he spent his days fighting his enemies and hunting the wolves that were so plentiful in those days in Britain. Rather than take the trip to Ireland himself, he resolved to send the best of his war band, the young warrior Tristan, to fetch Iseult from Ireland over the sea to Cornwall.

Iseult, for her part, did not want to marry the older king. She was sure he was generous and kind and brave, but he was too old for her and she protested to her father, the King of Ireland. But her father would not listen to her protestations. He said that Mark was a good man and he had resolved she would marry him. He would hear no more complaints. When the warriors from Cornwall came, led by Tristan, she would go over the sea in their ship and come to Tintagel.

Mark was a wise king and he knew the young woman would most likely not love him, so he spoke to his druids and procured from them a love potion. Before Tristan set off, Mark gave him the love potion and asked him to prepare a drink for her of fine Gaulish wine. But he must be careful to do it just before Iseult stepped off the ship in the harbour of Mark's fortress of Tintagel.

Tristan assured his king that he would do that. When Tristan's ship docked at Dún Laoghaire in Ireland, Iseult was waiting for him with her ladies. She bade a tearful farewell to her father and to Ireland and shipped with Tristan and Mark's soldiers for Cornwall. They were at sea only two days, but in that time, Tristan was stuck by Iseult's beauty as if by a lightning bolt fallen from heaven. But he put his love from his heart, because he could not betray his king. Instead he got the love potion ready for when they were about to land.

For her part, Iseult was charmed by the handsome young knight, as kind and gentle as he was strong and brave. She wished it were him she was going to marry. And then, with Cornwall in sight, Tristan brought out the potion. He was a man who could not lie and he said, "Take this my lady. I can tell by your eyes that this match is not one you have sought, yet if you drink but a sip of this, you will love Mark and your heart will be happy."

Iseult shook her head. "I will not do what men wish. My heart is my own. I do not care if King Mark is the best of all men — he is not my choice." But as to who was her choice, she kept her peace.

Tristan smiled ruefully. "Even so, it is best you drink," and he added the potion to the goblet of wine and gave it to her.

"I would not drink alone, Tristan. Will you not have this drink with me?"

Tristan considered and thought it would not be against his lord's command and so he poured himself a goblet of wine. They sat, she undrinking, though he didn't notice, and she charmed him with her conversation and her beauty. And then, when his attention was on her eyes as bright as the sun on the western sea, she switched the goblets and he drank of the wine with the potion.

From that time, he loved her deeply and forever. No other woman would enter his mind from that day until the day of his death.

They arrived in Cornwall and Iseult married Mark. Tristan made a show of congratulating the king but his heart was broken. Because he was the king's favourite he was often in the Queen's company and they would walk in the gardens among the summer flowers and neither would speak of their love for each other.

But one night, she came to him because she could do no other. She told him, "I love the king like a father. He is good to me and honest and kind. But my love for you is like the ocean and is like a fire at the same time if such a thing could be. If I cannot have you, then I must die."

"I will not have you die, my lady. For if you were not on the earth, I could not survive." And he kissed her and they lapsed into adultery.

The king found out and Tristan and Iseult fled, not back to Ireland for her father would not risk the wrath of King Mark, but rather over the sea to Brittany where they sought shelter with King Hoell who was at war with King Mark.

But wars do not last, and in due course there came talks of peace. King Hoell invited Mark and there Mark met Tristan again, the warrior he loved the most of all his men. He pretended to forgive him, but no matter how much he loved Tristan, he could not forgive him the crime of stealing Iseult.

King Hoell invited Mark to come hunting in the magic forest of Brocéliande. There they hunted the great man wolf, the loup-garou as they were later called by the Gallo. Tristan and Mark came across the werewolf in a secluded glade and they slew the beast. The beast had a terrible poison on its fangs and Tristan was wounded. As he lay there, dying, Mark said, "Tristan, I loved you best, but you took from me something I would never willingly lose and the loss of Iseult has broken my heart." He watched the young warrior fade into a sleep close to death and he closed his eyes, thinking he was gone, and left him there beside the corpse of the werewolf.

But Iseult was following the hunt and she heard from the retainers that Tristan was wounded and where he was. When she found him he was close to death indeed, but her tears of love flowed down him and with her hands she healed him for her love gave her power over death. And for that she was called *Iseult aux Mains Blanches* - Iseult of the White Hands.

Tristan and Iseult were never seen again in the lands of the Celts.

They went away into a far country and their fate is forgotten. But one thing is certain, they were never parted until death took them and even then, beyond the bounds of life, perhaps their love still endures and they return to earth to play out their legend again and again.

WHAT IS STRONGER THAN DUTY?

The answer is: love.

ABOUT THE AUTHOR

Tony Walker is the narrator of The Classic Ghost Stories Podcast. He is the author of several collections of ghost and gothic stories.

He does live storytelling events and lives in his native Cumbria.

ALSO BY TONY WALKER

Haunted Castles

Cumbrian Ghost Stories

London Horror Stories